Praise for Linda Jacobs and The Yellowstone Series

JACKSON HOLE JOURNEY

"A vivid portrait of ranch life and a devastating natural disaster."
—Lucia St. Clair Robson, Spur Award winning author of *Ride the Wind*

"Linda Jacobs writes with power and authority about people you care about in one of the most fascinating places and times."
—Robert Vaughan, *New York Times* bestselling author, Pulitzer nominee, and Spur Award winner

"A captivating page turner that lets us all know why Linda Jacobs is an award-winning writer."
—Jane Kirkpatrick, bestselling author of *An Absence So Great*

"*Jackson Hole Journey* is another 'can't put it down' by Linda Jacobs. I hated to see it end."
—Sherry Monahan, author, columnist, and Wrangler Award winner

2011 Spur Award Finalist — Western Writers of America (Audio Version)

2011 New Mexico Press Women Novel of the Year (Audio Version)

LAKE OF FIRE — Book 3 in the Yellowstone Series (Medallion Press)

"*Lake of Fire* is marvelous: well developed characters who grow in the course of the story, truly beautiful physical descriptions of place, and lots of action."
—Spur Award winner and bestselling author Kathleen O'Neal Gear

"Few writers can tell a story like Linda Jacobs. Her books tell stories that gallop out of our collective Western history, onto the page, and into our hearts."
—Rus Bradburd, author of *Forty Minutes of Hell*

2008 First Place Winner, New Mexico Press Women's Excellence in Communications Competition—novel category

2008 Third Place Winner, National Federation of Press Women's Communications Contest—novel category

2008 Spur Award Finalist, Mass Market Novel—Western Writers of America

2008 WILLA Literary Award Finalist, Original Softcover—Women Writing the West

Finalist, Historical Category—Gayle Wilson Award of Excellence, South Magic Chapter of Romance Writers of America

RAIN OF FIRE — Book 2 in the Yellowstone Series (Medallion Press)

"Linda Jacobs has created a thrilling vision of what it's like to be in the crater of an active volcano. Based on fact, the book details the signs, warnings, and the eruption that could take place in Yellowstone—tomorrow. Fast-paced, yet with touchingly human characters, *Rain of Fire* is a page-turner of the first magnitude."
—Robert Vaughan, *New York Times* bestselling author

"With *Rain of Fire* Linda Jacobs is in the zone. The book is a grabber for sure—I could hardly put it down. Jacobs has a gift for weaving story and reality, taking the improbable and moving it to the realm of the possible. Superb storytelling and her grasp of Yellowstone detail is uncanny."
—Bob Barbee, Yellowstone National Park Superintendent, 1983-1994

"Beautifully written with exceptional plot momentum and well

developed characters .... *Rain of Fire* is exciting, poignant and puts you on the edge of your seat .... A Perfect 10."
—Connie Ruebusch, Romance Reviews Today

4 Stars: "Jacobs masterfully combines scientific knowledge and suspense as expert scientists unite to predict the sometimes inexplicable forces of nature. The addition of the tension-filled romance between Kyle and Wyatt adds a human element to this swiftly moving, captivating read."
—Sheri Melnick, Romantic Times

"*Rain of Fire* is an exciting thriller that grips the audience with the tremors that threaten Yellowstone at a time when there seems to be an increase of major natural disasters. The story line is action-packed, warning people about the potential of natural disaster in a place where most people fail to realize the danger."
—Harriet Klausner

2007 WILLA Literary Award Finalist for Original Softcover Fiction

SUMMER OF FIRE — Book 1 in the Yellowstone Series (Medallion Press)

"*Summer of Fire* is at once a beautiful and disturbing voyage through the type of hell that only firefighters understand. Human, brutal, wrenching. Clare Chance is as genuine a character as they come— brave, vulnerable, well-trained and thrown by her own act of escape into a forested hell. Beautifully crafted and shudderingly real."
—John J. Nance, *New York Times* bestselling author

"A gripping novel about one of the most electrifying events in the annals of American wildfires—the great Yellowstone fires of 1988 .... [Jacobs] has done her homework well and the setting is completely accurate."
—Bob Barbee, Yellowstone Superintendent, 1983-1994

5 Stars: "Superb Reading Experience—A Real Page-Turner: Straight-line plot, background is detailed, characters are developed over time,

memorable and important secondary characters, will leave you feeling content, at ease, peaceful."
—Harriet Klausner

5 Blue Ribbons: "*Summer of Fire* is a tense but passionate tale that will keep you anxiously turning each page as you read of the struggles to fight the fires of Yellowstone Park. Linda Jacobs will keep your heart pounding as she describes the fires that tried to destroy Yellowstone in 1988 and the work that was done by the brave men and women who fought this fierce dragon."
—Brianna Burress, Romance Junkies

5 Fires: "Linda Jacobs does a magnificent job of recreating the scene, the heat, danger and the fatigue the firefighters face, while also telling the stories of four primary characters."
—Jeannine D. Van Eperen, Gottawritenetwork.com

WINNER of the 2006 WILLA Award for Original Softcover from Women Writing the West.

JACKSON HOLE JOURNEY

A NOVEL

JACKSON HOLE JOURNEY

A NOVEL

LINDA JACOBS

CAMEL PRESS

Seattle, WA

CAMEL
PRESS

Camel Press
PO Box 70515
Seattle, WA 98127

For more information go to: www.camelpress.com
www.readlindajacobs.com

Cover design by Sabrina Sun

Jackson Hole Journey
Copyright © 2013 by Linda Jacobs

ISBN: 978-1-60381-910-7 (Trade Paper)
ISBN: 978-1-60381-909-1 (eBook)

Library of Congress Control Number: 2012948385
Printed in the United States of America

10 9 8 7 6 5 4 3 2 1

Acknowledgments

Thanks to my agent, Susan Schulman, and to Catherine Treadgold of Camel Press for their faith in my work, and to Catherine for her incisive and inspired editing. I am also grateful to Dr. Lee Whittlesey of the Yellowstone archives, to Linda Franklin and Clayton Caden of the Jackson Hole Historical Society for assistance with research, and to Robert Vaughan, Spur Award Winner, *New York Times* Bestselling author, and Pulitzer Prize nominee, for valuable input on the manuscript.

Thanks to Harold Turner of the Triangle X Ranch for a look at modern-day dude ranching in Jackson Hole. Some books that helped me understand the early years of Jackson's Hole, as it was called until the middle of the Twentieth Century: *For Everything there is a Season*, Frank Craighead (Falcon Press, 1994), *The Diary of a Dude Wrangler,* Struthers Burt (Charles Scribner's Sons, 1924), *Legacy of the Tetons, Homesteading in Jackson Hole*, Candy Vyvey Moulton (Tamarack Books, 1994), *A Place Called Jackson Hole*, John Daugherty (Grand Teton Natural History Association, 1999). And, where appropriate, I have quoted directly from the *Jackson's Hole Courier*, as it was known during the 1920's. The paper ceased operations in 1961.

For information about the Ku Klux Klan in the West in the 1920's, I consulted the novel *Boldfaced Lies* by Charlene A. Porter (Rose City Press, 2006). For a modern day perspective on Rocky Mountain ranching, I thank a fellow member of Women Writing the West, Peggy Godfrey, and cite her DVD *Cowboy Poetry, a Woman Ranching the Rockies*, (Snowstorm Production, 2006). Tamsen Leigh Hert, of the University of Wyoming Library, produced a piece of dynamic research that brought Yellowstone's Canyon Hotel back to life. Tamsen also provided the dinner menu. Last, but not least, thanks to Scott Stowers of Lula, Georgia, for giving me a ride in his 1924 Model T.

Dedication

To the memory of American Book Award winner
Venkatesh S. Kulkarni

and, always, to Richard

I would like to thank **Medallion Press** for granting permission to reprint passages from two of my earlier books in the Yellowstone Series, *Lake of Fire* and *Summer of Fire*.

The first passage, from *Summer of Fire*, is reproduced in the first three paragraphs of Chapter 5.

The second, from *Lake of Fire*, appears between the two separator characters on page 90.

The third, from *Lake of Fire*, appears in Chapter 46 between the separator characters on pages 289 and 291.

The fourth and final passage, from *Summer of Fire*, begins with the last paragraph of page 300 and ends with the separator character.

This book is titled *Jackson Hole Journey* because of the worldwide name recognition of the valley at the base of the Teton Range. Throughout these pages, I use the name Jackson's Hole, as it was known for over one hundred years. Around 1830, explorer and trapper William Sublette named the valley after one of his trapping partners, David (Davey) Edward Jackson. The term Jackson's Hole stuck until the middle of the Twentieth Century, when it was simplified to its present form.

Today, a single working dude ranch remains within the National Park System. The Turner family have worked the Triangle X Ranch since 1926, and been concessionaires of Grand Teton National Park since 1950.

Chapter One
June 22, 1925

Francesca di Paoli's vision of Jackson's Hole as a peaceful haven barely outlasted her arrival.

When the wagon topped a rise north of Jackson Town, she caught her first glimpse of the Tetons, a sheer wall of jagged peaks beneath boiling black clouds. Dust devils danced on the valley's broad, sage-covered floor, harbingers of a windblast that sent sand stinging into her eyes.

While a curtain of rain swept down from the heights, she slipped her hand around William's arm. His muscles, tight from controlling the anxious team of bay horses, bunched beneath her fingers.

Lightning stabbed and split a lone pine, too close for comfort. At the blinding bolt, Francesca ducked and saw red, bisected by a streak of brilliance. The horses reared and plunged, crying shrilly as the stench of charred wood filled the air.

"Easy, Eli ... Jacob." William leaned his shoulder into Francesca's. "Missed us, by God." His voice sounded thick, as hers might if she tried to speak around the lump in her throat.

Thunder crashed, rolling like barrels down the cellar steps at the *Castello de Vigne.*

Storms had never alarmed her in her native Chianti. From the time she'd been tall enough to see out the window in the servants' wing, she'd always gotten out of bed at the first faint strobing over the Tuscan hills. Her older cousins might sleep, but she stood by the casement while lightning bathed the vineyards in violent illumination, dogs barked, and rain thrummed the clay roof tiles.

This tempest's violence reminded her she didn't belong in Wyoming.

Opening her eyes, she took in the range dominating the skyline. Beneath towering blue-gray thunderheads, the granite bulwark reached nearly seven thousand feet from valley floor to the pointed crest of the Grand.

Craaack!

Dio! At another dazzling display of lightning, Francesca's carefully practiced English deserted her.

"We're going to get wet," warned William.

The scent of rain hit first, shot through with an aroma of damp sage. A big drop splashed her cheek. Another thumped the top of her hatless head.

While William continued to fight the frightened team, wind tore loose her knot of hair, weaving dark strands before her eyes. The blowing spray became a deluge, drenching her.

She wrapped her arms around her torso and shivered. Steam rose off the horses' backs, where the chill downpour struck their sun-warmed coats.

Coming here had been crazy, as crazy as getting on a train in the middle of the night, leaving New York without knowing how far the money crushed in her trembling fist would take her.

With the squall behind them, William awaited the first sighting of their destination.

He'd picked up the wagon and team—left by one of the hands at the depot in Victor, Idaho—and negotiated the tortuous road over "The Pass," through the Teton Range. Francesca had seemed appropriately impressed by her first sight of the verdant floor of Jackson's Hole.

All the way up the Wilson-Moose Road and across the sage flats, he'd been anticipating her reaction to his home. Now, as they reached the edge of a fifty-foot bluff, the scattered buildings of the Snake River Dude Ranch came into view.

"It is very large," Francesca said.

"It takes almost as many hands as it does guests to keep things going."

At William's direction, Eli and Jacob descended the bluff, a river terrace of the Snake. On along the edge of a lower bluff, they pulled into the yard in front of the huge log edifice of the Main.

William dismounted from the high seat and lifted Francesca down. Her sleek ribcage bore not an extra ounce of flesh, yet well-formed breasts showed beneath the damp bodice of her yellow frock. Standing toe to toe, he confirmed she was an inch or so taller than his five feet ten.

Bringing her home was the kind of wild thing his brother Bryce would do. Perhaps that had been what had spurred William to action when he'd seen her on the railroad platform in Salt Lake City that morning. Determined to forge a link with the lovely woman who looked lonely and frightened, he'd approached and discovered the conductor had thrown her off the train for lack of funds.

What would his folks think of him bringing her to Snake River?

"William!" It wasn't a shriek. Laura Fielding Sutton never shrieked.

"Mother!" His arms around her, he spoke at her ear. "You should see Texas. God's country for ranching, only a couple dustings of snow a year."

At fifty-one, her green eyes remained brilliant and her sun-streaked brown hair bore only threads of gray. Dressed like a ranch hand in trousers and a blue cotton work shirt, she gave Francesca an expectant look. "Who's this?"

Before he could set his mother straight, the woman by his side straightened to her full height. "I am Francesca di Paoli, of *Toscana, Italia*. I am seeking the position of ... *chef* for your fine guest ranch."

William chuckled.

Francesca skewered him with a regal look.

"I'm sorry," he said, hastening to get out. From the moment he'd heard her speak, he had been charmed by her accented English, and the prospect of Prudence Johnston, a local blonde, had gone flying out of his head.

His mother, who had obviously concluded Francesca was his bride, looked regretful. "Jim Lovejoy's moved up from slinging hash for the outfit to working the Main. Our cook moved to San Francisco in the middle of the season."

"Must've listened to too many tales of California." William glanced at Francesca, who'd told him that was her ultimate destination, and went on, "Jim's not my idea of a chef. Maybe we should give Francesca a try." He realized he had no idea whether the woman he'd picked up in a depot could cook.

As Mother remained steadfast in her support of Jim, Francesca's manner chilled. "I thank you, William, for bringing me."

A frown furrowed Mother's brow as she studied the willowy young woman. "Don't think of leaving us. Even if we have a cook, you must stay until you find work."

"What kind of work?" asked a familiar deep voice.

William's imposing father grabbed him into a hug. He was six foot four, broad of shoulder where his son was average, with a fine thick head of hair turning gracefully to silver. "Glad you're back, son. We've needed you around the place."

William detected a trembling, almost a palsy, in the man he'd thought of as invincible. That is, until the letter Mother sent to Texas mentioning Father's failing strength. If not for the missive, William would be spending the summer working on the ranch near San Antonio, where people treated him as an independent man, rather than the owner's son.

Father's deep blue eyes, set in a sun-bronzed face, fixed on Francesca with the same familial interest Mother had shown.

William remembered his manners. "Francesca di Paoli. A cook ... *chef.*"

Father studied her. "How long have you been in America?"

"Since the spring of twenty-four," she said in precise English, "before the Immigration Act made it difficult to come. I cooked for a wealthy family, the Coldwells, in New York City for almost a year."

Father's brows knitted. "I hear they need a cook up at Circle X." At Francesca's questioning look, he gestured toward the east side of the valley, where a less rugged range of mountains rose. "Over there."

Mother stepped up and put her arm through Francesca's. "Let me show you around."

William thought the place looked good; the folks had a right to be proud. Only one thing could mar his homecoming and that was if someone else had also gotten a letter.

As the two women walked away, he ventured, "Bryce been by?" Casual-like, he eyed a new fence around the horse corral.

"Not since fall roundup." Father looked elsewhere as well.

Bryce Sutton held the letter gingerly, as if it were a snake. Another summons, no doubt.

Why his mother couldn't for once trust him to do the right thing was one of life's mysteries. He needed no reminder to go home next week for his parents' twenty-fifth anniversary.

He folded the pale blue envelope addressed to him in Idaho Falls and subsequently forwarded to the Driggs, Idaho, post office and shoved it into the pocket of his sweat-stained khaki work shirt. The small town punctuated Teton Valley's rolling high plains, emerald with summer wheat fields.

Six o'clock .... Sunlight bathed the gentle western slope of what a man raised in Jackson's Hole thought of as the wrong side of the Tetons. Whenever he happened to glance up sudden-like from his work mending ranch fences, planting potatoes, or digging irrigation ditches, the angle on the Grand always looked bass-ackwards.

Deciding to have a drink before reading the latest missive, he turned toward the nearest place serving bootleg liquor, The Rancher. Someone had painted over the word "bar" in honor of Prohibition.

At his shove, the old-time saloon door swung inward, releasing the smells of booze and furniture polish. The corpulent proprietor Luke was wiping down one of the empty tables.

"Lookee here what we got," came a mocking voice from a corner table. Though a card game was in progress, one of the men put down his hand and scraped back his chair.

Christ, it was Karl Good, all six and a half feet of him, known as "Tiny." Bryce considered a retreat, but dammit, he wanted that drink before he opened the envelope.

He kept his course for the mirror-backed bar. Held up a hand, casual-like, "Hey, Tiny." Looked away.

The tread of someone big and broad fell in behind him. He turned.

Tiny glowered down, making Bryce feel his six feet was small. "I'm ready to win back my money."

Last time Bryce had been home, he'd joined a game at the Jackson's Hole Clubhouse and taken Tiny for a couple hundred dollars.

"What brings you over the hill?" Bryce tried.

"Could ask what you're doing here. Word in the valley is, you work west of Idaho Falls."

That was the way Bryce wanted it. Should his folks catch wind he was close by, they'd start expecting him for Sunday dinner.

"Luke!" Bryce called to the bartender. "You gonna polish the top off that table while a thirsty man stands around?" He pulled a roll of bills out of his pocket.

Tiny's close-set eyes turned avaricious. "Whyn't you buy me and the boys a round?"

Damning himself for showing his wad, Bryce focused on Luke. "Tea or water?" the barman asked.

"Nice cold glass of tea." Bryce indicated his preference for bootleg whiskey over gin.

Luke scooped up ice, bent and disappeared from sight.

Tiny's big hand descended to grip Bryce's shoulder. "How about that round?"

Bryce pried off the big man's fingers.

Luke set Bryce's drink on the scarred wooden bar top. Tiny picked it up and threw back a slug.

Bryce grabbed for his drink, sloshing whiskey onto Tiny's soiled shirtfront.

The bigger man wrestled control of the glass and dashed its contents in Bryce's face.

With high-proof alcohol burning his eyes, he lashed out blindly. His fist connected with Tiny's jawbone, and it wasn't a thing like the choreographed fisticuffs in the movies recently shot in Jackson's Hole.

Hiding his sharp agony, Bryce reckoned he'd broken a bone in his hand. And almost missed seeing Tiny's meaty fist, on a collision course with his nose.

He tried to dance aside.

There wasn't time, but he did manage to convert a blow that would have pulverized his septum into a glance off his cheekbone. "That's enough, dammit!" he shouted, diving at Tiny's mid-section.

Someone grabbed Bryce from behind and dragged him back. "Settle down," growled Luke at his ear.

It took the three fellows who'd been playing cards with Tiny to subdue the big man.

Who was Bryce? Francesca wondered, while she and Mrs. Sutton walked through damp grass beside a pond near the lodge. Something in William's tone and his father's signaled the man might have the capacity to cause their family pain.

Of course, it wouldn't pay to get curious. Despite this place's staggering beauty, she would only remain in the area long enough to earn her train money to California.

With a slim hand adorned with turquoise and silver rings, Mrs. Sutton pointed out "The Main," where "guests took meals and socialized long past the hands' bedtime." The log building's pitched shingle roof topped twenty feet; huge peeled pine trunks braced the broad front porch. Next were the ice house, storehouse, garage, barn, saddle shed, granary, blacksmith shop, laundry, bunkhouses, and outfit dining hall where the hands ate. Scattered at graceful intervals on the bench above the Snake were guest cottages.

Beyond the cabins lay a pair of long stables. Horses and cattle grazed within a four-pole leaning fence of lodgepole pine that Mrs. Sutton called buck and rail. Within the fenced area, a huge black bull glared a challenge.

"Brutus thinks he owns the place," Mrs. Sutton said.

As they walked on, she continued, "Back around the turn of the century, Cord was part owner of the Excalibur Hotel in Salt Lake City. After he ... sold out, we moved up here to his family ranch and started taking guests in 1909."

Last, they came to a low-log building with smoke rising from the stone chimney. A covered porch floored with rounded river cobbles sheltered a chipmunk, who ducked into a burrow at the base of the foundation.

Mrs. Sutton stepped onto the porch. "Jim hasn't moved from the bunkhouse, so I'm putting you in the room off the kitchen. Until you get settled at the Circle X."

"They will hire me?"

Smile lines crinkled around the older woman's eyes. "Most valley natives are farmers and ranchers. It's not every day someone walks in with a talent." She inventoried Francesca—from her crown of curling damp hair to her serviceable black shoes. "You won't last long."

"*Scusi?*"

"Whenever an unattached young woman arrives, bets are laid as to how soon she'll marry."

Francesca looked away at the fenced plot beside the cookshack, with its neat rows of immature cabbages, squash vines, and tomato plants. "Your garden is doing well."

"Thank you. I have a hothouse where we keep a stove stoked during our long winter. Keeps us in produce year round, but there's no substitute for a summer garden."

"The climate in Chianti was ... *moderato,* with a good season for the garden."

Mrs. Sutton nodded. "I've never been a cook, but I have a way with growing things. Of course, at Fielding House in Chicago, I tended my rose garden and the house plants in the conservatory." She must have detected something in Francesca's expression. "I came from a wealthy family, but money doesn't solve everything."

Pressing her lips together, Francesca thought some cash would certainly help her situation.

Mrs. Sutton opened the cookshack door and spoke back over her shoulder. "I guess I mean, whatever trouble you're in will pass."

Francesca stopped on the porch and looked with pretended interest at a rack of antlers above the doorway. Was her jumpiness so obvious? She'd left New York so precipitously she didn't know if Vincenzo had called the police when he found the money missing.

Inside the cookshack, Mrs. Sutton said, "Here's Jim, making our dinner."

Jim Lovejoy, a burly blond with sunburned cheeks, looked like Francesca's image of a cowboy— well-worn boots, denim waist overalls, a plaid shirt, and a bandana around his ruddy neck. Clearly out of his depth, he wrestled a cast-iron Dutch oven smelling of watery beans out of the stone fireplace.

"This is Francesca di Paoli, a chef from Italy," Mrs. Sutton said.

Jim blanched and set the pot on the table. The cast-iron feet would leave scorch marks to match a score of others. "She gonna take over?"

Mrs. Sutton gave him a gentle smile. "She'll have the job up at Circle X."

Jim wiped his hands on his denims, leaving spots of flour, and shook Francesca's hand. "Pleased to meet you, ma'am." He ducked his head.

"I think it's 'miss,' " Mrs. Sutton gave Francesca a barely perceptible wink. "She's going to stay here until she gets set up."

Jim nodded, insulated his hand with a kitchen towel, and lifted the lid to inspect the beans.

The ranch kitchen was in its own way more welcoming than the one in the *castello*. There, Francesca had cooked in immaculate pots, put away each night in the pantry at *Signora* Rossi's orders, only to be taken out at four-thirty a.m. to make breakfast. Here, a ceiling rack displayed a collection of tarnished and battered copper cookware, and the place had a worked-in look.

Mrs. Sutton led Francesca through the kitchen to a small room with a lean-to roof. An iron-framed single bed against the log wall sported a many-colored quilt with a "wedding ring" pattern—or so she told Francesca. A washstand, a wall clock, a well-placed rocking chair before the window would allow one to look out at the Teton ramparts.

Even without the view, the room was far more pleasant than the one Francesca had slept in at the Rossi's. Once she had outgrown sharing a room with her male cousins, she had been relegated to a windowless space beneath the stairs.

"*Grazie*," she told William's mother, "very nice."

"We have flush toilets—elevated tanks and water piped from the river—for the dude cabins. I'm afraid you'll have to use the privy out back."

Back in the kitchen, Jim had his big hands, more suited to manual labor, in a mess of biscuit dough he was over-kneading.

If only he hadn't beaten her to this job.

A shadow appeared on the floor inside the door; William's sturdy shoulders made a backlit silhouette. He carried the scarred leather valise Francesca's father, Antonio, had passed on to her.

"It's too bad you're leaving," William told her, "but I'd be happy to drive you to the Circle X tomorrow."

After the sun sank behind the wall of mountain, twilight lingered a long time. Francesca bathed, using the bowl and pitcher on a marble-topped stand, and put on a clean cotton frock. Then she walked through the kitchen and outside, glad Jim was off somewhere.

Though Mrs. Sutton had treated Francesca as a guest, she recognized the difference between herself and the "dudes," the minute the group gathered on the front porch of the "Main." Of the twenty guests that represented a full house, more than half were men sporting a colorful parody of Western dress, chaps in red and orange, boots polished to a high sheen. The women wore divided skirts and blouses in jewel tones. The contents of pocket flasks transformed punch and lemonade into highballs.

Mrs. Sutton had explained that this was opening night for a round of dudes who would stay through the Fourth of July. "Dude," Francesca knew from today's tour, was not a term of disrespect. On the other hand, if a hand called a dude a "greenhorn" or a "tenderfoot," those constituted serious insults. Dudes claimed to want to rough it, but desired their rooms with a view and a vase of wildflowers.

Francesca stood beside the cookshack and looked across the gulf that separated her from these people ... as at the *castello*, and in the brownstone where she had served the Coldwells in Manhattan. No one had said anything about her joining the family and guests, so she went back into the kitchen, where firelight chased shadows into the corners.

While she was helping herself to a plate of beans, a biscuit, and a dry lettuce salad, Jim Lovejoy came in from the porch. "Got a grill round the side where I'm frying the steaks." He lit an oil lamp suspended over the table and watched her sample his fare.

As she'd expected, the beans lacked seasoning and the biscuit was tough.

"It's no good." He grimaced. "I wanted a promotion, but it's harder than I thought." With a glance toward the Main, he sighed. "It's time to serve, and I've got more meat to cook."

She should leave well enough alone, but ... "Why don't you let me dress the salad and you can take it over?"

Francesca rummaged among bottles on a table against the wall and went to work.

After Jim left with the bowl of greens seasoned with cider vinegar and oil, Francesca doctored the bean pot with salt and pepper. How plain this ranch fare without the zest of basil, rosemary, or garlic, all of which could thrive in Laura's hothouse.

Going out, Francesca checked the grilling steaks and did some more surreptitious seasoning.

On Jim's second trip ferrying food, curiosity got the better of her; she grabbed a platter and tagged along.

On the Main's broad front porch, a wiry boy on a ladder was lighting the hanging kerosene lamps. The flames reflected in the varnished yellow pine posts, making them appear to be afire from within.

Rather than enter the front door, Jim took a cobblestone path to the rear. Inside was another kitchen, smaller than the cookshack. He called it the winter kitchen.

Francesca peered through a porthole window into a single huge room with a high, beamed ceiling, knotty-pine bar, and a stone fireplace she could have stood in. The dining table before a panel of windows facing the mountains accommodated at least thirty.

The colorful dudes laughed and chattered, while a handful of bronzed men, the dude-wrangler squad, appeared taciturn. William sat at one end of the long table and his parents at the other; to Francesca they were Western equivalent of royalty.

Yet one detail surprised her. With the low-ranking jobs usually held by people of color in America, Francesca was surprised to see a man with coffee-colored skin seated at Cord's right hand. She guessed his age at around fifty, judging from the silver threads in his grizzled hair and smile lines at the corners of his eyes. The two men talked easily.

When Francesca came out of the kitchen, a male dude in orange chaps—who could have been handsome, with his wavy blond hair—watched her with a barely concealed leer. When she failed to hide her distaste, the leer became a scowl.

Without warning, the floor jerked beneath Francesca. Her fingers opened and a thick white china bowl of beans hit the pine boards and smashed.

The building was on the move, swaying. The Suttons and the dudes grabbed the table while their drinks toppled. In the kitchen, dishes crashed.

"Not again," Mrs. Sutton cried. "We had tremors last night."

Francesca transported back to *Toscana*, where earthquakes had often shaken the countryside and brought on the same feeling of utter helplessness.

She staggered and slipped in the spilled bean juice.

William shoved back his chair and rushed over to steady her, while the earthquake slowly subsided.

"Shakes are pretty common here," William told her as they left the Main an hour later. "During the one in March of twenty-three, it felt like my house had lifted up and settled with a thump."

A chill had come down, making the cookshack a cozy retreat when she and William went inside.

Jim was there, sweeping up broken dishes. Smells of strawberry preserves and vinegar pickles made an unfortunate mix. Though he was the owner's son, William pitched in, helping pick up broken glass and china.

After Jim left, William appeared ready to linger.

In the train terminal, she had gambled that a woman alone could trust this solid-looking man. So far, Snake River Ranch had appeared to be everything he had promised. But now, in his gray eyes glinting like silver coins in the lamplight, she detected a desire she was not ready to deal with after Vincenzo's betrayal.

"I am tired from the journey," she said gently. He nodded and brushed his sandy hair back from his forehead in a self-conscious gesture. "Goodnight, then."

Francesca waited until he had gone before she visited the outdoor privy. Then she walked back to the cookshack and stood outside with her face to the sky, in awe of more stars than she had ever seen. The dark wall of mountain was defined by the stars' absence, and a fingernail moon was setting.

She should be pleased at her good fortune. This morning she had been without a *lira*, hungry, with no hope of a meal. But something—the afternoon storm, the rawness of the land, the avarice in the eyes of the dude in orange chaps—portended violence.

As if in answer to her thoughts, another quake rattled the cookshack windows.

Chapter Two
June 23, 1925

The next afternoon, Francesca waited for William on the wagon seat while he adjusted the team's harness. Though Eli's ears twitched to repel a pesky fly, Jacob stood like a statue of polished mahogany, sunlight gleaming off his brushed flanks.

Francesca's valise rested in the wagon bed; no one expected her back this way.

She had thought Mrs. Sutton might come out to see her off, but the yard was empty. At breakfast William's father had announced his plan to ride up the Gros Ventre River past the Circle X to see the new bull at Red Rock Ranch.

Focusing on the high white clouds that posed no threat, Francesca nonetheless felt the same vague unease that had kept her awake last night. Would there be another storm or more earth tremors?

William swung up to the seat beside her. He wore a fresh shirt and his damp hair was tracked with comb marks. She smelled Bay Rum.

Wrinkles creased her best green silk. Worse still, it had a skirt to the ankle, rather than the fashionable short hems American women wore. She hoped it would do for meeting the Circle X owners and convincing them she was the proper cook for their staff ... *hands.*

She needed to pick up how people—*folks*—talked in the West. And buy some new clothes. Though she didn't fancy trousers like the ones William's mother favored. Perhaps one of those divided skirts ....

Or not.

She had to save her money for California.

Gathering the reins, William called, "Hi-yah, boys."

Eli and Jacob trotted off smartly.

A few miles south, at Menor's Ferry, William paid for them to ride a flat topped pontoon raft across the Snake River.

While he led the team and wagon aboard, Francesca walked on. The operator, feisty Maude Noble, who William explained had bought the business from Bill Menor six years ago, smiled at her. "The way this works, I set the pontoons at an angle into the current and it sweeps us across the river."

Francesca surveyed the Snake, a single-wide channel spotted with eddies that underscored its swift flood.

"Don't worry," Maude chuckled. "I haven't lost a passenger ... this season, anyway."

"I do not swim," Francesca said.

After her older cousins had finished dunking her, she'd climbed out of the local creek and refused to go back in.

"Good choice," William chuckled. "Almost the end of June and the Snake's no more than forty degrees."

They disembarked and headed east along the north bank of the Gros Ventre River.

Six miles in, at the small town of Kelly, Francesca's impression was of a scatter of wooden buildings thrown together at different times in varying styles. Here were rustic cabins constructed of chinked logs with shake roofs, there, homes made of sawn lumber. The little community had driven its roots into the rocky river banks.

"Has your family been in the valley long?" Francesca asked.

William nodded. "My grandfather, Franklin Sutton, was one of the first white men to winter over in this valley. He prospected for gold in the 1870's."

"Did he find it?"

"Enough to make ends meet."

"Is he living?"

William shook his head. "He and his wife died during the Nez Perce War of 1877."

"What about your father? He must have been pretty young."

"He was there when the Indians attacked," William said in an even tone. "Watched their homestead burn in the moonlight." His knuckles whitened where he clutched the reins.

Francesca shivered. "Are there Indians around here now?"

William shot a sideways look her way. "There are people with some native heritage. Mostly, you wouldn't notice."

Outside the Kelly post office stood a black automobile.

"There's Ranger Duran's Model T. He got here with his family a week ago to take over the Horsetail Station up the Gros Ventre." William gazed with longing at the bright brass rimming the auto's hood and decorating the

s. "I want a car, but Father would rather not have one on the
tolerate a truck to ferry the dudes, and a tractor, but he likes
ishioned, no electricity and all."

guided the team through Kelly and into the foothills. On the
north side of the valley, steep red sandstone cliffs dipped back into the
mountainside. "One of the settlers, Wilhelm Bierer, used to say the Gros
Ventre Indians stayed out of this canyon because they heard rumbling in the
earth."

"Like last night?"

He gestured at the high forested slope to the south. "Old Billy watched
Sheep Mountain."

"Watched for what?"

"He's supposed to have said, 'Up on that slope, if I lay my ear to the ground,
I can hear water trickling and running. Someday, we have a wet enough spring,
the whole mountain's gonna slip on that gumbo like a beaver's slickery slide.' "

"Does he still live here?"

"Sold out and moved back east to live with his daughter. Heard tell he died
in twenty-three."

Francesca surveyed the lively cataract of the Gros Ventre beside the road.
"This spring was wet?"

"Dry in Texas, but I heard tell of heavy snow here last winter. And Father
said it's been pouring nigh every afternoon for a month."

They drove farther into the canyon and Eli began to limp. William stopped
the team and handed the reins to Francesca.

She hesitated.

"You've driven before?"

Only a cart pulled by docile animals toiling the slopes of *Toscana*. Nothing
like the spirited pair in harness. Nonetheless, she nodded and William got out
to inspect the horse's right front foot.

"Threw a shoe," he said and walked back down the road.

As soon as he was gone, both horses swiveled their heads and fixed her
with liquid eyes. Perhaps if she stayed longer in this country, she would learn
to drive ... and ride.

A few minutes later, William returned with the metal horseshoe. "Piece
of luck finding it." He dumped it into the wagon bed beside her valise. "We'd
best stop at Hall's and see about getting the shoe nailed on." He stamped clay
off his boots.

"The gumbo Mr. Bierer spoke of?"

"Yep."

Around the next bend, they sighted a large home, which they reached by
crossing the Gros Ventre via a wooden bridge.

A slender brunette with her hair pulled back came out the front door, wiping her hands on her apron.

"Vera Hall," William told Francesca, then raised his voice. "Any damage from the quake?"

"Lost a nice wall clock. George must not have put it up properly."

"He around?"

Vera shook her head. "He plowed the lower field for most of the morning ... kept hearing rumbling and rock falls up on the mountain. About three, Foster Case and Lewis Pharr came down from Circle X to gather stray cattle. Then George went out on horseback to look for two of our head he'd discovered missing." A line between her dark brows said she didn't like it.

Francesca pursed her lips. In Italy, if you thought a slope unstable, you stayed off it.

"Mind if I help myself to a hammer and some horseshoe nails?" William inquired.

"Should be no problem."

He was already on his way toward the barn.

Vera looked Francesca over with shrewd eyes. "What brings you to our valley?"

"I am ..." Francesca smoothed her skirt while she searched for a word, "*seeking* the cook's job at the Circle X." By now, she suspected they didn't speak of *chefs* here, unless they were trying to impress an Eastern dude.

Vera gestured her toward the porch and a chair. "Circle X has got Asa Dean, who's better off tending stock, slinging hash. Their other cook got tired of the lack of female companionship hereabouts and headed to Chicago for a wife."

Francesca failed to react, recalling Laura Sutton's mention of the local demographics.

"Nobody needs to go all that way," Vera continued. "He could have tried the Heart and Hand Club."

"*Scusi?*"

"Men order a woman to come, and they marry her."

"One they do not know?" Of course, some *famiglie* arranged marriages, but often the participants had been friends since childhood.

"They write letters," Vera said, "send photos." She looked toward the barn where William had gone for tools. "Lots of folks been saying William should try Heart and Hand after he struck out with Prudence Johnston last fall." She paused. "Then again, maybe not."

Aware that she was being scrutinized, Francesca smiled gamely and spoke of what a lovely location the Halls had on the river.

A little after four, she and William said their goodbyes to Vera. As William drove the team back down toward the river crossing, Francesca looked up on the mountain and saw something beyond belief.

Santa Maria, it was trees on the move, bobbing and tipping in a drunken ballet.

Chapter Three
June 23, 1925

After William left with the mysterious Francesca, Vera Hall set about peeling potatoes and speculating about the young woman. Francesca seemed a little careful; she certainly hadn't risen to the bait about William.

Vera had mentioned the Heart and Hand Club partly in jest. Anyone knew a son of Cord Sutton would have no trouble finding a wife. William was just taking his sweet time.

Or rather wasting it. Take last summer when all the talk had been of him and Prudence Johnston. Any woman in the valley could have told him that girl was no good. Word was if a man snapped his fingers, she would lie down.

Vera didn't know what had happened to set William straight, but he'd lit out for Texas without succumbing to Prudence's tricks.

Setting aside the potatoes, Vera looked out the kitchen window. She'd asked George not to go up Sheep Mountain, and now she wondered if her fears had been well-founded.

She heard another rumble.

On the other side of the canyon, on a rutted track above the Red Bluffs, Circle X hands Foster Case, Lewis Pharr, and Bobby Cowan swapped lies. Whipcord lean and blond, young Bobby let his attention stray from the horses he was driving to find out what the other men had been up to lately. Foster, a burly braggart and the toughest of the three men, reported that the strays were out of Hall's meadow. Fifty-year-old Lewis, who moved more slowly than a man his age should, quietly kept an eye on the cows.

While Foster and Bobby visited, a few more rocks rearranged themselves with a clatter over on Sheep Mountain. It had been happening with some regularity all day, so when another commotion began, they kept talking.

Until the clacking and rolling escalated, and the earth began to rumble. "The hell?" said Bobby.

"Lookee there." Lewis pointed at dust swirling up to form a dense cloud.

"Mountain's goin'!" Foster shouted.

The slope turned elastic, spreading out at the base; millions of tons of rock, soil, and trees started overrunning the land above the Gros Ventre.

The remuda in Bobby's care started and whinnied, then took off up the canyon toward the Horsetail Ranger Station.

"Dammit to hell!" Bobby shouted. He started riding after the spooked herd, calling back over his shoulder. "I'll tell Ranger Duran."

Foster and Lewis tried to calm their wall-eyed, plunging horses, as a mile-long section of jumbled debris glissaded toward the Hall Ranch.

Laura Sutton was bringing a mess of fresh produce—she was particularly proud of the hothouse tomatoes—to a new mother. The father, Ben Raleigh, worked in the outfit at Snake River. The Raleigh's neat white frame house overlooked the Gros Ventre River west of the town of Kelly.

Laura rode horseback, which she preferred to driving a buggy. The mare, Bayberry, born of the breeding of a Nez Perce gray, White Bird, and Cord's fine black stallion Dante was not the horse either her sire or dam had been.

An odd thing, breeding. Laura had always expected any son of hers and Cord's would have her green or his blue eyes, abundant healthy hair, and a lean, long frame. Never had she expected William would come out a throwback to her father. Not only did he have Forrest Fielding's compact frame and fine, light brown hair, but every time she looked into her son's silver-gray eyes, she caught a glimpse of the father who had always wanted things just so. In a young man of twenty-four, that characteristic made him seem more mature.

It was difficult to believe Bryce, bold and brash, was only a year younger.

As Laura tied Bayberry to the hitching rail, the shudder of an earthquake rolled beneath her feet. Bayberry jerked her head and whinnied.

Up on Sheep Mountain Laura caught a motion where there should be none, what might be smoke or dust rising.

A second later, the hillside peeled away, raw earth exposed as though the mountain was unzipping from the top down. A moment later the sound arrived, a low unearthly rumbling.

৯৵

As Francesca watched the mountain with horror, Eli and Jacob spooked, dancing sideways and making the wagon veer.

"William!" she cried.

Accompanied by the oddest sound she'd ever heard—a weird yet sibilant growl that made her chest tighten—a huge hunk of Sheep Mountain began to peel loose from the top.

William looked back once. "Here!" he shouted to the team. "Gi-yah!"

The landslide gathered speed, its voice reverberating in the canyon.

Eli and Jacob turned runaway.

Francesca clung to the sideboard, braced to keep from flying out of the jouncing wagon. When William had spoken of this mountain sliding down, she wished she'd thought to spit for luck the way her mother had taught her.

As the slide gathered momentum, its angry vibration penetrated Francesca's bones and made her stomach heave. The wagon wheels leaped a rut, and she bit her tongue. Blood welled, salty in her mouth.

Beside her, William hunched over the reins connected to the galloping team.

Eli and Jacob swerved, and the wagon went up on two wheels.

৯৵

George Hall was riding along the lower river bench when the thumps and bumps he'd heard all day turned into an odd hissing purr.

Above on Sheep Mountain, beneath a cloud of strange brown mist, the forest transformed into a living thing, tossing and writhing as though some giant in the earth gripped the tree roots and shook them. The resonance became a roar, and on looking back, George saw a gigantic wall of debris sweeping toward him.

Even as he spurred his mount, the massive landslide tumbled behind his horse's heels. It had swept up fences, corrals, haystacks, cattle, chickens, and telephone poles. All the ranch buildings had been swallowed, and it had barely missed the house. When the mass of debris cascaded into the Gros Ventre River, the impact threw the river from its bed, water roiling upstream.

Though they were at least fifty feet above the bank, George and his horse got as drenched as if someone had thrown a washtub over them.

The mass of mountain churned on to slam into the red sandstone cliff face, four hundred feet up on the north canyon wall.

৯৵

Riveted to the sight of the pale scar spreading down Sheep Mountain, Laura shouted to the people in the Raleigh house. But the door was had already been flung open in response to the earthquake.

The first woman out was blond and buxom Prudence Johnston, wearing a fashionable short-skirted crimson dress, silk stockings, and crystal beads. For a time last fall, Laura had thought William might make Prudence a member of their family. She couldn't say she was sorry about their breakup.

Anne Raleigh emerged from the house next with her blanket-wrapped infant. Her sister-in-law Bettina followed, along with Larry and Benjy, her six and four-year-old boys.

"Another damned quake," Prudence swore. "I ...." She stopped and stared across the valley at the falling mountain. "Looks like it might be coming down on Hall's place." Her expression was one of unmistakable enjoyment at nature's destructive force.

Both Laura's husband and son were up the Gros Ventre.

She dropped her bag of vegetables.

In the yard of the Horsetail Station, Ranger Duran noted the earth tremor. He checked his watch, which read twenty past four, and went back to digging a trench. As a stranger to the Teton country, he'd found the earthquakes in the past few days unsettling.

But when he heard a strange grating and rumbling from down the canyon, he stopped work again and frowned. Not twenty minutes ago, he'd made the acquaintance of rancher Cord Sutton and seen him on his way downriver, riding his black stallion Lucifer.

What was happening down there?

Pounding hooves announced a rider barreling up the canyon. Duran expected to see Sutton coming back, but instead a long-legged young man on a sweating cow pony dashed into the muddy yard. He leaped to the ground, landing square on his long legs in what Duran found an improbable feat.

"Jesus Christ, Ranger. There's the whole mountain come down in the damned ... begging your pardon, Ranger. Fer chrissake, how's the river gonna get past the damned dam?" He touched the brim of his cowboy hat. "Sorry, sir, I'm Bobby Cowan from Circle X and I can't help swearin' for the life of me."

Duran headed for his Model T. "Leave your horse and let's go see."

When Lucifer detected the earth tremor, Cord had a deal of a time controlling him.

"Steady, boy," he soothed.

Then the strangest thing, a vibration in his collarbones and an accompanying growl. The pressure in his ears became painful.

Lucifer pranced, while Cord, who usually gave him his head, pulled hard on the reins. He saw it, then, up on Sheep Mountain. A rumbling, tumbling gush of earth's entrails.

His gaze traveled down to the wave front at the base of the slide and his gut clenched. Near the leading edge, Eli and Jacob were galloping flat out. The wagon, with William at the reins and Francesca on the seat beside him, veered and jerked drunkenly from side to side.

"Hold on!" William shouted.

Francesca tried.

Eli and Jacob struggled to stay up, side footing and going down in a tangle of extended necks and legs. Their screams pierced the pursuing slide's thunder.

The wagon began to topple. Francesca's valise tumbled out.

William threw away the reins and swiveled toward her. She had a fraction of a second to wonder what he was doing before he swept her over the back of the seat into the wagon bed and dove in after her.

The side of the wagon slid along the road. William snagged Francesca around the waist and hung on to the bottom of the high seat to keep them from falling out.

They seemed to grate along forever until the tangled-up horses finally came to a tumultuous halt.

Christo, they must have broken all their legs.

In the next instant, it seemed as if a giant slammed his boot into the wagon and dumped it bottom up. The brake handle and the back of the seat sheared off.

The light between the wagon boards snuffed out. Francesca's awareness narrowed to the sensation of William's arm around her, the cries of Eli and Jacob, and the ongoing thunder of the monstrous landslide.

Chapter Four
June 23, 1925

The horses' cries died away. The guttural voice of the slide dimmed. Sand grains sifted.

William pressed heavily atop Francesca, his chest and stomach against her back. He gasped like a beached fish. "Can't ... breathe."

"I'm ... breathing." For how long? The black air tasted of dust.

He went on hyperventilating.

"Crushing ... me," she managed.

A dozen heartbeats and he dragged himself off to settle on the dusty gravel at her side. "Sorry."

A hard ache twisted the back of her throat. Utter darkness surrounded them.

How many feet of debris buried them? Were their fates sealed?

"Fran?" William sounded as though he'd also abandoned hope.

"What ... can we—?"

"Make ... noise."

In case someone had seen them go under ... provided they were near enough to the edge.

If, if, if.

Francesca drew a breath to call out, but the weight of William's fingers landed half on her shoulder and half on her breast.

He snatched his hand away. "Don't yell. Not ... enough air."

The atmosphere did seem more stifling than even a moment earlier. "Then what—"

"Kick the wagon boards."

Francesca rolled over and aimed the heel of her shoe upwards.

Thunk.

Her open eyes filled with grit. "*Dio mio!*" Tears pooled in the hollow beside her nose.

William suffered a bout of choking. "Kick ... sides."

Her sandy eyes stung, but she struggled until she and William lay back to back and kicked.

Something to do, instead of waiting to die.

Cord flung himself off Lucifer's back and rushed the jumbled pile of dirt, rock, and shattered pines. His boots dug into the sandy surface; his ankle turned on a submerged rock.

There was the big sandstone slab he'd marked as being near where the wagon went under. When he reached it, he looked back to the ground and estimated the depth of debris at around ten feet.

More than he would be able to move.

His son was down there.

Cord dropped to his knees and started digging like a dog, scooping out debris and shoving it down-slope.

His breath came faster; he kept moving. Sweat beaded on his brow and popped out on his upper lip. In another minute, it was running down his sides.

He'd made a depression about three feet deep when his chest seized up. Three and a half and he knew he'd have to take a rest or black out.

With each thump to the boards, Francesca grew more exhausted. Behind her, William pounded his boot in a steady rhythm. Either his claustrophobia had passed or the man had an iron will.

What were the chances anyone had seen the wagon go under or that they could be dug out?

As a child she had become trapped in the cellar below the *castello* ... shrieking, alone in the gray light, wondering where her stout and comforting mother Carla was. In the kitchen pressing pastry dough into a pan, or slicing ripe pears to go into a tart with creamy, sweetened mascarpone? It had only been six hours since Francesca had eaten, but behind a locked door, the lure of food was doubly strong. What about her father Antonio, whose tall, lean physique she had inherited? He was the one who took her to Mass, who had gifted her with her grandmother's rosary, who taught her to pray in Latin.

Trapped beneath the wagon, she gabbled, *"Pater noster, qui es in caelis ...."* Her fingers convulsed as though gripping the onyx beads, but she'd packed them into her valise this morning.

Drawing a sharp breath, she started to scream.

At the muffled cry of horse or human, Cord resumed digging, trying to pace himself.

This desperate search took him back to a dreadful January day when snow lay in a deep and dazzling blanket beneath cloudless skies and shadows bore a bluish cast. In the Tetons, Cord, eight-year-old Bryce, and one of the wranglers Nordic-skied rough glacial chutes.

Bryce, graceful with a boy's quick energy, shot ahead and above the men.

"I don't like him up there alone." Cord dug in his skis and pushed through thick powder.

The wrangler, a stalwart twenty to Cord's forty-one, put on a burst of effort and followed the boy's tracks.

"Bryce!" Cord shouted. "Wait for Dan."

It began as an evil hiss on the still air. Within seconds, it gathered into a roar.

"Avalanche," Dan cried.

Big as hell, covering the slope at a fierce rate. The way it angled down the ravine, Dan would be engulfed by the thickest part, with Cord and his son caught on opposite sides.

Dan swore and pushed on toward the boy. Bryce looked up at the avalanche with stricken glass-green eyes.

"Ski!" Cord yelled. "Across its path."

Cord managed to sidestep out of the way, while the churning mass bowled over and buried both Dan and Bryce.

It was only natural to keep his eyes fixed on where his son went down.

When the maelstrom settled, he struggled through broken snow. On his way, he saw no sign of the young wrangler.

The tip of one of Bryce's ski poles protruded between blocky chunks. Praying it hadn't been torn from his hand, Cord started digging.

All the while, he knew Dan was dying.

For the rest of the winter—for the rest of his life—he would live with guilt, for shouting and perhaps starting the avalanche, and for not being two people, so he could have saved Dan, too.

They found the body with the spring thaw.

Now, instead of cold snow, Cord tore at grit and rock until his hands bled.

His heart threatened to burst in his chest, and he imagined he could hear it beating.

No, those were hooves, pounding on approach ... Foster Case and Lewis Pharr, shouting as they slid off their horses.

Francesca heard the sounds from above and kept screaming. William joined her.

If she used her last breath to call in help, so be it. Her throat was an aching wound; swallowing would not make the dry patch go away.

When she had been trapped in the cellar, her older cousins, along with Vincenzo, had happened to pass by and rescue her. They acted as though she was an ignorant child for getting shut in. Only when she grew older did she wonder if it had been a prank.

The scraping above grew louder. Francesca and William fell silent.

Dirt sifted down.

Shielding her eyes with her hand, Francesca spied daylight between her fingers.

Spent from helping the cowboys dig, Cord managed to gasp, "William! You there, son?"

"We're here."

"*Si, Si*." Francesca sounded hoarse.

Cord stood back and wiped his brow, trying to catch his breath. It would take a lot more to get them out, but now that they had an air supply, he must rest.

Bending, he laid his hands on his knees. He should be dancing because his son had survived, but the image of Eli and Jacob lying ruined beneath the rubble brought a wave of bile to his throat. William had learned to drive with those two. Small Bryce, not satisfied to be behind the reins, had ridden Eli bareback without so much as a halter.

Cord heard a rhythmic rattling and turned to see a uniformed Ranger Duran pull across the Hall's bridge in his Model T. Bobby Cowan leaped out, swearing, while he took in Foster standing astride the dusty wagon boards.

"They're alive down there," Cord said, "William and Francesca."

Bobby arched a blond brow at the exotic name and rushed to peer at the upside-down conveyance. Ranger Duran rummaged behind the seat for a rope and tied it around the auto's rear axle.

"Need to dig some more," suggested the stocky Foster. "Get down to something we can tie off on."

Cord sank onto a dusty log while the other men worked. His gut told him Laura knew about the slide and was wondering if her family was safe.

From the time they'd met, twenty-five years earlier, he'd sent up a daily prayer of thanks for the woman who'd been his helpmate, partner, and who had trusted him when no one else did.

Now he reached into his pocket and fingered what felt smooth like glass, with conchoidal surfaces and a sharp edge. His talisman of obsidian had been with him since he was six years old. He believed, in the way of the Nez Perce, that it soothed him in times of trouble, and allowed him to meditate on what would come next.

Were today's events bad omens?

An hour later, Francesca emerged from beneath the wagon into dust-laden air. Strong hands dragged her up; here were more of the lean, bronze men who seemed to be everywhere in Jackson's Hole. William's father, looking pale, rested beyond the bitter end of the slide debris.

With the men's help, she staggered down onto the gravel road. Looking back, she saw William, dun-colored from head to toe. Her dress, hair, and grimed skin were the same neutral shade.

"Water," she pleaded.

Three cowboy canteens materialized before her.

She grasped the nearest, unscrewed the metal cap and tipped it up. Liquid sloshed into her mouth, overflowed and ran down onto the front of her dress, turning dirt to mud. She swallowed and choked. Bent over, she rinsed her mouth and spat blood from her wounded tongue.

Finally, she managed to gulp enough liquid to make it possible to take in the larger aspects of her surroundings. Beyond the ruined wagon, she assumed that the slide concealed Eli and Jacob. William had told her the pair was the pride of Snake River Dude Ranch; he must have chosen them to impress her on the ride to the Circle X.

They'd run their hearts out, for their own sakes and to please their master. Had William been their friend? Had he curried them, offered oats and apples, and breathed into their horsy nostrils?

Spots swam in her vision. "Easy." William spoke close to her ear.

The spots coalesced into an ocean of ink, and she drowned in it.

Chapter Five
June 23, 1925

There has been no word from up the Gros Ventre. When the mountainside gave way, I saw curious plumes of dust rising. Trees danced and undulated and the hillside peeled away to raw earth. Finally, I heard an unearthly low rumbling as though a train passed.

Laura paused to compose herself and dipped her pen to continue writing in a new leather-bound volume of the journal she'd kept since childhood.

When the earth lay quiet, a-mile-and-a-half-long gash wounded it.

Jackson's Hole is not far south of the great volcanic field of Yellowstone. Here, the Teton fault has spawned great earthquakes, leaving behind the signs in fault scarps, flat triangle-shaped facets across the front range, where the mountains heaved up relative to the dropping valley floor. The quakes last night and this morning must have set off the slide.

After witnessing the catastrophe up the canyon, Laura had paid brief respects to Anne and the baby, then stood in the yard pondering where to go.

Part of me wanted to spur Bayberry over to Kelly and up the canyon to find Cord and William. Perhaps when I was younger I would have made a wild ride in search of my men.

I once followed Cord into the wilderness of eastern

Yellowstone even though the park's army custodians believed him guilty of arson and attempted murder. My staid father thought I was crazy—a city woman from Chicago—to refuse to return home, to marry Cord despite his heritage.

It was the only choice I could make, then and forever.

He is my life. It saddens me to see him growing older. His hair and beard have silvered as if the high altitude sun has bleached them while it burnished his skin. Creases at the corners of his eyes and furrows that cut from the base of his nose suggest he has done a lot of both squinting and smiling— signs of uncertain times, along with joy.

In every mirror, I see the same changes in my own features.

Laura put down her pen and looked around the simple homestead she and Cord shared. Though their dude ranch boasted grander edifices, this log house occupied the site of the cabin that had burned over his parents' heads in 1877.

She should go over to the Main and sit near the ranch telephone. How long would it be before messages came out of the canyon?

Thank God William was with his father. Unlike Bryce, he would be sure and see to things.

Bryce.

From the moment baby Bryce had opened his green eyes, mirrors of her own, she'd been powerless to resist him. While William had slept through the night from birth, Bryce had wrapped both his parents and the ranch hands around his colicky little finger. When he cried, there was never a dearth of offers to walk the floor with him. When he learned to read, everyone wanted to listen to him pipe out stories in a childish treble and turn the book back to front to show his audience the pictures.

Whenever their wayward son came home, he was the one who charmed the dudes, while William made sure everything ran smoothly and on time.

Suddenly, Laura had an image of William, before he had left the previous autumn for Texas. His features twisted, he'd burst out in an uncharacteristic display of rage. "It's always Bryce, Bryce ... and he's never here. I'm going to let you see what it's like without me for a while."

Francesca swam up from darkness, struggling for breath. She was in a coffin beneath tons of earth and buried alive inside the overturned box of wagon bed.

As she fought her way to wakefulness, she threw back the pale pink quilt, sat up on the wood-framed bed with carved pineapple posts and drew deep breaths until her stomach settled. When she swallowed around the raw spot in her throat, her bitten tongue sent out its own protest.

Someone had loosened the buttons at the neck of her filthy frock, removed her shoes, and bathed her hands and face. The bed was gritty with sand from her dress.

Gloria a Dio, she had survived. She should say a prayer, but her rosary, along with everything she owned, lay buried beneath the slide.

Francesca rose and caught her reflection in a shaving stand. Though her face was clean, her hair was a matted, earth-colored mess. Perhaps she could bathe before the Halls served their evening meal. Maybe Vera, though thicker and shorter, had something Francesca could wear.

It had been quiet outside the closed bedroom door, but now footsteps tramped across the porch and into the outer room. Male voices rose, along with a scraping, as though men were moving furniture.

"Steady now," said one fellow.

"This is the last we can get in this load," said another.

Francesca padded to the door and opened it.

Lewis Pharr and Foster Case, who had helped rescue her and William, were manhandling a behemoth of a china press. Vera Hall stood at her dining table for twelve, wrapping gold-rimmed dishes in cloth. From the smell of meat and potatoes, supper was simmering on the stove, forgotten.

William came in from outdoors. "The water's coming up faster than we thought. Don't know if we'll get everything out in time."

Francesca stepped into the main room, realizing the Halls' was no haven.

"There you are." William moved toward her, his gray eyes dark with concern.

Vera's hands, holding a crystal pitcher, stilled. "Are you all right?"

"I believe so." Francesca made a self-conscious gesture; she should have been stronger than to faint.

Vera shot a glance at William. "Between Ranger Duran's helping us, and the hands, we're doing everything we can here with one wagon. Why don't you and Francesca saddle a couple of our horses and ride them up to safety at the Circle X?"

Was time that short?

"You up to it?" William looked at Francesca.

Did she have a choice?

"You sure you don't need any more help with the stock?" William asked. "After George dug out that bull and calf—"

"I think eight or nine head are still missing," Vera replied.

Francesca went to the front door. Deep in the Gros Ventre Canyon, the summer sun was a memory, its last illumination high on the opposite canyon wall. Mud and slime coated the red sandstone cliffs fifty feet above the top of a dam several hundred feet high. While she'd been lying down, a new lake had begun to form.

A lake that might be as deep as the new mountain was high.

Francesca had hoped to hide her lack of expertise in the saddle from William, but he kept an eye on her awkward efforts. When she failed a second time to mount, he cupped his hands for her foot and boosted her to the saddle.

The big animal shifted; she was about to topple.

"Relax and settle into your seat," William instructed, as they set off.

The Hall's bridge was under and the horses picked their way across the rising lake, thigh-deep. Anything else coming out of the house would have to fit on a pack horse.

Near where Eli and Jacob lay buried, William drew rein. Although he'd lost his hat in the wild flight, he lifted his fingers and touched an imaginary brim.

"They were the best," he said. "Blood brothers." His Adam's apple bobbed.

Tears stung Francesca's eyes.

By the time they made their slow way up to the Circle X, she was barely clinging to the saddle. Thankfully, William's father came out with a lantern to meet them and caught her as she half-slid, half-fell off the horse.

William did not dismount. "I'm going back to help the Halls."

Mr. Sutton nodded. "I'll see to her."

"Have you let Mother know we're all right?"

"The phone lines are down."

A sturdy young man wearing suspenders took the reins of the horse Francesca had ridden and led it away. On the front porch of the Circle X's low log lodge, a stoutly built older man waited. Deep lines on his face attested to his being a smoker; the lit cigarette between his fingers confirmed it.

"This is Roland Howard," Mr. Sutton said. "He owns the place."

Mr. Howard took in her filthy dress and obvious fatigue. "Hungry, miss?"

She'd been starving, but she ought to remedy her first impression with a potential employer. "*Per favore*, a tub and some soap."

Francesca stripped off her once-green dress and ruined petticoat and bent to remove her shoes and stockings. A tub of water steamed before the fireplace, where a small blaze put out a welcoming glow. It might be June in the high country, but the temperature dropped rapidly after sundown.

Though she hated to be troublesome, she was so dirty that she'd had a second round of clean water brought. Lying back in it, she savored being safe and warm. So much that sleep nearly overtook her.

But she struggled up and toweled off. With her clothes a ruin, she found a white chenille wrapper in the wardrobe. She had nothing else to wear.

In a minute, she would call out to the men and ask them to rustle up a shirt and trousers, but right now she would lie down ... under the bedclothes, in deference to the night chill.

In California the climate would be more temperate, the hills covered with vines. Settling there was her dream. She had thought, once, that it was Vincenzo's dream, too.

Playing together as toddlers in the *castello's cucina*, Francesca and Vincenzo had banged spoons on pots and pans and babbled. She, the daughter of Carla and Antonio di Paoli, the chef and winemaker, he the son of the *construttore de barili*—the handmade barrels of Vincenzo's father were in demand at all the surrounding farms.

Francesca and Vincenzo had each inherited the prominent dark eyes, deep-hued hair, and warm skin tones of their ancestors. At times, people mistook them for brother and sister—twins, since they were the same age.

When they were fifteen, they took a walk beneath the full moon through the silver-washed vineyards to the hilltop village of Volpaia. From the crest, they surveyed the countryside, and, with the impetuosity of youth, found it wanting. Friends since the cradle, they swore an oath and sealed it by pricking their thumbs with Vincenzo's pocketknife and mingling their blood.

Someday they would go to America. To California, where they would own land, grow grapes, and make wine.

In 1915, Italy entered the War on the side of the Triple Entente—Britain, France, and Russia—rather than allying with Germany and Austro-Hungary, as they had in the past. The next year, Vincenzo became a soldier.

At the time, she had thought it a grand romantic gesture.

Nearly ten years later, under Mussolini's heavy-handed rule—with grapes and wine subordinate to a disastrously expensive state-ordained wheat crop— she no longer imagined Vincenzo's return.

To her surprise, one afternoon she ran into him beside the city wall of Radda, the closest town to the *Castello de Vigne*. She carried a net bag of spices, oranges, and onions; she'd taken over the *cucina* in 1918 when her mother passed away.

Though she recognized Vincenzo instantly, she no longer saw the boy who had been her friend, but a stranger. A scar slashed his forehead and eyes that appeared to see troubling things far away. He was still handsome, but in a dangerous way.

That night they walked again in the countryside. Dark eyes snapping, he took her down between the vine rows.

Lying beside her in the moonlight, his face, neck, and arms bronzed from working outdoors, he announced, "I came back because it is time for us to go to America."

Without a word of where he had been for a decade?

"Vincenzo—"

He put a finger to her lips. "It has been a long time, but I never forgot our promise."

If her father had still been alive, she would have refused. But he had died last winter, and, with Mussolini's Black Shirts throwing their weight around, Italy was no longer the land she had once loved.

"You have money?"

Shaking his head, Vincenzo spun a tale of rotten luck; only later did Francesca learn he'd lost at wagering. "If you have enough for our passage, we'll go to America."

She did, set aside through the years in a copper pot hidden in her wardrobe.

To celebrate, Vincenzo uncorked the season's grapey vintage of pure Sangiovese. The love they made was as raw as the wine.

Chapter Six
June, 1925

The next morning, Francesca awoke when the first pale light came through the bedroom window at the Circle X. An alarm clock on a table indicated it was almost five.

How could she have fallen asleep without speaking to Mr. Howard about the job?

Putting her bare feet to the plank floor, she sat up on the side of the comfortable bed. Last night, as he'd shown her to this room, Mr. Howard had quoted Struthers Burt, owner of a ranch near the Suttons. "Dudes need a ranching cot with a forty-pound mattress."

As she wasn't a dude, she'd been surprised at the royal treatment. The bath soap, scented with roses, had lathered smoothly. The towel on the washstand was thick, as was the chenille wrapper she reached for across the end of the bed.

A wall mirror threw back her reflection; she lifted her heavy hair and let it fall on her neck. Smooth chestnut ... like Carla's tresses, with a widow's peak in the center of her brow. Her eyes, dark and almond-shaped, shone as the morning continued to brighten. Though her skin was usually sun-tolerant, spots of pink on her sculpted cheekbones testified to the wagon rides of the past two days.

Francesca snugged the wrapper closer and walked barefoot to open the bedroom door. A faint clattering of pots and pans beckoned her through the dining room to a swinging door. She pushed through and was greeted by the smell of coffee.

The young man who had taken away the Halls' horse the night before turned from an open pie safe with a loaf of bread in his hand. "Wheeee," he said, blinking. Red suspenders held up his denim half-waists.

"Asa Dean?" Francesca guessed. The man Vera Hall said was better at tending the stock than the stockpot.

"That'd be me, miss." He set the bread on a wooden table and reached for a knife. "Just going to make toast."

Francesca looked around and located the flour barrel. "How about biscuits?"

Asa looked chagrined. "Lord, I can't get them to rise no how."

"I can." She gestured toward the wrapper she wore. "Provided I can get some clothes."

He scratched his head of prematurely thinning brown hair. "No ladies here now. That robe was left by a guest last season."

Asa was about her height, thicker through the middle. "If you can spare a pair of pants, I can probably hold them up with your suspenders. And a shirt, *per favore*."

He looked her over and blushed. "I'll get you something."

With the swinging door settling behind him, Francesca headed for the flour and started putting together a mess of biscuits she hoped would win Roland Howard over.

An hour later, wearing a plaid shirt, gray trousers, and a set of Asa's suspenders, Francesca helped him serve breakfast.

William and Mr. Sutton were there, apparently also wearing borrowed clothing, along with Roland Howard and nine ranch hands, including Bobby Cowan and Foster Case. There were no guests at the Circle X, Francesca learned, because Mr. Howard was building some new cabins to expand the dude business and needed all hands to complete the construction.

Once the repast of biscuits, fried eggs, and bacon sat on the table, Mr. Howard told her, "Grab a chair."

Surprised, Francesca took one of two left at the table while Asa got comfortable in the other. She didn't like the grave expression on Mr. Howard's face.

"First thing this mornin', I rode down the canyon and ran into Ranger Duran." He rubbed his prominent, veined nose. "He said more slides came down last night."

William leaned forward. "I got in from the Hall place after four in the morning. When we took the last load out on pack horses using an upstream bridge, there was eighteen inches of water in the house."

Mr. Howard shook his head. "From the height of that dam, this new lake may take out the Circle X as well."

Francesca pushed away her plate, though there was still food on it. First, Jim Lovejoy had beaten her to the job at the Snake River Ranch, and now ....

As the group finished breakfast, Cord asked Asa to have Lucifer saddled. The young man suggested a Circle X horse for William to borrow. "Laura's bound to be worried, so William and I will ride up over on the north side of the canyon."

During the discussion, Francesca remained silent. What was she expected to do?

Her answer came when Mr. Howard pushed back from the table. "Them biscuits were the lightest I've had in years." He looked at her. "I'd be obliged if you'd stay and cook for me and the boys."

She returned his smile. "*Mille grazie.* I will be most happy to."

Francesca settled into the Circle X routine with joy.

Asa Dean was glad to reclaim his role of stockman, and, as the cattle were in their summer pasture, he lent a hand building the new cabins.

For the first evening meal, she seasoned a pork loin with the juice of some tired oranges left over from winter citrus shipments. Roasted with glazed carrots and canned peaches to finish, she'd done all right with what she had to work with, based on the men's compliments.

The next day she went walking in the woods and found not only the first wild roses of the season, which she picked to decorate the table, but ripe strawberries. That evening, she prepared shortcake.

Mr. Howard and the hands treated her with deference, calling her "ma'am" and touching the brim of their hats, pantomiming the gesture if they weren't wearing one. Everyone seemed to welcome her except Foster Case. She wanted to like him—he had helped dig her and William out—but he seemed a brooding sort, watching her from beneath dark brows.

A week after the catastrophe, the Circle X group and Ranger Duran's family were the only ones in the area immediately behind the slide. The Halls had used a string of pack mules to move their belongings over to Jackson's Hole.

Each day Francesca walked down to the bend in the road to watch their house floating in the new lake.

By the night of June twenty-ninth, the lake level had risen to the Circle X and the Horsetail Station. Yellow clouds of pine pollen formed wave-washed lines at the water's edge.

It rained all afternoon.

Francesca's beef dinner turned into a somber affair. By the time she was pouring coffee to go with an apple tart, Mr. Howard was scowling.

Thinking he was refusing dessert, Francesca pulled back.

"Sorry, gal." He motioned for her to set the plate before him and replenish his mug. "It's just that we're losing the war here, and there's nothing to fight back with. Foster's already lit out to look for work elsewhere."

She filled Mr. Howard's mug and moved on to Asa.

The former cook looked sheepish. "I've been sort of hoping for the dam to break so this place would be saved."

Francesca's cheeks warmed, for she'd had the same thoughts. She needed this job.

Mr. Howard placed his hands flat on the table. His gaze traveled around the group, locking eyes with each of them. "One more night and it'll be time to go."

Francesca finished filling everyone's coffee and went through the swinging door to put the pot on the stove. She took a hand torch and went out onto the covered porch.

The steady downpour continued. There was no need to walk down to see the rising flood; its reflection sent back a baleful glitter.

Never mind the pleasant reception she'd had at the Circle X; it was coming to an early end. She was still alone, still "broke," as Americans called an empty purse. Mr. Howard had spoken of going to stay with his brother's family in Idaho Falls until "things settled down."

When she returned to the dining room, he was saying, "When I rode over the high trail and down to Kelly today, they were all in deathly fear of the dam breaking. Folks've been leaving their homes along the Gros Ventre and pitching camp in the foothills."

Asa set his mug down with a thud. "Think of a wall of water coming out onto the plain. There'd be nothing left of the town but chimney bricks and kindling."

Francesca washed the supper dishes and put them away. Part of her wondered why she bothered, but it gave her something to do other than think about where she would be tomorrow night.

With everything in its place, she looked out again at the rising waters.

Overcast blotted out the stars and waning moon; blackness surrounded the Circle X.

Francesca drew a denim jacket—one of the hands had given it to her—around her shoulders. Mist blew in beneath the porch overhang.

On a rainy night in the Chianti countryside, at least she knew that in the nearby medieval town of Radda everything shone bright—reflections of carriage lamps off wet brick streets, the welcoming lights of an *osteria* selling *minestrone* and *zuppa di porcini e fagioli*. Without the warming enclosure of a city wall, Jackson Town and the little settlement of Kelly stood open to the elements.

Much as she longed for home, more than the gulf of continent and ocean prevented her from going back. Even if she saved her funds, took the train back to New York and tried to board a ship, she might be on some police list. That is, if Vincenzo had reported her for taking back the money she'd paid for his sea passage.

With a sigh, she headed for bed.

She had added a few personal touches to her room. A green drinking glass from the kitchen held a bouquet from the meadow. A flowered china plate served as a soap dish. A smaller ivory bowl held the tortoiseshell hairpins that had not been lost when the wagon overturned.

Though the ranch hands had rummaged through their trunks and helped her put together a meager wardrobe of men's clothing, she ended each evening by slipping on the feminine wrapper. It made her feel more like herself.

She spit into the washbowl to ward off evil. Knowing what almost certainly lay ahead, she remained in her clothes. With care, she placed her hairbrush and pins into a cloth bag.

Then she lay down.

Francesca dreamed of vineyards where she was mistress of all she surveyed. A stone house, a rose garden, herbs in terracotta pots—lemon, limes, and oranges. Hers and Vincenzo's.

But her sweet dream turned to the nightmare. There he was in New York, his unshaven chin dark with stubble, straddling a chair at a table shared with other men. All of them wore undershirts in the sweltering Little Italy night. In the smoke-filled room, the cards were dealt. Vincenzo palmed them, rearranging his hand with cocksure certainty.

He might choose to destroy their dream of buying a California vineyard cheap during Prohibition—it could not last forever. He might refuse to work, spending his days and nights in an endless card game fueled by thick tumblers of rough homemade wine ....

The cook's job at the Coldwell's required her to live at their brownstone, where she spent her days and nights praying that through some magic the old Vincenzo—the one who had sworn an oath in blood—would return to her.

One weekend, when she was free to be away, she took a valise with her best green silk dress, now ruined, and returned to the room she and Vincenzo had shared. She would cook something nice; they would make love.

He was not there.

He must be playing cards again, losing more of their money.

Francesca slumped on the sofa, too weary to clean the mess of Vincenzo's dirty dishes. She should go.

A woman's laughter in the hall .... The door opened.

Vincenzo's arm was wrapped around an Italian girl who could not have been more than sixteen. Her face turned up to his, rapt, as he murmured endearments Francesca recalled from the vine rows.

She ran to the kitchen and fumbled all the money out of the jar where she and Vincenzo kept their funds.

Her plans in ashes, she was running, running ... from New York, fleeing in rainy darkness from the rushing of water. In nightmare blackness, her limbs seemed too heavy. She struggled and all she could think was that she couldn't swim.

A pounding. "Francesca!" Asa shouted. "We're getting out now!"

She came to consciousness, heard the evil hiss overlain with a rumble and knew it was real.

She tore open the bedroom door, shoes in hand. Asa's expression mirrored her fears. If she had not lost her crucifix and beads, if she had prayed her rosary after the Lord had spared her the week before, would she have to battle for her life again?

Trailing Asa through the main room and onto the front porch, she gabbled, "*Ave Maria, gratia plena, Dominus tecum* ... Hail Mary, full of grace, the Lord is with thee."

"Amen to that." Asa kept moving.

Outdoors, the sound of the mountain on the move grew more ominous.

"Here!" shouted a breathless Roland Howard. His voice came from somewhere in the dark behind his house.

Asa grabbed her arm, and they plunged off the porch. Rocks underfoot bruised her bare feet and she dragged to a stop.

She threw down a shoe and shoved her foot into it. Asa knelt and fumbled for the laces. With rushing water approaching, she cried out, "Go!"

Asa ignored her.

With one shoe half-laced and the other flopping loose, she started a shambling gait.

A new slide must have crashed into the lake and displaced the water. She'd heard of George Hall's wild ride, pursued by the Gros Ventre running uphill.

Francesca visualized the terrain around the house. Like the Hall place, the Circle X occupied a wide meadow on a bench above the river. The nearest high ground was at least a hundred yards behind the house. From the direction of the stables, Francesca heard the doors thrown wide against the walls and men shouting to the horses.

Ahead of her, Asa's boots pounded; she saw his white shirt as a paler shade against charcoal.

A male voice swore a vicious oath. It sounded like Mr. Howard, not twenty feet away.

Francesca stumbled up to him and Asa, who were scrambling through a barbed wire fence.

Expecting Asa to hold the wires apart for her, she bent over. Instead, he reached across the three-strand, thigh-high fence, seized her beneath the armpits, and swung her up off her feet. She lifted her legs as high as she could but got tangled in the wire.

They were running out of time.

With a struggle that tore her trousers and scratched her arms, she cleared the fence and wound up on hands and knees. Howard and Asa each grabbed one of her arms and yanked her up.

"Run!" Howard shouted.

As the three raced uphill, Francesca did not look back to see how closely disaster dogged them.

Once above the pasture fence, the terrain steepened. Her lungs on fire, Francesca forced her legs to keep climbing. From the panting sounds behind her, she knew she had out-distanced Howard and Asa.

A few seconds later, their renewed swearing alerted her they been overtaken by the flood.

Francesca reached the edge of the trees where the slope pitched up to thirty degrees.

Something clipped the back of her knees. Going down, she stretched to wrap her arms around a pine sapling. The flood swirled around her waist, to her neck, and covered her head.

She held her breath and clung to the tiny tree. Black water, foul and filthy; gritty and full of twigs and pine needles ....

Something solid struck her between the shoulder blades. Howard or Asa?

It bumped her again and then moved on. If it had been one of the men, he had to be unconscious.

Her chest heaved, her mouth opened. The vile fluid tasted of earth and gagged her into choking, which only brought in more to fill her lungs.

Another paroxysm, and she began a silent *"Pater Noster,"* believing they would be her last words.

Chapter Seven
June 30, 1925

Cord sat at the dining table in his house with ranch foreman Charlie Sanborn, while Laura poured cups of strong black coffee. She made it cowboy style over the woodstove, with a little cold water added at the end to settle the grounds in the blue and white speckled pot.

"That pot must be older than the boys," said Charlie, his deep brown eyes gleaming against his dark skin.

Cord studied the dents on the metal surface, along with dark spots on the rim where the enamel had worn off. "Could be older than I am. Ma and Pa had it in our cabin here when I was six, before ...." He cleared his throat. "Aaron found it when I came back to re-stake the homestead."

He pictured big hearty Aaron Bryce, his adoptive father, bending and poking in the weeds outside the long-charred ruin. "Hello," he'd exclaimed. "What's this?"

Cord cupped his hands around his mug. "It's one of the only things I have from the old place."

Laura went into the other room and Cord took the opportunity to dump a couple teaspoons of sugar into his coffee. She returned with a brightly painted elk hide.

The creases in Charlie's dark face shifted into a smile. "Reckon I've seen that before."

The first time Cord had seen the hide, it had been draped over the foot of his parents' bed.

Sarah had told Cord that long ago she lived with her people, who made such beautiful things. Before Franklin Sutton took her to live with him while he prospected the Teton wilderness for gold. Cord's father towered over most people, and, with his thick black hair and beard, he looked the part of a mountain man.

On that terrible night when his parents had burned to death, Cord's uncle, Bitter Waters, had taken two things away from the scene of disaster—six-year-old Cord, and his mother's blanket.

Charlie smoothed the hide, which was decorated with men on horseback aiming their bows at deer and elk. "I don't have anything like this from my family."

"You have your lucky piece," Cord pointed out.

"That I do." Charlie reached into his pocket and pulled out a silver dollar dated 1876, the year he was born. The coin, drilled and attached to a chain, dangled next to a gold-cased pocket watch. He touched the catch, and the lid opened.

Cord knew he wasn't checking the time as much as enjoying the inscription Cord had ordered when he gave Charlie the watch for his twentieth year at Snake River Ranch. *To my best friend, Charlie*, signed in engraved script, *William Cordon Sutton*.

"I got a couple of good luck pieces now," Charlie said. "But Lucy was my true luck. Can't believe me and her didn't have more years together."

Cord glanced at Laura, embarrassed that they had each other when Charlie had been left alone. Nothing had beaten Lucy's country ham and cornbread or her pecan pie. Her rich, full laugh had livened evenings in the Main.

Three years now since she came down with a misery in her lungs and died. The suddenness had thrown everyone at Snake River into shock.

And started a chain reaction of transient cooks who couldn't hold a candle to Lucy's talent.

Charlie harrumphed and put the watch and coin away. Cord set aside his coffee cup and Laura returned the painted hide to their room before taking a seat with them. She always sat in on ranch meetings.

So did William, but it was past their agreed time of three p.m. and he wasn't there.

Charlie glanced at the door. "Want to wait?"

"The boy knows how to tell time," Cord groused.

Laura broke in gently, "Maybe it's time to call someone who's twenty-four years old a man."

Quick anger flashed in Cord. "Time he stepped up and acted like one. If Bryce has no interest in this ranch, then William needs to find a wife and start planning the next generation of Suttons."

Charlie put up a hand. "Careful. He'll choose the wrong woman, like that Prudence gal who's got the wrong name for sure."

Laura's green eyes came to rest on Cord's. "Charlie's right about how it needs to be between a man and a woman."

"Like you and Laura," Charlie said, "and me and Lucy. Though the good Lord never saw fit to grant us children."

"If we're talking of William," Laura said, "why do you think he wants to be in Texas?"

"Damned if I know." Cord gestured at the Teton view. "God's country right here."

"Sometimes the place a man's born isn't special until he gets along in years," Charlie observed.

"I was born here like both boys, and I sure as hell appreciate it."

Laura interjected, "But you were taken away after the fire and didn't come back to homestead until you were older than William and Bryce."

Charlie set down his coffee. "And your father died when you were young, so you don't know what it's like for William Cordon Sutton, Jr., to live in your shadow. Or for Bryce to live in both yours and his big brother's."

Impatient with this line of conversation, Cord reached for the ranch ledger. "It doesn't matter why our sons aren't itching to take over the business. One thing's true, though. When William was in Texas, we learned the three of us can still run the place ... without him or Bryce."

Laura gave Cord and Charlie a thoughtful look. "Another thing's true, Cord. You and I couldn't do it without Charlie."

William was late. And getting later.

Seventeen-year-old summer hand, Ned Hanson, who had the crop of freckles many redheads sported, couldn't get the saddle on Bayberry for the afternoon trail ride.

William, dressed in a nice shirt and trousers and polished boots, because Father liked him to dress smartly for ranch meetings, stopped by the corral fence reluctantly.

"See, I just tightened it, and the girth's too slack." Ned demonstrated by reaching a thin arm, grabbing Bayberry's saddle horn, and tilting it back and forth.

The gray mare snorted and pawed.

William glared at Bayberry. "She makes a good dude horse because she's slow and gentle, but some days she decides she doesn't want to leave the barn."

Ned frowned. "So what do I do?"

The dudes stood around, including the fellow who affected ridiculous orange chaps.

William lost patience. "Didn't anybody teach you to saddle a horse?" He was sure he'd seen Ned getting lessons from Jim Lovejoy near the beginning of the season.

The boy reddened, reminding William that his own attempts to handle horses didn't always go smoothly. "Okay," he relented, starting to climb the fence.

Ned stepped back, and William bent to loosen the girth. "See how she puffs her belly when I let the slightest amount of slack."

"Yeah."

"Here's what you do." William brought his knee up sharply into Bayberry's middle. The mare gave the equivalent of a gasp, sucking in her stomach.

William slipped the strap and tightened it.

"Keen," said the lad. He headed to take the dangling reins.

"Not so fast." William loosened the buckle again. "I want to see you do it."

Chewing his lip, Ned went to Bayberry's side. William waited, wondering if the boy had the nerve to follow through. Hands who couldn't deal with large animals ended up mending tack or sweeping stalls.

Ned stroked Bayberry's withers. "You let me get that saddle on you now," he coaxed.

She puffed out her tummy.

"Guess you won't do it easy." In a burst of motion, Ned kneed the horse and tightened the girth.

"Good work," William said.

When he left the corral his polished boots were marred by horse dung. He tried to wipe them off on the grass. If Father noticed, he'd think William was being rebellious.

Twenty minutes late now, he hurried across the meadow behind the cookshack. Damned shame about Francesca having to work at Circle X. She had it all over Prudence. Blonde and buxom could get a man going, but brunette with eyes as big as saucers stuck in his mind. Something about Pru's sulkiness—call it true—bitchiness, made her a gal to tumble but not to tarry with.

On Sunday, he'd head up the Gros Ventre and pay Fran a call. Ask if he could take her driving in the buggy. When he got his Model T, going to see her would be easier.

Cutting in front of the Main, William heard the telephone bell's harsh grinding.

Hell. What difference would a few more minutes make?

He ran across the porch and inside, his boots shedding bits of dung on the polished floor. Picked up the earpiece. "Snake River Ranch."

"Cord?" Postmistress Ida Chambers sounded strained; William recalled her penchant for disseminating urgent news. On the day of the slide, Charlie had taken the call.

"It's William. Father is down at his house."

"That new lake up there," she began. "There have been more slides. Flooded out the Ranger Station and the Circle X in the middle of the night."

His heart bumping, William almost blurted a question about Fran. Then he thought better of advertising on the valley telegraph.

Instead, he tried to keep his voice steady. "Is everyone all right?"

Chapter Eight
July 1, 1925

Francesca awoke in a borrowed bed with tears pouring down her face. A nightmare, no, the truth. On the hillside above the Circle X, tossed by the water as if she were weightless, believing she would drown.

Gloria a Dio, the great wave had receded, leaving her sodden and clutching the sapling. Filled with immense relief, until the next surge seized her.

A new slide had sent water sloshing upstream and back down, the way water in a bowl agitates if someone drops in a load of pebbles. The new lake level stabilized with the Circle X lodge six feet under and a shivering Francesca looking for Mr. Howard and Asa in pitch blackness.

Ranger Duran and his family had arrived with the sun, fellow refugees. When they joined her search, they found the two men and all the Circle X hands, along with the horses. The cattle were not so fortunate.

Francesca turned over in bed and realized what had wakened her.

The mewling week-old boy's name was J.C. Raleigh, son of Ben and Anne, who lived near the Gros Ventre east of Kelly. When Francesca had asked the young couple who had taken her in what the initials stood for, she had learned about the peculiarly American custom of bestowing monikers like J.C., J.D., or J.R. on boy babies.

J.C. was apparently a good timekeeper: Jackson's Hole's early dawn had broken.

With further sleep out of the question, Francesca got up and washed her face. She used the brush Anne had loaned her to smooth her hair and wished she had asked to borrow some hairpins. Finally, dressed in one of Anne's blue drop-waist frocks with a pleated skirt, she went barefoot into the kitchen. There, Francesca cooked breakfast as silently as she could.

By the time Anne came out in a pink terry robe that matched her cheeks with the chubby baby in her arms, the aroma of coffee filled the kitchen.

Anne's blue eyes widened. "You shouldn't have."

"Of course I should."

"I was going to let Ben sleep a little longer after J.C. kept him awake half the night. But he's got to see this."

Ten minutes later, Anne had smoothed her tousled brunette hair and donned a loose dress. Her stout, dark-haired husband Ben wore work coveralls and a brimmed cap.

Francesca served delicate egg crepes filled with apples and cinnamon and drizzled with sweet cream. Alongside rested fried ham and eggs turned in the grease so the whites looked lacy.

Ben tucked into his plate, pausing between mouthfuls to sip coffee with cream so thick it floated. "I brought the dairy from Snake River."

At Francesca's inquiring look, Anne said, "Ben works at the Snake River Dude Ranch."

"*Si?*" Francesca abandoned English, as she did when flustered.

Ben put his fists on either side of his plate, clutching a knife and fork. "I had lunch in the Main yesterday, after guiding a morning trail ride. The food wasn't anything like this."

Anne studied her plate. "I thought crepes were French. Where did you learn to make them?"

"Italy is not far from France. And the mistress at the *castello* where I worked liked fine food."

"They're wonderful," Anne said.

"*Grazie,*" Francesca said.

After breakfast, Ben left for work and Francesca returned to the room they had provided.

Atop a lace doily on the wardrobe lay the money Roland Howard had dropped by the night before. A week's wages, plus two more he'd insisted on, "For notice," though her dismissal had been an act of God.

Was there enough for train fare to California? Perhaps, but without even a change of underwear, such a move seemed foolish.

Perhaps she could ask Anne about staying on a couple of weeks. Maybe she'd like to hire a temporary cook and housekeeper long enough to get over the birthing ... and for Francesca to put together a little more money.

Moving toward the bedroom door, she detected Anne's voice in the kitchen. From the tone, she was probably talking to an adult on the telephone rather than to the baby.

Francesca decided to wait outdoors. Picking up the bead-fringed shawl that matched the kick-pleated flapper dress, she slipped out through the living room. On her way, she overheard Anne laughing into the phone receiver. "She said she worked at some castle in Europe. You should have tasted her crepes."

With a smile, Francesca let herself out the front door. If Anne were enthusiastic enough to call a friend, perhaps she'd keep her on.

On the other hand, if Ben worked in the outfit at Snake River Ranch, they couldn't have a lot of extra cash. Their neat frame house was plain, befitting a young couple starting out.

Francesca descended three raw wooden steps between a pair of pink-blooming rosebushes. The front of the house faced west with the Teton view, so it was in the chill morning shade. She pulled the shawl tighter around her shoulders as she rounded the side yard to find the sun. Inside the rustic wooden fence with posts propped to form an "X" was a river cobble patio. A circle of split-willow lawn chairs surrounded a fire pit still smelling of smoke.

Francesca took a seat and watched the valley's display of wildlife. Beside the Gros Ventre, a moose in velvet wandered among the cottonwoods. The meadow blooms were predominantly yellow; Asa had identified the fading flowers of yellow balsam root, along with little sunflowers and several varieties of cinquefoil coming into their prime. The tip of the Grand Teton peeked over the forested promontory of Blacktail Butte.

The sun moved higher, and she let the shawl fall from her shoulders. The contrast between this warmth and the freezing flood the other night suffused her with a sense of well-being.

On the other hand .... She stared at the river, perhaps a hundred yards away. Here, the river was behind a terrace. There was none upstream in Kelly, which could explain why the Raleighs did not feel the need to sleep in the hills.

Pushing aside unpleasant thoughts of what might happen if the slide dam failed to hold, Francesca lay back. The energy to move and even to think drained away.

William parked the Dodge truck in front of the Raleigh place and procured his hat from the seat beside him.

As he started for the front door, he noticed someone lounging in the side yard. With those long legs and dark hair that hung over the back of the chair, it had to be Fran.

As soon as Ida Chambers had said the Circle X had flooded, he'd planned to find Francesca and bring her to Snake River. Moving in closer, he realized she was fast asleep, and her repose afforded him the opportunity to study her at leisure. In the sunlight, her hair shone like burnished metal with bronze highlights. Her dark lashes made crescents against her lower lids where faint shadows lurked.

With her legs a-sprawl in the fashionably short dress—modern folks were no longer calling them "limbs"—he had a view of bare thighs, and though the dress did not hug her waist, its jewel-toned silk clung to her breasts.

Francesca opened her eyes to find William Sutton. He immediately swept his cowboy hat off and held it before him. "I didn't want to wake you, you were sleeping so soundly."

His flush spelled too clearly the picture she must make.

She didn't want a man .... On the other hand, William had none of Vincenzo's calculated smoothness.

Flattered by his discomfort, she pulled her knees together and sat up straight, careful not to snag Anne's dress on a nail head in the willow wood chair. She reached behind her, gathered her sun-warmed hair into her hands, and twisted it into a loose knot at the nape of her neck.

Still holding his hat below his waist, William put out a hand. "Your hair ...."

She gave him inquiring look.

"Looked fine the way it was." His blush deepened, and she couldn't help but laugh.

Quick hurt reflected in his eyes. In a formal tone, he said, "I've come to take you back to Snake River."

Joy surged at the prospect of returning to the retreat by the river, but .... "I can't take any more of your family's charity. I've got a little money Mr. Howard paid me and—"

"You don't seem to have trouble taking Ben and Anne's charity," he flashed. "They have less to offer than I do."

Francesca flashed back, "You think because I didn't have a *lire* ... penny ... and I went with you without knowing who you were or where we were going ...."

William pulled up the nearest chair. "I think you've misunderstood. It's my fault for not telling it straight. The word is out in the valley from the Circle X hands about what a first-class co ... *chef* you are. You're to come back to Snake River and cook for the Main. Jim Lovejoy is going back to slinging hash for the outfit." William turned his hat in his hands.

Francesca weighed her options.

"Mother even said she'd like to learn from you."

"She did tell me she was not a cook."

"She's not. The ranch could really use you."

He didn't say he wanted her to come and that stung a little, but she had nowhere else to go.

Mr. and Mrs. Sutton came out as soon as William pulled up in front of the Main. Jim Lovejoy came running and scooted to a stop, red-faced, in front of Francesca. "I wanted to tell you nobody's making me give up the cook job, so you mustn't feel a bit bad. What this place needs is a chef like the one they have over at the Bar BC. And I'd appreciate some pointers on cooking for the outfit, especially how to make the men stop ribbing me about the biscuits being made of lead."

Francesca laughed and climbed out of the truck.

Mrs. Sutton hugged her. "Welcome back ... and call me Laura."

"*Grazie*. I am ready to work."

"Nonsense." Laura waved that aside. "It's true Anne Raleigh had my mouth watering when she called about your cooking, but you need to rest after what you've been through. Plan on serving your first meal in the Main tomorrow evening. Tonight Jim's doing roast beef and mashed potatoes."

Did these people eat nothing but meat and potatoes?

Two dark-haired women stood to one side. For a moment, Francesca thought they might be Italian, but a closer look at their almost Indian bone structure made her suspect they were Mexican.

Laura gestured them over. "This is Rosa Flores."

The shorter of the two, dressed in a faded blue dress, bobbed her head. "*Señora*."

"*Señorita*," Francesca corrected in Spanish; she spoke a smattering of French, as well.

"Maria Gonzales," Laura went on.

Francesca greeted a statuesque beauty only a few inches shorter than herself. Maria carried her height proudly; her divided skirt and jacket in burgundy fit her exquisitely.

"Maria is a skilled seamstress and manages the ranch laundry. During dude season, Francesca, you can just put your clothes in a basket in your room and they'll come back cleaned and pressed. Rosa is our dishwasher; she'll be cleaning up in the Main, and also setting the tables."

Next Francesca met Tom, the wiry, dark boy who had been lighting the lamps of the Main. He was about seventeen, with a Welsh accent; his job was to bring wood to the cookshack and build fires in the stone fireplace and black iron woodstove. He also assisted the head roustabout with keeping the wood boxes in the guest cabins stocked with fuel and overseeing the evening fire in the Main.

Other introductions followed, until Francesca knew she'd have to meet everyone at least twice to get them all straight.

Laura walked her to the cookshack. "You've yet to meet our ranch foreman, Charlie Sanborn. And at least ten of the wranglers."

Francesca took her meager belongings—Asa Dean's denims and flannel shirt—into the lean-to. There, she had a pleasant surprise. A green silk robe lay across the bed and on the wooden dresser rested a silver-backed comb and brush set.

She turned to find Laura smiling. "I thought you would need a few things."

Francesca would have to spend some money on material and pay Maria to make her some clothes ... as long as those purchases did not eat too deeply into her savings for California.

Once Laura had gone, Francesca took a walk around.

The ranch seemed bigger than she recalled, as she tried to remember the purpose of each building. One particularly nice frame house with white paint and a picket fence sat apart in a grove of cottonwoods. A sign on the gate said, "William Cordon Sutton, Jr."

Francesca ended up at the edge of the bluff overlooking the river in its deepest cut. The Snake's wide, braided channel spread out before her, littered with tons of fallen snags. Rapids rippled, and from over a hundred feet away, she heard water burbling. Rounded river rocks beneath her feet testified that the river's turbulence had once reached this level.

Below, the water threw back the sky's reflection and that of cottonwoods and spiky firs along the banks.

Wishing she had her rosary, Francesca sent up a prayer of thanks for her safe return to Snake River Ranch.

The next evening, Francesca prepared her first meal for the Main—dinner for twenty dudes, the wranglers and guides, the Suttons, and a plate for Jim Lovejoy, who was standing by in case she ran into problems.

After researching what was available in the ranch stores, the hothouse, and the garden, she decided on legs of lamb seasoned with mint and sorrel, new potatoes sliced thin with lemon juice, garlic, and fresh cream butter, and wilted lettuce with a sauce of egg yolks, sugar, and cider vinegar.

Even as she considered making bread, unsalted Tuscan-style, she created the expected ranch biscuits, considerably more airy than Jim's. While she rolled them out and used a water glass to cut circles, she gave him pointers on biscuit making.

About ten minutes before serving time, William strolled into the cookshack bearing a bottle of French Bordeaux. Francesca had not seen a decent wine since she had served in the Coldwell's brownstone in New York.

"A gift." He handed her the bottle and she placed it on a shelf next to a tin of baking powder.

"*Grazie.*" Something fluttered in her stomach.

"I came to tell you about the rodeo up on the flats above the Bar BC tomorrow. Everyone goes, and there's a big pre-Fourth of July barbecue, so huge we won't be making dinner here tomorrow night." He looked around. "Anything I can help with?"

She could have used an extra hand carrying things over to the serving kitchen, but it would look unseemly for the owner's son to serve at table.

Before she could demur, William picked up the bowl of wilted lettuce salad and the potatoes. "Father taught his boys there was no chore on this ranch we should not master."

"Boys?" She had thought him the only son.

But William was already out the door. If he had a brother, or brothers, where were they?

Moments later, she watched him in the Main, chipping ice at the bar. Once he filled the crystal ice bucket, he started slicing oranges and carrying on a conversation with a bob-haired flapper whose smile said she was smitten.

Francesca turned her attention to carving the lamb. With William bringing her wine and helping her serve the ranch guests, she had almost forgotten the gulf between his station and hers.

Chapter Nine
July 3, 1925

When Francesca arrived at the rodeo on the sage flats above the neighboring Bar BC Ranch, at least two hundred people had assembled. Horses at hitching rails stood patiently, twitching their tails at flies. Wagons and buggies, and a line of automobiles and trucks filled a field.

The oblong ring looked enormous, with swinging gates at intervals around it. A grandstand of redolent, raw pine boards provided seats for the local dignitaries. Behind the grandstand, concessionaires sold coffee, drinks, and pastries.

Not knowing what to expect, Francesca stayed with Rosa and Maria while they pointed out the staging areas for each event. Jim swapped stories with Asa and Bobby Cowan; the two men from Circle X had joined the Snake River outfit yesterday.

Everyone there seemed to have learned how to ride from when they'd been carried on horseback at their mother's breast. They knew how to shoot and hunt meat, even bear—eaten smoked, salted, or dried. When she asked how it compared to *prosciutto*, Jim and the boys didn't know what she was talking about.

Without warning, a metal cup appeared before her nose, held in a masculine hand. She turned.

It was William, offering a cup of lemonade. He was wearing a pair of alpaca chaps over his denims, and his polished brown boots were already gathering dust. Rosa, Maria, and the guys drifted away while she felt her cheeks warm at being singled out.

"*Grazie.*" She sipped the sweet-tart drink and shook it to enjoy the clinking of the ice. "You did not get one?"

William's silvery-gray eyes twinkled beneath the brim of his brown beaver hat. Lifting his hand to hers, he brought the cup slowly to his lips. Just before he would have touched the rim, he paused. "May I?"

She nodded; that little catch was back in her midsection again.

He drank, released the cup and her hand. "Don't forget to root for me in the bronc riding."

Laura sat in the grandstand and watched her son flirt with their new chef. Tapping Cord on the forearm, she asked, "Did you see that?"

His dark blue eyes, with a midnight ring around the iris, connected with hers. "You mean William and Francesca?" He looked amused. "Summer ... I seem to recall a time when two people met on the twentieth of June and—"

Laura laughed low in her throat. "And married on the Fourth of July."

Cord slipped his arm around her shoulders. "Happy Anniversary ... tomorrow that is."

"Twenty-five years. When I see our sons, I know it has to be true."

"I remember our first winter on the ranch. About the time when I started thinking about us having children. I imagined a boy, pushing his way with chubby hands through the sage."

"I felt the same."

"Back to the subject at hand .... Wild oats get sown, especially on dude ranches."

Laura looked up at Cord. "When I spoke with Francesca, I got the impression she was in some kind of trouble."

"What trouble?" Cord scowled. "Best she not think she can palm someone else's brat off on William." He gestured at his son, who was striding toward the corral where the horses awaited their turn at becoming "bucking broncos."

Much as Laura wanted to like Francesca, Cord's insinuation gave her pause.

Cord left Laura and wandered over to shake Struthers Burt's hand. One would never know the principal owner of the Bar BC was a Princeton graduate and best-selling author. *The Diary of a Dude Wrangler* had appeared in installments in *Life Magazine*, and last year the book had been published by Scribner's Sons.

Though raised in the East, Burt had transplanted thoroughly, riding and roping with the best. His wife, Katharine, was also an author.

Burt greeted and reached into his pocket to offer a smoke. Cord waved it away. The last few times he'd tried tobacco, he'd felt breathless for an hour.

Burt gestured with his cigarette in the direction of the parking lot full of automobiles. "More and more of those beasts every season."

"I don't like tin can tourists any better than you," Cord replied. "Won't have an auto on my place, even though William's angling for one."

"I never thought I'd be a conservationist," Burt mused. "When I started ranching, I believed in private enterprise in this valley above all."

Cord had, too. In 1898, after he had reestablished a homestead on his father's land, the Director of the United States Geologic Survey had recommended the Tetons be designated a park.

He had been dead set against it.

In 1916, when Department of the Interior Director Stephen Mather and Yellowstone Superintendent Horace Albright decided the Tetons should be added to Yellowstone, Cord and Burt had stood shoulder to shoulder in opposition.

But by 1920, Albright had made it clear he favored a park that would include the Tetons and Jenny Lake and leave the rest of the valley in private hands.

"What I believe in is my ranch," Cord told Burt, "and the old ways."

"The old ways ...." A man spoke in a mocking voice from behind Cord. Burt's pleasant expression altered only slightly, as Cord knew it did when his friend was forced to suffer fools.

"The old ways are done," went on fellow dude rancher Dieter Gross. "You might as well get used to it. Nothing's come of your 'Jackson's Hole Plan.' "

Cord turned and took in the shaved cannonball of head, heavy black brows, and matching handlebar mustache that failed to hide Dieter's moue of distaste.

Dieter referred to an idea that had come out of a meeting on July 26, 1923, between the National Park Service and local interests, held at Maude Noble's place beside Menor's Ferry. Out of their discussion had come The Jackson's Hole Plan, to create a recreation area that would preserve the "Old West," with rustic log architecture mandated. In addition, they would seek private funds to purchase land and restore it to a pristine condition.

"I don't know why you aren't on our side," Burt said. "Your Lazy D would be part of the preserved area."

"I don't have the kind of romantic notions about the 'Old West' that you do." Dieter's glare included Cord and Burt. "Next season, I'm building a gas station on the Jenny's Lake Road."

"That's all we need." Cord started to walk away.

"Hold on, breed," Dieter called after him.

Cord's shoulders stiffened; he did not turn back.

"Dieter!" Burt abandoned all pretense of politeness.

Still walking, Cord missed the reply.

During the singing of the national anthem, William spied his parents in the grandstand and Fran sitting prettily on the fence. She wore a pink flowered dress that came down to her ankles; he preferred the blue silk from the other day for the expanse of leg it had displayed.

In the center of the paddock, Asa Dean, who had signed on at Snake River as a stockman yesterday, used a megaphone to announce the bucking horse competition. The horses weren't really unbroken animals, which made it a matter of showmanship. The cowboy who got his horse to buck the highest and stayed on through the clock won.

By the time ten men competed—several on horses that refused to buck—William knew the man he had to beat. Tiny Good had worked at Snake River half a season, picked a fistfight with Bryce when he was home, and called Charlie a nigger. Cord had fired him, and for the past three seasons, Tiny had worked for Dieter Gross at the Lazy D.

Astride a mean-looking black gelding, Tiny waited while one of the hands from the Lazy D blindfolded his mount. At Tiny's signal, the man removed the blindfold and waved the cloth in the horse's face.

Horse and man put on a thirty-second virtuoso performance.

Up last, William held the reins of Crackerjack. The little strawberry mare stood hands shorter than the other broncs but had a feisty energy.

At Asa's direction, William led the horse into the arena. Aware of every nuance of the crowd, he noted he had Tiny's attention. He found his parents and saw that his father wasn't watching; his attention was on a knot of cowboys leaning on the fence.

Fran was looking, though. "Be careful," she called. Prudence Johnston, who stood a few feet down, frowned at Fran and then waved at William.

He blindfolded Crackerjack, mounted up and got a gloved hand beneath the leather strap across her withers. Jim Lovejoy waited for William's signal.

He took a couple of deep breaths and turned his free thumb up.

Jim ripped off the blindfold and waved it. "Hiyah!"

Crackerjack threw out her hind legs in a mule kick and started to buck. Anyone who knew the gentle mare understood her performance was worthy of Theda Bara. Though spurs were part of the costume, Crackerjack didn't need them.

William had discovered long ago that he did worse if he counted the seconds; this time he found himself doing it. All went well through five.

Without warning, Crackerjack started at something or someone outside the buck rail fence. Rather than continue as an almost perfect bronco, she lost focus and dropped her hind legs.

Losing count, William dared a glance at the audience.

Tiny slouched beside the grandstand a few feet below Dieter's seat. Both men were laughing. Foster Case, who'd joined the Snake River outfit along with Asa and Bobby, stood close by.

For the first time in his life, William spurred Crackerjack.

The mare went berserk, becoming a whirling dervish. With both a twist and a vertical component, it was all William could do not to let her unseat him.

Would the horn ever sound? His ride had turned into the kind rodeo champions got from wild horses.

With a baleful glare, Crackerjack planted her front hooves.

William's legs lost their grip and he found himself hanging off the side.

Crackerjack started another contortion. It yanked William's arm and he feared dislocating his shoulder.

To hell with it.

He let go and landed on the broken turf, while Crackerjack aimed a kick at him.

Francesca watched Jim Lovejoy go to the now-subdued Crackerjack and take her by the halter. While he escorted the mare out of the arena, Asa Dean handed over the megaphone to the mayor of Jackson, who presented the bucking bronco trophy to Tiny Good of Lazy D.

An older, bald man with a startling black moustache came into the ring and took the trophy from the rider; Francesca assumed he must own the ranch and the bucking horse.

On the far side of the arena, she spied William heading away across the sage meadow. Intending to follow him, she jumped off the fence and found another of the ubiquitous bronze, slim-hipped cowboys blocking her path.

Wearing faded denims, well-worn brown leather chaps, and boots bearing scuffs and scars, he appeared to be the real thing. His eyes bore the glint of green bottle glass; a dark mote near the outer rim of one served to make him less than perfect, along with his couple days' worth of beard. He took off his hat to her and the sun picked up gold streaks in his thick, tawny moustache and hair.

With a courteous nod, he stepped past her.

"*Scusi!*" she called.

He stopped, his hat halfway to his head. Gave her a rich grin. "*Si?*"

Had he really meant to answer in Italian, or was he speaking Spanish? She smiled at him. "Are you going to ride a bull?"

"If he doesn't throw me."

Leaning against a tree beside Cottonwood Creek, William pulled out his sack of Bull Durham and papers. With unsteady hands, he rolled a cigarette.

He'd had two women watching, not to mention his parents, and had been primed to win. What in hell had Crackerjack suddenly found so fascinating in the crowd?

William stuck the end of the cigarette in his mouth and brought out a box of matches decorated with the Snake River brand, a sinuous "S" curve holding up a leaning "R." He struck a match on his boot heel and lighted his smoke, hoping to calm down before the branding and roping exhibition.

The stream sparkled and burbled. Born in the mountains, it meandered across the valley floor to join the swift flood of the Snake just above Menor's Ferry.

This was where he belonged .... Why couldn't he forget that in Texas he'd been a man, not someone's son?

Inhaling smoke, he cursed whatever impulse had incited him to spur Crackerjack. She was without a doubt one of the sweetest animals he'd ever ridden. He'd been fifteen when he found out she liked to play at bucking and would make a good show bronc.

William started back to offer Crackerjack an apology.

The bulls, in contrast to the well-groomed horses, were behemoths. Whenever a man stepped near, their nostrils flared and they pawed the earth and stamped, throwing up wet clods and digging deep pits into the muck.

Wondering if William would compete in this event, Francesca looked around.

Laura caught her eye and beckoned her to the grandstand. "Are you enjoying the rodeo?"

Francesca couldn't say she enjoyed watching men flung into the mud, even if it was the local culture.

Before her lack of reply became obvious, William's mother went on, "I imagine his pride suffered more than his backside ... especially with you watching." Something in her tone warned Francesca she might be good enough to cook dinner, but not to aspire to the Suttons' son.

Looking over at the blonde who had waved at William, Francesca replied, "I believe he was riding for someone else."

Laura followed her gaze. "Prudence Johnston took a shot at William last summer." Her tone said she was glad the blonde had failed.

Francesca flushed.

"Do you like my son?"

What did the matriarch of Snake River want to hear?

Francesca kept her expression neutral. "When the slide came down, he saved my life."

Asa's amplified voice began to announce the bull riding, and Francesca took the opportunity to move away.

"Oohh," the crowd gasped.

Francesca looked into the ring as the biggest bull she had ever seen tore out of a narrow chute. Brutus from Snake River, with the cowboy who had tipped his hat to her astride.

Her hands curled into fists. This event appeared far more dangerous than the bucking horses; they had been led docilely or ridden calmly into the ring and incited to their gyrations.

The spectators shouted encouragement. Francesca held her breath.

Seconds ticked. If the monster pitched the cowboy off, those hooves could pound him to death.

A horn sounded the end of a successful ride, and the cowboy leaped from the bull's back, landing lightly on both feet. Blood pounding, Francesca raised her fist and cheered.

Though Asa announced the next rider, Francesca left the ring.

At loose ends, she passed a whole steer turning on a spit. One of the men watching it sopped a rag and plastered sauce onto the meat.

She struck out toward a line of trees that marked a clear, swift-flowing creek. The sounds of the bullhorn and the crowd receded, replaced by the drone of bees pollinating the summer wildflowers.

Drinking in the floral scents, she leaned against one of the cottonwoods. She had learned their name when she commented to William about the drifts of "cotton" released from their seed pods.

The midday sun beat down; she lifted her heavy hair off her neck and a rivulet of sweat ran down the middle of her back. As she recalled the slow way William had lifted the lemonade to his lips while touching her hand, a heavy languor stole over her. Vincenzo had made her feel that way before they arrived in New York.

From downstream came the approaching chatter of children. A pair of boys, a towhead about six years old, the other smaller and darker, splashed in the shallows, their boots throwing up rooster tails. With each splatter, they giggled.

"Hey!" the older boy called, waving at someone downstream.

About fifty feet away, propped against a white aspen trunk, stood the cowboy who had successfully ridden the huge bull. He straightened and lifted a hand to the children.

Francesca ducked behind the cottonwood.

"You sure showed 'em."

"That Tiny, he never had a chance."

"Larry and I knew you'd win."

"No, Benjy wasn't sure."

At least the ugly fellow who had taken the bronc trophy had not ridden off with the one for bull riding.

The cowboy knelt and put an arm around little Benjy, who wore short pants. "You guys know how to skip rocks?"

Larry, in longer coveralls, nodded. "Benjy doesn't."

"Then we'll have to teach him."

The man poked around in the gravel bar beside the creek. Selecting a smooth, flat stone, he took Benjy's wrist and pressed the rock into his fingers. "Hold on to that, buddy."

Picking out a similar missile, the cowboy pointed out an area of smooth water, cocked his wrist, and flicked the stone out. It struck the surface, glanced off, and landed again. Two times, four. "Now you, Benjy."

Dark eyes focused, the boy frowned and chucked his stone into the creek. With a gulping splash, it sank.

Larry snickered. The cowboy quieted him with a glance. "Let's see you do it."

The blond boy bent for a skipping rock, set his thin arm, and released. His stone bounced off the water once and augured in.

"Good work!" said the man.

"Let me try again," Benjy entreated.

The sun made diamonds on the water, puffy clouds sailed over the Tetons, and the sky was a bowl of pure cobalt. Laughter mingled with the babble of the brook.

The cowboy did not look old enough to have sons the boys' age, but she sensed his love of children.

When Larry and Benjy declared they wanted to head back to the ring and watch "William ride the cutting horse," Francesca followed the threesome at what she hoped was a discreet distance.

She wasn't careful enough, though, for when she climbed on the fence to see the roping and branding exhibition, a low male voice spoke at her ear. "It's beautiful down by the creek."

She turned and looked into green eyes twinkling with mischief.

"Perhaps the bull should have thrown you," she came back.

Asa was back in center ring, lifting his megaphone while the crowd quieted. "Today, for our guests who haven't seen roundup, we have a special treat. William Sutton of the Snake River Ranch and his team will show you how it's done."

On the far side of the arena, a man opened the gate leading into a stock pen. Inside the confined area were half a dozen calves and William, riding a sturdy black and white paint horse.

"Chester is one of the best cowponies in the valley," narrated Francesca's companion.

William appeared as one with his mount while he and Chester attempted to herd. With a deal of chaos among the calves, lots of doubling back to the rear of the pen and bawling, they got into the open ring.

There Foster, Bobby, and another slim sapling of summer cowboy she'd met at the corral yesterday—Ned Hanson—waited near a charcoal brazier with a couple of branding irons heating. "Good thing Foster's riding herd on those boys," the cowboy said.

As he appeared familiar with the local hands, Francesca dared, "Do you work in the valley?"

He shook his head. "I'm in from a place near Idaho Falls. A big spread."

"Oh."

"Watch how William handles Chester."

With a slack rein and barely perceptible nudges of his knees, William directed the horse. Cutting a red and white calf out of the group, Chester pivoted.

William lifted the coiled rope from the saddle horn and twirled it over his head in an almost lazy motion. Man and horse gained on the fleeing animal.

The lasso curled sinuously to land around the calf's neck. Chester planted his front hooves and the rope jerked the calf off his feet. The muscles in the paint horse's rump stood out as he backed away.

Foster grabbed the calf's neck and Bobby and Ned each seized a hind leg. Together, they tried to wrestle the squirming animal to the dirt. Chester kept tension on the rope.

Bleating with each breath, the calf continued to fight. Finally, with a knee on its neck, it was down, squalling.

One of the cows in the pen bellowed.

The cowboy pointed. "That's mama yelling at the boys to leave her baby alone."

Looking for the mother, Francesca missed the branding.

The calf was up, running blindly, stumbling into a mud puddle, bouncing off the fence. William had Chester follow, guiding the frightened animal to the gate Foster held open.

"Nice work," the cowboy commented. He joined the crowd in applause.

Clasping her knees, Francesca looked at the fire heating the irons. "They have to burn the calves?"

"You could put a tag in their ear, or a collar on them like a dog, but cattle are too good at rubbing them off on the nearest tree. Branding works."

After some of the things she had seen in the War, this practical means of dealing with livestock should not disturb her. Yet it did, more than she cared to admit in front of a man for whom wrangling cattle must come as naturally as breathing.

The last calf turned out to be the largest, a sturdy young bull. The Idaho cowboy told Francesca he was an Angus and estimated him at three hundred pounds.

Each time it seemed that William would rope the young animal, it outran Chester. At last, when the rope snaked through the air and fell to earth, the Angus stepped into the circle with a front leg.

Chester started backing off. Foster grabbed the trapped animal by his horns and twisted, throwing the thick neck to the ground. Bobby went after one hind leg and Ned the other.

The Angus kicked out, throwing his weight to the left and right. Francesca heard Bobby swearing. Foster hung on.

"Look out, Ned," William shouted, as the green hand lost hold of the leg.

A hoof connected; Ned went flying. The cowboy Francesca had been sitting with leaped off the fence and raced across the clodded dirt. He dove headlong and caught the Angus.

William jumped down from Chester's back. The riderless cowpony kept the rope taut while the Idaho wrangler ran for the branding iron and pressed it to the calf's flank. Not thirty feet away, Francesca heard the hiss of contact, saw smoke rise, and smelled the stench of scorched hair.

The flesh caught fire.

Francesca clutched the fence rail and willed herself to remain in place.

In the ring, William pulled a knife from his pants pocket, reached between the bull calf's hind legs and gathered his testicles. Drawing them out away from the body, he sliced through the stretched-thin skin of the sack and cut them off. The newly minted steer screamed.

Francesca jumped off the fence and ran to hitch a ride back to Snake River Ranch.

Chapter Ten
July 3, 1925

In the stillness of early evening, while the people at the rodeo ate beef, Francesca gathered delicate young carrots, sweet onions, and baby spinach leaves from the garden. In the glass-walled hothouse, she selected red and yellow tomatoes, intending to sun-dry a supply rather than canning them as Americans would.

On her way back to the cookshack, she paused to watch the sun slip behind the mountains. A bank of clouds rolled up behind the range, their underbellies shot with vermilion. Up on the Grand, lightning streaked.

Francesca took her basket inside and lighted the lamp. A draft swirled around her ankles, lifting the pink flowered skirt. More lightning flashed, and the refreshing breeze brought the scent of rain.

Using pages from the previous week's *Jackson's Hole Courier* as kindling, she started the woodstove fire and the one on the hearth. About to burn the rest of the newspaper, Francesca noted a headline.

"All Quiet in Slide Area on Gros Ventre River."

Standing, she read by firelight.

> Little news is filtering down from the big slide. The water is slowly backing up.
>
> A.A. Bean of this city has been placed in charge of a crew of men and is busily engaged in building a pack trail around the slide. This work will probably be completed in a few days.
>
> Recent showers have practically assured a good grain yield, hay crop prospects are good, tho there may be no second cutting of alfalfa, and in that respect will the big slide affect the

farmers and ranchers of the Gros Ventre River Valley.

State Highway Engineer Corwin today made a survey of the slide. He announced that according to his measurements, the slide was approximately 180 feet deep. Yesterday, the water rose four feet. A raise of forty-five more will put it over the slide.

What would happen when the lake reached the top?

Safe on the opposite side of the valley, Francesca washed her harvest and decided to bake a loaf of Tuscan bread. Scooping out flour from the wooden barrel and mixing dough in a thick pottery bowl brought back memories of working beside her mother.

How she missed her, even after six years.

When the War had ended in November of 1918, the joyous celebrations on every continent only served to spread the Spanish influenza that roved the land. People who were well and playing cards in the evening were dead by morning, suffocated by viscous mucus in their lungs. Gauze masks failed to stop the scourge's leap from person to person.

Francesca could never recall having been so sick, but she had fought through. When she awoke to find her father at her bedside, smoothing back her fever-dampened hair, something in his manner struck fear in her heart.

"Mama!" She struggled to sit up.

"Sleep now, *cara*."

"I want Mama." Eighteen years old, but her sickbed emotions were that of a child.

Antonio shook his head.

With her mother gone, responsibility fell on her slender shoulders—in the *cucina*, and caring for her suddenly aged father.

His only animation came with remembering. "The first time I saw Carla, I knew there would be no other woman. She had her hands in flour, kneading dough in the lemon light that fell through a window at the *castello*. Her hair shone like the rich copper of the pots above the brick oven." Antonio wiped his tears from both cheeks without shame. "She pinched off a bit of bread from a cooling loaf and offered it to me on her open palm. I shall never forget the sense of warmth that gave me, of coming home."

Homeless, yet with a roof over her head, Francesca chopped the vegetables with precision and mixed them with broth in a pot on the woodstove. Outside the rain began its steady drumming. Every so often, a drop would bounce down the chimney and land in the fire with a hiss.

Soon the soup's ripe aroma blended with the smell of baking bread.

While she waited, Francesca went into the lean-to and sat in the rocking chair. Outside, the deepest dusk rimmed the tops of the peaks.

The rain continued to pour off the eaves, splatter on the ground, and sheet down the windows. Above the din, footsteps pounded, someone running through the storm.

A squeak of hardware announced the door opening.

"Hello?" A male voice, not William's. "Anybody here?" Boot heels struck the plank floor, approached. "Barry?"

Francesca went to the lean-to door. Silhouetted against the fire and lantern light, his eyes were all dark pupil, but she recalled their gimlet hue.

"You," he said. "Where's Barry?"

Smoothing her long skirt, she stepped out of her bedroom. "The cook who was here has gone to California."

"Always figured him for a wandering man ... not unlike myself." Dressed now in rain-darkened denims without his scarred leather chaps, the man reached up to tame his curling damp hair and took in the floured table. "Don't tell me you're cooking for the Main."

She remained silent. He cocked a sandy brow.

"You said not to tell you."

He burst out with a merry peal. "By God, I did."

What was the Idaho cowboy doing here? He had spoken as if he was familiar with William and Foster at the rodeo, turned up riding Brutus, asked after Barry and mentioned the Main ....

He sniffed. And frowned.

"Oh!" Francesca ran for the woodstove.

He beat her to it, grabbing the handle and opening the oven door. She scooped up a pair of potholders and pulled the round loaf off the metal rack. Thankfully, the top and sides appeared a rich golden.

He looked at the bread, then at her. "I haven't seen anything so beautiful since I was in *Toscana*." He spoke Italian.

As if in a dream, Francesca pinched off a piece of the bread crust, placed it on her palm and offered it to him.

"*Grazie.*" Bryce took her offering, chewed and swallowed. It was as fantastic as the woman before him. "I was afraid we might have to waste good bread," he went on in Italian.

She studied him with those astonishing eyes. "You are too young to have been one of the Americans who came during the War." She spoke English, either because she took pride in doing so, or because she detected from his syntax that his command of Italian was rusty.

"It was after. A humanitarian mission. We went to help with Mussolini's Battle for Grain. To teach farmers who were used to growing grapes and fruit about wheat."

She spat and swore a condemnation of Mussolini's mother. "It drove up the price of wheat and made us all hungry."

"I'm not surprised you say that. We learned, from talking to the people, that we had taken the wrong side."

"You did not know our country," she accused.

"And you don't know bull riding or branding."

Their gazes clashed. She looked magnificent with her chin thrust forward and dark eyes shining, an echo of ancient Rome.

"Let's agree." He spread his hands. "I know no more about your country than you do of mine."

He went to the front window, looked out at the rain, and found himself telling her things he'd pushed to the back of his mind. "This is wonderful country for ranching. It doesn't matter that it's cold and snow-covered six months of the year. This season makes up for it, when the light doesn't fade until after ten. The garden leaps, the grasses spring up before your eyes, and corn grows a foot a week." He turned to her. "Let's eat ...?"

"Francesca," she replied. "Francesca di Paoli."

Pulling bowls from a closed cupboard, he waited for her to ask both his name and how he knew his way around.

But she must have figured it out, or someone at the rodeo had told her, for she turned her attention to slicing bread and placing it into the bowls. He found a ladle and spooned soup atop while she cut more slabs from the loaf.

Inhaling, he named the dish. "I love *ribollita*."

"Would you ... like some wine?"

He moved to get a bottle of Bordeaux he'd spied on the shelf, slid open a drawer and extracted a corkscrew. She selected juice glasses from the shelves.

He poured for them and raised his glass. "What shall we drink to?"

Francesca stared at him, unable to think. He seemed more alive than anybody she could remember meeting. His enthusiasm for the art of the rodeo, his lean body riding the bull and leaping into the ring to help when Ned got hurt, his professed love for food and wine ....

Most of the time one toasted birthdays, weddings, accomplishments ... perhaps she could toast his bull riding trophy.

She tried to think, but his green gaze was mesmerizing.

This kitchen with its hanging copper pots, and this food, reminded

Francesca richly of home ... or rather, the *concept* of home. When she was a child, she had seen the Rossi's kitchen that way. Only later did she learn a servant has no home.

Perhaps when she reached California she would find one. Lifting her glass, she proposed, "To journey's end."

"To coming home," he replied.

He must have seen her quizzical expression, for he stopped with his glass raised. "Do you know who I am?"

Without the warning of footsteps, the cookshack door opened.

William took in the tableau; soup bowls steaming, glasses raised, and a pretty flush on Fran. Chilled, his rain wet hair plastered to his head, he declared, "Well, if it isn't my wandering brother."

Fran's eyes went wide.

William laughed. "Ever the ladies' man—toasting you without even an introduction."

Bryce addressed Fran as if William weren't there. "I had assumed my reputation preceded me, but ... Bryce Aaron Sutton, named after Dad's adoptive father, the son who came along a year after the firstborn, William Cordon Sutton, *Junior*." He emphasized the last word.

Francesca murmured something in Italian. Bryce replied in an equally low tone. Excluded, William felt his face warm.

Bryce glanced over. "Just the pleased to meetchya, and likewise, Brother."

"So you decided to come back during slack time," William parried.

Summer was the slowest time for real work at the ranch. With the cattle driven to the high pastures, long days and extra hands on board, it seemed easy to get things done ... like equipment repair, fixing corrals and fences.

Bryce tilted his chair back onto two legs and lifted his boots onto the table beside his soup bowl. "That's me." He smiled. "A lazy bum." With a gesture at his scratched and worn footwear, he went on, "Plum wore these boots out sittin' on my ass over in Idaho." His expression hardened. "When I come home for the Fourth of July, I expect a vacation like most working people."

The rain increased its din, with the added rattle of hail. William stepped closer to the fire, holding out his hands.

Bryce rose and clapped a hand on his shoulder. "Come on ... there's plenty of soup."

William had eaten his fill at the rodeo.

His brother moved with the lithe grace William envied to the shelves and pulled down another juice glass. "Have some wine and swap some lies." He shot a wicked glance at William, reminding him of the little brother who had always made him laugh. "We'll talk about how I saved the roping demo this afternoon."

"You saved it?" William took up the challenge. "In a pig's eye." But his tone softened.

Bryce poured wine. William shrugged off his damp jacket and took the glass. The bottle he'd planned to share with Fran was half empty.

Bryce pulled out a chair next to his for William. "Who was the kid lost hold of the hind leg?"

"Ned Hanson. Son of one of our Philadelphia dudes last summer. Good kid, he's learning."

"Lucky he didn't take more than a glancing kick."

"Thanks to you. Say, was it you in the crowd who got Crackerjack distracted?"

Bryce grinned. "Sorry about that. When she saw me, she must have wanted to check my pockets for treats."

Francesca compared the two men. William, shorter and sturdy, with sharp gray eyes, did not appear to favor either his mother or father, while Bryce had his father's tall and rangy physique, his mother's clear green eyes, and her hair—the color of brown sugar taffy when first pulled. Though they differed in appearance, Francesca detected a similarity in mannerisms. The way the brothers cocked their heads while talking, for instance.

She sat back, listening to them catch up.

"We heard about the slide over in Idaho," Bryce was saying, "but when I came up the Wilson road yesterday, I had to pick my jaw up off the ground." He looked at his brother. "Where were you when it happened?"

William related the story of their trip up the canyon, the horrifying realization of the mountain's collapse and their wild flight. Of lying beneath the wagon, believing he was dead.

"You did not act that way at the time," Francesca said. "You kept me hoping."

Francesca saw the way Bryce's eyes flicked back and forth between her and William, evaluating. After a little silence, he asked quietly, "What team were you driving?"

"Eli and Jacob—"

"Dammit to hell!"

Lest Bryce think William could have saved them, Francesca began, "There was no—"

William cut in, "Both horses are buried under the slide. They suffocated the way Francesca and I almost did."

Bryce bowed his head. When he raised it, his eyes were awash in tears. "You did what you had to, Brother. Thank God you came through."

Finally, William spoke of rescue and how gray and drawn their father had been.

Bryce leaned forward. "Mom wrote me that he wasn't well. I didn't know if it was a ploy to get me home. He looked fine yesterday and today."

"I've only been home from Texas for a week and a half. She wrote me the same."

"Hard to think of Dad being anything but the strongest man on the place."

Both men went silent, while Francesca divided the last of the wine between their glasses.

Chapter Eleven
July 4, 1925

Five p.m.

"The Fourth of July dawned clear and rain-washed," Laura wrote in her journal.

We had a late lunch on the lawn—Francesca made sandwiches of thinly sliced roast pork on homemade bread. With them, she served a salad of raisins, nuts, and greens, dressed with a sweet oil and vinegar that bore a hint of dried rosemary.

I have decided to send one of the hands over to the nursery in Idaho Falls for a truckload of plants. Herbs: parsley, dill, rosemary, oregano, basil, fennel, and tarragon. Having never had a chef like Francesca, I had not seen the sense in growing them fresh.

After lunch, William and Bryce carried out an enormous triple-tiered layer cake. Frosted with butter cream and decorated with red and blue lettering, "Happy Anniversary, Laura and Cord, 25 Years."

Our first wedding cake, baked by the wife of Yellowstone's Acting Superintendent, was small, devoid of decoration. Without family or friends, Cord and I stood up together in borrowed clothing.

Today, he surprised me with the dress I might have longed for. A white silk tailored by Kelly seamstress, Harriet Lawrence, who knows my measure—Cord sent Charlie to fetch it last evening in the nick of time. With beaded fringe and hand-embroidered designs, it is the most elegant gown I have worn in years.

It makes me feel young as a bride, and the fine dark suit Cord wore for our luncheon made us the picture of elegance. I look forward to this evening at Struthers Burt's Bar BC, where I shall pretend the musicians play each tune in our honor, and the fireworks are our celebration.

Francesca slipped the blue silk dress from Anne Raleigh over her head. A look in the lean-to's mirror showed that yesterday's rodeo and today's picnic had renewed the sun flush on her cheeks. She brushed her hair over her shoulders and reminded herself to buy some hairpins. Sitting on the bed, she pulled on the silk stockings Maria had pressed on her, along with a pair of black, flat-heeled slippers.

William was waiting on the porch. The silver aspect of his eyes gleamed, as they surveyed her from head to toe. "Ready?"

"I was ... going in the buckboard with the rest of the help."

He gestured at the ranch's Dodge truck, idling in front of the Main. "I'm taking them."

Jim, Foster, Bobby, and Asa were in the truck bed, while Maria and Rosa sat on the buttoned upholstery in the rear seat.

There was nothing to do but get into the front seat beside William.

Bryce leaned against the river rock chimney on the Bar BC's outdoor dance floor. The moon was rising from behind the eastern mountains; the brilliant disc would be full in two days.

With the sun nearing the western horizon, over a hundred people from a number of dude ranches crowded inside and outside the Bar BC's main building. The low log structure with red rolled roofing lacked the grandeur of the Main.

Struthers Burt had thrown up the ranch buildings the spring before his first season. The cabins were mostly cheap hog-trough construction, stacked logs with end pieces nailed on.

The party was livened by music provided by Ben Raleigh on guitar and Ned Hanson on fiddle. He sat to play, a bandage on his thigh from the rodeo incident. A Victrola also stood by; there'd be a lot of repeat requests for that new rage, the "Charleston."

Bryce liked Burt's parties, always had. Back when he and William had been fourteen and fifteen, before the U.S. had entered the War, the brothers had taken their first drink of whiskey, legal then—the liquor, not their age. They'd rolled their first cigarettes out behind Burt's saddle shed. And, though their mom suspected her boys' sexual initiations had been at the hands of her dudes, their first times had been at one of Burt's galas.

The summer he turned sixteen Bryce had tumbled a sturdy Montana girl who worked as a Bar BC dishwasher. William claimed a woman dressed as a white rabbit had lowered his trousers and showed him the way of it during one of the Bar BC's impromptu costume parties.

Speaking of sex, there was Pru Johnston. Not that Bryce had rutted in this particular communal trough.

He hoped she might sashay on by, but she stopped before him, sending her double strand of pearls swinging over bodacious breasts. The silky turquoise of her flapper dress stretched tight over the matched assets.

"Lo, Bryce." Her uncannily pale eyes sought his.

"Lo, Pru."

She hadn't been a bad sort when they'd been in school, until she turned fifteen and started laying any man who'd have her. He'd often wondered if she'd taken money from the soldiers on leave during the War, but perhaps she'd only been doing her patriotic duty.

"Surprised to see you," Pru said.

"Couldn't miss my folks' big anniversary."

She scanned the crowd. "I saw at the rodeo that William's back from Texas ... I didn't get a chance to speak with him."

Bryce couldn't resist. "I reckon he might be with our new chef from Snake River." He gave a low whistle. "Real looker. Biggest brown eyes I ever saw."

Pru gave him a dirty look and walked away.

He took a turn by the punch bowl and brought his parents cut-glass cups of spiked juice.

"Did you stay at William's house last night?" Dad asked.

"Slept on his sofa ... spent some time talking over a libation." He and William had polished off some decent bootleg whiskey after retiring from the cookshack.

"He tell you we're running more head of cattle?"

"Lord, no." Bryce sighed. "You're an optimist. A lot of spreads have cut back on their herds, what with prices in the toilet."

"Things have got to firm up by auction time," Dad insisted. "If you're here, you'll see."

Mom put a hand on his sleeve. Next would come the less subtle hints, then the direct appeal for him to come home and take his place under William.

With an effort, Bryce kept his smile in place.

William helped Fran out of the truck and spied his parents drinking punch. Predictably, Bryce was there, the young prince enjoying his vacation while William had to wait until the dudes and hands were all transported to the party before he could begin to enjoy his evening.

Nonetheless, he plastered on a pleasant expression and started to lead Francesca over. Halfway there, he realized she had melted into the crowd.

Mother lifted her cheek for his kiss, keeping her hand on Bryce's sleeve. "There you are, William." She looked around. "Did I see you with Francesca?" Something in her tone sounded chilly.

Odd. The other day she'd seemed thrilled to have Fran back at Snake River.

William affected nonchalance. "She's around somewhere."

Surmising William was going to greet his parents, Francesca decided not to accompany him. Bad enough the hands knew he'd waited outside the cookshack for her. No need to draw Laura's ire at the servant who did not know her place.

Anne Raleigh waved her over and let her hold J.C. The soft bundle of baby tugged strings inside her, reminding her of Bryce's easy way with Benjy and Larry. Ben came over from a break in making music, towing his brother John. The family resemblance couldn't be missed, another broad-shouldered ranch hand with a head of thick dark hair.

Francesca learned the two little boys were his sons, J.C.'s cousins. John and his family lived on Mormon Row.

Ned Hanson limped by and Francesca asked how the leg was doing. His mature façade crumbled; he blushed at having let the bulldogging team down.

Asa Dean, in a white shirt, red bow tie and blue suspenders in honor of the Fourth of July, joined them and danced attendance on Francesca, bringing her a glass of punch.

She tossed back the cold sweet drink to quench her thirst, figuring out too late there was liquor in it.

With her head a little muzzy, she wandered away. The music and chatter of the guests faded.

Irrigation ditches cut the flat between the main building and the river, and she crossed several board bridges over their quick flow, ending up on the riverbank. As before, the Snake's power stunned her. The darkening current, shaded from the setting sun, swept past ten feet below a vertical cut bank. She stayed back from the edge, unable to tell if it were undercut. Swirling eddies like those she'd seen at Menor's Ferry spoke of depth and turbulence; she spotted a dead tree floating past.

With a suddenness that shocked her, someone seized her upper arms. She had heard no footfalls; he—from the iron grip she did not believe it could be a woman—had come up silently on the soft riverine soil.

Dio, let it be an ill-conceived joke. Bobby Cowan's kind of immature approach. "You gave me a start ..." The words died in her throat, as she twisted her head and recognized the dude who had leered at her in the Snake River dining room.

In as pleasant a tone as she could manage with him holding her fast, she said, "Shall we join the others?"

"I was thinking what luck to find you alone."

"A friend is on his way ... to bring me a drink."

"Sure, I believe that."

She struggled. He dug in his thumbs.

"Let me go!" Her voice rose.

He chuckled. "No need for unpleasantness, darlin'. I'll be happy to pay." He leaned in, blew a gust of hot halitosis and suggested something so vulgar it made her gasp.

"I am not for sale."

"I'd question that. Don't you bring food to the table at Snake River for money and a roof over your head?" He released one of her arms, shoved a hand down her dress, and took her breast in a cruel grip.

She cried out.

He lifted his other hand and covered her mouth. "Not so high and mighty now."

She tried to kick him. He pulled his feet back.

"I said I'd pay, you Eyetalian tart," he gritted. "Look down at all that swift water and think it over."

The river roiled past, exhaling frigid air. One shove and she'd be tumbling and struggling in dark water. After the night she'd escaped from the Circle X, she did not think she could face it again.

She kicked back once more, striking him in the kneecap.

The dude screamed like a girl. And released her with such abruptness she staggered forward. Her arms windmilled.

She stared at the current and prepared for the sickening plunge, to be swept away. If she tangled in the logjam a few hundred feet downstream, her body would never be found. People at Snake River would believe she had moved on.

Someone grabbed her dress in the middle of her back. Not the dude, he was down somewhere behind her, swearing.

Her rescuer dragged Francesca back from the brink and let her go.

She turned to find Bryce Sutton forcing the dude onto hands and knees and making him look over the precipice. "I'd suggest you look at all that water."

"I'm a guest at Snake River," the dude blustered.

"My family owns Snake River. You get the hell away and don't show your face until you're ready to leave with your group in the morning." With eyes like chips of green glass, Bryce gave him another shake and let him go.

Holding up a hand in case Bryce swung his fist, the dude climbed slowly to his feet. Favoring the knee Francesca had kicked, he shambled away.

Bryce watched until he was sure the dude was gone before he turned to Francesca. The last cherry light of the setting sun caught her eyes and glinted in her tousled hair before the sun slipped behind the mountain, leaving the Bar BC in the long shadow.

"Are you all right?" He resisted the urge to smooth a chestnut curl back over her shoulder.

Her Adam's apple bobbed. "I am ..." he thought she searched for a word," ... tough." But she rubbed her shoulders where the dude had hurt her.

"I heard the sunnavabitch offer to pay you."

Her shoulders stiffened.

"Hey, I know he had the wrong gal."

Wariness remained in her regard. "He stared at me in the dining room ... I gave him a look ..."

Something in her expression made him guess, "You gave him the evil eye? The one the old ladies in the villages gave us foreigners."

Her smile confirmed she was tough. "Something like that."

Bryce reached to his pocket and brought out a pewter flask of bootleg brandy. "Here."

Hands out, she began to demur.

"Hell, you need a drink. I thought he was going to throw you in the river. When you lost your balance I was sure you were going in." He took a slug of brandy. "Maybe I ought to pour some over my hands to disinfect where I touched the scum."

He offered the flask again.

৵৹

Francesca drank.

A moment after the liquid fire went down she did feel better. Her racing heart settled into a slow and steady cadence, as if she had known Bryce a long time.

They stood close to each other, focused on the remains of sunset. Golden rays radiated from behind the Tetons' dark silhouette like wheel spokes stabbing the crimson sky.

"It always makes me feel like I'm in church," Bryce said. "Like a cathedral with spires all the way to heaven."

She nodded.

"I've always thought every church in the valley should have a picture window."

"I have heard they are building a chapel near the ferry with a window behind the altar," she offered.

"No kidding?"

"I would not ..."

Bryce laughed.

She did not blush as she had last night, when he caught her with, "Don't tell me you're cooking for the Main."

He touched her arm lightly and withdrew. "No kidding is a saying—one you couldn't know."

The place where his finger had grazed her skin felt warm.

"As for religion," he said, "I've been raised with so many beliefs I've never decided on one."

"I have been Catholic all my life."

"I've been taught the Protestant story of Jesus, the Book of Mormon ..."

"*La chiesa mormone*? With more than one wife?"

Bryce laughed. "My dad's adopted father is Mormon; he had only one wife. That's true of most of them since the LDS Church renounced polygamy in 1890 as a condition of Utah statehood. I've never understood how a man could handle even one wife."

With the tingle still on her flesh from his touch, she noted his warning.

"I've also learned the way of the Nez Perce." He pointed to the Tetons' silhouette, to a peak south of those flanking the Grand. "That's Nez Perce Peak there ...."

After a moment of silence, he went on, "When I was boy, Dad built a sweat lodge down by the river. We'd go in naked and sit until we were weak, then rush out and plunge into the snow or the Snake if there wasn't any snow, hollering to beat hell." He offered the flask.

The next sip was pure fire. She both did and didn't want it.

Bryce took his own long swallow. "I envy you that this is your first time to see all this. Sometimes I wish I could come to this valley fresh."

A wistful note in his voice made Francesca sad.

"But you are always traveling?"

"We don't appreciate properly what we know too well." In the gathering darkness, it was difficult to make out his expression.

"You do not live here because you do not ... appreciate it? When you spoke of ranching and the growing season ..."

A beat of silence passed. "Place only needs so many bosses. Dad and Charlie run it fine."

"And William?"

"When he went to Texas, things rocked along, but Mom and Dad want him here."

"They must want you as well."

Bryce gave a vague shake of his head. "William's the firstborn."

A shrill whistle erupted.

"*Caspita!*" she cried. Red light radiated above in an expanding star, followed by a sharp crack and boom.

Bryce touched her arm above the elbow. "Steady. You've never seen fireworks?"

On New Year's Eve in New York, she had wanted to go out and watch, but Mrs. Coldwell had insisted she serve champagne to her guests at the brownstone.

Crimson sparks made graceful arcs.

The next shell startled her less, a pale cascade turning the surrounding sage to silver. Bryce slid his hand up to her shoulder and pulled her against his side.

After the fireworks, guests gathered around the deck where Ned and Ben tuned up. Bryce walked Francesca over, placing a light hand at her waist as they ascended the steps. Beneath the blue silk, she was all muscle and sinew.

Struthers Burt, dressed in a summer suit with dark hair brushed back from his forehead, held up a hand for order. "Of course, you locals know the Fourth is the Sutton's anniversary. As this one is their twenty-fifth, I'd like us all to congratulate them."

Amid a round of applause, Burt went over to Bryce's folks, shook Cord's hand and kissed Laura on the cheek.

Bryce, clapping with the rest, saw his mom scanning the crowd. Her eyes locked on his brother and she beckoned. William went to her with swift steps and hugged her, to more approbation.

Too late, she looked around again. "Where's Bryce?"

He went forward and congratulated his parents.

"For the first dance," Burt called, "let's have the Suttons and their boys," he grinned, "and a couple of young ladies."

Without a second thought, Bryce started for Francesca.

When he was about a third of the way there, he got a funny feeling. William was traveling in the same direction.

Recalling his brother arriving at the party with Francesca in the passenger seat of the Dodge, Bryce almost veered off. But the memory of her hip soft against his while they watched the fireworks had him forging on.

From the corner of his eye, he noted Pru Johnston angling for William to choose her, pushing herself to the front.

William kept to his trajectory.

Both Sutton men ended up in front of Francesca.

⋙⋘

Two brothers, alike, yet vastly different. Surely, they did not expect her to choose between them.

Putting out both hands, Francesca shook her head.

William stepped in close and seized her hand. "You came with me. Let's dance."

"I do not know how." She kept her eyes on William, but she could feel Bryce's gaze upon her like heat.

Burt let out a laugh. "Come on, boys. You're holding up the works."

"Please, no," Francesca said.

"All right," William agreed. Though his expression was bland, a muscle formed a hard bunch at his jaw. "I'll teach you to dance for the next party."

He turned away and chose a young matron with black hair curling around her alabaster forehead, the wife of one of the Snake River dudes. Her husband smiled at the honor of his wife opening the dancing.

Francesca looked at Bryce, apology in her eyes. Their interlude during the fireworks hung between them.

His expression remained hard. "You should have told me it was like that between you and William."

She wanted to say it wasn't what he thought, but the musicians played a few notes and Burt chided, "Bryce, we need you on the floor."

⋙⋘

His jaw set, Bryce selected a petite blonde dressed in summer white.

On the last night of her western interlude at the Bar BC, she seemed to be looking for adventure. Fine with him.

"What's your name, sweetheart?"

"Carrie."

"I'm Bryce."

As soon as the waltz ended, he led her from the dance floor. She wore a white dress with eyelet embroidery, trimmed in enough lace to make it look like it might be an undergarment. He walked with his hand on the exposed skin of her back where the dress dipped low.

After a stop at the punch bowl for a little more of the mix—the proof level got higher each time he sampled—he guided her out into the moonlight. Near the base of the bluff, he ducked into the saddle shed and pulled a couple of blankets off a stack. Carrie laughed, low and sultry.

They skirted the edge of the trees and came to a small log cabin. He happened to know the dishwasher who bunked here was helping clean up.

"Look," Bryce chuckled, opening the door to reveal a narrow bed. In the murky dimness, he made out rumpled white sheets and quickly spread the blankets over them.

Carrie leaned against the door frame. Her blond hair and white dress looked silvery, silhouetted against the night.

Bryce pulled her against him. "Carrie," he murmured. "Where you from, Carrie?" All the while, he let his hands roam lightly over her back.

"Dubuque," she said.

"Tell me, Carrie from Dubuque. Did you ever do anything like this at home?"

She lifted a shoulder. "Well, sure—"

"Okay." He urged her toward the bed.

By the time he had her horizontal, she had hold of his belt buckle.

He slipped the white lace straps off her shoulders, mouthed her ample breasts until she pumped her hips against him.

He was out, in her hand, in her ... going at it fast and furious since she was setting the pace.

The worst part was that when it was over and he saw blond locks spread over the pillow, he damned himself for slaking his desire with the wrong woman.

What a shame Francesca belonged to his brother.

೪৶

Francesca slept poorly.

Vincenzo visited, dressed in cowboy chaps. He jumped off a fence and doffed his western style hat. There was Bryce, dancing with a blonde, taking her off into the darkness. Francesca tried to get free, to run after him, but Vincenzo slid a hand down her dress and squeezed her breast until she cried out. A dark voice, "I suggest you look at all that water," and she was in the river. Choking, crying, and flailing because she had never learned to swim.

She awoke with a start.

When she ferried the first load of breakfast over the Main, she found Laura alone before the cold fireplace, hugging herself. Her shoulders formed a defeated posture, her hair in disarray. Twin tear tracks streaked her cheeks, and her eyes were pink. "He's gone." She thrust a piece of paper at Francesca.

After a brief hesitation, curiosity got the better of her and she took it, noting the bold slanting script.

> Mom and Dad,
>
> Enjoyed your anniversary. The place looks great under your management and with Charlie's hard work. Wish I could stick around and sample more of Francesca's fare.

Her fingers closed on the edge of the note and crinkled it. "How ... often does Bryce come home?"

Laura dashed at her cheek. "Not often enough."

Chapter Twelve
Summer, 1925

Summer at the Snake River Dude Ranch warmed through July. Francesca borrowed a book on wildflowers from the lounge in the Main, and, on walks in the foothills, identified many species—white *spirea*, the blues of flax and lupine, and scarlet Indian paintbrush.

She also read Laura's subscription to the *New Yorker* in an effort to soak up sophistication. Having already gone through the short stack, she read in the February debut issue that the magazine "was not edited for the old lady in Dubuque." Laura said Dubuque was a town in the Iowa farming country.

In one of Laura's ladies' magazines, Francesca found recipes for ice cream using Borden's evaporated milk. When fresh summer peaches and cherries came over The Pass, she set the men of the outfit to cranking the freezer almost every evening.

By the end of July, the huckleberries ripened, and Bobby, Asa, and Jim brought her buckets full. She fashioned them into pies, added them to the evening ice cream, and transformed them into jams and jellies.

Though she managed to sneak in some Italian recipes, Cord warned her not to try it too often, citing a recent study revealing that Americans were primarily steak eaters.

On each weekly payday, Laura stopped by the cookshack for a cup of tea and a chat. The older woman had not turned out to be nearly as warm-hearted as Francesca had believed when she first met her. Of course, she might have been dismayed when both her sons asked a hired hand to dance on the Fourth of July.

In answer to Laura's questions, Francesca told of her childhood in Chianti, of her training with Carla di Paoli. She had come to New York, she said, because post-war Italy under Mussolini had become a difficult place to live. No mention of Vincenzo or how she ended up penniless on the train platform in Salt Lake City.

Each time Laura left her, Francesca rolled her bills and placed her nest egg beneath a loose floor board. Based on her progress, she determined to strike out for California after fall roundup, when the seasonal workers departed.

In spite of his father's objections, William continued to plan on buying a Model T. He pointed out that Peter DePaolo—he teased Fran about the similarity in their names—had won the Indianapolis 500 at over one hundred miles an hour and assured his parents the Ford would be tame in comparison.

With Bryce gone, William settled into the summer routine he knew so well. Dudes came and went at two week intervals. William engaged where it pleased him and withdrew when he craved solitude. Riding up to the summer pastures to check on the cattle consumed several weeks.

On the trail, he rode alone. At night, he slept in his bedroll beneath a panoply of stars and tried to decide what to do about Fran. Part of him wanted to mount a whirlwind campaign, but she was ranch staff and Mother hadn't warmed to her the way he thought she might. If he had a modern affair with the chef, he suspected it would not be overlooked the way his fling with Pru had been.

Something else prevented William from making a move; he half expected Bryce to return and work his wiles on her—the way he had when William found them drinking wine in the cookshack. They had also been conspicuously absent during the fireworks, long enough for any number of things to have happened.

It shouldn't matter if Bryce had tumbled her, but it did.

William didn't want to be Fran's second choice.

July 31, 1925

Francesca's coming has been like a stone thrown into a pond. All the male dudes under fifty, every unmarried hand— and some married—for miles around are all a-ripple with the impact. Men ride in almost daily, on horseback, in buggies, and work trucks, making their first stop the cookshack, as if they cannot find the way to the Main. At that point, it is right in their face.

> Yet, as attractive a nuisance as she is, she shows no interest in men's admiration. As for Cord's suggestion she might be with child and planning something with William, I see no signs of thickening at her waist.
>
> She might be one of those with a long back who carry their babies invisibly. It is too soon to be sure.
>
> With William in the high country so much and Bryce God-knows-where, I worry over the fate of this ranch. Cord's father, Franklin Sutton, eked out a spare life, panning a little gold and acting as geologist on the early expeditions through Yellowstone ... Cord's mother Sarah traveled with him and bore her son here without benefit of doctor or midwife.
>
> After over fifty years and three generations, one of our boys must commit to making a future here or all we have worked for ....

The words blurred on the page. A tear dropped and turned the last word into a spreading puddle of ink. Laura pushed back from the table and went to the dining room window.

Above the bluff, the Tetons towered. They had captured her heart one summer dawn in 1900, with the rose glow of sunrise touching the peak of the Grand. No matter the weather—be it day or night—they were as changeable and as dear as a lover.

She wiped her tears and went back to the table.

> Uncertainly permeates not only our place, but everything in the valley. Since the slide, engineers have assured us it is stable and that the Gros Ventre River can simply go on flowing beneath, but I wonder.

Sven Nygaard, a young valley man studying for his PhD in engineering at UCLA, clambered over the massive Slide Lake dam. For the better part of an hour, side-footing and stepping between blocks of quartzite or from log to log, Cord and Ranger Duran had followed him. Finally Cord, with his denim shirt stuck to his skin and sweat pouring down his back, suggested that he and Duran repair to an outcrop of the Red Bluffs overlooking the lake.

While he caught his breath, he noted water lapping at the slide debris, six feet below the spill point.

"A couple good rains and she'll be over the top," Duran noted.

Hall's inundated ranch had been reduced to a slim apron of emerald against the darker spiky forest. In the upper reaches where the canyon narrowed, doomed trees stuck out of the water.

Duran selected a piece of sandstone and sent it flying in a flat arc into the lake. "Every engineer who looks it over says it can sit there forever." Duran tossed another stone, which fell short of the water.

"Trying to convince yourself or me?" Cord asked.

"Some of both, I reckon. The folks in Kelly have moved back to their houses. No more camping out in the foothills."

Cord studied the muddy water. Perhaps by winter the suspended sediment might settle.

"I wish my family and I could have stayed up at the ranger station," Duran went on. "In Kelly, I sleep with one eye open and an ear on the canyon."

Sven started up in their direction. At home with his family in the valley for a week, he had asked the ranger to show him around the slide. Duran had agreed, on the condition Sven give his professional opinion. Cord, who had ridden up the canyon that morning to go fly fishing in Crystal Creek, had happened to run into the two men by the slide.

When Sven reached their perch, it was all Cord could do not to start questioning him. Nonetheless, he and Duran waited while Sven set down his metal clipboard and shrugged off his backpack. His chest rose and fell rapidly beneath his khaki shirt; sweat greased the sunburned vee at his neck.

Standing with one booted foot on a ledge of red sandstone, he swigged from his canteen and wiped his mouth with the back of his hand. "You've got Tensleep Sandstone over the Amsden shale on a dip slope. That's where the tilt of the rock parallels the mountainside. Along the river, there's a bunch of springs running out of a sandstone strata—the water hits the sticky layer below and can't sink deeper." He pointed across the slide. "Before the slide, the river had eroded through one side, weakening the base, plus there was a lot of heavy precipitation." He studied the jumbled mound. "This is one of the biggest slides I've heard of ... fifty million cubic yards, at least."

"What do you think about it holding?" Duran prodded.

Sven capped his canteen with maddening slowness and replaced it in his belt holster. His gaze wandered up over the scar running almost to the top of Sheep Mountain. Then he scrutinized the slide block again and the water lapping below the top. "I don't like it."

Cord cocked a brow at Duran, who gave Sven a sharp look. "That's not what the state engineer and his chief deputy said."

Sven nodded. "I've read the report. One of my major professors knows the man who came here to inspect." He gestured at the broad expanse of debris. "I can see why they came to the conclusion they did. This dam has a stable shape for an earthen barrier. The canyon walls are good and steep, with sandstone bedrock on either side."

"What don't you like?"

"Three things." Sven pointed to the top of the slide block where it abutted the scar and ticked a finger. "Any further slippage from uphill might scoop out a low spot, creating a zone of weakness."

Cord chewed on a grass stem.

Sven ticked another finger. "This differs from an earthen dam in that it has not been compacted; it's probably twenty-five to thirty percent trees and doesn't have a clay layer. Water seeps through and out the bottom."

"Isn't that what's keeping things stable?" Cord asked.

"Yes, and that's what led to their conclusion. They forgot just one thing. An earthquake of considerable magnitude set this slide off. With the dam saturated, another trembler could liquefy it and shake it loose in a heartbeat."

Duran swore and squinted at Sven. "Do me a favor and write up what you've said."

"Oh, no, sir," the young man looked at the ground. "As a student and not yet licensed, I've said too much already."

Chapter Thirteen
August 23, 1925

On a Sunday afternoon in late August, Francesca strolled on top of the bluff overlooking Cord and Laura's home on the lower river bench. To escape the relentless late summer heat, she sought shade beneath a lone cottonwood.

Below, on the river, anglers on a quest for cutthroat trout arced their fly-fishing lines through the hot still air. That evening, Francesca would prepare their catch—fried or grilled with sage and mint.

It was the Sabbath, so she performed her ritual of the rosary. Though she had no beads—a trip to both the Catholic Church in Jackson and the general store had yielded none—she imagined holding the crucifix, made the sign of the cross, and began her prayers.

A trail ride angled up the slope. The sweating horses carried torpid riders in a slow file. Not at all the kind of exuberant horsemanship the hands exhibited when they rode out for a solitary gallop.

Francesca had not been on a horse since she and William had ridden from the Halls' up to the Circle X.

As the sun traveled across the sky, she enjoyed her slack time before the work to come. The trio of men who had declared themselves her suppliers—Jim, Asa, and Bobby—had gone into the foothills with buckets, promising a load of golden currants and chokecherries. Though she would dry the currants, the astringent chokecherries would require jam and jelly making.

She was about to start back to the cookshack when an approaching automobile engine caused a herd of pronghorn antelope to scatter. As the car drew closer, she recognized William behind the wheel in his Sunday suit.

He didn't respond to her wave, for he was speaking with his passenger, a man who must be in his eighties, his hair in long white braids.

As she moved in the direction of the cookshack, ominous charcoal clouds reared up over the Tetons. Moments later, a blast of arctic air struck, turning up the pale undersides of the leaves.

Gathering her skirt, she began to run, and, by the time she reached the cookshack, the peaks had disappeared in a black shroud. As she forced the door closed against the blustering wind, she pitied the hands caught out with the berry pails.

While waiting for William, Cord read the *Jackson's Hole Courier*. Local preparations for the Frontier Days Rodeo the following weekend were in full swing, with a baseball game planned in addition to "Dude races." Only bona fide guests riding horses owned by a dude ranch could run.

But the rodeo appeared eclipsed by more spectacular news.

"Fox Film Company Selects Jackson's Hole For Filming Super Production."

> The Fox film company has picked Dead Man's Bar, one of the famous spots on the Snake River ....
>
> Only a few miles upstream, the gravel bar had been the scene of a grisly triple murder. In the summer of 1886, a fishing party discovered three of four placer miners dead; the fourth partner was arrested, tried, and acquitted.
>
> .... as the scene for filming a large part of what is claimed will be the screen classic of all times. The advance men have now been in Jackson two weeks getting ready for the arrival of a company of 200 actors and actresses.

Cord hoped they got their movie made quickly and left.

Light from the window faded on his paper; a threatening overcast had rolled over the mountains. After Friday and Saturday's frost had wilted Laura's squash and potato vines, they didn't need more bad weather.

Laura, sitting opposite Cord at the table, paused with her pen poised above a page of her journal. A couple of ink blots testified she tended to press her fountain pen too hard. "I hear them."

Rising, she secreted the leather-bound book away in its silver box on the mantle.

Then Cord heard the approach of a motorized vehicle as well. "Doesn't sound like the truck."

"It must be someone else .... I'll start tea."

Cord opened the front door and spied William behind the wheel of a new

Model T. Bitter Waters occupied the front passenger seat.

"It *is* them!" Cord called over his shoulder, his jaw set.

William pulled the shining black car up before the stoop and cut the engine.

"Where's the truck?" Cord clipped, in a voice as chill as the wind.

"Bobby's driving it back from the dealer in Idaho Falls."

In deference to the man in the front seat, Cord stepped past William. "We'll discuss this later."

He opened the passenger door. "Welcome, Uncle."

Who was the elderly man with William, Francesca wondered. He appeared to be Indian. Perhaps he was selling turquoise jewelry.

Laura had a nice collection.

Shivering, Francesca built a fire in the lean-to woodstove and settled into the rocking chair. Rosa and Maria had warned it could snow here any day of the year. And that she must have true winter clothing if she planned to stay past dude season.

"I will be leaving then," Francesca had told them.

As early twilight descended, fat raindrops struck the window, rolled down and blurred the view. In a little while, Tom would build up the fires so she could prepare dinner.

In the meantime, she lifted the loose floor board and withdrew her leather pouch. The bills and coins amounted to more than enough to travel to California.

As for her clothing, if the weather held until dude season ended, if there was an Indian summer—she was unclear on why people used the term for a warm spell in the fall—she should have what she needed.

Francesca looked up from her money to find fat white snowflakes spiraling to earth.

"I bring you greetings from the People, Blue Eyes." Bitter Waters spoke in the stilted formal English he had learned from missionaries.

Blue Eyes was the pet name bestowed by Cord's mother before she had died ... before his uncle took him away on the Nez Perce's flight for freedom through Yellowstone ... before six-year-old Cord made his pilgrimage in the high wilderness above the Lamar Valley to seek his guardian spirit.

Alone on a bare mountain peak covered in loose cinders, in the Yellowstone backcountry, he had hugged himself against the night wind. The moon rose, tinged red by the smoke of late summer forest fires, but he did not believe it to be what he was looking for.

Cord's mother had taught him that in the Nez Perce way, a spiritual protector, or *wayakin,* revealed itself in many and varied forms. A jackrabbit might pause to sniff at the wind, a distant mountain peak catch the illumination of the setting sun, or a *hohots* (grizzly) could happen by.

Sarah had told Cord how Heinmot Tooyalakekt—or Chief Joseph, as the white men called him—had discovered his *wayakin* in the hills overlooking the Wallowa Valley. After ten-year-old Heinmot had watched and waited for five suns without food or water, a storm poured fury upon the peaks, sending down jagged lightning bolts and rain that soothed his parched throat. Thereafter, Heinmot was known as "Thunder Rolling in the Mountains."

Though twelve-year-old Sarah Tilkalept bore the blood of a white father, she, too, had gone to search for her *wayakin.* After wandering alone for a day and a night on her pilgrimage, she was attracted by the crisp tinkling of water pouring over a ledge of sandstone to a crystal pool. From that day forward, her guardian spirit became "Falling Water."

Cord had waited on the mountaintop for hours, falling into a sort of trance between sleep and wakefulness, when the moonlight fell onto a pair of yellow eyes glowing in the darkness.

He fumbled on the ground for a stick, a rock. There was nothing, and his wild heartbeat threatened to burst his chest, until his hand closed over an angular sharp stone.

Drawing his arm back, he threw the rock as hard as he could.

A sharp "kiyah," and the wolf leapt from the rocks and disappeared.

Cord picked up another missile, felt a sharp edge, and looked down to see what he held. Black and glassy, and glowing like a diamond, the obsidian reflected the light of the full moon.

Bitter Waters looked to Laura. "You have smoothed the sharp edges from our Obsidian and turned his brittle character strong."

Cord smiled and fingered the glassy rock in his pants pocket. "I would hope I have mellowed a bit in twenty-five years."

The older man sipped the tea Laura had brewed. "All has worked out for you. Your woman, your ranch, your sons."

As if in answer to a summons, William entered with snowflakes sticking to his hair and clothing. "What with the weather, I put Lucifer in the stable."

"Thank you." Cord also thanked providence he had at least one reliable son.

Bitter Waters focused on William, who shucked his coat and sat at the opposite end of the table. "You have grown tall since last I saw you."

William had been in his teens at his uncle's last visit.

"Am I correct that you have no Nez Perce name?"

"I'm only one-eighth," William argued.

His great-uncle waved that aside. "Have you searched for a guardian spirit?"

William looked exasperated. "When I was ten, my father encouraged me to go into the hills. No *wayakin* appeared."

Bitter Waters nodded. "I recall that, now. Thank you for reminding a forgetful old man."

Like hell, he was forgetful, Cord thought. Clearly, Bitter Waters still hoped William would follow the advice he'd once given Cord: "Always honor your mother's people, the Nimiipuu, as well as your father's."

Both Laura and Cord had always believed William's lack of faith in his ties to the tribe had eventuated the fruitless outcome of his search. In later years, Cord had occasionally inquired whether William wanted to try again.

"Where is Koyama, our mighty lion?" Bitter Waters asked with obvious affection.

Bryce, though a year younger, had insisted on going out when William had, hiking higher into the foothills of Death Canyon than his brother. He had come back with a tale of encountering a mountain lion—*Koyama* in Nez Perce—of waiting motionless among the rocks until it padded away.

At the time, William had accused his little brother of lying. Cord had listened to Bryce and detected no youthful duplicity.

Bitter Waters's seamed face bore an expectant expression. "Will Koyama join us for dinner?"

Laura poured more tea. "Bryce has been working away from here for years. This season, he's at a ranch in Idaho."

"I am sorry to have missed him."

William rose, knocking the table with his knee. "I must go and see to our guests."

A blast of cold air marked his exit.

Chapter Fourteen
Autumn, 1925

Crystal days and diamond clear nights. Snow dusted the peaks and held off in the valley. Coyotes came down from the mountains and attacked the fat geese feeding by the Snake River Ranch pond.

Francesca rose each dawn to find frost painting the meadow. The maples turned red first, blazes of color on the mountainsides, then the aspen brightened the foothills with gold.

Laura worked daily with her hands in soil, setting up the hothouse for winter. Now that she was certain Francesca was not trying to pin a pregnancy on her son, she stopped by the cookshack and took tea with her more often.

With the shortening hours of light came the time to gather the cattle from the mountain grazing allotments.

William was in his element. He rose before dawn and sat in the saddle for ten or more hours, working with Bobby, Foster, Jim, and Asa. Charlie, Ben, and Ned rode as a separate group during the day. They all came together to camp.

Having received lessons from Francesca, Asa had concocted a camp spaghetti and called it "*bologonese*," approximating her accent. He caught hell until they tasted it.

Cord joined the roundup for a few days, but when the men ascended above ten thousand feet, he started feeling the altitude and rode Lucifer home. With the approaching cattle auction and prices still depressed, he was glad Bryce wasn't home to say, "I told you so."

Of course, that wasn't true; he wanted his son to come home no matter what he said.

As for the business, dudes remained the best way to earn a buck.

Other ranchers must have noted the pinch, for Struthers Burt called a series of fresh meetings to discuss the valley's status. In short order, ninety-seven landowners signed a petition indicating a willingness to participate in either extending Yellowstone Park or founding a separate one. With one important caveat ... the grandfathering of dude ranching.

While Cord, Burt, and the rest of the ninety-seven agreed, some of the townsfolk and Dieter Gross of the Lazy D wanted the valley to stay private— all of it, including the site by Jenny Lake where he planned to build his gas station.

During a meeting of about twenty ranchers at the Bar BC, Cord held the floor.

Everyone listened politely until Dieter shook his bald head and glared at Cord with his bottomless black eyes. "America was built on free enterprise, Sutton." He made an aside to the others. "A mighty fancy English name for an Injun."

Cord started to rise, but Burt laid a light hand on his arm.

He subsided, noting that none of the other men present chuckled at Dieter's little joke.

After the meeting, Burt detained Cord for a private word beside the river. "You ever hear why Dieter's such a bigot?"

Still steaming, Cord said, "I don't know and I don't care."

Burt went on as if he hadn't spoken. "I was talking with Foster Case, who had it from Tiny Good. Dieter's family farmed in Virginia back before the Revolutionary War, just across the mountain from Jefferson's Monticello. Slave labor was the norm."

"You going to tell me he's entitled to hate black men and red men because his family kept slaves?"

"Not at all. Story is his family didn't keep them. During the Reconstruction, when Dieter was a babe in arms one of the free blacks got into some kind of altercation with his father ... and killed him."

Cord stared at the river's endless flow. Everyone died, one way or another.

"I'm sorry he lost his dad," he told Burt. "But just because Dieter's father ran afoul of a black man doesn't make them, along with every other person who isn't white, subhuman."

A couple days before the men would drive the cattle home, Laura watched the sunset outside the Main with her head against Cord's shoulder.

"I love this time of year," he said, "when the motors have gone and the only dudes we have to entertain are a few serious deer and elk hunters."

"Do you suppose Bryce will come home before the roundup and cattle auction are over?"

"He usually does."

Geese honked their nightly approach to the pond, their silhouettes dark against the last lavender in the sky. They came in high, flared, and sank to the pewter surface, breaking its perfect mirror.

Bryce should be here to see it.

"I have a feeling he's not coming this year," she said.

Cord slid his hand over hers. "If you say you have a feeling, I've learned not to dispute it. But I'd like you to at least hear your reasoning."

"Do you recall how William brought Francesca to the Bar BC on July fourth?"

"Can't say I do." Cord considered. "I've begun to like that young woman, though. She's not like these modern girls, talking slang and swearing, calling people 'kid,' being fresh."

"I like her, too. I'm sorry we thought ill of her."

"So what does she have to do with Bryce staying away? I'd think she'd have him salivating like the rest of the men in the valley."

"On the Fourth, when William got to the Bar BC, he had a number of the folks from the outfit piled in the Dodge truck; Francesca was in front with him. He took her arm to help her out when he parked."

"If you say so."

"After the fireworks, I saw her and Bryce coming in together from the darkness. Then both boys tried to get her to dance the first waltz with them. First thing in the morning, Bryce was gone."

When the outfit drove the cattle back onto Snake River acreage, Francesca top-railed the fence and watched the men work. Though William and Charlie took apparent charge of the herd, Cord supervised from astride Lucifer.

One at a time, William and Chester cut the animals out. Depending on their sex and age, the men shunted them into different pens.

Charlie, his coat and shirt off in the brisk air, stuck his arm into the birth canal of each cow to check whether she was pregnant. If not, she was for the auction. The ranch could not afford to feed a barren cow over the winter.

Cord and William examined the young bulls, selecting one to challenge their stud, Brutus. The rest, they castrated.

Francesca sat on the fence and watched without flinching. She understood the business now that Laura had explained the cycle of cattle ranching. One thing she did refuse to do, though, was to prepare "calf fries," for the hands.

Undeterred, they would build a fire and roast the testicles themselves.

Francesca noted the lines of Cord's face etching deeper with weariness.

Cord dismounted from Lucifer and joined her. William continued to look to his father for a thumbs up or down on each young male.

A shadow on the ground of a large man wearing a cowboy hat alerted Francesca to someone's approach. She glanced over her shoulder to find the bald rancher with black brows and handlebar moustache whose bronco had won the rodeo bucking contest. The same horse stood a short distance away with his reins on the ground.

The man eased an elbow onto the fence and stared at her breasts. "Looks like Sutton's got a new addition to his menagerie."

❧

Cord rose to his full height. He'd been sick and tired of the bigoted Dieter Gross ever since the man had arrived in the valley five years earlier.

Dieter spread his hands. "I was just talking about what a hodgepodge you've got here. Old Charlie from Africa ...."

"His great-great-grandfather was in America before 1800."

"All his fathers were slaves. You call Charlie 'foreman'; I call him 'nigger.' "

Cord told himself to control his temper.

"Now you've got those Mex gals and a ...?" He poked Francesca, who was sitting stiffly, in the ribs. "What country you from?"

"Francesca is from Italy," Cord said coldly. "She'll thank you not to touch her."

She clambered off the fence, ducked around the men, and rushed away without looking back.

"I'll bet you touch her—"

"You filthy—" Cord seized Dieter by the shirtfront.

Now what? His opponent wasn't as tall, but he outweighed Cord by twenty pounds.

Dieter sneered and slapped Cord's hand away.

Cord told himself to disengage.

"I'll bet you and your half breed boys all share the gals." Dieter glanced at Charlie. "How about the nigger ... he get a piece, too?"

Cord's fist curled, shot out, connected.

A mist of blood sprayed from Dieter's nose, as Cord swore, spears of pain shooting up his arm. He couldn't help but be glad Francesca wasn't a witness to this.

Dieter reached around beneath his leather jacket and came out with a mean looking pistol.

Charlie tensed and aimed a long rifle square at the center of Dieter's chest. His index finger, laid out along the barrel, fairly itched to move onto the trigger.

Chester trotted over and planted his hooves in classic cowpony style, while William leaped from the saddle over the fence, to land on his feet beside Dieter. His arms went around the nasty bigot in a wrestling hold.

Charlie had been in the valley over twenty years now; he and Lucy had been some of the only folks of African heritage—he hated the term "colored," as much as he did "nigger" or "negro." They all sounded about the same to him, although some people used "negro," to show they were being careful not to use the more disparaging version.

The insult about him sharing the ranch's women stung, but he'd heard worse. The one thing he didn't want was for Dieter to catch wind of his friendship with the widow Harriet Lawrence, a Kelly seamstress. The fly in the ointment was that Harriet, new in town last fall, was white like almost everyone else in the valley.

As William and Dieter scuffled over the gun, Charlie barked, "Don't move, Dieter!"

The man ignored him, and William kept getting in the way of his aim. "Come on, Dieter. Give it up!" Charlie called. "My pa was a buffalo soldier. Taught me to shoot when I wasn't any taller than the sagebrush."

Charlie was ready to fire, but the ugly brute relinquished the gun, and, with a glare at Charlie and a black look at Cord, stood with his hands at his sides.

William stepped back from the now-subdued Dieter with due care. He leaned over, pulled his rifle from Chester's saddlebag, and held it ready to snap up. "Don't come round here looking for trouble, Mr. Gross. You'll find it."

"You'll find it, too," said a gruff voice.

Charlie turned to find Tiny Good seated atop a roan horse, his rifle aimed at the middle of William's chest.

"Stalemate," said Tiny. With guns pointed at both William and Dieter, Charlie held his breath.

"Look, everybody just settle down," Cord ordered. "Nobody's going to shoot anybody here."

For another endless moment, Charlie held his aim steady, watching Tiny to make sure his finger wasn't on the trigger.

Then Dieter nodded at Tiny, who lowered his gun.

Cord gave Charlie a nod and he stood down.

"William and Charlie will escort you to the edge of the property," Cord said. "He'll give you your pistol there, Gross."

Dieter went to his horse and mounted. Gathering the reins, he shot Cord a look of pure hatred. "You'll pay for this, Sutton."

ജൽ

That same afternoon, William went to the cookshack and tapped on the door.

Francesca did not answer, so he pushed open the portal. Through the open door to the lean-to, he saw her lying on the bed in a striped housedress.

"Fran?" he called.

She put her feet to the floor and came out into the kitchen with reddened eyes.

"What's wrong?"

"Those men ...." She started to move past him to the pot of beef stew over the fire.

"That can wait," he said. "I've come to teach you to shoot."

Her eyes widened.

"In case anything like this afternoon happens again, and none of the men are around."

"Oh, but—"

"But, nothing."

She came with him, out to where the hands had set up a practice firing range with a backdrop against the upper bluff.

He drew his Smith & Wesson from his holster and held it in his right hand, pointed downrange. "See how I push forward on the thumb release on the left side and rotate the cylinder out of the frame." He carried it with five cartridges and an empty chamber under the hammer. Closing the cylinder, he pulled the hammer back with his thumb, rotated the cylinder to bring up a live round, and cocked it.

With care, he aligned the front sight with the notch at the rear of the frame and squeezed the trigger.

At the loud report, Francesca jumped.

"Now you." He passed it across. "Hold the gun in your hand, like this, with your feet about shoulder width apart, and sight along the barrel. Put your finger on the trigger, draw in a breath, let out half, and squeeze, don't yank the trigger."

She was an apt pupil, putting together a tight group on the target before dinnertime.

After the cattle auction, where the Snake River livestock commanded a disappointing pittance, a number of the outfit said their goodbyes for the season. Tom, the fire keeper, was going all the way home to Wales. Rosa and Maria intended to work at the Excalibur Hotel in Salt Lake City, still owned by Cord's adoptive family

Francesca, too, needed to leave, especially while The Pass was still open to automobiles and trucks. Once the snows settled in, gargantuan avalanche chutes would turn horse-drawn sleighs—the only form of winter transport— into targets.

It was time to go, but one Indian summer day melded into another. She surveyed mountain peaks aglow with aspen gold and considered the unknown consequences of uprooting her life yet again.

One afternoon in late-October, after returning from guiding an elk hunt, William came to the cookshack. With the quiet look of admiration she recalled from their first meeting, he said, "Now that you can shoot, it's time for you to learn to ride."

"I know how. We rode up to the Circle X."

Though she protested, he persisted.

An hour later, dressed in denims and boots, she faced a wall of gray horseflesh.

"You must always check the saddle girth to make sure it's tight," William said, tugging on the leather strap. "Horses panic at the dumbest things. If a saddle turns, they get crazy."

He must have seen her look of dismay, for he went on in an upbeat tone, "Of course, a dude horse will take care of you. They're trained for the least experienced rider." He patted the gray's neck. "Bayberry, here, is fifteen and has worked off most of her steam."

Francesca swallowed.

"Put your left foot in the stirrup." William stood by to boost her as he had done at the Halls'.

She considered. "I think I would do better getting on from the other side."

"Indian ponies will let you, but white man's ponies will kick you if you try it."

Determined to get up without a boost, Francesca seated her left foot in the stirrup, put her weight on it, and swung her leg over Bayberry's back.

"Hold on with your knees. Use the reins to tell her you know what you're doing."

Francesca gathered the leather lines in both hands and waited for William to mount the strawberry mare, Crackerjack. Before he could, something shifted under Francesca.

William said, "Dammit, she did it again," just as Bayberry took off at a dead run.

Francesca used her legs, as he had instructed, to hold fast. She leaned to try and make up for the left list of the saddle.

Behind her came rapid hoofbeats. "Hang on!"

Tiring fast, she considered how to dismount without breaking bones.

Crackerjack galloped alongside on her left. William shouted, "Haul back hard on the reins with both hands!"

Both horses came to a skidding stop.

William reached and yanked Francesca off the saddle. Held her one-armed—she had no idea he was that strong—let her down gently so her boots touched the browning grass.

He slid down after her. They stood between the sweating horses, feeling the heat pouring off their flanks. The sun beat down.

Without warning, they started to laugh, the merry helpless mirth of children, guffawing and bellowing, bending and slapping their thighs. "Wooo ... hooo!" William got out. "You should have seen your face when she took off."

"You should have checked the girth." She was still giggling.

"I swear I did. Bayberry's too sly for me."

Their gazes met and held. William's expression sobered. "Fran ...."

"*Sì?*"

"I know you told Rosa and Maria and everybody you want to leave."

The sun turned his eyes, usually plain gray, to silver. "Everybody who's wintering over at Snake River wants you to stay."

She waited, breathless, for him to speak his mind.

When he did not, she forced out, "And you?"

William's Adams apple bobbed. "I'd like you to stay, too."

Autumn colors faded, and the leaves blew away. The snowline marched down the mountains to the foothills. The first true blizzard of the season, with almost a foot of snow in the valley, signaled the move from using the cookshack to preparing meals in the Main.

Soon it would be time to plan Thanksgiving dinner.

From listening to the hands who remained at Snake River, Francesca learned Menor's Ferry would be beached and replaced by a winter bridge. Men from all over the valley would form a construction crew—Maude Noble had carried on Menor's tradition. If people wanted a river crossing, they had to pitch in.

Another snowfall piled a half foot on the first blizzard's accumulation.

Francesca and Laura sat on couches before the big fireplace in the Main, drinking tea. A coating of white veiled everything beyond the big windows.

"I'm glad you're still with us." Laura gave Francesca a frank look over the rim of her cup. "We would hate to lose you."

"*Grazie.*" Francesca went on with her now-automatic response. "When William rescued me in Salt Lake, I was on my way to California."

"Have you family there?"

"I thought to find work—"

"You have work here."

"The wine country—"

Comprehension dawned on Laura's features. "You thought it would be like your home in Tuscany."

"*Sì.*"

"Is this place not acceptable?" Laura gestured, encompassing the Main, the valley, and the mountains. "Has someone hurt your feelings or made you feel unwelcome?"

Laura must have heard about the altercation with Dieter Gross and the nasty remarks that set it off. Francesca pressed her lips together. "People at Snake River have been more than kind, better than any place I have been."

Laura's eyes lit up. "You may work for us, Francesca, but that doesn't mean we can't be friends. Charlie works for us, our son works for us ...."

Though William had asked her to stay, he had not given her the slightest encouragement in these past weeks. But he had made himself indispensable, helping with the dishes and the cooking fires in the Main's kitchen, treating her with the same affable cheer he used for dudes and the rest of the outfit.

Francesca knew she should leave, but she was held back by the memory of Indian summer heat, of her and William's untrammeled laughter after Bayberry had run away with her ... of the way she sometimes turned her head and found him looking at her with a smokiness in his eyes.

"Word is they're using sleighs now on The Pass," Laura went on.

Outside, the snow deepened.

At Snake River, Francesca had warmth and friends, and—though Laura might be appalled that a servant would consider loving her son—the prospect of being able to trust a man again.

"Why not stay?" Laura urged.

The answer came simply, as though a weight lifted from Francesca's shoulders. "I will need some winter clothing."

Chapter Fifteen
December, 1925

As winter set in, Slide Lake remained brimful.

In spite of the engineers' assurances the dam was stable, the residents of Kelly watched it with wary eyes. Francesca heard Cord discussing it with Charlie and William several times. The Snake River men's gut sense, and the assessment of engineering student Sven Nygaard, was that there was trouble to come.

Still without a rosary, Francesca sent up a prayer that the season of peace on earth would see Kelly safe and prosperous.

By Christmas Eve at Snake River Ranch, icicles as large as her arm hung from the eaves. Snow heaped on the meadow, almost covering the buck rail fences.

Winter clothes had not been a luxury but a necessity. Francesca put on layers—thick German socks that reached far up her legs, woolen drawers, trousers—she had seen the wisdom of following Laura Sutton's mode of dress—new thick boots, and a heavy shearling coat.

All this just to walk over to the Main and prepare Christmas Eve breakfast. Trips to anywhere else required snowshoes.

After the meal, she returned to the cookshack, bolted the door, and built up the fire.

Using a nutcracker, she shelled almonds until her kitchen scale read four pounds. She added the almonds to a large pan of boiling water to blanch them; then she pounded them a little at a time in a stone mortar until each batch formed a fine paste.

Two pounds of sifted sugar went into the mix. Creaming butter with more sugar, she beat in egg yolks, stirred in flour a little at a time, and fashioned the dough into shapes.

While she was mixing food coloring, a knock came at the door.

Francesca lifted the latch and peeked out at Laura. The older woman was inside before she could stop her, stripping off her gloves and going to the fire.

Laura turned back to her. "I came to talk to you about my son." She smiled with eyes that still reminded Francesca of Bryce's.

Had he met with an accident? Or come home for Christmas?

"It cannot have escaped your notice that William ...." Francesca let out her breath, "has had his eye on you for some time."

"I am sure you are mistaken," Francesca replied automatically. He would have declared himself by now."

"A woman knows these things," Laura insisted, "and you know."

William's arm around her beneath the wagon, while they fought for life, his eyes following her when he thought she wasn't looking .... Francesca's heart rate accelerated.

Laura had been nothing but kind in recent months, but the distance between the cookshack and William's bachelor house was not measured in feet. She waited for Laura to forbid a servant to be courted by her son.

Instead, Laura said, "There were people who censured me for marrying Cord."

Francesca could not imagine why, but then recalled Laura's mention of "Fielding House" and surmised Cord must have come from a more humble beginning.

Her backbone straightened. "You equate my being poor—"

Laura's features softened. "You misunderstand me. I merely want to say, if you and William were to ... *find* each other, Cord and I would not only be pleased but proud."

Stunned into silence, Francesca almost burst into tears. Of all the Christmas presents Laura might have offered .... It must have taken a great deal for an American couple to decide an immigrant could join their family.

"I'll leave you to your baking." When Laura reached the door, she turned back. "Don't forget we're all going to the Chapel of the Transfiguration for candlelight mass this evening."

"I am not Episcopalian." Francesca longed for the chapel in Radda, to take communion with her mother and father.

"I'm not, either. In fact, I don't think we have an Episcopalian on the place. But we're all going." With her hand on the door latch, she warned, "Dress warmly."

❧

William drove the sleigh, with Cord and Charlie on the rear seat. Francesca and Laura faced backward, tucked beneath buffalo lap robes, with hot bricks warming their feet. The only thing cold on Francesca was her face.

With winter's early evening darkness, stars spangled the black canopy and dry snow squeaked beneath the runners. William had lobbed a snowball at Francesca before they started, only to have it fall at his feet in a puff of powder.

The harness jingled, and Laura began to sing, "Sleigh bells ring, are you listening?"

Cord, Charlie, and William joined in, while Francesca learned the Christmas carol.

When they arrived at the Chapel of the Transfiguration, a raft of sleighs suggested almost everyone in the valley had come for Christmas Eve service. The small church bore a load of snow on the roof. With its brown wooden walls, it looked like a gingerbread house awaiting decoration.

The Sutton party passed through the vestibule and up the aisle between rough wooden pews lashed together with rawhide. By day, the picture window behind the altar would permit the glorious landscape to serve as decoration. That evening, candlelight reflected from the glass.

Though Francesca would have taken a less prominent seat, William's hand at her elbow brought her along to the second row.

As the service began, he nudged her.

When she turned and to meet his intent gray eyes, he gestured for her to look down.

On his open palm rested a rosary of blue crystal beads, bearing a gold cross that sparkled even in the dim light. Francesca sucked in her breath. Laura must have known.

William bent and put his lips to her ear. On a warm breath, "I was going to give it to you tomorrow for Christmas, but ...." He pressed the beaded chain into her hand, using his other to close her fingers over it.

"*Grazie*," Francesca whispered. She sensed Laura watching from a few feet away.

The next day Cord surveyed the Christmas feast from the head of the table in the Main; two ten-pound turkeys with crisp golden skin, a ham decorated with pineapple slices and studded with whole cloves, and a beef roast, along with mashed potatoes, sweet potatoes, green beans, squash, hot rolls, and pickled beets and olives.

At his left hand, Laura. How could she be more beautiful than on their first Christmas together? William smiled from the foot of the table; if Bryce were there, it would be perfect.

With the last platter on the table, Francesca sat down beside William.

Cord bowed his head, reached and grasped Laura's hand on one side and Charlie's on the other. While he was thanking the Lord aloud for the food, he prayed silently that at least one of his sons might find happiness as complete as his and Laura's.

When the turkey carcasses were picked clean, the beef roast reduced to bones, and the other dishes empty, Laura urged her extended family to gather around the fireplace.

Gifts surrounded a twenty-foot spruce decorated with popcorn and cranberry garlands, and delicate ornaments of German glass. Though the family had already exchanged gifts, they had each brought tokens for everyone who wintered over.

Cord played Santa, picking up each package in turn and reading the label.

When the mountainous pile of presents had become a drift of paper and ribbons, Laura noticed Francesca had not offered anything. Yet, she wore a smug look when she went to the kitchen for "something special," as she called it in her lovely accented voice.

William jumped up. "I'll help you."

A moment later, his and Francesca's laughter mingled behind the swinging door. After a few minutes, which Laura hoped her son was taking advantage of, the two of them came out, flushed and smiling.

William carried the silver urn used for morning coffee during dude season, set it on the bar, and returned for a tray piled with Laura's best Limoges china cups and saucers. While the mouth-watering scent of spiced cider filled the room, Francesca bore a silver tray covered with tea towels.

She slid it gracefully onto the bar. "I have something for everyone."

When her slim arm lifted the towel, the rich almond scent of baking in the cookshack came back to Laura.

Picking up the first shape with care, Francesca called, "Mr. Sutton," with a smile.

"Cord," he corrected.

He came to the bar, and Francesca handed him a marzipan figure in blue pants and shirt, his trademark black hat, and boots. He laughed. "I swear you've captured my face, as well."

One by one, Francesca gave out her culinary artwork, each adorned with a personal detail. Jim's had his ruddy complexion and blond hair. Asa's wore suspenders, Charlie's his best gray Stetson. Laura's likeness wore trousers, but the slim waist, brown hair, and green eyes distinguished her from the others.

No one ate them.

With another enigmatic smile, Francesca went into the kitchen and brought out more shapes, bananas, cherries, oranges, each flavored with extract. The group made short work of these.

Laura watched William, who sat with his marzipan portrait wrapped in a napkin, his eyes on Francesca.

Chapter Sixteen
New Year's Eve 1925-26

On Thursday, December 31, the command appearance for everyone wintering over in the valley was the all night-dance at the Jackson Clubhouse. Around seven p.m., William came round to the cookshack with the sleigh driven by Romulus and Remus, the spirited young bays that had replaced Eli and Jacob.

Not that they could be replaced.

William crunched over the cold snow to the porch, a bit nervous. After giving Fran the rosary on Christmas Eve, he had had nothing for her at the gift exchange. Now, holding a new shearling hat from Deloney's Store behind his back, he knocked.

Fran opened the door, holding a hairbrush. Her chestnut tresses, longer than when she had arrived in summer, flowed over her shoulders and down her back. "William!"

"Am I early?"

"I think perhaps I am late."

Inside, the lamp glowed over the big wooden table and the vented kerosene heater brought in for winter had the place downright temperate. He shut out the cold and took in the rest of her.

She wore a dress he'd never seen, a burgundy wool drop waist that fell in a single smooth line to below her knees. A silver-buckled belt encircled her hips, and pearl buttons tracked down the center from neckline to hem.

"I picked it out in the August patterns from McCall's and had Maria make it up in winter wool before she left."

"It's great." Bryce would have waxed more eloquent, he thought.

Fran didn't seem to notice William's simple delivery. Turning away, she walked toward her bedroom in the lean-to and spoke over her shoulder. "Can you help me with my hair?"

His throat constricted. "Sure."

Still hiding the hat, he followed her sinuous passage to the door of the room where she slept.

She slipped inside and came out cradling wire contraptions in her hand. "I bought these new style bobby pins. I am having trouble getting them right."

"What do you want to do?"

"Pin this on?" She showed him a cloche, a bell-shaped hat that matched her dress.

"That won't be warm enough this evening." Already well below zero, it was the coldest night of the winter so far.

She studied her hat. "That's true."

William brought out the shearling. "This might be better."

Fran's eyes brightened. She took the hat, smoothing her fingers over the suede, digging into the thick wool. She leaned in, taller than any woman he'd been this close to, and kissed his cheek. "*Mille grazie.*"

He considered kissing her lips, but didn't want to rush.

Moments later, he helped her into the sleigh and spread the buffalo robe over them both. Snuggling in, with warming bricks at their feet, he pointed out the moonrise, where bare cottonwoods made a lacework against the rising orb.

"The dance will truly last all night?" she asked.

He nodded. "There'll be a midnight supper at the Clubhouse and breakfast in the morning."

When they neared the town square, the sleighs ahead threw up a fine snow mist, starring Fran's hair where a few locks peeked from beneath her new cap. Her almond eyes appeared huge as she took in the holiday lights on every building near the square. Farm families who had moved to town for the winter so their children could attend school waved from the windows of the Crabtree Hotel and several boarding houses.

No question about it, everyone's expression said William and Fran had just become the valley's latest item.

Reluctant to leave their cocoon, Francesca watched William unhitch Romulus and Remus and walk them into Wort's livery off the square. He moved with quick efficiency, making her aware of his rugged build.

It was happening the way Laura had said it might. And Francesca had a decision to make. After Vincenzo's betrayal, was she ready to risk her heart again?

On the surface, William seemed the steady son, as Laura called him. He lacked the fire of Bryce, who had breezed into Francesca's life for a single weekend, shared soup, philosophy, and fireworks.

And disappeared.

William assisted her down from the sleigh with an arm around her. Aware of the many eyes on her—not only her, but on the scion of the Snake River Ranch—she held her head high.

On the walk over to the Clubhouse, he told her the huge frame box with a hipped roof had housed the Jackson's Hole Gun Club from 1897 to 1908, and also served as courtroom, gymnasium, commercial building, and now the Jackson Post Office.

Now it housed the social hall upstairs, from whence came strains of music and laughter. They were about to ascend the outside stairway when they saw Prudence Johnston leaning over the rail. Hatless in the cold, she had let her golden hair fall in fashionable hot-oiled waves over her coat collar. She brought a cigarette in a pearl-handled holder to her rosy lips and drew in the smoke.

Her companion was the cowboy who had won the bucking bronco competition ... and who had pointed a rifle at William.

William clenched his jaw. Of all the rotten luck.

"Lookee here," said Tiny Good in a falsely jovial tone.

Pru bent over and showed off her cleavage. "Why, it's William and ... I don't think I know the name of that Mexican cook."

Tiny leaned in to Pru, confiding, "She ain't no Mex. She's an Eyetalian."

"Hell!" Pru showed off her modern bent for swearing.

William, his hand behind Fran's waist, kept climbing. "Evening, Pru ... Tiny."

"Lo, William." Pru used a sultry, knowing tone. "You haven't been round to see me."

William glowered as he and Fran reached the top step. Tiny and Pru blocked the door.

For a sickening instant, William had an image of Tiny giving him a shove. He braced himself to make a grab for the banister, hoping the lummox wouldn't end up hurting Francesca.

Pru picked at Tiny's sleeve. "It's cold out here, hon."

The big man stared at William a moment longer, then turned away.

Inside the hall, the party was in full swing. Ben Raleigh strummed his guitar and an older gentleman sawed on a fiddle. Beyond the musicians, long tables groaned under the weight of food prepared by the ladies of Jackson Town.

"Oh, no," said Fran. "I should have brought—"

William touched her arm. "Tonight you are not the cook."

"That is not what Prudence Johnston said."

He started. "How'd you know her name?"

"When she was cheering you on at the rodeo, your mother told me about her."

"Lord, what else has she told you?" William tried to keep annoyance out of his tone.

Grace Miller approached Francesca. She had been Jackson's first female mayor back in 1920 and 1921, heading up the nation's first all woman town council. Of tough pioneer stock, Mrs. Miller had a firm, no-nonsense mouth.

"You must be the chef at Snake River I've been hearing so much about. Come sample my bean casserole and tell me what I could do to liven it up."

Her regard expanded to include William. "How nice you two look this evening. William, why don't you take her coat to the cloakroom, while she and I have a little chat?"

Over the next several hours, Francesca felt fortunate to have read today's *Jackson's Hole Courier*, as locals argued both for and against the southern expansion of Yellowstone. The paper's front page had contained little else, opinion by Rock Springs attorney T.S. Taliaferro, Jr., on the illegality of park extension, and a reprint of his wife's editorial from the *Wyoming Clubwomen*.

Mrs. Taliaferro had stated:

> It seems strange to law-abiding residents of Wyoming that people from other states should request us to give them our Teton Mountains, for when we go to any of their parks the first sign we see is, "KEEP OFF THE GRASS."

In addition to politics, there was comic relief. Fred Lovejoy, a cousin of Jim's, said he had surrounded his haystack with lighted lanterns at night to keep the elk from eating it. Whereupon a big bull elk scooped up a lantern onto his horns and trotted away with it.

Each time William brought Francesca another cup of spiked punch, her smiles grew wider. She even decided she would dance.

But as soon as the waltz began, she had trouble following.

Sotto voce, William spoke instructions at her ear.

She glanced down at their feet, made a misstep. His breath puffed against her cheek. "One two three ...."

In a few minutes, he said, "You've got it."

At first, he held himself in such a way that their hips did not touch. Later he drew her closer.

At ten, the dancing stopped for the wireless broadcast of the New Year's celebration in New York City. Then more dancing, until a break for the observation of midnight.

The fiddler laid aside his instrument and raised a hand for quiet. Holding his pocket watch, he called, "Five, four, three, two .... Haaapppy New Year!"

William drew Francesca away from the central chandelier into a darker corner and pressed his lips to hers. The kiss suffused her body with warmth.

For midnight supper, he brought her the best of the buffet. He must have paid attention to what she served herself since joining the family at table, for there was not a slice of beef, a ladle of beans, or a bite of potato on her plate.

When the dancing began again, William held her flush against him, making no attempt to hide his desire. Surely everyone could see her high color.

Over the past week, since he had given her the rosary, their eyes had met and lingered many times. Each evening, he had walked her to the cookshack, fueled the kerosene heater, and stoked her bedroom woodstove before leaving. Not once had he attempted to kiss or hold her, but she had seen in his eyes that it was only a matter of time.

If a man wanted a woman just for a tumble, would he go to such elaborate lengths to make her feel special? As they danced, she found herself dreaming of sharing William's house, though she would have preferred to build on the bluff. Of being the mother of the new generation that Laura and Cord so richly desired and deserved.

William shifted his hands over Francesca's back, sending shivers through her.

It had been long months since Vincenzo, but her woman's body, once awakened, craved the physical expression of love. Pressed against William, all her blood seemed to pool in her loins.

His lips at her ear, he murmured, "I know a place."

Keeping her hand in his, he led her down the inside stairs to the first floor. The party had spilled over here; the men's smoking room was packed and cloudy blue.

William drew her along, down a hallway past the men's and women's latrines that emptied into a trough outside. At the corridor's end, he opened a door to the subzero cold and a narrow alley between the Clubhouse and another building behind.

"What ...?"

William put a finger to his lips, pulled a key ring from his pocket, and unlocked a door on the wall a few feet across. She rushed across the space between buildings, hugging herself against the weather.

Inside, elk antler chandeliers with electric bulbs shed a glow upon a brown leather sofa facing a stone fireplace. It was warm, probably from a coal furnace, but William pulled out a box of matches decorated with the Snake River brand and lighted the kindling and logs laid upon the hearth.

"A friend's townhouse," he offered. "He owns a ranch up by Moran and keeps this for when he wants some civilization."

Odd, to hear Jackson Town described as "civil," when she had seen *Roma* and New York, but Francesca had not been up to the small settlement of Moran near Jackson Lake Dam. Perhaps it was all relative.

William came to her with a look of rare determination on his face. "I've been waiting for this."

Francesca waited, too. For him to tell her she was beautiful, to speak of where this might lead.

She had wanted their first time to be the kind of dream-come-true his mother had given her blessing to, but her urgency had dissipated while passing the latrines and traversing the cold alley.

Perhaps it was just as well. She had gone with Vincenzo without a second thought and this time she did not want to be "easy," a term she had heard used to describe a woman who was too available.

She and William needed to talk. About his dog, Sophie—she had seen the spotted bitch with pups and a boyish William in a photo—Laura had supplied the dog's name. That and ... Francesca wanted to know everything about him.

William touched her cheek. With the heels on his boots and her flat shoes, they were the same height.

He dragged her against him, his hips moving insistently against hers.

She waited for the glow to come back.

He drew her over to the large leather sofa and took her down with him. His fingers parted the buttons at the collar of her dress.

It was going too fast.

"I thought we would—"

He mouthed the side of her neck. "We are."

His hand found her breast and the renewed tug of his touch spread in her womb.

"After tonight," William whispered, "you can come to my bachelor house. If you come round the back by the cottonwoods, no one will see you."

"No one will *see* me?" Francesca gasped.

His suggestion froze her, as if he had thrown her out coatless into the arctic night. She should have foreseen it, should have known all he wanted from an employee was a tawdry secret affair.

She struggled up and shoved at him. He slid on the smooth leather and landed on the floor with a thump.

"Hell!" He got up on his knees. "What did you do that for?"

"Who do you think I am?" She poked a finger on his breastbone.

"Ouch! Dammit!"

"You think I am *puttana* ... a ... whore ... you can use ..." To her horror, tears welled. He must not see them.

He intercepted the path of one of her tears with his thumb. "Men don't spend time trail riding and talking, helping out in the kitchen with a woman they don't want to be with. If I really thought you were a whore, I'd deserve to get shoved on the floor."

He started to climb back onto the sofa with her.

Still wary, she put her hand up, palm out. "But you said for me to sneak ... I thought—"

William looked genuinely puzzled. "You thought what?"

Recognition dawned on his features. "Don't tell me you thought I was asking you to marry me?"

They stared at each other. A log collapsed with a hiss in the fire.

Francesca gathered the sides of her dress together. She thrust the buttons into their holes, smoothed the dress front, and swung her feet to the floor.

William still knelt, their faces on the level. "You're taking this all wrong."

With breakfast and sunrise hours away, she longed for her bed. She wanted to order William to get the team out of livery, to drive the sleigh back to the ranch.

But it must be twenty below. The wind had come up, beating at the window panes and whistling around the doorframe.

Nor could she go back and dance as if nothing had happened.

Squaring her shoulders, she tried to keep her voice steady. "Go. Come for me when it is time to leave."

William ran a hand through his hair, tousling the dark strands. He looked so bereft, part of her wanted to take it back, to be his lover. "God, Fran, I swear I didn't mean to insult you." He put out his hands. "Let me stay and ...."

In the dead of the night, in the middle of the coldest winter she had ever known, she wanted nothing more than to snuggle against his warmth ....

But he did not love her. If he did, in even the smallest way, he would say so. After believing she loved Vincenzo, she could not settle for less than a man's whole heart.

"Perhaps with time," he began.

"With time what? If a woman lies down for you in secret, she is no better than a whore. And once she agrees to it, what will happen to change ...?"

His face reddened, his brows came together in a dark vee. "Don't try and tell me you've never been with a man, that you've been saving it for your husband, not after the way you plastered yourself to me on the dance floor."

That was when she had believed ....

His chest heaved. "You came to the ranch without a *lire*. You've been lying in wait with your cool and aloof act, thinking I'd get so hot for you I'd ask you to marry me."

"No, I ...." Hadn't she? "Your mother said ...."

His color rose again and she knew she'd made a fatal mistake.

"Everyone, including you, thinks I live to please my parents." He pushed to his feet and glared at her. "I'll have you know I'm my own man, and if Mother picked you out for me, I'll have to pass."

William slammed out; the door shuddered in the frame. The shotgun space between the buildings made a tunnel through which a winter gale whistled.

He turned right and staggered upwind to open air. Despite his gait and some spiked punch, he wasn't drunk. Not yet.

Coatless, hatless, he made his way across the side street in the direction of old man Meyer's speakeasy. There, he'd get an honest drink without facing the town gossips.

Of course, hiding out wouldn't make a difference. Every nuance of what had passed between him and Fran upstairs had certainly been noted and duly dissected by the valley folk, right down to their sneaking away, flushed and eager.

Christ, it was freezing!

He blew into Meyer's on a gust of frigid wind.

"Hey!"

"Shut the door!"

"Were you raised in a barn?" This last from Tiny Good.

A half second later, the big man loomed over him, smelling of whiskey.

After the falling out with Fran, a bar brawl with Tiny was exactly what William needed to blow off steam.

Except it was what Bryce would have done. William tried to move past the bigger man.

Tiny started to block him.

Old man Meyer called, "Next round's on me, folks. For the New Year."

At the promise of free booze, Tiny veered off. William found a seat at the opposite end of the bar and knocked back two whiskeys in quick succession.

Then slowed, but continued to sip, staring into his glass. How dare his mother imply to Fran that he would marry her?

Of course, he had only Fran's word. Maybe she had made it up.

A hand touched his shoulder.

Tensed, he turned with the care he used when drinking. If Tiny were back....

Pru stood behind his chair. All the sulkiness had drained out of her.

William looked around and saw his adversary throw back a shot, put on his coat, and turn toward the door.

Pru's china blue eyes met William's and held, reminding him of when he'd seen them glazed with passion. On this night she appeared exhausted and vulnerable.

"Lo, William," she said in a husky voice.

"Lo, Pru."

Chapter Seventeen
Winter, 1926

The January days began and ended under pale skies that spit snow or drove it in whirling torrents. The only colors were the trunks of bare trees, the deep hues of evergreen peeking from beneath a draping of snow, and the shaggy coats of elk and moose come down from the high country to browse.

Jim and Asa took Francesca to the National Elk Refuge just north of Jackson Town. William had told the boys he would drive them, but when he saw her waiting beside the sleigh, he said he had forgotten something he needed to do.

Even so, she enjoyed the trip, marveling at the magnificent antler racks on the males. How did they hold up their heads?

How did she?

Eating in the Main's dining room had been fun before, laughing, meeting William's eyes over the boards for a gaze lasting an extra significant second. Now, they talked around each other.

What a fool she had been.

Of course, she had no way of knowing what might have happened had she melted into the leather couch and let nature take its course. Perhaps if they had begun a modern affair, as so many did, affection might have metamorphosed to love.

When Laura asked what had happened to their promising start, she deflected. "It seems we do not want the same things."

The wall clock in the lean-to became her enemy.

Each dawn she woke too early and bundled up for the ordeal of hiking to the Main; the path stamped down at least three feet in snow. On days when a blizzard made a white-out, she followed a stout rope tied to the cookshack porch pillar and a hook beside the Main's rear entry. By the time she reached the kitchen door, she sweated beneath her layers of clothing, while hoping her nose and cheeks beneath her muffler escaped frostbite.

Before the men who wintered over—Charlie, Jim, and Asa—arrived, she worked alone, starting biscuits and coffee. Breakfast always waited until William took the sleigh down and brought his parents up.

At night Francesca lay in her narrow bed, staying awake too late, listening to the clock's rough ticking. Time after time, she replayed the night at the Clubhouse. Her mind knew she had made the right decision, but when wind-driven sleet rang against the lean-to's window, and she curled under the covers trying to forge a warm spot with her breath, she imagined his warmth ....

Her hands felt full with longing; she slid them over the sheets. Her treacherous body longed for another chance on the soft leather sofa in the Jackson town house. When the ache grew acute, she considered the frigid distance between the cookshack and his house.

In dreams, he came to her. They blended, seamlessly, until she woke, filled with shame. She must leave, no matter the conditions on Teton Pass.

Yet each dawn she counted her blessings to be working for people as wonderful as Cord and Laura. She looked out at the mountains that seemed to float above a layer of winter ground fog and could not imagine a place more beautiful.

She would not stay for William, but for herself.

෨෬

Sunday, February 28, 1926

It is difficult to believe today is the last day of February. At least the darkest days are done.

We have lost two of our valley elderly to pneumonia. In addition, as we have every year since 1918, we fear the onset of influenza. Thankfully, this year it felled only a few for a week of misery and spared us at Snake River.

No matter how many winters I spend in the valley, with the coming of March, I always begin looking for signs of spring. Perhaps it comes from a gift Mother gave me when I was a child. On the colorful calendar, with the months in the shape of a clock, each season bore a different color: summer, the gold of wildflowers, autumn, the burnt orange of maple leaves, winter, the blue of shadows on snow, and spring, green. Each year I recall the transition from cold cobalt to verdant hue on the first of March and begin to hope.

Though Mother died when I was ten, giving birth to my baby brother who lived for a day and a night, I knew her well enough to believe she wanted me always to hope.

If only there had been more time to know her better.

When Violet Fielding entered a room, the rustle of skirts and the scent of lemon verbena always preceded her. And if the breeze off Lake Michigan died, and the flies of August droned, her hands always felt cool.

Once she was gone, Father and I imagined she helped us decorate each year's Christmas tree. In our hearts, she was still the slim woman with sleek brown hair drawn back in wings, frozen forever in a silver frame on the mantel.

If only Father had not also frozen into inflexibility after her death ....

I worry about William, and whether his resemblance to his grandfather will dictate his destiny. It appears he has not made further overtures to Francesca. I fear his stubborn streak is showing.

Even Charlie, in our talks over his favorite Lapsang Souchong tea—I cannot abide the smoky taste—has revealed how with Lucy gone, he especially hopes for one of the boys to marry and bring new life to our shared endeavor.

Perhaps when spring comes, the mild air and bursting forth of life will soften William toward Francesca. But we have months to go before mud season.

Laura lay down her pen and looked fondly at a piece of lined tablet paper beside her journal. With a smile, she opened it. A pencil scrawl, Bryce's habitual quick energy:

Dear Mom and Dad,

Just a note to let you know I'm still above ground. I decided to try William's trick of last winter—getting out of the deep freeze. So I'm working at the Phelps Dodge copper mine in Morenci, Arizona. It sounds like a great adventure and it has been, seeing parts of the country for the first time. Me and C—

Another tall letter followed the capital "C" with both of them scratched out. Laura lifted the paper to the light for the third time. Clara, Claire, Chloe? Or just another Charlie?

drove up to the Grand Canyon for a few days at Christmas. Tell Dad I bought a Model T. I promise not to bring it anywhere near the ranch.

Anyway, the Grand Canyon is the biggest damn ditch you'd ever hope to see, miles across and a mile deep. Outside of the valley, it's the most spectacular scene I've had the pleasure of seeing.

As for the work, it gets cold down here, too. Mostly, I drive a truck with a bad heater, but last week they hit a new vein of the sulfide ore they smelt from a few percent copper to the pure metal. I got shanghaied into going underground and swinging a pick—primitive stuff. Pretty soon I'll have a better looking set of muscles than Mike Yokel.

Bryce referred to a young valley man who owned a Wilson gas station, hauled freight and was a world class middleweight wrestler about to set off on a nine month tour of Australia.

It'll serve me well if I get into a fight.

Well, that's about all I can think to tell you. Sorry I didn't make it for the holidays. Happy belated Christmas and New Year's. I'll try and stop by when I come north to start ranching in a few months.

Love and a hug,
Bryce

Laura put away her journal and took out her stationary. She ordered the pale blue notes, custom monogrammed by the same company that did the ranch brochures, along with their trademark wooden matches. Each note was discreetly engraved, "Snake River Ranch, Moose, WY," allowing guests to tell the outside world what a time they were having playing dude.

Her thoughts went back to the best part of last year's season, the Fourth of July, and calculated. There might just be a way to get William off square one where Francesca was concerned.

Laura picked up her pen.

February, 28, 1926

My Dearest Bryce,

It was so good to get your letter. Your father and I worried about you when the holidays passed with no word ....

৩০৫

Bryce stood in the Morenci post office, reading his mother's letter. The second week of March had brought real heat to the copper pit; he stood inside to avoid the direct sun.

> Arizona! I always thought to get there someday, but the years slide by and we spend our time in Jackson's Hole. Of course it has the most spectacular scenery.
>
> I confess I never imagined you working in a mine. You and your friend—is that someone who works in the pit with you or a lady?—must have enjoyed seeing the Grand Canyon.

Try as she might, Mom couldn't help but be nosy.

> As far as the Model T goes, you know you're welcome anytime, no matter what you're driving. William bought one, too, late in the summer. At first, I thought Cord would take him to task, but he let it pass. Probably because Bitter Waters was visiting.
>
> Your great uncle asked after you—called you Koyama, his mighty lion. His face really fell when he learned he would not see you.

She also couldn't help dishing the guilt.

But the mention of Bitter Waters brought back the cold night on a mountain when a shivering small boy pressed himself into a cleft in the granite and prayed for the lion to take himself elsewhere.

> William is fine. He enjoyed his car until the snows set in and we brought out the sleighs. He spends hours in the shed behind his house taking off the tarpaulin and wiping the car down. For his sake, I hope it starts in the spring.

Bryce glanced out at the southwest sun. No sleighs in the streets here.

> One bit of excitement. At Christmas, William began to squire Francesca. You remember our new chef? A tall willowy brunette with huge dark eyes.

Bryce frowned. He'd expected when he left that William would move in on her. Why had it taken until Christmas for Brother to lose his timidity?

> Cord and I have come to care for her greatly. How excited
> we are to think one of our sons will settle down and give us
> grandchildren to enliven the old place.

Bryce gripped the paper. Why did she think it had to be William? Bryce happened to know his brother didn't even like kids. Not like Bryce did.

He'd been thinking about it the past few months, no doubt because of his relationship with Charlene. She was a wonderful cook, if you liked enchiladas. Her ample curves enveloped him in bed, and her merry disposition showed on her round, smiling face.

She was thirty-two and had hinted last night about getting married and starting a family.

The trouble was that when he considered settling down, he got an image of companionship by a fire, of sharing soup, bread, wine ... and fireworks.

What a damnable shame that Francesca would settle for William.

> I will close now and give this to Asa, as it is his turn to ski
> down to Moose for the mail.

Bryce folded the letter and put it in his pocket. He had a date to take Charlene to dinner.

Chapter Eighteen
May, 1926

Spring arrived in Jackson's Hole with agonizing slowness. Snow lay in patches between areas of muddy bare ground. Though the ice finally began to break up and melt on the lakes and the ranch pond, the mountains remained white from crown to foothills. By the middle of the month, flowers began to bloom: the first arrowleaf balsamroot, yellow violets, and buffaloberry.

In Salt Lake, Rosa and Maria said their goodbyes at the Excalibur Hotel. In Wales, Tom bought his steamship ticket to return to America.

Young Ned Hanson looked forward to the end of his freshman year at La Salle University in Philadelphia. He had signed on for another summer at Snake River, hoping this year to encounter a female dude, or perhaps a laundress or maid, who would help him get rid of his pesky virginity.

With the taking down of the winter bridge and the reopening of Menor's Ferry, Maude Noble started to remark upon Charlie's frequent trips. He kept his counsel with a smile, though he sometimes whistled as the current pushed the pontoon raft across the Snake.

Spring weather meant he and Harriet no longer had to meet *accidentally* on the covered porch of the Kelly Mercantile—shopping and exchanging polite pleasantries whenever anyone got close and speaking in low and significant tones when they believed they were unobserved.

As the days grew warmer and softer, Harriet and Charlie rode out on horseback and met in the forest. She brought picnic lunches of fried chicken, potato salad, and home-baked brownies.

Charlie remained deferent, but he was beginning to drop his early pretense of feeling nothing but friendship. Harriet's bright blue eyes, soft red hair, and porcelain skin haunted him noon and night.

At first he worried over what Lucy would think. But the two of them had talked years ago and agreed that if death took one of them, the other should not dwell in the past, but seek out the warmth and pleasure of a new relationship.

Lucy and Harriet could not have been more different.

Charlie's wife, older and rounder, had been both unabashedly sensuous and a source of deep and calming comfort.

Harriet was sharp, almost electric, in her quick movements and was fast on the draw with her opinions. Her husband had been an inventor in Bozeman, where they had lived together until he dropped dead in a field while testing an automatic feeding device for livestock.

What would Harriet do if Charlie kissed her?

One thing for sure, she'd let him know one way or the other.

Laura started working the garden soil in preparation for setting out plants from the hot house. She made a few new acquisitions for the ranch interiors: a percolator for Francesca to make coffee in the Main's kitchen, and a Congoleum rug to place in front of the huge fireplace. The durable material, printed up in a blue and vermilion pattern to resemble an Oriental rug, was designed to withstand stains from spilled drinks and cigarette and cigar ashes.

In late May, Laura had a letter from Bryce, suggesting he would be coming north and planned to stop by. She announced the news to Cord and William before lunch, hoping it would be soon. Her theory of last winter—that if Bryce knew William was interested in Francesca, he might come home to compete—had not yielded results, leading her to conclude that the person whose name started with "C" must be female.

What if Bryce brought her home with him?

On the same pleasantly warm afternoon that he learned of Bryce's impending visit, William arrived at the cookshack with a pair of baskets over his arm.

Surprised he had come alone after months of avoiding contact, Francesca met his gaze warily across the table where she was preparing pasta for her own dinner. The mix of flour, eggs, a little water and salt, was dry enough to roll and she was flattening it vigorously with a rolling pin.

"Lo, Francesca," William said.

She nodded.

"What would you say to ... gathering mushrooms?"

Her mother had taught her to recognize the edible varieties when she was old enough to be trusted. Sliced and sautéed in butter, tossed with strips of pasta, cream, and shallots ....

"I need to finish this." She gestured with the rolling pin.

"I'll wait." He set the baskets on the table, pulled out a chair, and straddled it backward. The sleeves of his blue cotton work shirt were rolled back to expose strong forearms, already bronzed from outdoor work.

He watched without saying much, except to make a few comments about the weather and calving season. She rolled the dough, giving up when it was thicker than ideal, wanting to be outside in the soft spring air.

William waited some more while she changed into denim trousers, a long-sleeved shirt, and boots for the mud.

Outside, he led her down to the Snake River bottom. Starting at the base of a cottonwood, he passed a clump of bright green scouring rushes and moved on to some deadfall. "Aha!"

Francesca approached; there was the spongy texture and bland color of the morel. The more she scanned, the more seemed to pop out.

She and William returned to the cookshack with full baskets.

"What shall I make with them?" she asked, certain Cord would not care for her pasta recipe.

"Beefsteak and mushroom gravy," William replied without hesitation.

She smiled. "And mashed potatoes."

He grinned. "But not for you."

Francesca expected he would leave, but he pulled out the chair again. For something to do, she got a soft brush and started cleaning the mushrooms. "We've got so many. I'll have to dry some."

"Think so? You haven't seen how many I can eat."

As it got closer to dinnertime, and she started getting busier, William rose and gathered the baskets. "I'd better get to the stables and help the boys muck out."

He started for the door.

"William."

He turned. "Yes?"

"Thank you for taking me to find the mushrooms."

His smile recalled everything she liked about him. Her pulse edged higher.

In the doorway, he was backlit against the setting sun; she couldn't discern his expression. "Mother said Bryce should be coming soon," he said abruptly.

"That ... will be nice," she replied softly.

❦

That night, Francesca lay in bed and stared at the darkened window, while the wall clock continued its infernal ticking.

After months of thinking things were over between them, William's visit had her back in a quandary. Had the lonely nights of winter and the slow-warming spring worn him down, the way they had her?

Perhaps he, too, had tired of pride keeping them apart.

She'd been an idiot on New Year's just as he had. For her part, why had she acted like a shrinking virgin when she was not? Why set herself upon a pedestal, in these modern times when affairs were the norm? She had read about them in magazines while improving her English and learning American ways. Even Struthers Burt had alluded to such goings-on in his book, *The Diary of a Dude Wrangler.*

William was, after all, a man of few words. When he had gotten her onto the leather sofa and things had gone wrong, stress had gotten the better of him. Words had tumbled out that he might now be regretting, based on the unwavering regard he had turned on her today.

Then he had dropped his bombshell about Bryce coming home.

Glinting green eyes, passionate, yet patient when teaching Larry and Benjy to skip rocks. How he'd rescued her from the ugly dude, the way he'd gazed up at the mountains ... "It always makes me feel like I'm in church."

William doled out his words, while Bryce's conversation flowed like a lively waterfall. It caught her up and swept her along, making her forget his charm was ersatz, his commitment to family lacking. How much damage had this casual charmer inflicted on his parents, and whatever woman he turned his focus on?

With a sense of time running out, Francesca threw back her bedcovers. As soon as William heard Bryce might be coming, he had come to her. Because he was afraid of his brother's gift of talk and its effect on her? Because he believed Bryce's physical beauty—there was no other word for it—made his own rugged looks ordinary?

Her hand went to the yoke at the top of her nightgown. Beneath the cloth, her heart beat quickly. All her senses on overload tuned into the whisper of her breathing, the smell of her woman's musk, the texture of muslin too rough on her swelling breasts.

The taste of regret.

She must go to William. Before Bryce breezed in and starting toying with her the way he did everyone else. Bryce could break her heart far worse than Vincenzo had.

William was safe. Safe was what she needed.

The wall clock's hands etched a single black line against the pale face.

Mezzanotte, midnight, when one might run into *stregas*—witches—or evil spirits abroad in the night.

Francesca slipped the green silk wrapper over her nightgown, put on socks and boots for the mud. Over it all, her black wool coat.

She would go as far as the privy then decide.

In a few days, the moon would be full; even tonight it shed enough light to navigate by. She followed the worn trail to the outhouse and took the opportunity to empty her bladder. Then stood at the juncture of paths.

Back to her bed, the sane alternative?

In William's bachelor house, a single light shone in a rear room. Was he wakeful, too? If she took this crazy step, knocked on his door or found the rear passage by the cottonwoods ....

It needn't been so dramatic, she bargained. She would go to the front. Say she'd had trouble sleeping.

In her mind's eye, William would be wearing a heavy silk bathrobe in burgundy or black, pajamas, and leather slippers.

"Lo, William." She would try to sound modern.

He'd usher her in out of the night chill. "Would you care for a brandy?"

"That would be ... swell."

He'd smile, taking in what a regular gal she could be. Offer to hang her coat; his pupils would widen at the slippery green silk beneath. He would pour liquor so potent she could smell it across the room. Bring her a drink and raise a toast, "To new beginnings."

He would explain how sorry he was for bungling New Year's Eve.

Francesca made her careful way toward his house. In the yard, the trees wore spring leaves, pooling inky shadows on the ground. She opened the gate in the white picket fence, winced at its creak, and passed through. When she was three steps from the front porch, a dark shape lifted off the roof.

Stifling a scream, she ducked. A shadow passed over her—a barn owl with great black eyes in a pale face—an omen.

Gathering saliva, Francesca spit and retreated beneath the trees.

The lamp still burned in the rear room—William's bedroom?

With careful steps, she moved in the direction of the window. The curtains were half open, the lamp on the table beside a rumpled bed.

Amid a tangle of covers, a naked William straddled a woman whose legs sprawled. Her big breasts, pressed by his chest, bounced with the impact of each thrust. A pearl-handled cigarette holder lay on the bedside table.

William's body was everything Francesca had imagined. Though his skin was winter-pale, his broad shoulders tapered to strong-looking flanks. An obscene sloppy slapping sounded each time he seated himself to the hilt.

White hands with scarlet-polished nails gripped his buttocks.

"Baby," William groaned.

"Give it to me," his paramour begged.

His pace increased. He rose up, braced on his hands, revealing her.

A pair of knowing blue eyes clashed with Francesca's through the window. On the outside, looking in, she watched Pru Johnston bucking her hips beneath William.

William lay on Pru, heavy with post orgasmic languor. She shifted beneath him. "Get off."

He complied, rolling to the side. And wished, now it was over, that Pru would simply evaporate.

He'd told himself he wasn't going to do it with her anymore; he hated how empty he felt after. But each time she came creeping in the night, leaving her family's auto parked in a grove of trees off the Moose-Jenny Road, every time she slipped in through his unlocked door and bared those luscious heavy breasts, his brain went on vacation.

Could a man be blamed for taking what was freely offered?

Pru looked toward the window. "My, my."

"What?"

"You've been burning your candle at both ends," she chided, with a nasty edge.

"What the hell are you talking about?"

"I'm talking about her." Pru pointed to the window.

"Who?" William leaped from bed and ran to look out. "I don't see anyone."

"She was out there. Your cook, peering in with her eyes wide."

Despite being drenched with sweat, he went cold all over. "Fran?"

"Whatever her name is."

He kept looking. On a low limb sat a huge barn owl. Its face in the shadows, pale against darker plumage, did resemble a human's. It even had a widow's peak like Fran. It blinked; lamplight spilling into the night defined baleful dark eyes.

"Prudence, you twit. It's nothing but a damned owl." William drew the curtains together with a jerk and turned back to the bed.

She lolled on her back, fingering herself down there. Her other hand toyed with one of her nipples. "You think I don't know the difference between an owl and a woman ...."

He started warming up. "That's right. I think you're a dumb blonde."

She kept fiddling.

He hummed "Five Foot Two, Eyes of Blue," a song just out this month. She licked her lips.

How long had it been? Not more than a few minutes and he was rising to attention.

Pru gave him a triumphant smile. "I'm smart enough to get you."

Francesca lay on her narrow bed in the lean-to with rage swelling her chest.

At herself, for sneaking up to a man's window like a spy, a low-down eavesdropper. At William, for acting as if he wanted her, while he was "screwing"—yes, that vulgar slang word—Prudence Johnston. The worst of it was Francesca knew he wasn't taking Prudence out publicly in the valley. Their relationship must be only of the night.

If he would do that to one woman, he would do it to her. He had suggested as much on New Year's Eve.

Lying alone, sick to her stomach at the memory of William's undulating white buttocks, Francesca plotted her revenge.

Bryce ….

Chapter Nineteen
May, 1926

Cord gave Lucifer his head in the forest near the foothills. Signs of season's warming were coming on everywhere.

When he'd left the house, he'd checked the river level and found it still rising. But the spring runoff in the Snake should peak soon. As for the Gros Ventre, the reduction in flow would help the folks downstream sleep better. After almost a year, Kelly residents were beginning to believe the Slide Lake Dam was safe.

Cord still had misgivings.

In a copse of pine, he and Lucifer surprised a bull elk with a well-developed rack in velvet. The refuge north of Jackson was emptying, as the herd returned to the high country.

Next week, dude season.

Riding the trail, Cord rubbed at his chest and damned the mediocre lunch that Asa had offered. Francesca had been ill for the last few days. He vowed to ride home, take down the blue glass bottle of Bromo-Seltzer, and have a dose. If he were lucky, Laura would be working in the hothouse and wouldn't see and worry.

As his discomfort continued to increase, Cord decided to dismount in case lunch came up.

He got down, placed Lucifer's reins on the ground and sat with his back against a stout pine. The pressure behind his breastbone made him feel as though he were caught in a vice. In spite of the cooling shade and a pleasant breeze, he broke into a sweat.

❧

As the clacking train wheels carried Bryce closer to his home country, the image of Charlene faded, as he had expected it would. He'd left Morenci, telling her he'd return in the fall, but doubting it. To keep her from getting weepy, he'd presented her with the Model T and the keys.

Now, with each mile he traveled to the north, the memory of a tall, slender woman with a widow's peak grew more vivid. So much that when the train pulled into Idaho Falls, his chest tightened, knowing he would soon learn whether Francesca and William had already tied the knot.

It had been over a month since he and Mom had exchanged letters. He'd passed along the approximate date of his coming north and suggested if she needed to get in touch with him close to that time, his post box in Idaho Falls was still a good address.

A pale blue envelope peeked out from behind the little glass door.

He spun the dial.

May 25, 1926. Four days ago.

> My Dearest Bryce,
>   I know you believe I send missives intended to manipulate you into coming home …

He was about to crumple the paper when a chill touched the back of his neck.

> But I thought you should know. Yesterday afternoon, your father went out riding on Lucifer. We had scheduled a meeting to discuss ranch business at three. You know you are always welcome to come and take your part in making decisions …

And watch William play crown prince, cutting off his ideas at the knees.

> Charlie and William arrived on time.

The chill spread inside his chest.

> We waited an hour. Then William, Charlie, Asa, and Jim mounted up to search.

Bryce looked around the post office. No place to sit.

He pushed out the door. If Dad were dead, Mom would have started, "Bryce, I am devastated to tell you ..." Wouldn't she?

He folded down on the curb; his duffle splashed into a puddle.

They found him at dusk ...

God, no.

> ... sitting against a pine with Lucifer nearby. He said he was just tired, but the doctor insisted he go to St. John's Hospital.

Bryce checked his watch: four p.m. No trains until morning.

At the Porter Hotel, he entered the one-story stone building and asked to use the telephone. Dialing the number for the ranch phone in the Main, his finger trembled; Mom and Dad had never run a line down to their place.

The phone rang once. Twice. Twenty times.

Bryce booked a room for the night.

After dropping off his bag, he walked over to the local Latter Day Saints church. The doors were open, no one there. Bryce took off his hat and walked up the aisle.

He liked to think he wasn't a believer, but he said a prayer for Dad.

At six p.m., he tried the phone again. Imagining the instrument on the round walnut stand in the Main, he willed someone to walk across the polished pine floor and answer.

An accented female voice said, "Snake River Ranch."

At the unmistakable cadence of Francesca's voice, Bryce almost dropped the mouthpiece. William would never have believed a woman rendered his brother speechless.

"Uhhh, this is—"

"Bryce!"

"Francesca?" He pictured her expressive eyes.

"Your mother said you might be coming home." It sounded as if her English had improved. In almost a year, it should have.

Bryce gripped the receiver. "I got Mom's letter about Dad when I got into Idaho Falls this afternoon ... written Tuesday."

"He is in St. John's. Laura is with him."

Bryce let out the breath he'd been holding. "Do you know when he's coming home?"

"I am sorry, no."

"That's all right," he told her, though it wasn't. "If Mom calls tonight, tell her I'll come by St. John's tomorrow when I get into Jackson."

"I will."

Bryce heard in her voice that she was preparing to hang up.

"Thanks, and ...?"

A little silence ensued.

"How's William?" he finished.

"Very ... busy."

As frightened as Bryce was for Dad, a leap of elation flared at the flatness in Francesca's tone.

Cord rode in the passenger seat of William's Model T, past the turn for the Bar BC and onto his land. How he loved the pungency of sage, the cinnamon scent of cottonwood and the ripe aroma of river bottom soil. How terrified he had been of dying without gazing again upon the land he loved.

When William would have driven down toward the house, Cord pointed ahead. "I'd like a look around before you and Laura put me to bed." He glanced over his shoulder at his wife, who rode in the back seat. Though the lines beside her mouth appeared deeper than he'd ever seen them, her eyes were bright with joy at his homecoming.

"The doctor said activity is always better than lying in bed," he argued.

Laura took Cord's arm, and they walked together to the porch of the Main. Since his attack on Tuesday, he had improved steadily. Today, if she hadn't known what had happened, she wouldn't have believed it—his color back to normal, his stride as strong as she recalled.

Almost.

The doctor said that after such episodes people often came back to around ninety percent of their former health. And again, each time, in a deteriorating spiral.

Francesca came their way from the cookshack, taking her apron off over her head. "Will you be wanting tea?"

Laura looked to Cord, who replied, "After William and Charlie show me how things look, tea would be fine."

Though her focus was on Cord, Laura didn't miss the way William's and Francesca's gazes collided and bounced off.

William feared Fran's smiling greeting didn't include him, but he grinned back. "I heard you were sick."

"I am fine." She didn't look directly at him.

Because her illness had cleared up so suddenly when Father took sick, he wondered if she had been hiding out. If she had seen him and Pru.

He ought to get her alone and flat out ask. But how would that work without admitting something he didn't want her to know? He might say he'd heard something outside his house a few nights back and wondered, hoped ....

If she had seen him with Pru, she'd no doubt come out swinging. If not, she might get her drawers in a twist again like she had on New Year's; accuse him of not respecting her for suggesting she would come to him in the night.

What a mess.

Charlie came over from the stables and embraced his boss. "What you thinking, laying up in that hospital? We've got work to do and dudes a comin."

"That we do." Father surveyed his domain, leaving no doubt he was still in charge at Snake River Ranch.

Two hours later, Francesca and Laura waited for the men in the Main, the table set for tea.

Francesca consulted the mantel clock. "Perhaps they will be ready for something stronger by the time they come back."

"The doctor said a small dose of spirits might be good for Cord." She made a choked sound. "I may have something, myself."

After Laura's bravery this past week, Francesca recognized a woman about to fall apart.

"I ... didn't cry all the time he was in the hospital," a tear broke and ran down Laura's cheek, "but I ...."

Francesca went to the bar where she poured brandy, neat, brought it back and put the glass in Laura's hand.

"Th-thank you." Laura stammered. She took a small sip and dashed at her cheek. She drank again, more deeply. "I've ... never been so scared as when William and Charlie brought him down. I ... don't know what I'd do without him."

Francesca tried to imagine what it would be like to spend over twenty-five years with a man one loved as deeply as Laura clearly loved Cord.

"I wish you and William ...." Laura ventured shakily.

Francesca wished she had a brandy. If she did, she might tell Laura her son was a lout who rutted in secret with a slut.

Footsteps on the porch announced the men's return.

"Here," Cord spoke from the doorway, "what's this?"

Laura raised her tearstained face. "I'm crying because ... I'm so happy you're home."

Cord strode across to her. She rose and went into his arms.

Charlie ambled in. "Can't keep a good man down."

William went to the bar and poured himself a shot. He tossed it off and his gaze met Francesca's with a pained expression. Sorrow for his father's illness? Regret? Did he know that she had caught him with another woman?

If she had her way, he never would.

From the doorway came a new voice. "Dad!"

Bryce took in the scene.

Charlie, leaning on one of the lodgepole roof supports, clapped a hand on his shoulder. "Good to see you back, kid."

Francesca's fantastic eyes locked on Bryce's; her hand went to her throat.

From the dark look William bestowed upon her reaction, Brother hadn't given up. But if he had wasted a year without capturing her heart, it was Bryce's turn.

He dragged his focus away from Francesca and onto his parents. Mom looked like the waterworks had been on, but the sun came out in her smile. Dad's color was good. He looked a lot better than Bryce had feared when he'd spoken with the doc at St. John's.

"I'm so g-glad you're here." Mom's tears started again. He heard her fears, for Dad's being in the hospital, for him on his endless wanderings, and embraced her for a long moment.

Dad jostled her playfully. "Let me get one of those hugs."

Tears stung Bryce's eyelids. Dad and Mom did need him. Perhaps it had been true all along and he'd been too blind to see, or maybe Dad's illness had brought it home.

Without planning to, Bryce said, "I'm home ... home for good."

Chapter Twenty
June, 1926

Cord and Laura sat at their kitchen table over the remains of breakfast. Cord had come home from St. John's Saturday; now it was Tuesday. Each morning he sent up a prayer of thanks for his life, his family, and his land.

Catching up with the latest issue of the *Jackson's Hole Courier*, from May 27th, he zeroed in on the ongoing controversy over extending Yellowstone to the south. The paper had printed a letter from the Honorable Senator John B. Kendrick, of the State of Wyoming, beneath the headline:

"Kendrick Favors Teton Area Being Set Aside As Separate National Park."

> In our Committee yesterday, I asked Mr. Horace Albright if he had not, during his long service as Superintendent of Yellowstone Park, met thousands of people who were astonished to find themselves in the State of Wyoming. From the day I first beheld the Grand Tetons, to this hour, it has been to me a continuing source of satisfaction and even pride that our State lines included within their boundaries this, the most magnificent mountain range, as I believe, on all the North American continent. At any rate, nothing that I have ever seen is comparable to it in grandeur and even sublimity.
>
> Therefore, if it is to become a park, it must essentially be known as the Grand Teton National Park ....

Cord pushed his bowl of shredded wheat aside. When the doctor had insisted on no more sausage and eggs, Laura had proposed to observe the change with him. And suggested it would be better to have their meager repast at home rather than in the Main, with Francesca's more tempting fare.

Cord loved her dearly, and she had the best intentions, but he was sick of shredded wheat.

"As of last night, the outfit is all here," he observed. "I ought to be supervising." The first round of summer dudes would arrive in four days.

"You agreed to rest this morning and go up at lunchtime," Laura countered.

Cord scowled and reached for the mail.

"Here's our account from Deloney's Store." He whistled. "For three hundred bucks, you can send a kid to Harvard for a year." He waved a bill from the fuel company. "Twelve cents a gallon for gasoline."

"That ought to explain why Bryce left his Model T with his friend and took the train."

Cord shook his head. "Stop defending his irresponsibility. He leaves his car behind, then changes his mind and decides he's staying here."

Laura reached for the store bill. "Coffee's thirty cents a pound. We've got no choice but to keep the urn full when the dudes and the outfit are in."

Cord allowed her to change the subject.

One more bill, from the livery in Jackson. And a plain white envelope without a return address. The writing looked shaky yet familiar.

Frowning, Cord slit the envelope with his letter opener and pulled out a folded piece of cheap white paper.

"What's that?" Laura leaned forward and he showed her the greeting "Blue Eyes," written in a barely legible hand.

My God, Cord thought, *something terrible must have happened to make a man's penmanship deteriorate like that.* "It's from Bitter Waters."

He read aloud. "The misery in my stomach started during the winter snows. I find I need more help than I am willing to take from my friends and neighbors."

An ink blot filled the last "o."

"Could you find it in your heart to let me make my last journey to your home?"

Cord met Laura's gaze.

Laura held out a hand and he gave her the missive. She read it silently, with a slight frown. "This couldn't come at a worse time," she said. "With the dude cabins booked and the Fourth of July rodeo only a few weeks away." Thankfully, she stopped short of waving the red flag of his health.

Just when he was beginning to worry she would be against having Bitter Waters, she raised her head. "Of course, there's no help for it. If his health is failing, we have to take him in."

"He took me in once, as blood of his blood," Cord mused. "I repaid him by running away from the Nez Perce way of life."

"If you had not run, you might have died in the cattle cars or in the filthy camp at Leavenworth with so many who went on the long march," Laura said tartly. "And if you had not been adopted by Aaron Bryce, we would never have met."

Cord looked pensive. "Strange how life works. One decision leads into the next and pretty soon your path is set."

The first indication Francesca had that Cord's uncle had arrived was the recognizable rattle of the Dodge truck as it pulled up very slowly in front of the cookshack on Friday afternoon.

She removed her apron and went to the door.

William and Cord stood by the tailgate. The man who lay on blankets in the truck bed had skin the color of old leather and long white hair. With a shock, Francesca recognized the elderly Indian who had been there last summer for a single night, the one she had decided must be selling jewelry.

Cord bent to touch his uncle, who opened his eyes.

"I'll do it." William muscled his father out of the way and helped their patient to a sitting position. The old man's seamed face twisted; he guarded his abdomen with his free hand.

Cord saw her watching. "Francesca, this is my uncle, Matthew Tilkalept, known as Bitter Waters."

The old man's keen eyes sought hers. Though his body was failing, a proud and indomitable spirit shone through.

"Hello, sir," she said.

"Francesca is our chef, and she's going to help us take care of you."

Bitter Waters gave her a dignified nod. His expression became a grimace when William slipped one arm beneath his shoulders and another behind his knees. Lifting him looked like easy work; his limbs appeared sticklike beneath his black trousers and jacket.

William approached the porch, and Francesca stepped out of the doorway. Their eyes met. "Now you know," he said.

Francesca stared at William's back while he carried his great-uncle to the lean-to. Laura had suggested he stay there, so Francesca could look in on him while she worked. The outfit was stretched to the maximum with the dudes arriving the next day.

Swift footsteps announced Laura's arrival. She must have heard her son's statement, for she touched Francesca's arm. "Perhaps William means you weren't aware Bitter Waters is Nez Perce."

"No one mentioned it."

Laura gave her a steady look. "Why should they?"

Francesca recalled the Christmas Eve when Laura had said people had censured her for marrying Cord. Now she knew why.

The two women went through the kitchen and into the room off it. William stood looking out the window. From the bed, Bitter Waters reached out to Laura.

She put her hand in his. Eyes overly bright, she admonished gently, "Your letter didn't say you were this ill. Had we known, we would have sent someone to travel with you."

Bitter Waters shook his head. "One of my old friends from the Dreamer Church came on the train with me as far as Victor."

"He should have come and stayed with us before going back," Laura said.

Bitter Waters glanced at William's back. "You have people who might not appreciate having a Nez Perce." When Laura's face clouded, he amended, "With your guests, you do not have room."

William cleared his throat. "I guess I'll go check on the calving."

Though Francesca flattened herself against the door, he brushed past closer than necessary.

She followed him through the kitchen onto the porch. "William."

He stopped. It was a moment before he turned.

She shielded her eyes with her hand against the sun. "What was that about 'now I know'?"

He pressed his lips into a line. "You remember last summer, you asked about folks with Indian blood and I said something like, 'Not so you'd notice.' Well, now you know I'm one-eighth Nez Perce."

She took in his unhappy expression. "I suppose some people like Dieter Gross do not care for that. But why are you," she searched for a modern word, "*touchy* about it?"

"Touchy!"

She stepped up and put her hand on William's forearm. He looked at their contact, and beneath her fingers, a muscle twitched beneath his plaid cotton shirt. When he raised his eyes to hers, she saw that, despite the other woman, he still wanted her.

She removed her hand. "You may not agree with me, but I believe I know how you feel. I was not born in this country and you remember things that have happened: Dieter, and Tiny and Prudence."

"Sounds like there's times you get a mite touchy, too."

"I do." She tried for composure. "But I am proud of who I am and where I came from. From what I saw of your great-uncle, he is also someone to be proud of."

William glanced toward the cookshack. "I care for all my folks, including

Bitter Waters. But I'm only one-eighth Nez Perce, and if I don't care to identify with it, or be made to feel small because of it, that's my right."

When the dudes arrived on Saturday afternoon, Cord and Laura waited to greet them on the steps of the Main.

Cord tipped his Stetson to the men and shook hands, removed the hat and bowed over the ladies' hands, and knelt to talk to the three small children in the group. Rosa and Maria came out with trays of drinks.

Slipping a hand into his pocket, Cord touched his obsidian talisman. Surely, the start of a new season was a good omen. With plenty of sunshine and Francesca's good food, both he and Bitter Waters would recover their strength.

Laura made the rounds, wearing her western costume, a brown suede divided skirt, matching boots, a white blouse, and a turquoise and silver squash blossom necklace.

Summer had arrived to welcome their guests. The first yellow blooms of bitterbrush brightened the meadows surrounding the Main. The sun rode in a sky of brilliant blue—it would not set until almost eight, plenty of light for the chuck wagon dinner.

The hands arranged tables and chairs on the banks of the pond. Rosa and Maria set out silverware, plates and glasses, and rolled napkins into rings crafted of elk antlers. Near the cookshack, Asa and Jim tended the barbecue pit where an entire young steer roasted on a spit. Last year at the rodeo, when Francesca had first seen this technique, she had found it barbaric. Now she was used to it.

Passing by the beef, she pointed out a dry spot for Jim to sop with sauce. Inside the cookshack, great caldrons of beans seasoned with sage, cilantro, and parsley bubbled over the fire.

Going to the woodstove, Francesca stirred a smaller pot of soup and studied its texture. The bits of beef had been minced, the tomatoes pureed, and the greens were soft and fine. Poured over a piece of her home-baked bread, the *ribollita* should be soft enough for Bitter Waters to chew and digest.

She pulled down a soup plate, reached for the loaf and a knife, and sawed off a slice. Laid it in the bowl's bottom and ladled on the aromatic liquid. She needed to hurry if she were going to get some pies baked.

"Let me take that in to him," Bryce said from the doorway. She met his eyes across the big wooden table where the bread and knife had been set beside the soup plate; the evening of their meeting lay between them. They had not been alone since his return to the ranch.

He moved toward her with his catlike stalk.

The rap of knuckles came at the kitchen door.

Francesca jumped.

Framed in a rectangle of afternoon light, William peered in. "I came to see if I could help you with dinner .... Oh, hello, Bryce."

As if he had not seen his brother heading this way and followed.

Bryce took up the soup plate and started for the lean-to.

William advanced into the cookshack. She expected he would go in to see Bitter Waters, but he spoke to her. "You've got so much to do, with a full slate of dudes and ...." He jerked his head toward the sick room.

"Everything is fine," she began. But the dried apples needed to be hydrated and the dough rolled for the pies.

William was already in position by the table. "I'm not a chef, but I can take direction."

Bryce carried the soup into the room where Bitter Waters lay propped on pillows. Behind him, he heard his brother's sly approach on Francesca.

As he set the bowl on the bedside table, he caught the pungent scent of barnyard ... of a man whose gaze met his with frankness and a touch of shame.

The chamber pot lay on the floor beside the bed, but evidently the strength to rise and squat over it had ebbed from the bones of Bitter Waters. Bryce made a note to suggest that future meals be prepared in the Main rather than so close to the sick man.

"Got dinner here," Bryce said matter-of-factly, "soon as I help you clean up."

Bitter Waters looked regretful. "Koyama, you should not be doing this."

He shrugged. "We could hire someone to take care of you, but they would not do it with love."

A sensation of eyes on his back made him turn. William leaned against the doorframe, causing Bryce to wonder if he had heard.

Bitter Waters lifted a hand. "William! You have not come to sit with me."

William approached the bed and bent to kiss his great-uncle's forehead. "I should have, but I've been busy getting ready for the dudes and dealing with the calving. Brother just got in the other day—one of his vacations." He glanced at Bryce. "I'm sure he'll be leaving soon."

Chapter Twenty-one
June, 1926

As June warmed, the snow receded from the foothills, pulling back into the high country. Francesca slept on the living room couch in the cabin Rosa and Maria shared, while Bitter Waters occupied her old quarters.

When he had been at the ranch about two weeks, Francesca awoke in the middle of the night and couldn't get back to sleep.

She threw back the blanket and put on her dress and shoes. No more running around in the night in her gown and wrapper.

Pulling on a sweater, she stepped out onto the porch.

A faint illumination shone through the curtains at the cookshack's rear window. Had Bitter Waters lighted the lantern?

Francesca wended her careful way along the dark path. To reach the cookshack she had to pass the privy, and was debating whether to take advantage of her proximity, when a man's shape loomed. Her heartbeat became a gallop.

"Francesca," said William.

"You startled me."

"Sorry." He nodded at the door marked with a crescent moon. "Someone in there?"

She shook her head and hugged herself against the rising night wind. "Do you make a habit of walking around late at night?" he inquired.

There it was. She could not see his face because of the swiftly scudding cloudbank, but something in his tone .... Prudence Johnston must have wasted no time telling him about her peeking through the window.

She waited for his accusation, but he appeared to be waiting for an answer.

"I was ... on my way to check on Bitter Waters. There's a light on ...." She was babbling. "He has been eating poorly."

"Of course he's eating poorly," William said savagely. "The man's dying." His shadowy hands drew into fists. "Why did he have to come here when Father needs peace instead of something more to worry over?"

Francesca took in something stark in William's eyes. "You must have been terrified when you found him in the foothills," she guessed.

He stepped closer. "It scared the shit … pardon … out of me. First I saw Lucifer with his reins on the ground, riderless." She heard him swallow. "All I could think was something had spooked him. Damn horses and their fears! A bear or a mountain lion … and Father had been thrown." Words rushed from him. "I got off Chester and went to see if Lucifer was clawed up and I saw …."

At the emotion in his voice, Francesca touched his arm above the elbow. His leather jacket felt cool beneath her fingers.

"He was lying at the base of a pine, his back to me, his hat on the ground. I didn't see any blood, but his neck looked … strange." William took her by the shoulders. "Francesca, he was gray!"

"It is a shame you had to be the one—"

"No, I wanted to find him for Mother." His fingers gripped her upper arm; she did not pull away. "I didn't call to him. I thought if he hadn't moved at the sound of Chester's hooves, or when I spoke to Lucifer …."

William pulled her into the circle of his arms; he was trembling. He spoke at her ear, "I walked over. A stick cracked under my boot and he opened his eyes. 'Just resting, son,' he whispered, 'Time we went home to your mama.' "

Francesca forgot Prudence. Though they rode rough seas in separate small boats, William needed her. He drew her closer, his breath on the side of her neck.

He was a rock, who handled the ranch problems without a word of complaint, who helped her in the kitchen and the bar. If she had gone to him on New Year's Eve, Prudence Johnston would never have had a chance. Bryce might have returned to find her and William married.

Enveloped in his embrace, she sensed the moment when his emotional scale tipped from concern over his father to awareness of her body's press against his.

"Fran," he murmured. "Why can't we get this right?"

Why, indeed? She felt the evidence of his desire … but there was no magic.

Because Prudence Johnston shared his bed? Because seeing them together had raked up Vincenzo with his arm around a different blonde?

William kissed the side of her neck. She clenched her shoulder up.

"Dammit, Fran …."

She shoved him.

"What the hell?" He fell back, tripped, and staggered, narrowly missed landing in a sagebrush.

She raised her voice, heedless of Bitter Waters sleeping in the cookshack yards away. "I will tell you what is the hell! You and that *puttana* who comes to your house in the night and leaves the same way."

William's face was a paler shape in the darkness. They stared at each other, chests heaving.

Before he could speak, a lazy drawl came from the direction of the cookshack. "This is all very charming, but a sick man, and some of the rest of us, are trying to sleep."

William looked from her to Bryce and back. "You've got the nerve accusing me. You were on your way to meet my brother."

Francesca started to deny it, but closed her mouth.

Starting up the path to the cookshack, she made out Bryce's white shirt at the corner of the porch. When she was almost to him, she looked back to find darkness had swallowed William.

In the shadows, she caught her toe on one of the cobblestones. Bryce took her arm to right her and released it as if touching her burned his palm. When he spoke, his voice was less than steady. "I wouldn't mind making Brother jealous ... unless you have an arrangement?"

She glared at Bryce. Did her eyes catch the reflected glow of the hearth fire the way his did? "You think we have an arrangement? I was not clear?"

"Clear as mud." Bryce strode inside.

"What does clear as mud mean?"

A match flared; he lit the kerosene lamp. She blinked at its brilliance.

Bryce spread both hands wide on the table. "I mean you don't yell at someone unless you care." The lamp threw his flickering shadow on the wall.

She did not answer.

"Shame William's still after that little tramp Pru," he lifted a single eyebrow, "but perhaps his loss might be someone else's gain."

Francesca became aware of the pulse in the sides of her neck. It did not beat faster, but with a measured emphasis.

"Tea?" Bryce inquired as if it were his kitchen, which she supposed it was.

She shook her head. A glance around revealed a brown leather sofa against the wall outside the lean-to.

He followed her gaze. "Jim and I carried that in tonight. I thought someone ought to be here ...."

Francesca went to the door and looked into the sickroom. A wedge of light from the bedside lamp she'd seen from outside fell across Bitter Waters— he looked like a corpse, pinched nose and sallow sunken cheeks—William's anguished cry that he was dying came back. In the dimness, she made out an upholstered armchair beside the bed that had not been there earlier.

Gently, she closed the door so they would not disturb the sleeping man.

Despite her refusal of tea, Bryce put the kettle on a hook over the hearth fire he must have built up. He took down thick white mugs and selected teabags from the tin. "He didn't eat enough today to keep a bird alive."

"I am not sure he can." She trod lightly, for she did not know if Bryce had accepted his great-uncle's fate the way William had.

The kettle boiled, and he poured and dunked teabags with restless energy. Handing her a cup, he led the way to the sofa.

She sat, while he fell into pacing, his cup cradled in both hands. "One thing I've always wanted to know is about the night my grandparents died. Apparently, Bitter Waters showed up during the Nez Perce War with some braves .... My grandparents Franklin and Sarah ended up dead. The cabin burned over their heads in front of Dad, who was six years old."

"William mentioned that to me." Francesca had not pressed anyone at the ranch for more information, thinking to keep to her place.

"Bitter Waters took Dad, a little kid, on the Nez Perce's flight through Yellowstone." Bryce's voice cracked. "I suppose there must have been other children, babies even. I listened to Dad's story and read some things about it, how part of the tribe refused to go on to the Reservation."

"I have wondered how your father ended up with a Mormon family in Salt Lake City."

"He ran away before the Nez Perce were captured." Bryce stopped and looked down at her. "The hell of it is, if Dad felt he had to run away from Bitter Waters, why did Mom and Dad teach me to love him?"

"If your father or Bitter Waters wanted you to know about all that, they would have told you." Francesca set her empty cup on the floor and rose to her feet. Spoke Italian to be sure she said it right, "But you would have loved him without being taught. I have come to love him in only a short time. How does the heart decide who we love?"

Bryce stopped pacing.

They stood toe to toe. He cupped her cheek with his hand. "No one knows how we decide who to love." He spoke English.

Her face flaming, Francesca stepped away. "Thank you for the tea and bringing the sofa and chair." She was talking too fast. "You should not have to do so much. I will take turns spending the night here."

He looked as if he wanted to close the space she had placed between them, but did not. "Thank you for offering, but I can sleep when it's over."

∽◆∾

June 23, 1926

"It is difficult to believe a year has passed since the Gros Ventre Slide," Laura wrote in her journal.

Anne and Ben's baby, J.C., is pulling himself up and trying to walk; he's the delight of everyone in Kelly and over on Mormon Row. Since the runoff peaked, most folks have decided the engineers have called it right and the Slide Lake Dam will be a permanent fixture.

Not so with Cord. He still worries and even asked Ben about moving over here to the ranch. As it would save Ben having to cross the Snake every day, he was in favor, but Anne and her mother, who lives close to their house by the Gros Ventre, put an end to it.

A year since the slide—a year since Francesca came to us. A year since she met William, and still those two haven't worked it out. His resemblance in looks and manner to my father, Forrest Fielding, grows greater each year. Of course, like his grandfather, he can outwork any two men.

When Bryce returned, I expected he would head up the drive to take the stock to the summer pastures as he used to do years ago, leaving William to work with the dudes. This year there are fewer head of cattle than we have ever had. After last year's poor auction and with prices still depressed, Charlie and I convinced Cord to cut back, though he hated doing it.

As for the drive, Bryce did not offer to go. I am certain it is because of Bitter Waters. I expected Charlie would take over, but William suddenly packed his gear and insisted Charlie stay here.

As for Bitter Waters, Bryce has become his caretaker, along with Francesca. Bryce has always loved his great-uncle and I can see the strain in him as he watches him slip away.

Late last night I went to the cookshack. With the lamp off and the fires burned down, I expected Bryce would be on the sofa he had brought in, but he was in the lean-to.

He sat in the chair by the bed, keeping watch over a sleeping Bitter Waters.

୨∾ଓ

Francesca bent to spoon soup between Bitter Waters's lips. Only yesterday evening, Bryce had told her he'd taken some. This morning he pressed his lips together.

"*Mangia*," she encouraged, opening her mouth, realizing too late it was the gesture one would make to a baby.

His eyes, dark and shining, stared into hers with pride and understanding, even as he shook his head on the pillow.

She spoke to the window and the summer meadow, burgeoning with mustard-colored flowers. "If you can eat, try and get up."

What incentive could she offer?

After the noon meal, Cord sat beside Bitter Waters's bed. His uncle had not taken any reasonable amount of sustenance since arriving at the ranch, yet today he was unusually talkative, picking at the covers with index fingers and thumbs. His black eyes seem to burn with an inner fire.

A number of the valley elderly had exhibited the same behavior; Cord believed this burst of energy would be his last. With each passing day, the bones of Bitter Waters grew more prominent, his skin drew tight over his eye sockets and cheekbones and sagged on his arms, legs, and abdomen.

William had come by earlier before leaving to drive the cattle to the summer pastures.

Cord had sat outside the lean-to door on the sofa. He had not been eavesdropping, he told himself, but a few things had drifted out. Bitter Waters had entreated William to accept both his mother's and father's ancestry, to take pride in being Nez Perce, as well as French-Canadian and English.

Cord had failed to hear his son's reply but hoped the wish of a dying man might persuade William.

Now, at Bitter Waters's bedside, Cord said, "Perhaps William might someday find his guardian spirit." As always when the subject came up, in thought or conversation, he touched the glassy talisman in his pocket.

The sick man eyes wandered to the world outside the window. "My *wayakin* is the sunrise, so I am always on edge at night." He picked at the bedding again and sighed. "Each time I see the sun set beyond the mountains, I believe it may be my last."

Cord did not demur.

Without warning, Bitter Waters broke into a smile and raised both his hands in a blessing gesture. "I told William he is the rock, not your fiery obsidian, but the granite holding up mountains. If he does not accept it, it cannot help him stand strong. He may wander."

"He went to Texas back in twenty-four, stayed over the winter."

Bitter Waters nodded. "Koyama also wanders far, like the lion, but he will find his way back."

"He says he's come home for good."

Bitter Waters waved a chastising finger. "He says."

Chapter Twenty-two
June, 1926

Laura sat at her dressing table and brushed her hair, one hundred strokes, as her mother had taught her. It kept her mind off Cord sitting up with Bitter Waters this evening.

Envisioning the sickroom, she told herself their patient was probably asleep, Cord in the big chair beside the bed. Bryce might be with him or catching a nap on the sofa so he could take the graveyard shift.

Thank God Bryce was home to lighten the load with William making the cattle drive. Of course, his departure had something to do with his brother's arrival; the ranch was no longer big enough for both the boys ... men.

Finishing her hair, Laura unscrewed the top from a jar of rosewater-scented cream. She began by rubbing a dollop onto her hands, then smoothed the emollient up her left arm. The lamplight was kind to her mirrored reflection, hiding the tracery of lines around her eyes. Cord was four years older than her fifty-two. Until recently he had looked as youthful as she.

"Halloo!" he called from their front porch, his signal so she would not be alarmed when he opened the cabin door.

"In here," she answered.

When he came in, looking pale beneath his summer tan, she slipped her arms around him. "How is he?"

Cord's sigh stirred her hair. "I've stopped praying for a miracle."

She pulled back and searched his strained face.

He gave her a gentle smile. "I remember when we had it all ahead of us. Then your father and Aaron went. Once Bitter Waters goes, we'll be the ones on the leading edge."

"I still feel twenty-five inside," she said, "but folks around us, even our generation, have started dying." Feeling cold inside, she pressed her cheek against Cord's chest and listened to his heartbeat. Tonight it sounded as strong as ever.

During Bitter Waters's first weeks there, Francesca had discovered he liked milkshakes made from the ice cream churned by the hands in the evenings. But, today he picked at his bedding and looked at the glass with listless dark eyes. He pursed his lips around the straw; his cheeks hollowed.

No liquid moved into his mouth.

Francesca got a spoon.

He opened his mouth for her, but immediately screwed up his face.

"You know you love this," she pleaded.

"I know it is good," he gave her an apologetic look, "but it tastes ... terrible."

She left the lean-to and went into the kitchen, casting about for anything that might appeal. If not milk, what about broth? Very sick people would almost always take it.

Getting her sun hat from the hook inside the cookshack door, she went out. The chicken coop was on the far side of the ranch, past the stables.

At the corral, she saw a shirtless Charlie studying a lone brown cow. As Francesca drew closer, she saw blood covering the foreman's arm and shoulder.

"Just helped this gal here birth her calf." He smiled, teeth white against his cocoa skin, and she noticed the small, soaking-wet bundle of spindly limbs beyond the cow. "She's way late past the calving season, but better late than never."

The mama moved between Charlie and the little bull calf and used her thick tongue to clean off mucus.

Going to the spigot, Charlie turned it on and hosed himself to remove the bloody birth fluids. "Good to see new life." His dark eyes took in Francesca. "Time I was your age, me and Lucy'd been married for years. Waiting and hoping for new life."

"Charlie, not you, too!" Francesca protested. "Everyone in this valley wants to rush me into starting a family."

"Everybody's right. Modern young folks all holding out for God knows what."

"I am not modern. But I am holding out for—"

"You take a good man, someone rock solid, and love'll come quick enough."

"You mean William."

"I mean someone like William, or Bryce—"

"Bryce? No one thinks of him as solid."

Charlie chuckled. "He and his brother both have some growing up to do. Mark my words, folks don't know yet who's going to turn out how."

Francesca went on to the chicken coop.

In the mid-afternoon heat, the flock of about forty stood around in a desultory manner; she studied them before opening the door to the wire enclosure. In *Toscana,* she had normally gone out to the coop in the early morning. While the fowl were still somnolent, she would snatch one up by the legs before it could evade her. A chopping block had waited outside the door to the *cucina,* the heavy oak stump dark with stains of old blood.

Francesca entered the ranch coop. The strutting, pecking flock scooted for the far corners and eyed her with beady suspicion. Setting her sights on a plump Rhode Island Red, Francesca used a slow and steady approach.

When she made a grab for it, chickens exploded into futile flight, wings beating the wire.

She waited for the melee to settle.

The red hen would be wary now, so on her next stalk Francesca seized a white one by a leg. It flapped and squawked; she held it at arm's length and got a handful of future chicken broth under control.

So as not to tip off the other fowl as to what would happen to their cohort, she exited the pen and carried the now-subdued hen to the cookshack. There, she broke its neck and cut the jugular.

Once the blood had drained, she plucked the feathers, saving them in one sack and the down in another for Maria to use for pillows. By the time she singed the last feathers off over the fire and removed the entrails, she heard a weak call from the lean-to.

Bitter Waters lay flat, his alert black eyes watching for her entry. In the weeks he'd been at the ranch, he had shrunk terribly, his emaciated limbs barely mounded the covers. With a gesture, he conveyed he wanted to use the chamber pot.

Wondering if, in his weakened condition, she would be able to get him out of bed, she folded back the covers. His exposed chest, above striped pajama bottoms, looked pale. Even his richly bronzed skin had faded. She considered suggesting a bedpan, but a proud lift of his chin made her want to let him try. With care, she slipped her arm beneath his shoulders.

As soon as she lifted, he gave a cry and reached a hand toward the misery in his stomach.

Perhaps with extra help ....

As if summoned by her silent entreaty, Bryce appeared in the doorway. His bottle green eyes took in the scene, and he set aside his dusty hat.

"He wants to get up," she said.

Together, they got Bitter Waters into a sitting position on the mattress, his bare feet with rough yellow toenails on the floor.

Bryce reached for the chamber pot, and Francesca stepped to the window. Behind her, she heard the rustle of cloth and a weak dribble into the pot. Beyond the glass lay summer, the garden spiked with sprigs of green onion and tufts of ruffled lettuce pushing toward the sun.

"Ready," Bryce said.

Francesca went back to help Bitter Waters lie down, but he struggled. "Need to ... stand up."

Each supporting an arm, she and Bryce brought him to his feet. His thin legs folded; they held him upright. Bitter Waters stared down at his emaciated arms and legs, where the skeletal structure showed clearly beneath sagging skin, as though just discovering how far gone he was. With a sigh, he subsided onto the waiting bed.

Francesca left Bryce alone with his great-uncle.

She was mad as hell, as Billy Cowan would call it. At Bitter Waters for not being able to eat, for being too weak to squat to move his bowels, and now for being too far gone to stand without assistance. He should cling to life, not lie hour after hour with his eyes on the bright day or the night sky, becoming ever more silent and indrawn.

Savagely, Francesca sliced off the chicken's head and feet and delivered the carcass to the waiting pot of hot water with a splash.

Bryce came up behind her and touched her arm. She turned. "Why doesn't he try?"

A corner of his sun-bleached moustache went down. "He just did."

He turned his attention to the chicken. "Something on the menu tonight besides beef?"

Her throat tight, Francesca permitted the change of subject. "I'm making broth for him. He has to eat something!"

It took her back to the *castello*, when her father had lay dying of pneumonia.

She had sat at his bedside, offering a spoonful of chicken broth, the final resort once he started choking on solid food. "If you do not eat something!" she railed. Immediately, she was sorry. "Papa ..." She burst into tears; the spoon clattered to the floor.

Antonio di Paoli's gaze was beyond the walls of the sickroom. With tear-bright eyes, he lifted Francesca's hand in both his trembling bony ones. He was so weak it took him a long time to draw her hand to his lips and kiss it.

In the cookshack, Francesca's rage transformed to a piercing ache. Bryce traced one of her tears down her cheek. "You're working too hard."

"What of you? You work from before dawn and sit with him all night."

"We're doing what we have to." He lowered his hand and looked at the boiling chicken. "I'll pull some green onions."

❧❧

Six-year-old Bryce and seven–year-old William capered in the sun, while Uncle sat on their cabin's porch in the shade and whittled wooden whistles for them. With all the impetuosity of his years, Bryce demanded the first one completed be his. William stomped a foot in his diminutive cowboy boots and claimed he had been born first and had it by right.

Bitter Waters raised a calloused palm. "Boys!"

Bryce skidded to a stop in front of Uncle. There was nobody he found more fascinating. Sure, he loved Mommy and Daddy and Brother, when he wasn't busy figuring out how to catch up with William's "being older," but Bitter Waters wasn't there all the time.

William piped up, "At school, Jimmy Johnston said you were an Injun!"

Bryce didn't go to school yet, another gross injustice. Pea green with envy at William knowing a word he didn't, he took up the cry as if he did. "Injun!" He danced on his small bare feet. "An Injun!"

Bitter Waters flat lids covered his keen dark eyes. Tiredly, he pocketed the whistle, set aside his knife, and took William by his small shoulders. "Do you know what that means?"

"No," Bryce blurted.

William wiggled. "Na ... nasuh."

Bitter Waters looked out over the flats beside the river, where Mommy's garden burgeoned. "Come on, boys, let's pick some green onions for the dinner salad."

Though Uncle spoke with his habitual cheer, young Bryce sensed something profound and dark had touched his world of sunlit ranch and river.

❧❧

When Bryce finished his story, Francesca asked, "Do you mind that you are Nez Perce?"

"Mind?" He looked as if the concept were foreign. "It's part of me, like my mother's eyes and my father's height."

"Your brother does not seem happy about it."

"No, he pretty well rejects it."

He went out to the garden for the onions.

On his return, he spoke volubly about his *wayakin*, the mountain lion, and William's failure to find a spiritual guardian.

The broth continued to bubble.

At three o'clock, Cord and Laura came for their afternoon visit with the sick man. After two hours, they left, murmuring that he never opened his eyes. They paused on the porch and Francesca heard them, *sotto voce.* "You can't start sitting up with him and losing your sleep," Laura argued. "Bryce and Francesca will tell us ... if ... when ...."

Cord grumbled something unintelligible.

Francesca and Bryce did not look at each other.

About thirty minutes after the older Suttons left, Asa and Jim arrived with Rosa and said they would take care of dinner in the Main kitchen. Asa also indicated Bryce would not be needed in the stables or corral that evening.

The death watch began.

Chapter Twenty-three
June, 1926

Bryce sat in the armchair beside Bitter Waters's bed and watched the afternoon shadows lengthen. If only William were there, instead of off driving cattle. When he had departed, there had still been a chance at denying Bitter Waters's outlook.

Or had there? William, ever practical, had probably said his mental farewell before hitting the trail. Bryce imagined him looking down at Bitter Waters with a bracing smile, gray eyes twinkling to hide the ache inside. At the doorway, he would have paused and looked back, memorizing Bitter Waters's pain-wracked features, the morning sun on the bed, in case it turned out to be the last time he saw his great uncle.

Better to be stoic like William than to sit there wiping away tears with each fresh wave of realization. Bryce had believed Bitter Waters would always be around, fixed in his ordered life on the reservation, visiting at odd intervals, sending his neat, formal missives.

At seven, Francesca came in with a white china bowl and spoon. If she saw the tear traces on Bryce's cheeks, she gave no sign.

He rose. "May I?"

She passed the aromatic offering.

"Uncle, Francesca has made fresh chicken broth."

Bitter Waters's graying brows drew together. His eyelids clenched tighter, then fluttered open. Bryce dipped the spoon and brought it to lips thinned by dehydration.

Bitter Waters used motions of his eyes to convey the negative.

"Please," Bryce prayed aloud.

His great uncle relaxed his mouth and permitted a few drops to pour over his lower lip. He did not swallow.

Bryce refilled the spoon.

Bitter Waters began to sputter. He coughed, once, twice, and choked. His face reddened and he struggled for breath, while a liquid bubbling began in the back of his throat.

Francesca grabbed a rag and wiped the pink froth of phlegm foaming from his lips.

"God." Bryce dropped the bowl; it bounced on the boards and broke into thick white rinds, spreading broth; the spoon tinked once and landed with a clatter.

§∞§

Though it was high summer outside, in the sickroom there was no season and no time. For the next two days, Bitter Waters lay without speaking, eating or drinking. His labored breathing was punctuated by moans and the occasional incoherent cry.

On the third day, the doctor came in the afternoon, left a bottle of opiate drops for pain, and suggested their liberal use.

After the dudes had eaten dinner, Laura left them to their flasks and flirting, draped a shawl round her shoulders and came across to the cookshack with a lantern. Cord stayed a little later, then came to join the vigil.

After midnight, Francesca sat beside Bitter Waters's bed. Her gritty eyes burned with her effort to keep them open.

She drew out her rosary. As always, she began with a quick prayer for William ... for his safety on the cattle drive. Her mother had taught her that if someone gave her a rosary, one should always pray for that person.

Today, as she envisioned William and the men of the outfit around a campfire, a sharp ache pierced her. Was he well? Was he thinking of her?

Francesca began the comforting, rote ritual of prayers, but before she could murmur more than a few words, Bitter Waters gripped her hand with surprising strength. "Sa ... Sarah ...."

"What about Sarah?" Francesca leaned in to hear his agitated whisper. His eyes focused above the end of the bed, as if he saw someone there; his face contorted and, despite his dehydration, tears squeezed from the corner of his eyes.

Francesca got the pain medicine and put a dropperful on the back of his tongue.

§∞§

"Bitter Waters can't seem to let himself die," Francesca told Laura, while she poured tea the next afternoon.

Laura brushed back her mussed hair, wiped her hands on her breeches, and took the blue and white speckled mug from the worn boards of the cookshack table. She glanced toward the sickroom, where Bitter Waters was going about his solitary business of dying, and walked out onto the front porch.

Francesca followed.

Turning and leaning her shoulder against a twisted pine support, Laura stared at the mountains. A lone hawk circled. "Has he said anything about his sister?"

"He was muttering about someone named Sarah last night."

"His sister ... Cord's mother," Laura replied.

"His eyes were staring ... at something. I spoke to him, and he glanced at me as though what he was seeing was more real than I."

"It probably seemed so." Laura lifted her cup and drank, her troubled green eyes so like Bryce's. The two women followed a path down the terrace to the river. A herd of about twenty elk spooked and ran, splashing through shallow water and disappearing into a thicket. "Some days I get busy and forget how beautiful it all is, until a sight like that reminds me."

Francesca watched the animals' retreat. She wanted to ask why the memory of Sarah disturbed Bitter Waters, but accepted Laura's change of subject.

৩৵

Later that evening, Francesca caught a couple hours of fitful rest in Rosa and Maria's cabin. When the women returned from work around eleven-thirty, she went back to the cookshack.

Bryce lay on his side on the sofa outside the lean-to, dressed in a clean blue work shirt and denims. The lamp over the table guttered; shadows cast his face in angles and planes.

Francesca went to the lean-to door and found a single candle burning inside. Cord sat in the big armchair with Laura cradled in his lap. Both of them bore a drowsy look, but came to alertness.

"He's still skip-breathing," Laura said. "Cord gave him some more drops a little while ago. I don't think he hears us anymore."

"Do you two want to go down to your house to sleep?" Francesca offered.

"I don't want to leave him," Cord said.

"How about we nap here in the chair while Francesca sits with him?" Laura suggested.

Francesca went to the kitchen for a straight chair and perched on it. Though she had rested a short time, fatigue made her dopey. Hopefully the hard wooden seat would ensure she kept the watch.

Past midnight, the wind came up and played a moaning dirge, making the big window shudder in its frame. Its keening cadence reminded Francesca of winter, when fierce gusts battered the cookshack.

Laura slept with her jaw slack. The irregular cadence of Cord's snoring helped keep Francesca from nodding off.

She pulled out her rosary and murmured in Latin, "Hail Mary, full of grace, the Lord is with thee. Blessed art thou among women, blessed is the fruit of thy womb, Jesus. Holy Mary, mother of God, pray for us now and at the hour of our deaths ...."

She found herself counting the seconds between Bitter Waters's breaths. He would inhale, chest heaving, then his lips would seal. Ten, thirty, forty-five seconds—by the relentless ticking of the wall clock—until, with a panicked snort, his mouth gaped like a fish's on the bank and he continued to live.

Hours passed and the clock wound down and stopped. Francesca stared at it and at Bitter Waters, but the cessation of the ticking had not marked his passing. Finally, the realization that she hoped each time he stopped breathing would be the last drove her from the room. Cord and Laura still slept.

Bryce lay on the sofa, his head pillowed on his arm. She touched his shoulder and for a moment, they looked into each other.

"My turn?" His voice sounded thick.

Francesca moved so he could swing his long frame around to sit up. He stabbed both hands into his hair and made the sleep-tousled mess worse. "How is he?"

"The same."

Bryce put a sinewy hand on each thigh and pushed to his feet. "The suspense is killing us all," he said in a husky voice. "God strike me dead for wishing it over, but what he has now is not a life."

The living hell of slow suffocation, whether her father with fluid buildup in his lungs, or Bitter Waters' ....

In the flickering light, the kitchen clock said it was nearly four. Less than an hour until summer's dawn would paint a seam of silver gray above the Gros Ventre.

Bryce went in to Bitter Waters and she lay down. The leather on the couch was still warm. The door to the lean-to opened onto blackness .... The candle had burned out.

Shifting her position, she tried to ease the places where knives seemed to have been inserted beneath her shoulder blades. She moved her restless legs. Hunger pangs roiled, but she did not want any broth.

Giving up on sleep, she went to the fireplace, stirred the embers and added two logs.

From the lean-to, she heard a rasping breath, followed by silence. Her shoulders hunched, her bare toes curled on the chill stone in front of the hearth.

Without warning, a wave of relief washed through her.

She seized the lamp from its hook and ran to the lean-to. In the wedge of light across the bed, she made out Bryce, sprawled awkwardly on the straight chair, asleep. His extended hand covered Bitter Waters's.

Cord and Laura also slept.

Francesca tiptoed to the bedside. Bitter Waters mouth hung open; he did not blink at the light.

Though she felt certain his soul had departed, she stood a minute, and another, giving Bryce and his parents a little longer to live in the time before Bitter Waters died.

Chapter Twenty-four
July 1, 1926

Bryce started awake at a touch on his shoulder and blinked his scratchy eyes. At some core level he knew it was Francesca. He pushed to his feet and, in the lamp's less-than-adequate light, made out Bitter Waters's sagging jaw.

Gently, he closed the staring eyes, not wanting Mom and Dad to see them with the opaque look of death. When the slack mouth would not stay shut, he adjusted the angle of the head. Wordlessly, Francesca assisted, tucking an extra pillow behind the neck. Bryce lifted the claw-like hands and folded them atop the heart.

Francesca placed the lamp at the head of the bed and came to stand beside Bryce. He put his arm around her slender yet strong shoulders; she fit against his side.

Nothing more to do. Where he had expected pain and tears, he felt emptiness. Francesca also stood quietly, dry-eyed.

In the armchair, Mom stirred and murmured, "Oh, no."

When Francesca and Bryce emerged from the cookshack, dawn had broken. Laura had insisted she and Cord take over, saying their goodbyes, phoning for the undertaker, getting out Bitter Waters's good black suit that Maria had already cleaned and pressed.

With first light, the wind had subsided. Francesca walked beside Bryce, who had his hands in the pockets of his denims, thumbs hooked over. When they reached the path to the cabin where Rosa and Maria would be catching the last of sleep before their alarm clock jangled at five, neither Francesca nor Bryce turned aside.

"I don't believe I could sleep," she said.

"The boys at the bunkhouse will be making a racket getting up," he replied.

They passed in front of William's house, behind the bunkhouse and stables, and up the bluff. Dead sage trunks crunched beneath their feet; neither spoke.

Out across the meadow was a mounded hill with steep-treed sides. People called it the Timbered Island, out of place on the floodplain, existing because of a well-drained glacial mound.

Francesca had expected to cry, but her mind was carefully blank. Everything seemed at a distance.

Until they climbed up onto the island and the forest of pine and fir closed around them. A heavy pulse started at the base of her throat and spread down through her woman's softness. The breeze caressed her skin and swirled her skirt, soughing in the trees. The sharp scent of resin mingled with the musk of the man beside her.

Did he feel it, too, the overwhelming need not to be alone in the rising morning?

She stood still, faced him, saw in his eyes that he knew what she was feeling.

"Dear God!" Bryce seized her. Bent his head and plundered her mouth. His hands clutched; there would be bruises.

Equally desperate, Francesca kissed his lips, his cheeks, his eyelids, tasted salt tears and sweat. His hands claimed her breasts; she didn't care that her dress and camisole were sour from perspiration.

She found his shirt buttons, fumbled them to reveal his pale chest. She put her mouth to the sunburned triangle at the base of his neck and found his thundering pulse, slid her lips over to the hollow between his shoulder and collarbone and inhaled the aroma of aroused man.

They went down together onto a prickly bed of pine straw, a stone at her back. He lifted her dress and pulled her loose drawers to the side, plunging his hand into her moist cleft.

God, she couldn't see his eyes in the dimness; his must be as sightless as hers. This was crazy, but she only she knew she wanted Bryce with a hunger and ache she had never imagined.

She found his zipper, lowered it with a rasp. Opened for him, clamped her legs around his thighs while they rode the waves in their separate oceans.

She grabbed and hauled him home, over and over. He stiffened, broached.... His primal cry lifted her, and with each crushing spasm, she arched and moaned.

Bryce collapsed on her, chest heaving. She released her death grip on his flesh. He pulled away.

With her eyes shut tight, she detected his movement onto hands and knees and up to his feet by the rustle of pine needles and the whisper of clothing.

"Francesca."

She peeked out through her eyelashes.

He stabbed his hand through his hair again. "I don't know what ... how ...."

She had expected he would hold her close while their hearts slowed together.

Instead, he stood over her, his voice filled with uncertainty. Did he wish they had not done it?

Suffused with shame, she pushed her dress down. Bryce must think she was like Prudence Johnston, to have rutted with him in the dirt like an animal.

Francesca flung her arm across her eyes so she would not have to see the ambivalence in his.

She heard his harsh breathing a moment longer, then listened to his retreating footsteps.

Drying sweat made her curl into a shivering ball. The tears came.

Cord sat with Bitter Waters all day, while warmth ebbed from the lifeless husk. It was his duty to stay until the undertakers came.

After embalming the body and dressing it for the final journey, they would take Bitter Waters to rest beside his wife, Kamiah, and Chief Joseph in Nespelem.

Cord had scarcely known Kamiah, only for a few weeks on the trail through Yellowstone in 1877. While the tribe camped in the high meadows above the Lamar Valley, gathering camas roots to grind into flour, resting seven hundred people and two thousand horses, a small boy had plotted his escape from the man he blamed for the murder of his parents.

How little he had understood.

A last look at his uncle's face .... As he'd noted before, the dead seemed to drop their earthly burdens before they stepped into the light. Bitter Waters's formerly wrinkled brow lay smooth; the deeply incised lines from the base of his nose to his chin had disappeared.

Cord bowed his head and prayed to the God of his adopted father Aaron Bryce's church, that of the Latter Day Saints. Then he removed his talisman of obsidian from his pocket and held it until it warmed. Bending to kiss Bitter Waters on the forehead, Cord slowly lifted the quilt and drew it over his uncle's head.

With the dead man shrouded, his lips forever silent, Cord discovered a thousand questions he had failed to ask.

In the kitchen, Francesca tended a cast-iron pot, suspended over a bed of coals. He smelled stew, but wasn't hungry.

She came and slid her arms around him. "I am so sorry."

Her youthful freshness reminded Cord that he and Laura were now on the leading edge he'd envisioned, the oldest generation in their family. "Thank you," he said, "for helping see him home."

Outside the cookshack, he found it was later than he thought.

What was death like? In the midst of the sharpest pain, or when the loss of life's blood brought the most profound cold, would there be relief, a beckoning light, or would it be the way it had been before he had been born—Genesis-like, with darkness upon the face of memory?

The sun hung on the western horizon, spreading golden warmth on his face in spite of the chill at his back. But all too soon, the glowing orb touched the tip of Nez Perce Peak ... the first sunset Bitter Waters would not see.

Chapter Twenty-five
July, 1926

The next day, Bryce and Cord accompanied Bitter Waters's coffin over The Pass to catch the train at Victor, and on to the Colville Reservation and the town of Nespelem in Washington State.

Bryce worried about his father, who looked exhausted to his toes. He was glad to have been able to go with him, since William had not returned from driving cattle in the high country.

Now the tables were turned—the steady son away, the wandering one elected to take up his unaccustomed place. Bryce thanked God and his guardian spirit, the mountain lion, for the chance to accompany Bitter Waters home.

As they traveled, Cord spoke of his first visit to the reservation, when early January snow had drifted against the row of small squalid houses. The creaking wagon Cord and Laura had hitched a ride in from the railroad siding had brought them to find Bitter Waters's wife, Kamiah, laid out before the altar, dressed in her beaded burial dress.

Twenty-six years later, a truck carried Bitter Waters's coffin; Bryce and his father sweated in the mid-summer sun. The taciturn Nez Perce driver let them out in front of the small, wood-framed Dreamer church, with a bell tower above its steeply sloping roof.

Once he alighted from the truck, Bryce found himself forced to reconsider his momentary impression of squalor. In the houses and the church, glass windows gleamed brightly; lace edged the curtains. Next to the church stoop, beds of transplanted wild roses bloomed riotously, as if in honor of Bitter Waters.

Bryce told himself he'd done his crying, but during the service, he wiped tears from his cheeks unabashedly. The grave, near Chief Joseph's tall white monument, lay beneath a lone tree. It reminded Bryce of the cottonwood on the bluff at Snake River, a place that had always felt sacred to him. He'd seen Francesca walking there a time or two.

God, what was he going to do? He'd had violent sex with her when he had imagined they would make love. And been repaid by her covering her eyes, unable to stand the sight of him.

Left behind at Snake River, Laura helped Charlie entertain the dudes. One evening she wrote in her journal:

> I think Charlie was relieved to be off the hook when William took over this summer's cattle drive, as he's been going to Kelly whenever he gets the opportunity. He doesn't talk about it, and I've heard no rumors, but Cord thinks he visits Harriet Lawrence.
>
> Both of them widowers, I wish them the best. But it would be another reason for Dieter Gross to sling arrows at those of us at Snake River.
>
> The Ku Klux Klan's post war re-emergence distresses us all. I don't think it has made its way to our valley; there aren't many Colored like Charlie, but I understand Klan members are against anyone who is not completely white, Protestant and American born. That pits their kind against Jews, Catholics, and our immigrant employees, including Francesca, Rosa, Maria, and Tom, as well as my husband and sons for their Nez Perce blood.
>
> And me for marrying Cord.
>
> I know that he had to see Bitter Waters home to lie beside Kamiah, but I miss him terribly. Each day, I watch the driveway for Bryce bringing Cord home, and the hills for William's return.
>
> Each day I am disappointed.
>
> I am beginning to wonder which of the boys Francesca misses more. My hopes for her and William, a year in the making, have not materialized. And, while she and Bryce spent time together nursing Bitter Waters, she did not come out to the truck to bid him goodbye when he and Cord left for the reservation.

Cord and Bryce had been gone nearly a week, and Francesca was out picking vegetables with two ladies from Pennsylvania who enjoyed gardening. They chose early carrots, green peas, and selected fresh mint leaves, while she weighed what she would do if she were pregnant with Bryce's child.

Of course, she might not have to worry about telling him if he stopped off in Idaho and did not return to Snake River.

As she bent to snap off the fragrant mint stalks, the slow cadence of hooves came from the trail along the high bluff. Probably a trail ride returning.

Francesca looked and saw horses angling down the bluff road. Once they reached the upper bench where most of the ranch buildings were, she recognized Ned Hanson in the lead. He was waving and speeding ahead of Bobby and William.

As soon as they drew near, William dismounted and placed his horse's reins on the ground. She stood in the garden, waiting for him.

"How was the drive?" she asked, aware of the female dudes as audience.

William's jaw set. "We lost a couple of this season's calves."

"Oh, dear," said one of the women.

Bobby blurted, "Damned mountain lion started a stampede. Brutus trampled the little ones."

Francesca's stomach lurched, while the women oohed and murmured. Though there was clearly no connection, William had probably assigned some sort of blame to Bryce.

She spat to ward off the evil spirits.

William shifted his weight from one foot to the other and finally seemed to realize this was no place to speak with Francesca.

As she was preparing dinner, a familiar cramping informed her that she was not expecting. And, though she seldom cried, hot tears sprang to her eyes. She had not realized how much the possibility of having Bryce's child had embedded itself in her consciousness. How she had dreamed it would make the wandering Sutton son settle down .... Bryce had told his parents he was home for good this time, but she was certain neither of them believed it. Now that his father seemed well enough and Bryce had seen Bitter Waters home, there was nothing more to hold him at Snake River.

He would leave for Idaho, Arizona, or the California that had been Francesca's dream.

She wiped away the tears with her apron and turned the biscuit making over to Rosa while she went to freshen up. She would have liked to have lain down with a hot water bottle on her stomach, but she had to finish making dinner for the dudes.

That evening, as she was placing the last bowl of carrots and peas seasoned with mint on the dining table, William touched her arm.

She jumped.

He looked up at her and jerked his chin toward the vacant chair on his left. "Have a seat."

Francesca hesitated, both because she had never joined the group during dude season, and because of Bryce ....

But what about Bryce? He could have come to her the night before he and Cord left with Bitter Waters's remains. She had lain awake on the sofa in the cabin Rosa and Maria shared, unwilling to go back to sleep in the cookshack lean-to, waiting.

She pulled out the dining chair.

As soon as the dudes headed for their cabins, William appeared at Francesca's side and walked with her toward the cookshack. A pair of rocking chairs, which had not been there earlier, stood on the porch.

"I ... am not staying here anymore," she told him.

William nodded, as if he understood her aversion to sleeping where Bitter Waters had died, but gestured at the rockers. "We can still sit on the porch, can't we?"

She weighed the hot water bottle against being alone with her thoughts and sat.

"Tell me about it," he urged.

"Tell you what?"

"Like ... did Father sit up with him at night?"

"No. Laura insisted he get his rest."

"Did you and Bryce stay with Bitter Waters through the nights, then?" His tone was even.

"We took turns," Francesca evaded.

"You want to be careful of Bryce, Fran."

She did not reply.

"He paid off his latest conquest in Arizona—her name is Charlene—with a Model T. Just up and left her."

Francesca's stomach tightened. "How ... do you know?"

"He told me."

She took a moment to digest it.

"My brother knows his way around women ... better than I do."

She made a small disbelieving sound at the pot calling the kettle black. She'd seen him in bed ....

He stopped the movement of his chair. "I don't see Pru anymore," he said gruffly.

Francesca rocked, her eyes on the crescent moon going down behind the Tetons.

"I want us to get this right." William reached across and took her hand. His skin was warm, calloused from hard work.

Bryce had gotten up and walked away, left her shivering and crying on the ground.

William rose and pulled her up to face him. "I'm sorry I wasn't here when Bitter Waters was dying."

He took her in his arms, but not in an insinuating way. Rather, he held her tightly, the way he had the night he'd spoken of finding his father sitting by the trail with his skin an ugly shade of gray. "I ... can't stand the sight ... the thought of anyone dying. I've always been superstitious—"

"There are evil spirits but Bitter Waters's spirit was a good one."

"Yes, and I should have been here. But someone had to head up the drive, take the cattle to the high pastures," he argued. "Father needs someone he can count on."

She needed someone she could count on, too.

William bent his head and she believed he was going to kiss her. Feeling wooden, Francesca was trying to decide whether or not to let him when headlights swept across the porch.

William dropped his arms from around her and stepped back. He shielded his eyes with his hand, while she heard the cough of a truck taking the turn down toward Cord and Laura's house.

"It's Father and Bryce," William said. "They've come back."

Chapter Twenty-six
July, 1926

Upon learning of Cord's and Bryce's return to the ranch, Struthers Burt invited everyone at Snake River, dudes and the outfit, over the next evening for an impromptu party. Cord spoke with Laura over their spare breakfast about the appropriateness of going so soon after burying Bitter Waters.

She suggested it would do them both good to get out. "While you and Bryce were gone, I've been entertaining dudes. The new folks who got in Saturday don't know we had a death."

Cord scowled. "William doesn't seem to know, either. He gave no word of condolence when I returned."

Laura took her cereal bowl to the sink and pumped water. "You know William's never been comfortable with his Nez Perce heritage."

Cord brushed that aside. "Bitter Waters used to play with both the boys when they were young. He must feel something!"

"He's never been good with words like Bryce is."

"Perhaps not, but he seemed to be communicating pretty well with our cook the other night when Bryce and I drove in late."

Laura's hands stilled with a bowl in them. "Oh?"

"William and Francesca were on the cookshack porch, looking mighty close."

"Indeed." Laura appeared to digest that while drying her hands.

She came to Cord and rubbed his shoulders. "I really think we ought to go to Burt's this evening."

But when it came time to leave, Cord pleaded fatigue and Laura stayed with him.

❦

Bryce tethered Lucifer to a Bar BC hitching rail and watched William arrive in his Model T with Francesca. Brother made a show of going around and opening her door.

Pretending an indifference he did not feel, Bryce went to speak with Struthers Burt.

The rancher took him aside. "I was hoping your father could make it." His bright dark eyes were troubled.

"He wanted to, but since he's been ill, and the long trip ..."

Burt nodded. "I wanted to tell him John D. Rockefeller, Jr., is coming to the valley. Horace is bringing him down from Yellowstone Wednesday."

Though Bryce had been away, he knew Horace Albright, the Yellowstone Superintendent, had been interested for years in protecting the Tetons and the Jenny's Lake area from rampant development. Rockefeller, a wealthy philanthropist, seemed to share their desire to prevent further eyesores like the Elbo Ranch that had opened the week before with tourist cabins and a permanent rodeo grounds, located uncomfortably close to Snake River Ranch. A new billboard proclaimed the Elbo the "home of the Hollywood cowboy."

Not to mention Dieter Gross's new gas station and store with garish pennants waving in the wind.

Burt lit a cigarette. "Horace and the Rockefellers are stopping here and I thought to bring them to Snake River afterward. The more folks we have lobbying for a park in our front yard, with the authentic ranches forming a living history museum …."

"I'll tell Dad and Mom," Bryce promised.

Burt sobered. "Tell Cord he has my sympathy. I know he set a store by Bitter Waters."

Because Burt was a friend, Bryce spent some time telling him about his visit to the reservation. "Those folks live in real poverty, whereas, being raised here in the valley, being only part Nez Perce, I haven't had to put up with too much."

Burt frowned. "Even so, don't forget that part Indian is as good as all for some people." He glanced around before going on, "I'm hearing the Klan is coming in."

Bryce mentally ticked off valley candidates for Klan membership. At the top of his list sat Dieter Gross and his thug Tiny, whom Bryce had fought in the bar in Driggs.

❦

Dusk gave way to a sky spangled with stars, while Bryce stewed over Francesca staying by William's side. What kind of woman was she, to go from him to his brother without even a word?

Last night when he'd seen them together on the cookshack porch, he'd at first been unable to believe what the truck's headlights had revealed. Then disbelief had given way to a rage so powerful he'd spent all last night trying to decide whether he wanted to kill William, Francesca, or both.

Today, he'd thrown himself into hard labor, mucking out stalls and currying horses, hoping their placid nature would calm him enough that he was no longer dangerous.

It had worked for a while, but seeing the two of them together this evening had raked it all up again.

As the party was breaking up, Bryce saw Francesca go inside alone to use one of the flush toilets in the lodge. Taking his chance, he waited until she came out onto the deck and stepped into her path.

She glanced around. Afraid William would see her talking to him?

Bryce grabbed her wrist, harder than he intended. "Come with me."

The instant he touched her, the old compelling urge seized him, the one that had ended before with them in the pines.

"Come with you where?"

"Anywhere we can sort out what the hell happened the morning Bitter Waters died." And what she was doing with his brother.

Francesca lashed back. "What in hell do you think happened?" Her swearing sounded awkward. "I have heard you know your way around women."

"Heard from whom? My brother?"

Her eyes flashed. "Who else? He told me about Charlene ...."

From the dining area, William called, "Fran?"

When she heard William's voice, Francesca tried to look away from Bryce. William called again, a little louder.

She ought to walk away, after Bryce had taken her in the copse and left without a word.

"Fran?"

She could not tear her gaze from the vivid intensity of Bryce's eyes, torchlight reflecting twin flames in them.

It might be crazy, but she let him tow her down toward the river. They ended up near the place where the dude had attacked her. Cottonwoods bent over the swift dark flow.

In the darkness, she became aware he still held her wrist.

Now he slid his hand around and twined his fingers with hers. "Francesca," he said in a low and tortured tone.

"*Si?*"

"Why? Why did you go with me when it's William you want?"

The current flowing between her and Bryce swept all thought of William and the woman called Charlene away.

"Why did you make me believe—?" Bryce gritted.

"Nothing has happened between William and me. Not like ...." Nothing like the morning on the Timbered Island.

"When I came back yesterday, you were with him. And you sure seem a lot friendlier now than when you were accusing him and Pru."

"He doesn't see her anymore."

"Is that what he said?" Bryce dropped her hand. "Do you want him?"

Did she? Only last night she had imagined him as someone she could count on, while Bryce ....

Her silence went on too long, as his expression went from hostile to wary. "Were you just passing time with me while he was on the cattle drive? Is he the reason you didn't talk to me when I came back?"

How could he call their caring for Bitter Waters "passing time?" Francesca raged, "Since you came back, you have not even looked at me!"

"You would not look at me, after—"

"I was afraid you would think me a whore, the way I—"

He cut her off. "Francesca, even as I walked away, I wanted to stay. When Dad and I drove in the other night, I saw nothing but you ... and that you were with William."

A dreadful suspicion took hold of Francesca. Was she merely a pawn in the brothers' game?

"Is this about anything other than beating William down?" she challenged.

Bryce stared at her for what might have been a telling moment. "I won't dignify that," he blustered. "Now are you and William—"

"Forget William!" Could she? Should she?

Bryce's hand came up and cradled her cheek with a gentleness she did not expect. "I can't fathom what's going on with us, much less with you and William." His eyes were shadowed. "I only know I want to take you in my arms ...."

Her breath made a little hiccup.

"And that I won't do it until you ... figure things out."

He removed his hand from her cheek, leaving it cold.

"You do not want—?" she began.

He broke in, "*You* don't."

"What?"

"Your English is good, it's time you learned to talk with contractions. Say, 'We don't want' instead of, "We do not want.'"

She caught the sheen of moonlight on his eyes and decided not to accept his changing the subject. "What if we do?"

"Oh, Lord." He dragged her against him and buried his face in her hair. "Francesca."

Joy surged. Touching him was like being against a live wire; she had no thought of safe or secure, only that she wanted ... needed him like a parched plant must have water.

She felt his answering need, but he said, "Don't make me do the wrong thing again. Two wrongs won't make a right."

If they made love, everything would be right. "Perhaps what we did is the only thing right."

"God, Francesca. I want you so much I'd take you here beside the river ... the way we did before ...."

She waited for him to kiss her.

He set her aside.

"Bryce?"

"But I won't touch you again ... until you tell me I'm the only man you want."

Her fist came to her mouth. She did want him, in a different way from William, but would he stay at Snake River or leave again, this time taking her heart?

Her hesitation lasted too long.

Bryce strode away toward the lights of the Bar BC.

Chapter Twenty-seven
July, 1926

July 14, 1926

At any moment, a cloud of dust on the road from the Bar BC will signal the arrival of Horace Albright and John D. Rockefeller, Jr., to visit Cord, who awaits them on the porch of the Main. So much is at stake in the valley.

The Jackson's Hole Plan, conceived at Maude Noble's cabin three years ago, has not moved forward. Several trips to the east by representatives of the ranchers did not find a benefactor to purchase private lands.

The cattle business is still off, the valley economy is terrible, with a full page in the paper devoted to people owing back taxes. And now Albright brings Rockefeller, who has the Standard Oil money behind him ... perhaps to be our benefactor. If only he would agree to buy up all the rag tag businesses near Jenny Lake, including Dieter Gross's gas station; then we dude ranchers could carry on our business in peace and perhaps in prosperity.

Cord watched one of the White Motor Company's Yellowstone auto stages, an open-topped yellow touring car, come trundling along the bluff. Moments later, he shook hands with Albright, whom he knew well. The Superintendent wore his uniform, a white shirt and tie tucked into a buttoned flap-pocket jacket, trousers bunched at the knees and folded into polished high boots. A flat-brimmed, high crowned hat completed the ensemble.

"Horace," Cord said.

John D. Rockefeller, Jr., stepped forward. The only son of the billionaire industrialist of Standard Oil fame, he was a rather stern-looking man who appeared to be in his early fifties. Although Cord knew that he had a daughter and five sons, only sixteen-year-old Laurance, fourteen-year-old Winthrop, and eleven-year-old David accompanied John D. and his wife Abby. As one would expect, the family wore expensive-looking leisure clothing.

Laura's lemonade and a platter of Francesca's sugar cookies were duly praised and lightly sampled, for the Rockefellers had lunched only a little while earlier. After introductions, John D. and Abby admired the Main and the ranch's "ideal" location.

Before re-boarding the touring stage, the guests walked out to the bluff overlooking the lower terrace and the Snake River. Cord came along.

"There's nothing like this in all of North America," Albright said.

John D. nodded, while Abby turned in a circle to absorb the entire vista. Afternoon shadows had begun to soften the sheltered valleys on the Teton front, while sunshine still bathed Antelope Flats and the land around Blacktail Butte. Abby asked about the scar of the Gros Ventre slide and Albright filled her in. "Over a year, now, and the river flows out from beneath the dam created by the landslide."

John D. looked toward the Moose-Jenny's Lake Road and said to Cord, "You're fortunate that from here you can barely see the ugly construction."

Cord spoke up, hoping Rockefeller would take the bait. "All those buildings are on private property—the dilapidated old dance hall, the bootleg joint, and the billboards. The owners can do what they like."

John D.'s thick brows furrowed and a significant glance passed between him and his wife. "Horace," he ordered in a corporate command voice, "submit a map to me and a list of the offending properties. Along with estimated costs to buy them."

Cord made a conscious effort to keep from smiling. Here, three years after the meeting in Maude Noble's cabin, was the man whose personal power and fortune could alter the valley's future.

Albright nodded. "I'll get that right to you, John. Confidentially, of course."

Burt had told Cord that Rockefeller was traveling under his middle name, Davison. Cord had assumed it was for privacy's sake, but now he suspected Rockefeller intended his role in Jackson's Hole to be a clandestine one.

⁓

Laura waited for Cord on their porch, pondering the fate of Jackson's Hole and Snake River Ranch.

She had no control over the one—time would tell if Rockefeller proved a help or hindrance. As for the future of the ranch, she had seen that the apparent war between the boys for Francesca was heating up. And felt helpless in that regard, as well.

Perhaps the three young people suffered from the same restless discontent that she did after Bitter Waters's death. Each day and the next passed with a dull sameness and, though each group of summer dudes was unique, she now found no joy in their sunburned, eager faces.

They all needed something to shake up their routine.

That evening, Francesca did not sit beside William at dinner. Bryce would have taken it as a good sign, but later he saw William slip away from the Main and figured he was leaving to be with her.

For a distraction, Bryce chatted with Riley Grogan of Charleston. The stocky dude in his early thirties, with bushy black brows, identified himself as a mountaineer who hoped to climb the Grand Teton.

Bryce had heard that before from city men. "It's 13,770 feet ... not an easy thing to do."

Riley smiled and spoke in the soft cadence of the South. "Ah understand two teenagers climbed it a couple years ago in cowboy boots. How hard can it be?"

Bryce gave him a grudging nod. "You've done your homework. Paul Petzoldt was sixteen, went up with his nineteen-year-old buddy, Frank Herron. But did you know they almost died of exposure?"

The climber refused to be discouraged. "Ah figure on doing it with better planning and better footwear than cowboy boots. Ah've already talked with Billy Owen." He named the first man to have conquered the Grand, back in 1898, along with fellow climber Frank Spalding.

Bryce threw back another jolt of the whiskey he was using to forget Francesca. "Where all have you climbed?"

"On Mont Blanc in the French Alps," a little shrug, "Colorado, California." It sounded as though Mr. Grogan might know what he was doing.

Something shifted inside Bryce, or perhaps it had happened a while back. With Bitter Waters buried and Francesca unwilling to choose between him and William—and not to decide was to decide—he'd started thinking about leaving the ranch to find a new challenge.

Perhaps it was right here. "You're really thinking of going for the summit?"

"Hell, yes," Riley said. "That's what ah came out here for, not to ride your tame dude horses."

A slow smile spread over Bryce's face, as he imagined the cold wind at the top of the Grand, of seeing a hundred miles in every direction—something to take his mind off grief for his great-uncle and rage at Francesca and William.

Bryce bent toward Riley and spoke in a conspiratorial whisper. "Got room for me to go along?"

When Francesca heard about the expedition to climb the Grand, a wild impulse to go along seized her. They would need someone to cook, of course, but primarily it would be a break from Snake River.

She loved the ranch, but needed some kind of closure after Bitter Waters's death. Cord and Bryce had been able to take him to Nespelem, to see him placed into the earth, while she kept waking each morning believing she must rush to the lean-to and see to him.

The next evening after dinner, she approached Riley Grogan in the big room of the Main after dinner. "Mr. Grogan, I wonder if I might go along on your climb?"

"Call me Riley."

She waited for him to refuse her for lack of experience, but before he could, Laura spoke up. "I wonder if my husband and I might go, as well." She glanced at Cord, as if this were the first she'd spoken of it and wondered what he might think.

Standing in front of the big fireplace, Cord looked jaundiced, or perhaps it was the leaping ochre light from the flames. "I've just come back from a long journey," he said gently. "You try if you want."

Laura started to demur, but Cord drew her against his side and said in a low voice that nonetheless carried to Francesca. "Please go, my love. I've lived here all these years and never felt the need to go up."

Francesca waited for Riley to say the climb was no place for them.

Instead, the Charlestonian grinned. "Since ah can't be the first one to ascend the Grand, ah've decided the way to make this expedition famous is to bring along a whole group of folks who've never climbed. If young Paul Petzoldt can guide a fifty-nine-year-old woman up, I can take you two."

"A woman has climbed the Grand?" Francesca asked.

Bryce spoke from where he leaned against the mantle. "Paul took a valley resident, Geraldine Lucas, up two years ago. She was the second woman to summit after Eleanor Davis from Colorado in 1923." As he answered, his eyes met Francesca's for the first time since their altercation at Burt's.

William, who was working behind the bar, set down the glass he was polishing. "Of course, I'm going, too."

"Of course," Bryce said dryly.

William looked at his mother. "So a few women have gone up, and Francesca can be our cook and sit out the summit effort if need be ... but you can't be serious."

Before Francesca could tell William he needn't worry about her sitting out something a woman over twice her age had done, Laura's chin rose and a determined light shone in her eyes. One Francesca realized she had not seen in them since Bitter Waters's illness had worsened.

"I am perfectly serious, son. I'm not too old to want a challenge before I am unable to meet it."

Chapter Twenty-eight
July 22, 1926

A week later, the ascent on the Grand began.

Before dawn, the climbing party—Riley Grogan, Laura, William, Bryce, Francesca, Asa, and Bobby—gathered in the foothills south of Jenny's Lake. Laden with packs carrying tents, sleeping bags, ropes, and food, they said goodbye to their drivers, Cord and Charlie, and set off.

At first, the procession contoured along a well-traveled trail in deep forest at the base of the range. Most of the expedition wore heavy jackets, caps, gloves, and stout leather boots with thick lug soles Riley had selected with Bryce on a trip to Idaho Falls.

As the pitch steepened and they negotiated several switchbacks leading in and out of forest, the sun marched down from the high peaks and burst upon them. Bobby started to swear about the heat and everyone stopped to shed layers of clothing.

Above nine thousand feet, the trail gradually became a faint track, then disappeared into solid rock on the south side of Disappointment Peak. Laura started to lag, and William dropped back to walk with her. She noted he kept a keen eye ahead on Francesca, who was close to Bryce.

Near ten thousand, they stopped at the base of a waterfall. After a light repast of bread, cheese, and fruit that Francesca had put together, they worked their way around the falls. At the head of Garnet Canyon, Middle Teton towered, a dark vertical dike cutting up toward its summit.

The group climbed the valley between Middle Teton and the Grand, beside Middle Teton glacier. Jumbled boulders of moraine, bulldozed up by the ice, made for rough going. Though the glacier appeared white from the valley, up close it was a filthy mess of slush and icy puddles, embedded dirt and rock fragments, and red algae. Only in a few places did the deep aquamarine of true glacial ice peek forth.

By mid-afternoon, with the air thin above eleven thousand, their evening's camp was in sight. They planned to overnight in what Billy Owen termed the Lower Saddle.

Toiling and sweating, Francesca was beginning to believe they would never reach the saddle when she looked up to discover a wall of leaden clouds pouring over from the Idaho side.

Within moments, the sun was swallowed, and a cutting wind sent them all reaching for jackets. While Francesca struggled to take off her pack and get her coat, lightning stabbed over the peaks.

William caught her arm. Cupping his hands so she could hear him over the rising gale, he shouted, "Get down."

Riley and the hands were already sitting, spreading oilskins over themselves and curling into balls with their heads on their knees. Bryce helped Laura.

Francesca yanked out her oilskin, which flapped wildly. William seemed to be having better luck untying his from where he'd rolled it atop his pack.

A curtain of silver rain struck, stinging Francesca's face and hands like needles. It brought back the storm that had caught her and William her first day in the valley.

A bolt of electric fire struck too close, exploding a boulder into flying shards. Blinded by the flash, with an eerie feeling of her hair standing on end and her heart quivering, Francesca lost her oilskin into the void.

William tackled her and shielded her with his body; rock fragments rained around them.

Held beneath him, with lightning etching purple streaks on her closed eyelids, Francesca felt grateful for his constant vigilance.

As rapidly as it had blown up, the squall gave way, revealing the daylight rise of a nearly full moon over the Gros Ventre. Asa and Bobby struggled, but managed to build a fire of wood they had collected near tree line and roped onto the base of their packs, while Bryce and William staked out tents in the lee near a rock wall.

Laura sat gratefully beside the fire, drying her clothes and writing in her journal, while Francesca started a pot of beans seasoned with bacon, brown sugar, and dried mustard. Bryce went wandering and upon his return struck up conversation with Riley. William prepared a pot of cowboy coffee.

The hot drink warmed, and a plate of beans and bread further strengthened Laura, so much that she decided to follow William's lead and take a walk.

By the time she reached the crest of the Lower Saddle the sun was sinking over the fertile Teton Valley, its wheatfields and pastures a checkerboard of greens and gold. Above, on the Grand, ruby light cast a glow over scattered snowfields.

If only Cord had been able to climb, but he could not have made it this far. Clutching her coat around her against the sharpening wind, she raged against the sun setting upon their years of managing the ranch.

Darkness descended, yet she stayed, watching for shooting stars. One traced a long line over Idaho.

William came back to the fire from his twilight exploration.

"Where's Mother?" he asked Bryce, who had moved over next to Fran in William's absence.

Bryce nodded up toward the Lower Saddle.

"You let her go alone?"

"I can see her from here," Bryce pointed up a hundred yards at a lone figure silhouetted against the western sky.

Taking care with his footing, William clambered up. In the cutting wind atop the saddle, he became aware that his coat was not quite dry.

"I wish Father were here," he told Mother.

"I've been missing him, too." Her shadowy form appeared delicate against the gargantuan setting. "Now that I've come this far, I realize he could never—"

"It doesn't stop you wishing." William touched her arm; there should be more he could say.

"How I want to make it to the top, for both of us."

"I'll help you," he promised.

They stood together in silence, then turned back toward the bright beacon of the fire.

Fran's clear laugh ascended.

Knowing Bryce was the one amusing her cut William to the quick. He turned and looked down.

Mother also faced the camp. The moon illuminated enough of her features for him to see consternation. "I've held back asking why it hasn't worked out...."

He tried to speak lightly. "You know, parents can't be the ones doing the proposing."

She detained him with a hand on his arm. "If your intentions are right …."

William squirmed inwardly at her accurate assessment of his past behavior. "And if they are?"

"Then you mustn't let anyone whose plans might be less worthy interfere."

William almost gasped aloud. Did she mean to say she would back him over her beloved baby Bryce in the matter of Fran? Did she, too, realize Bryce would bed Fran and leave the ranch without a second thought?

As Bryce's and Fran's mingled laughter rose on the night air, he said, "It may be too late."

&

When Mom and William came down from the Lower Saddle, she looked at Bryce in a searching way that seemed to include Francesca … and made Bryce wonder if she and William had been discussing them.

With a smile that included Riley and the hands, Mom excused herself and went to the tent she was sharing with Francesca.

Bryce watched William take a seat by the fire on Francesca's other side and steeled himself to observe.

"The view up there is dynamite." William smiled at her, showing teeth. "Tomorrow evening after our climb to the summit, let's watch the sunset from there." His tone said he wasn't inviting the rest of the crew.

Francesca turned away from Bryce. "It will be lovely. If it does not rain."

Bryce's blood surged. Sooner or later, she was going to have to choose.

The thought occurred to him, as it had before, that her failure to decide was a decision. In the days since they'd spoken at the Bar BC, she could have come to him anytime and told him she didn't want William.

Bryce pushed up from his rock seat. He stepped across in front of Francesca and looked down at her. She met his gaze and he jerked his eyes to the side, indicating she should come with, or at least, follow him.

Francesca lowered her focus to the fire.

Gritting his teeth, Bryce shrugged on his sheepskin coat and walked away. Had she chosen, then? Was that her message, despite her willingness to smile into his eyes and laugh when Brother wasn't looking?

Keeping to the edge of the rocks where they would climb the next day, he went about a hundred feet beyond the ring of light and relieved himself.

Hoping against hope, he moved on and found a place where glacial boulders formed a shelter from the night wind.

&

Francesca had to trust the firelight to hide her flush. If she had misread Bryce, and he had merely gone to answer nature's call, he would be back by now.

As time passed, she sat next to William and pretended to listen to Riley tell stories of past ascents.

William leaned forward to make a point in the conversation she wasn't sharing in. When he sat back, his shoulder brushed hers, then settled against her. Her arm warmed, bringing back the Christmas Eve service in the Chapel of the Transfiguration when he had given her the rosary she carried in her coat pocket. Filled with dread at how he would feel if she got up and followed Bryce, she remained rooted.

If only William were more forceful, more definite, more articulate about what he wanted. If only his touch bore the kind of live wire intensity of Bryce's ....

She knew that the penalty for not choosing, and for not choosing now, was that Bryce would leave the ranch again, despite his promise to stay.

A shaft of pain drove through her. No surprise, for there was no outcome in which someone would not be hurt.

She could stay beside William, live out her life at Snake River.

Choosing Bryce would mean they must leave the ranch, take up a life of wandering, of living on the transient wages he and she might earn. But oh, the electricity that surged through her at the prospect of seeing the world at his side!

She rose, plunging without fear into the fire that only Bryce's touch sent coursing through her veins. She envisioned growing old beside him, laughing and loving the way Laura and Cord did.

William saw she was on her feet and shoved up.

"I just need to ...." she nodded at the darkness.

"I should come along."

At her sharp look, he flushed. One could see it by firelight. "I'll look the other way," he persisted. "You wouldn't want to run into a mountain lion."

Caught out, her voice went sharp, "I'll be fine!" She extended her hand, palm out, to stop him following her.

From the nearby tent, Laura called, "What's the trouble?"

William looked into Francesca's eyes; she saw his hurt and anger.

And, though her stomach ached at making him feel this way, she pretended not to see.

William spit out, "Go, then." He turned his back and stared at the fire, shoulders hunched, hands shoved in his jacket pockets.

She stood a moment longer, looking at the unyielding set of his head, then turned to go.

As she moved away, silver from the full moon replaced the fire's gold. Her night vision was poor, and she wasn't sure which way to go.

Being out there alone brought home the vulnerability of being human. William's warning about mountain lions, though meant to refer to Bryce as Koyama the lion, had not been idle.

Despair washed over her. Her bold move had been foolhardy, she would never find Bryce ....

She heard a trill, that of a whippoorwill.

Bryce's sense of irony, crying "poor will" in a place where there could be none of the birds, made her grin. Footsteps crunched toward her.

"Steady," Bryce murmured.

All sense of being alone, or vulnerable, blew away on the night wind. His arms captured her and drew her against a rock wall into the lee. He nudged aside her coat collar and brushed his lips along the side of her neck.

"I didn't think you would do it. I told myself you'd play it safe."

"I'm here," she breathed, like a promise.

William stood with his fists at his sides, watching Bryce seduce Fran. When he'd left the fire, night blind, he'd had troubled tracking her, but finally succeeded in the moonlight.

Her head fell back, her lips parted .... Everything in him wanted to leap forward, tear the lovers apart.

He could barely breathe. His teeth brought blood, salt where he bit his tongue.

What if Mother knew her choice for him was a little whore, who played both ends against the middle, who sat with him beside the fire and pressed her shoulder against his? Who didn't care that Bryce, all bullshit and banter, was incapable of love?

Fran wrapped her slender arms around Bryce, her body bent back and pressed against a rock face. William was suddenly fiercely glad she had seen him fucking Pru. The blonde might have round heels, but at least she was honest about it.

Bryce moaned in his throat. Lust, or one of his put-ons to get a woman going?

What was William going to do here?

Rush in and make a fool of himself?

He loosened his coat, let chill air in onto his neck and chest. Another man might have resorted to violence, but that was not his style. He must walk away, find his sleeping bag and pretend to lose himself in pleasant slumber. Wake in the morning for their pre-dawn start, hearty, hail-fellow-well-met.

Some might call it cowardice. He preferred to think of it as pride.

Chapter Twenty-nine
July 23, 1926

Before dawn, Asa was beating a spoon against the metal coffee pot. He fired up the single burner Primus camp stove and made coffee and tea. Though the sun would not rise until just after five, the climbing party got under way the moment it became possible to tell a black thread from a white one.

Boots still wet from slogging through slush by the glacier, they left their tents and large packs at the Lower Saddle. Riley, Bryce, and William carried lightly laden knapsacks with nuts, chocolate, and dried fruit to dispense to the others for energy. Everyone carried their own canteen on a belt that could serve to cinch up their jacket behind them when they became overheated.

Riley led the way with authority, a coil of rope slung across his chest. An eager Bobby followed. Next, Bryce climbed above Francesca, then William above Laura. Sturdy Asa, at Riley's instruction, brought up the rear.

After an easy upward walk of five hundred feet, they discerned a thick black dike of rock similar to the one that bisected the face of Middle Teton.

In his element, Riley studied the route in the rising light. He chose to go left around the dike, staying to the west. Likewise, he avoided the roughest part of a promontory of rock by staying to its left. After several false starts, he found the way around a chimney and back to the right, where he crawled through a tunnel-like opening. There, waiting for the rest of the party to catch up, he savored the sunrise brightening the peak of Middle Teton.

Bobby scrambled through the Needle's Eye, as Billy Owen's map termed it, with ease. Bryce let Francesca go next; the men above could give her a hand. He waited while his mother went up, as well. With an ironic bow, William sent Bryce ahead of him.

Once everyone had threaded the needle, they moved up through a gully to the high saddle. On their left was the Enclosure, a satellite peak about three hundred feet lower than the Grand's summit.

They pulled out their canteens and looked back. The camp was in morning sunlight now, nearly two thousand feet below. As they rested, Riley told how the first superintendent of Yellowstone, Nathaniel P. Langford, had, on the 1872 Hayden Expedition, climbed the Grand ... or not.

Langford had definitely reached the peak he named the Enclosure, for he had described, on its apex, a structure of boulders turned up on end to form a circular breastwork. Inside the circle, there were no stones, only fine grained granite sand. Indians might have made it during the past few hundred years, or natives in a much more distant time.

The trouble was that Langford described the feature as being "on top of the Teton," and later climbers found no cairn or marks on the summit of the Grand. Riley had read the war of letters that erupted between Owen and Langford, published in the outdoor magazine *Forest and Stream*. Each man claimed his party had been the first to summit.

As he finished his story, Riley studied the group and its dynamics. The only one he had complete confidence in was Asa, who seemed to have a good head on his shoulders. Young Bobby, though he tried to appear fearless, might have a nervous streak. Mrs. Sutton seemed game; she'd make it if they went slowly and the weather held. The brothers Sutton acted like a pair of dogs quarreling over a bone—in this case, the ranch's lovely chef, Francesca. The tension, almost a vibration between them, was particularly frightening, since they all needed to be a team.

Riley rose and addressed the group. According to Owen's instruction, the next challenge was to traverse north across the bottom of the west slope before beginning a direct ascent on the summit. Because of the inexperience of his fellow climbers, he told them, he'd chosen the easiest route.

Nonetheless, they had to cross a large detached slab with a steep pitch and a major drop-off below. Most sat, straddling the awkward exposure, and inched across the ten foot challenge.

From there, Riley pointed out their traverse back to the south along a series of slabs Owen had termed the Catwalk.

Laura took one look at the sheer drop below and demurred.

"It's only a little way across, Mother," William urged.

She studied the distance between the rocks. "My legs are too short to make that."

"Bryce and I will help you, one above and one below," he insisted.

"I'll climb up and tie off a rope," Riley suggested. "Anyone who needs to can use it to pull themselves along."

"I'll help you, Mr. Grogan," Billy offered.

Laura shook her head again.

Francesca moved up next to her. "I'll wait here with you."

"With your long legs, you can make it."

"With everyone's help, you will, too," Francesca said. "Cord ... and Bitter Waters ... would want you to."

Laura made it up both the slab and the Catwalk without using the rope. From there, the route to the citadel was an easy boulder scramble.

So simple that she could hardly believe she'd made it.

After years of looking up at the distant austerity of the Grand, never imagining she might reach the pinnacle, she rubbed her hand across the summit rock of banded gray and white gneiss; it bore rusty-looking patches where iron-bearing garnets had weathered.

Riley photographed the group. Standing close together, each heard the others' rapid, harsh breathing.

Laura hugged both her sons. William grabbed Francesca up against his side in a vice-like grip.

As soon as the picture-taking ended, everyone drank in the three hundred sixty degree view. Seven thousand feet down to the hazy floor of Jackson's Hole .... Bryce pointed out the ranch and they all waved for Cord and Charlie.

Francesca hugged Laura, women pioneers on the summit, with only two before them.

Laura whispered, "I think of you as family."

Francesca's face got hot despite the buffeting wind. Laura believed she was involved with her older son, the rock.

Or did she? Having heard last night's squabble by the fire, Laura might have realized Francesca was going to Bryce in the darkness.

After less than fifteen minutes of celebration, Riley pointed out approaching clouds over Idaho.

Bobby shoved to his feet. "Time to get the hell down."

Mindful of yesterday's storm, everyone prepared to descend.

Laura had made it to the exposed slab near the base of the Catwalk, when lightning struck the top of the Grand.

Instantaneous thunder cracked. Everyone ducked.

Laura looked at the drop ahead of her and shook her head. She should never have gone up; she knew going down was always tougher.

Blue gray clouds cut off sight of the summit.

"Come on, Laura," Riley called from below in a commanding tone. He, Bobby and Asa had already descended the pitch.

"I ... need the rope."

"I'll free climb beside you," Bryce said.

William and Francesca waited above. A line of rain swept toward them.

Don't look down, Laura told herself, sitting on the edge with her face turned away. She had plenty of strong young men with her who wouldn't let her fall.

She held the rope and eased over the edge, pressing her boots against the rock. Letting one foot down, then the other, she stopped to catch her breath.

The squall struck, wetting her to the skin. No one had rain gear.

"Take it one move at a time," Bryce cautioned, sliding down beside her on the treacherous wet gneiss.

She looked down at her boots and caught sight of the abyss beyond. Already dizzy from the thin air, she felt her foot slip, and she crashed into the slab with her shoulder. She cried out and her other foot lost purchase.

Why had she taken such a chance? For Bitter Waters and Cord ... but one of them was dead, and she wasn't a believer in spirits who lingered and watched the living. If she fell to her death, Cord would never forgive her for leaving him for fifteen minutes of oxygen-deprived ecstasy atop the Grand.

Hanging, her arms losing strength, Bryce trying to take some of her weight ....

He'd never be able to hold her and not slip off the wet rock.

"No," she cried. He was young and had his life ahead of him.

"I won't let you go, Mom."

Blinded by the driving rain, she heard from below, "Let her down. We've got her."

Scraping down the rough face, Laura felt her feet and then her calves collected by Bobby and Asa's strong hands.

His mom was safe, but Bryce was hanging out. Trying to hold her up, he'd moved over into an area where the footholds were slim. With one leg dangling, he reached for the rope and missed.

The toe of one boot stuck to the gneiss; he strove for the top of the slab. Above, he looked into Francesca's black almond eyes, her mouth opened in a silent scream.

Adrenaline—sheer terror—surged down all his nerves. His arms and hands stung.

If he got out of this, he would tuck Francesca into a soft bed and make love to her until the world looked square. If William didn't like it, if Mom and Dad thought his big brother ought to be the one for her, let them all go to hell.

Bryce's heart rate must be three thousand .... The rope was tied off about six feet to the right of Francesca, with William on the side away from it.

Somebody had better get it to him pronto.

Francesca tore her gaze from Bryce's stricken one and smashed her fist into William's upper arm. "Get him," she shouted.

He wasn't moving.

Dio, what had she been thinking, to raise ire between William and Bryce on the night before they climbed?

Below, Bryce's wet knuckles turned pale, yellow cartilage showing through, and she knew he couldn't hold on much longer.

"Help me," he gasped.

With William still immobile, she plunged forward, the rock slab cutting her middle, her arm extended. "Bryce!"

Her hand seized his.

She started to slip forward, head down over the edge. For a sickening instant, she looked down thousands of feet over Bryce's shoulder. Their joined hands started to slide apart.

"Noooo ...." she cried.

Arms caught Francesca around the waist. "I've got her," William called.

He dragged them both to safety an instant before their grip broke.

On the miserable, rain-drenched trip down to the Lower Saddle, William brought up the rear.

He loved his brother, he wished him joy. He recollected baby Bryce with his grubby fingers in his mouth, while Mother called William her "big boy."

What if his second of hesitation had cost his brother's life? How could he have lived with that? How could he have let a woman get under his skin to the point he would even have considered a world without Bryce?

Pray God Bryce had not noticed. He also prayed that God had not, but feared he was out of luck in that department. Nonetheless, he promised whatever power might decide a man's fate that he would never wish his brother dead again.

When they got to the camp in the Lower Saddle, he approached Bryce and put out his hand. "Damned fine job you did getting Mother down that face."

Bryce gave his trademark tough grip and grin, but the skin around his lips was drawn tight. "Good job you and Francesca did. For a moment there, I was starting to wonder if I was heading for the long rappel."

He turned away.

William should take him aside, apologize for freezing up and not moving faster, but the moment got away from him.

Later, when they camped for the second night, with the wind keening up from the Idaho side, he still said nothing.

Chapter Thirty
July 24, 1926

The walk out to the foothills was far easier than the prior day's descent from the Grand. The weather had cleared overnight; the sun warmed their faces. Riley, Asa, and Bobby were in high spirits, trading stories and jokes on the trail. Francesca walked with William behind her and Bryce ahead.

By four o'clock, Cord and Charlie had ferried the climbers back to Snake River.

After kissing her husband, Laura announced she would not appear at the evening's chuck wagon dinner for new dudes. She couldn't wait to get into a hot bath, treat the blister on her left heel, and get into bed with Cord's arms around her. Two nights away from him, after so many years together, had been far too long. Part of her even wished she had not gone; her achievement was sure to further underscore his diminished capacity.

Though Francesca longed for the luxury of an early night, she took a bath and insisted on helping Jim with dinner. Asa joined them, limping from a stone bruise.

William came out in clean clothes, with his damp hair combed back, and offered to gather wildflowers for the tables if she'd join him.

"No," she snapped. "I need to pick vegetables for a salad, but that isn't why I won't. On the mountain ... Bryce could have fallen, and you didn't move!"

He reddened and his jaw set. "I did move! I pulled you both up."

"You stood there for what felt like forever!"

William's manner changed; his anger becoming contrition. "I'm sorry ...."

I've been beating myself up over not leaping right for the rope, but at the time, with Bryce dangling there, my brain just seemed to freeze."

Francesca studied him for a long moment. His clear gray eyes held hers.

"Didn't that happen to you up there, for a second, too?" he challenged.

And she was back on the mountain, leaning over the precipice and looking into Bryce's terror-stricken eyes, her mouth open in a silent scream.

Bobby and Foster met the dudes with horse-drawn wagons at the Moose-Jenny's Lake Road and brought them in to the ranch. With Cord and Laura away, William and Charlie played host. By the time the serving line opened, Bryce was still nowhere in sight.

Francesca took her place at the head of the spread of beef, beans, potato salad, green salad, and assorted vegetables, and greeted the new dudes with smiles and mindless pleasantries.

If she couldn't see Bryce now, she would later. Her stomach flip-flopped as she recalled the night before last. Their need unfulfilled in the chilly darkness, he had whispered, "I want all night, all the nights."

How could that happen with him sleeping in the bunkhouse, and her in the cabin with Rosa and Maria? There was the lean-to, but Bitter Waters ....

Francesca spat to ward off evil.

Where would they spend the nights Bryce had spoken of? Did he expect her to settle for a blanket beneath the stars, for sneaking around like Prudence Johnston?

Bryce woke and didn't know where he was. Then the narrow cot reminded him he was in the stables. After showering, he had decided that the room where a hand slept if a horse needed overnight monitoring would be quieter than the bunkhouse.

Outside the flyspecked window, shadows lay long.

He was hungry.

On his way up to the chuck wagon area, he pondered what to do about Francesca. They needed a solution that did not involve sneaking around like Brother and Pru. From the way Francesca had screamed at William by the privy, he knew she'd never settle for that.

At the opposite extreme, he could take her over to the Chapel of the Transfiguration and ask the Episcopal priest to marry them.

A knot in his stomach at the thought of pledging himself until death suggested there had to be a middle ground.

Beside the pond, some of the dudes were still at the tables. William was talking up some new arrivals, and Francesca was behind the serving line.

Bryce gave her a smile as she piled a plate for him. "Come sit with me," he urged.

Unfortunately, another wagon load of dudes arrived and she had to stay on the line.

Bryce scanned the tables and joined a group that included Riley Grogan. The climber, who was leaving the next morning, could not say enough about his excellent private adventure.

Bryce had a sudden idea that might solve his problem. Would some of the dudes want to enhance their Western experience with a jaunt to Yellowstone?

Never one to waste time, he commandeered the floor and began to propose another adventure, one not listed in the ranch brochure. Immediately, several guests were hanging on his words, and from the corner of his eye he saw Francesca's fork stop halfway to her mouth. William looked suspicious.

Bryce kept his regard on Ila Cox, a repeat guest he'd met last summer. The wealthy fiftyish New Yorker, in a tent-like linen dress, resembled a ship under full sail. Her bobbed black hair was almost blue, suggesting a dye job. She might be said to have brought along her quiet husband Macy, rather than the other way around. Their boisterous teen-aged twins, Harry and Hamm, were chunking rocks at the ducks on the pond.

Bryce affected nonchalance. "We could motor up to Yellowstone Lake, have the horses trailered, and ride around the Grand Loop Road beside the waters. Then sleep and dine in luxury at the Canyon Hotel."

"Count us in," Ila declared, "provided we go after our two weeks here. I wouldn't want to miss any of the trail rides."

"Of course." Bryce pitied the dude horse that had to carry her.

"How much extra will it cost?" Macy Cox put in.

Ila lifted her hand, as if to brush away a fly. "Now, Macy, you know we have plenty of money."

"We could throw in the transportation since tours are inclusive here," Bryce negotiated.

Ila fiddled with the opera length double strand of pearls over her enormous bosom. "So, then the four of us and ...." She gave Bryce an almost coquettish look.

He smiled. "I will be your guide, of course. And Francesca di Paoli, one of our chefs from Tuscany, will go along to see to our lunches."

క్లా

"*One* of our chefs?" As soon as William got a chance to separate Bryce from the group, he challenged him. "You know Fran's the only one who can cook worth a damn around here—"

"And I know a lame excuse when I hear one." Bryce's moue of amusement infuriated William further. "We just took her and one of our other cooks, Asa, to the top of the Grand, leaving Jim in charge of the kitchen like before Francesca got here."

"Charlie said the dudes weren't happy with the food while she was gone."

Bryce shook his head. "Let's get to what we're really talking about. You've had over a year to get Francesca in your court. And wasted it on Pru Johnston." His long-legged stride took him farther from the guests; William had to hustle to keep up.

Stopping in the sage meadow on the other side of the pond, Bryce fixed him with a keen look. "Do I smell some of your prejudice in play? She's foreign so she wouldn't be right for you to have children with. You like to imagine we're not Nez Perce."

"We're not, dammit!"

"We are! And if you had an ounce of respect for our heritage, you would have been here when Bitter Waters died."

William wasn't about to tell Bryce that if he could turn back time, he would have swallowed his aversion to sickness and been the one to nurse Uncle with Fran. He did need to explain that to Father, whose disappointment in him was all too obvious.

Staring at his brother, William cast about for different ammunition. "When Fran figures out what a bounder you are, the shoe will be on the other foot," he declared.

Bryce burst out laughing.

William had to remind himself again that he loved his brother.

Plucking a long grass stem and chewing on it, Bryce continued to smile. "Tell you what. For the next two weeks, until we leave for Yellowstone, you pull out all the stops with her. I'll lay back and give you every chance."

William gave him a suspicious look. Had Fran already made her decision and Bryce hoped he'd make a laughingstock of himself?

"Go ahead," Bryce taunted. "Ask her to marry you."

"Well, I didn't ..." William sputtered. This was the last thing he'd expected. If he asked her, and she turned him down—as Bryce was all too confident she would—William would never be able to hold his head up again.

"Aha!" Bryce threw down his blade of grass like a gauntlet. "You don't think she's lily white enough to marry. You who don't want to believe you're Nez Perce."

"That's not it."

"Two weeks," Bryce repeated, and walked away.

Chapter Thirty-one
August 7, 1926

Two weeks later, Francesca woke before dawn in the cabin she shared with Rosa and Maria. The two women had helped her pack the evening before, Maria unveiling a below-the-knee white linen dress she'd "run up for her," and Rosa offering a scarlet silk shawl.

"The Canyon Hotel, *la musica*." Rosa sighed.

"I'm only going to make the lunches." Since Bryce had not pressed the advantage she had given him during their ascent on the Grand, she wondered if that really was the only reason for her going. How difficult it had been during the past two weeks not to try and find him at some solitary ranch work and demand to know why he had pulled back after she had accepted his challenge.

Maria's black eyes sparkled. "Only for lunch? Everyone know you going for Mr. Bryce. Mr. William, it make him *loco*."

Francesca shook her head. "Not crazy enough."

The evening of their return from the mountain, William had walked her out of the Main with a definite hand at the small of her back. "I've got a bottle of wine on ice at my house."

There was a time when she would have wanted this. "I don't—"

William used the hand at her back to turn her toward him. "This can't be a surprise. You've known I ..."

Francesca ought to tell William straight out that she had chosen Bryce, but .... "Before you say another word," she said, "are you still expecting me to sneak around in the night?"

Quick anger showed in his indrawn breath. "You know I regret our misunderstanding about that."

"Misunderstanding?" Her voice rose. "You made it clear you wanted me to be a modern and have a secret affair. When I refused, you went back to Prudence ... if you ever left."

"I've regretted that," William went on. "You must know."

"How would I know? You've never told me. You never say much of anything."

His lips pressed together. Then he burst out, "I know I can't talk as well as my silver-tongued brother, but I'm the one who cares for you."

Francesca put out her hands in a "stop" gesture. "If you had said all this when you should have ...."

After Bryce, could it have made a difference?

"I'm saying it now."

Without hesitation, Francesca came back, "It's too late."

The words hung between them. Faint thunder rumbled over on the east side of the valley.

Francesca walked away, half-expecting he would come after her.

When he did not, she knew he had no honorable offer to make.

By eight a.m., the entourage to Yellowstone got under way. Bryce had borrowed two Franklin touring cars from the Bar BC; he drove one with Ila and Macy in back. Harry and Hamm rode with Bobby Cowan, who drove the other. The Snake River's Dodge truck carried the Cox's copious luggage, foodstuffs, and outdoor cooking gear, with Ned Hanson at the wheel and Francesca beside him.

As the Grand Teton receded and Mount Moran became more prominent, they stopped to eat at Lunch Tree Hill near the Amoretti Inn on the Jackson Lake Shore. Bobby and Ned put up folding tables and chairs for lunch and Francesca brought out the picnic hamper with fried chicken, potato salad, and pickles.

Harry, Hamm, and the men from Snake River made sure there were no leftovers.

After lunch, they carried on to the north, leaving the lake behind for the dense lodgepole forest. By mid-afternoon, they reached Flagg Ranch.

Named by owner Ed Sheffield because the United States flag had flown over it when it was a military outpost, Flagg had been open with accommodation in tent houses since 1910. Nowadays, Ed offered trout fishing in the Snake, camping supplies, and fifteen rooms in the main building for a dollar a night. Meals were also a dollar.

The touring party alighted before the log lodge. While Harry, Hamm, and Ned rushed off to the swimming hole and hot springs on nearby Polecat

Creek, Ila let her considerable bulk down into a rocking chair. With a glance in Francesca's direction, she ordered, "Unpack my russet dinner dress and my riding habit for tomorrow."

Francesca opened her mouth and closed it.

A moment later, Bryce came out from seeing to their check-in. He must have heard, for after Bobby brought the luggage to each room, he showed her to Ila and Macy's chamber.

Francesca expected Bryce would leave her to serve as maid, but he came in and leaned against the heavy wooden bureau while she unfastened the leather straps on the suitcases and identified which one held feminine apparel. To her surprise, he stepped forward and peered into Macy's bag. "If she's wearing the russet, I'll hang his brown suit and," he riffled through the clothes, "this tie with orange stripes."

He stopped with Macy's beige dress shirt in his hands. With the bed between them, they looked at each other.

"Tomorrow night," Bryce's voice sounded thick, "at the Canyon Hotel."

Francesca had seen black and white photos of Yellowstone Lake, but they failed to do it justice. When they arrived by motor at West Thumb Geyser Basin, she caught her first glimpse of reflected sky turning the broad expanse of water ultramarine. Stretching away miles to the east, the lake lapped at the feet of the Absaroka Mountains, touched with snow on their peaks even in midsummer.

Though the plans were to picnic on the shore, Bryce refused to let her start preparations until she had a tour. Hissing pots of thick pink mud were surrounded by cracking crusts. Placid turquoise pools gave off pale steam, and springs lay rimmed by algae in hues of lime, chartreuse, rust, sienna, and mustard. Along the edge of the clear lake, bubbles emerged from the bottom, marking more thermal vents.

After lunch, riding Bayberry along a lakeshore bridle path, Francesca felt like a lady of leisure. For the next two days, she had no culinary responsibilities, nothing to do except sightsee, wear the lovely clothing in her valise, select her meals from a menu, sleep on a wide soft bed ....

With the anonymity of the Canyon Hotel, Bryce evidently meant for them to be together.

What should she do?

While she didn't want to be a modern girl and had no interest in a casual affair, she could not believe that was what Bryce intended.

A warning voice told her only time would reveal his true intentions.

Though their destination was the Canyon Hotel, they planned to dismount from horseback at the Lake Hotel, an impressive building with porticos and tall white columns overlooking the water. Bobby and Ned saw to the horses, getting them ready for the hands to trailer back to Snake River. Bryce led the way into the hotel, where at five o'clock they were not out of place in riding clothes.

Ila commandeered a seat in the lobby while Francesca went to a window overlooking cobalt waters. Rowboats and small fishing vessels berthed below the bluff at wooden docks, alongside gleaming cabin cruisers renting space for the summer. Harry and Hamm dashed down the drive to throw rocks into the lake.

Bryce joined Francesca at the window. Behind them, Ila said, "Look, Macy, do you suppose those two ...?"

Francesca did not catch the reply. Were she and Bryce so obvious?

If he heard, he did not show it. "This place was much different back in 1900 when Mom and Dad fell for each other here. A single wing of rooms and a smaller lobby over near the fireplace." He pitched his voice a little louder. "Expansions took place in ought-four and ought-five, designed by Robert Reamer, who built the Old Faithful Inn at about the same time."

"You sound like a tour guide."

"I am." He glanced at the Coxes and moved farther away.

Convinced they had privacy, Francesca said, "I thought you stayed away from home because you didn't like dealing with the dudes."

"Not at all." Bryce kept his regard on the vista. "I stayed away because there isn't room for both me and William. My parents have made it clear which son they want to take over."

"You said you've come back for good," she said carefully.

"I did say that."

Ila Cox raised her voice. "Bryce? Can we get a drink here?"

He put on his dude wrangling mask. "I'm so sorry, Mrs. Cox, but the bootlegging in the park was put out of business five years ago. The Lake Hotel Assistant Manager, head porter, and front clerk got caught doing business." He lowered his voice. "I've got a flask in my luggage for when we get to Canyon."

Macy chimed in, "I've got some 'medicinal' brandy in my bag, too."

When the time came to head north, Bryce put a hand on Francesca's arm and led her to the passenger seat of the car he was driving. He whispered at her ear, "If the Coxes are on to us, it doesn't matter."

As the two Franklins and the Dodge truck traveled north in caravan along the Yellowstone River, the sun slanted lower. For a few miles, the Grand Loop Road meandered through dense forest, redolent of pine. On their right, the shining silver stream of the Yellowstone River flashed in the sun. Within an hour, sulfurous fumes from the Dragon's Mouth Spring and the Sulphur Caldron swept across the road.

A mile farther on, the thick forest gave way to a vista of broad valley, covered with a sea of grass and sage. The Yellowstone meandered across its floor. As they drove on, Francesca spied the red roof of the Canyon Hotel on a hill, nearly ten miles away.

"Back in 1890, there was a single wing," Bryce said. "Then in 1910, this million dollar structure took shape over a single winter."

"I cannot believe there is such a huge hotel in the middle of Yellowstone," Ila marveled from the rear seat.

Bryce chuckled. "The building is supposed to be over a mile around the outside."

Francesca expected they would go directly to the hotel, but Bryce took a side road at the lower end of Hayden Valley to view the Grand Canyon of the Yellowstone before they lost the sun.

From the smooth surface of the river in Hayden Valley, one would never expect the sudden gorge that cut twelve hundred feet into rocks made rotten by the invasion of hot mineral-laden waters. Steep slopes topped with cathedral-like spires had been carved by wind and water into fantastic shapes.

The river that powered the trenching ran swiftly and cascaded in great waterfalls, pouring in a green flood to the brink of the cliff, then plunging through the narrowed neck in a white roar.

Once the caravan started on, Francesca got her first close sighting of the hotel.

The massive edifice had a long central wing, with additions angling off in several directions. A wide drive inclined up hundreds of feet to the crown of the hill and split into an oval that ran beneath a porte-cochère at the grand entry.

Porters with wheeled carts whisked the luggage away and valets drove the vehicles to the parking area.

Bryce escorted Francesca up the covered walkway to the main entrance. "The hotel staff will see to the Cox's unpacking. All you have to do is bathe and dress for dinner."

Feeling like Cinderella, Francesca found the scale of the interior staggering, at least five hundred feet from end to end. Abundant columns divided the vast lobby into conversation pits furnished with leather furniture. Pillars also marched through the dining room, a short flight of steps down.

A grand staircase from the lobby ascended to the hotel's stunning focal point, the lounge. Huge trusses supported its ceiling, creating an unbroken space nearly two hundred feet long and a hundred wide.

While Francesca took in the largest building she had ever been in, including the cathedrals of *Firenze*, Bryce approached the desk across from the main door.

When he retraced his steps across the gleaming wood floor, he carried a handful of skeleton keys.

"Suites for Ila and Macy, and one that connects for Harry and Hamm," he said. "Rooms in the old wing for Ned and Bobby."

Bobby took his key. "Ned and I want to go back down to the falls. We'll get dinner in the café."

Harry and Hamm chimed in. "Can we go, too?"

"May you—" Ila prompted.

"May we?" the boys chorused.

Their mother nodded.

Bryce placed a key on Francesca's palm. Etched into the shining brass tag, the number 327. A glance at his showed 329.

All too soon, Bryce and Francesca stood in front of a pair of doors. Before he could speak, the creak of wheels signaled the porter with luggage cart. "Mr. Sutton ... Miss dee Pauli?"

"Close enough." Bryce fingered the bills in his pocket for a tip.

They handed the porter their keys; he unlocked her room first. After arranging her valise on the luggage rack, he assisted Bryce. The rooms were mirror image, brass beds and willow furniture.

Bryce stepped back out into the hall.

Francesca's door was half open. Inside, she stood by her open bag, pulling out a white sleeveless dress he would have given six months of Morenci mine wages to see her in ... and out of.

He advanced into the room, looking over the long bathtub. "Looks like you can get cleaned up," he said inanely. Where was the gift of gab William always gigged him over?

Something about Francesca, her regal bearing, made him feel like a stammering schoolboy. "I'll meet you downstairs," he finished.

Francesca arrived in the lounge before Bryce or the Coxes and took a seat at a writing table against the wall. A rack of postcards pictured aspects of the hotel and the park; she wished she had someone to write to.

But who would she send a missive to? William? Laura?

As she riffled the cards, her stomach tightened. With Laura's hopes for her and William, what would she say if Francesca and Bryce returned from Yellowstone a couple?

As if summoned by her thought, Bryce appeared at the top of the stairs. With his sun-streaked hair brushed back, he cut an elegant figure in a fine dark wool suit.

Francesca re-racked the cards and drew the scarlet shawl around her. The feeling of being Cinderella returned when Bryce sauntered over and dropped a kiss on her cheek. "You look beautiful. I wish we didn't have to play host and hostess."

She suppressed a leap of excitement at being termed hostess to his host.

With his hand beneath her shawl, touching bare skin where the white dress cut low, Bryce guided her toward the bar. "Seltzer, please, with lemon. Two times."

Taking the glasses to the writing desk, Bryce brought out a flask and poured a colorless liquid into the drinks. "Gin, gin, the wages of sin," he chuckled. "Will you sin with me, Francesca?"

Whatever they did, she did not think she would feel sinful.

Bryce handed over her glass and clinked his against it. "What shall we drink to?"

Praying his wandering days had truly passed, she repeated the toast she'd offered the first time they drank together. "To journey's end."

Before she could gauge his reaction, Bryce whispered, "Don't look now, but Mrs. C is coming our way with hubby in tow."

In the spacious dining room, Francesca sat at Bryce's left hand, the Coxes across. Their waiter, Thomas from Illinois, passed the menus and they ordered more set-ups for Bryce's gin and Macy's medicinal brandy.

Francesca studied the *table d'hôte*, lettered in red beneath a line drawing of the Lower Falls of the Yellowstone.

As a chef, Francesca enjoyed imagining how she would prepare each dish. She visualized what the uninitiated would term chaos in the hotel kitchen, while the men and women assigned to breads and pastries, salads, meats, vegetables, and dessert went efficiently about their business.

After they ordered, talk turned to the new boyish fashions that designers had unveiled in Paris for spring. "You'd look absolutely smashing in them, my dear," Ila suggested to Francesca.

Bryce gave a wry chuckle. "My mother's been wearing trousers for twenty-six years."

Over the appetizer, Macy mentioned he either wanted to purchase a new Cadillac LaSalle, a twenty-five hundred dollar car, or a Chrysler 72 Crown Sedan at eighteen hundred. He sought Bryce's opinion, who said he wasn't familiar with those models but did enjoy driving the Franklin.

© BY HAYNES, ST. PAUL

Menu

TABLE D'HOTE

Sunday, August 8, 1926

Dinner rolls
Consomme Rice   Cream of Lima Beans
Pearl Onions   Garden Radishes
Medallion of Salmon, Victor Hugo
Boiled Potatoes
Casserollette of Fresh Crab Meat, Dewey
Boiled Silver Bow Bacon, Spinach
Homemade Noodles   Saute Polonaise
Stewed Tomatoes   Mashed Potatoes
Broiled Sirloin   Steak Minute
Salad en Season
French or Epicurian Dressing
Peach Charlotte
Pistachio Ice Cream   Assorted Cake
Cottage Cheese   Saltines
Tea   Coffee   Milk   Iced Tea

CANYON HOTEL   YELLOWSTONE PARK
Souvenirs and Curios—The Canyon Art Shop—Entrance from the Lounge

Ila focused again on Francesca. "What do you think of the ruling finding Mae West guilty of indecency in her Broadway production of *Sex*?"

Francesca lifted her chin. "I'm afraid I'm not familiar with the show. It's been almost two years since I walked down Broadway." While carrying Mrs. Coldwell's fur to storage, she peered at the theater posters with longing.

Sometime between the crab casserole and the salad, Bryce slipped off his shoe and slid his sock foot up Francesca's calf. She looked everywhere but at him, the tips of her ears hot.

Ila fixed Bryce with the direct and demanding gaze of the schoolteacher she had been before marrying, revealed over her Medallion of Salmon, Victor

Hugo. "I'm wondering if you might let us in on something." Her black eyes moved to Francesca, her small mouth pursed. "Is your girl here the future chatelaine of Snake River Ranch?"

Francesca choked. Bryce lifted his water goblet and brought it to her lips in a solicitous gesture.

She swallowed, coughed again. Perhaps with this distraction, Bryce wouldn't have to answer.

Ila was like a dog with a new bone. "Macy," she said slyly, "I think he's shy."

"Not at all, Mrs. Cox," Bryce said smoothly. "I've been trying to convince Francesca to marry me, but I'm afraid she prefers my brother."

When Ila laughed, Bryce knew he'd made a mistake. He grabbed Francesca's hand under the table and willed her to look at him, but her expression could have frozen the ranch pond in August.

When she spoke, it was to the Coxes, the pitch of her voice too high. "Bryce likes to joke. I appreciate your interest, but I ... I'm afraid neither of the Sutton men have made me any kind of honorable offer."

Thomas from Illinois inquired if they wanted anything else. Bryce asked for the check.

Moments later, they entered the lobby. From the lounge came the strains of the orchestra. "One dance?" he hoped.

She kept moving in the direction of the spiral staircase and brought her key out of her pocket.

"Francesca, please."

She stopped, stiff-shouldered, her back to him.

"Dance with me," he said humbly. "It's an honorable offer."

She turned her head, her silken hair rippling; he wanted to put his hands in it. "I don't ...."

Bryce gently urged her up the staircase to the lounge. He faced Francesca, got her hand in his and placed his other at her waist.

He drew her closer. She fit well in his arms; he'd never danced with a woman he could look in the eye.

When the song ended without her thawing, he drew her out of the traffic pattern behind a pillar. "Everyone thinks I'm a bounder, based on past history." He swallowed. "I've stopped wandering."

"You say so, but I can't handle jokes about ...."

He'd been stupid to mention marriage. Having done so, he'd painted himself into a corner.

Why had he brought it up?

Francesca was so damned beautiful; her eyes tear-bright in the illumination from the mammoth art glass lanterns. Always beautiful, whether dressed for dinner or sweating over the cookshack fire, changing Bitter Waters's soiled linens, or risking her life on the Grand to yank him back from the precipice.

Had Bryce's subconscious mind brought the truth to the surface? Had his trip to bury the last of the generation before his father's made him realize it was time to stop simply saying he'd changed and find out if his and Francesca's separate journeys might end with each other?

He took her face in his hands. "It wasn't a joke, Francesca."

The seeds sown the summer before, when a rodeo cowboy came into her kitchen, blossomed into flower. Like Cinderella in a role that would brook no midnight, Francesca walked with Bryce up the spiral staircase.

At her door, he accepted her key, escorted her inside, and closed out the world.

His eyes darkened; the corners of his moustache went down. He hooked his thumbs in her shawl and drew it down to bare her arms.

The room had cooled with the night chill—by morning, it might dip to freezing outside—but Francesca could not conceive of ever being cold again. When Bryce picked her up effortlessly, one arm at her back and the other behind her knees, she wound her arms around his neck.

He lowered her onto the bed and lay down beside her. "Better than a carpet of pine needles."

Beginning with the top button of the white dress, Bryce trailed his lips down her skin as he revealed it. Basking in his appreciative gaze, Francesca forgot all the months spent yearning for his return.

Tonight, there was certainty.

And sensation, rippling down her spine, when he put his hot mouth over her pebbled nipple. She bit her lip to suppress any sounds that would cue those in neighboring rooms.

He moved gently to worship her other breast, then helped remove the rest of her garments. All the while, she detected his ever-present electricity.

Naked before him for the first time, she lifted her chin and her ribcage with pride. His pupils dilated, his indrawn breath told her everything she needed to know.

Never again would she envy better endowed women.

Bryce's torso, bronzed from working shirtless outdoors, bore springy sun-bleached curls that brushed her nipples and sent shocks skittering down her nerves.

They kissed, slowly and deeply, until passion overcame their attempts to savor the experience.

"Bryce ...."

He fumbled out a condom and soon they joined, hot and desperate, sweat slick, striving.

Both muffled bittersweet cries, he in the pillow, she with her teeth pressed against his shoulder.

It wasn't perfect.

By the third time, long and slow, and sweet, Francesca was beginning to think it might be.

Chapter Thirty-two
August 9, 1926

Francesca, Bryce, Ned and Bobby returned to Snake River late, after dropping the Coxes at the Crabtree Hotel in Jackson and the Franklin automobiles at the Bar BC. Lights in the Main, along with silhouettes of people on the porch, indicated the dudes had not yet called it an evening. No sign of the elder Suttons, but Francesca spied William sitting in a rocker next to an attractive blonde who couldn't be Prudence Johnston, but resembled her.

Bryce drove the Dodge truck with their luggage to the equipment shed, where Francesca waited while the men offloaded bags. As soon as Bobby and Ned took off for the bunkhouse, Bryce and Francesca gave up their efforts not to exchange the kind of looks that would give them away.

Everything had changed and yet was the same.

"I suppose we could go to the lean-to ...." Bryce trailed off. "Or we could take some blankets to the Timbered Island and get eaten by mosquitoes." His light tone made her heart sink.

Had bedding her been his goal? Had his talk of marriage been a joke, after all?

They walked up the road together; he carried both their bags.

Their silence lengthened.

"Ah, hell," Bryce said, "we've got to do something about this."

"What?" Francesca held her breath.

"Tomorrow, we'll go down to Mom and Dad's, during your lull between lunch and dinner, and tell them about us."

∽∾

Next morning at breakfast, Bryce had trouble keeping the news to himself. After eggs and bacon, he brought his plate into the Main kitchen, dropped a kiss on Francesca's full warm lips, and cast about for how to spend his morning. If he wanted to socialize, he could guide a trail ride, or work off his restless energy mucking out stalls.

Instead, he found himself on the bluff overlooking the lower bench, near the lone cottonwood.

Having an idea that Francesca would share his appreciation of the site, Bryce started to pace off dimensions. A spacious living room here, with a fireplace that also opened into the master bedroom. Windows at both ends, one facing the Tetons and the other the river view. It wouldn't be a thing like William's simple bachelor house or his parents' modest home, but a place of style and beauty for Francesca.

Gathering rocks from the soil, he began placing them in lines, marking the exterior and interior walls. Here was where his future with Francesca would play out. After they saw his folks this afternoon, he'd bring her here.

"What the hell you doing, Brother?"

Bryce turned to William with a smile. Nothing could spoil his mood today. "Building a house for Francesca."

William studied the outline of the plan. "Little large for a woman alone."

Bryce tossed the rock he'd been about to place along the living room wall from one hand to the other. "She's not gonna be alone. There'll be room for me and our kids."

William's expression went from bland to murderous. "Oh, no, you don't."

"I don't what?"

"You don't waltz in here after being gone for a year and take Fran ...."

"Away from you? Got some news, she isn't yours."

"Or yours."

"You had a year to win her. And a bonus two weeks. Time's up."

William scowled. "You'll run away from her the way you do everyone. It's bad enough you come and go and break Mother's and Father's hearts—"

"Forget breaking hearts. I've asked Francesca to marry me."

Bryce saw William make fists.

"You'll leave, all right," William cried. "And when you do, Fran will see who the real man is." He and his brother had engaged in plenty of fisticuffs when they were kids and traded tough talk once they reached manhood. Never had Bryce seen such pure rage in William, as his shoulders squared and his hands came up in a prize-fighter stance.

Bryce became aware of the rock in his hand, his fingers curled around it so tightly they were going numb.

William spoke through gritted teeth. "I ought to beat you senseless for toying with Fran."

As clearly as if it were happening, Bryce saw what would come next. William would throw a punch ... Bryce's own hand fortified with stone ....

He let the rock fall from his nerveless fingers. Quietly, he said, "What happens isn't up to you or me, but Francesca."

He walked away, his back muscles drawing up like drying leather. Would William attack from behind?

He did, with words. "You don't have the guts to stay long enough to build a house, much less marry and have kids."

Bryce kept moving, letting the wind sweep away William's voice.

To avoid another confrontation with William in the Main, Bryce ate lunch in the outfit dining hall. Awaiting the appointed hour when he was to meet Francesca at the cookshack, he wandered the bluff again.

With his stomach sour from the less than stellar meal Jim had prepared, he tried to calm down. Now wasn't the time to let his lifelong competition with William get in the way. Not when even Francesca had questioned whether he cared for her or just wanted to take his brother's toy as he might have at age four.

Cared for her?

Lord, he hadn't told her he loved her. Hadn't formally asked her to marry him, just told her he hadn't been joking with the Coxes.

What was wrong with him?

According to William, words were Bryce's stock in trade. But Francesca had a way of striking him speechless. Perhaps it stemmed from his desire to keep his tongue from running away with him, to be sure he spoke only the truth to her.

Bryce wished he had a ring, a diamond that would put everyone's eye out with its brilliance. He'd get down on one knee before Francesca, to solemnize that he'd found his journey's end.

When Bryce reached the cookshack, he tapped on the door. "Francesca?"

The portal swung open a few inches. Something in the quality of the stillness told him she wasn't there.

Checking his watch, he decided she must have gotten held up in the kitchen over in the Main.

Whistling, his thumbs slung through his belt loops, Bryce hurried along the path. He considered going in the front door and discarded it to move on light feet to the rear entry.

No Francesca, but there were voices beyond the kitchen.

Bryce despised eavesdropping, but when he heard William's voice, he forgot his scruples.

"... cockamamie nonsense he'll build you a house. He's never followed through on anything in his life."

A female reply ... unintelligible.

Bryce looked though the round glass window in the swinging door.

William and Francesca stood in the space before the fireplace. Brother's face was red, his bunched fists on his hips, her expression anguished. Worst of all, Mom and Dad were with them.

Mom put a hand on Francesca's shoulder. "I hate to agree, but I'm afraid William's right. He has always been a gadabout."

Bryce shoved into the big room, just as Dad chimed in, "I find it hard to believe Bryce actually asked you to marry him."

Francesca lifted her tear-stained face. "He hasn't—"

"Stop it!" Bryce shouted. Even as he advanced on them, he saw on their shocked faces that his outburst played into their hands. "I'm twenty-four, old enough to know what I want." He moved toward her and found William blocking his way. "Brother, I warn you—"

"Or you'll what?" William sneered. "Beat me up like a kid on the schoolyard?"

Dad's hand came down heavy on Bryce's shoulder. "Come on, son. The time's past for you and William to fight."

Bryce knocked the hand off. "We're not fighting over a baseball or whose turn it is to use the Flexible Flyer for a sled run. I told this son of a bitch," he saw his mother blanch, "that Francesca and I are getting married, and he's unwilling to accept that I won."

Looking from Dad to Mom, he rushed on, "I came home this summer in good faith, because Dad was ill. I helped nurse Bitter Waters and traveled to see him home." His voice broke and his focus shifted to William. "But nothing has changed here. The firstborn is still favored, and he'll stop at nothing to set me back on the road to ensure his status."

Pushing past everyone, Bryce took Francesca by the shoulders.

She looked into his face, and saw doubt and rage radiating from him. Where was the certainty with which he had taken her at the Canyon Hotel?

Was his family right? Did they understand Bryce better than she did? Had she been swept off her feet by smooth talk?

"Tell them, Francesca," Bryce drilled. "Tell them about us."

She opened her mouth ... to say what? That she'd gone to bed with him?

"Francesca," Bryce said. "This isn't the way I wanted to do this, but ... I love you. I want you to marry me." His tone wasn't lover-like but strident. As if he were a child demanding his toy.

He turned to the others, slashing his hand sideways. "Will you get out of here so Francesca and I can talk?"

Laura blinked. Cord took her by the shoulders. "Come on."

They started to move in the direction of the big doors. William stood his ground until Cord turned back. "Son."

William didn't look at Bryce or Francesca as he followed his parents.

As soon as they were gone, she expected Bryce would sweep her into his arms to quiet her doubts.

Instead, he began to pace. "Have you any idea," he asked the fireplace, "what it took for me to say that in front of them? With their looks of disbelief saying plain they thought I was just talking to hear myself?"

Francesca twisted her hands together. "Bryce ...."

He stopped and came to her at last, crushed her to his heart. "We'll get married. I'll build us a house on the bluff you love. William will go to Texas."

With a gasp, she tore herself from Bryce's grasp. She staggered; jerked away to avoid his outstretched hands. "Damn William and damn you. Growing up a servant, I'd have given anything to have a place like Snake River Ranch. I'd gladly have shared it, even with my cousins who joined Mussolini's Black Shirts. It's criminal that you and your brother can't see past your petty penchant ...." At Bryce's raised brow, she blasted him. "Yes, I said *penchant*. I'm no longer a helpless immigrant who knows little English and has to accept charity. I could walk out of here today and take care of myself, because I have the pride to refuse to be a pawn on yours and William's chessboard."

When she stopped, struggling for breath, Bryce faced her with tears in his eyes. "God, Francesca, if I thought it would make a difference I'd get down on my knees."

"Go get down on your knees to your parents and ask them to forgive you for all the years you haven't been here for them, because you think you've been somehow wronged. Tell your brother there's room for you both on this land I've come to love so much."

Bryce shook his head. "You don't believe in me, either."

He started for the door.

Pain sliced through Francesca, cutting off her breath, making her understand that one's blood could run cold. She did love him. She wanted nothing more than to marry him, to see their sons grow up to ride the range, as more than brothers ... as friends. "Don't ...." she choked.

He stopped. Twin tear tracks made paths into his moustache; his eyes were red-rimmed. "If you can honestly say you believe in me, that you'd stake your life I'd never leave you ...."

Did she believe she could be his journey's end?

They needed time to get to know each other better, to sit on the porch in rockers in the evening and talk about their day. Perhaps, then, she could stake her life on not waking up some morning and finding him gone.

They looked at each other without speaking.

He walked away.

Bryce threw his clothes into his duffle. Thank God, the bunkhouse was empty at this hour.

The bunkhouse!

What kind of place was that for the Suttons' son? Dad had bankrolled William's bachelor house, had the outfit do the work. Had anyone ever suggested Bryce should have a place to come home to? Had they even thought that if he had a place here, remotely equivalent to the firstborn's, he might come more often and stay longer?

Amazing how wrong he'd been. He'd believed, even in his darkest hour of gritting his teeth over William playing crown prince, that at some level his parents loved him best. Brother might be the rock, but Bryce had always been the family showman, the darling of any gathering.

Never had he imagined his folks saw him as unreliable. A wanderer, sure, with the cachet that accompanied the designation—a seeker of adventure—but never had he suspected they viewed him in such low regard.

And Francesca felt the same. She might want him, might even love him, but he'd seen plain on her face that she doubted he was husband material.

Feeling as though she and his parents had driven a spike through his chest, Bryce saddled Bayberry. He left a note for one of the outfit to get the horse from Wort's livery in Jackson.

Chapter Thirty-three
Autumn, 1926

When September ended, Francesca was still at Snake River. One, she lacked the heart to move on, and two, what she had told Bryce was true. Even if the Sutton sons did not appreciate the place where they had been born and grown up, she did. The valley, the Tetons, and the Snake River Ranch had insinuated themselves so deeply under her skin that no other place held any allure.

Day by day, she worked at making appetizing meals for the Main, ate, and tasted nothing. She no longer went riding or tended the garden; not even in sleep did she find respite for the pain behind her breastbone.

The trouble was that each time she fell asleep, she risked dreaming.

Dreams ... a two-edged sword. Would her nightscape be one of living and loving with Bryce atop the bluff, or a monster scenario? Of a hollow-eyed Laura handing her a telegram from Morenci: *Mr. and Mrs. Sutton stop Regret inform you mine accident stop Await instructions per remains stop.*

Whether her dreams were joyful or horrifying, they ended the same way. With tears streaming down her temples and pooling in her ears.

Why hadn't she died when Bryce left? How could one suffer such pain without the release of death?

Fortunately, or unfortunately, Carla and Antonio had not raised her to succumb. Each morning, Francesca dragged herself upright, squared her shoulders and kept them that way until she lay down again at night.

As for William, when she stopped appearing in the Main's dining room, he didn't ask why. He spent a lot of time entertaining the dudes, especially the youngest and prettiest female in each group. If he bedded them, Francesca neither knew nor cared.

Each day when the mail arrived, she had to admit there was a third reason she stayed. Only there might she get word of Bryce.

Hating herself for her weakness, she waited.

ᖇᖇ

William stayed away from the ranch, and Fran, as much as possible. He volunteered to take the dudes on extended campouts into the Tetons, where he salved his ego with female guests who sought romance with a cowboy beside the campfire. Bobby had caught on to the campouts for the same reason, even cleaned up his language a bit.

The key difference was that Bobby went through a supply of prophylactics, while a single tin of three remained unopened in William's pack. Sure, he paid extravagant compliments to Mary from Milwaukee and Paula from Petaluma, but kept to the bounds of propriety.

Because he lacked interest in any woman but Fran.

With roundup next month and the dude season winding down, he had some decisions to ponder. Should he go to Texas and start a new life, as he'd mentioned to Father a few weeks earlier? Should he go to Fran and suggest—demand—that she leave the ranch to end his torment?

As the weeks following Bryce's departure flowed into months, William weighed options and found them all wanting.

One day, while walking on the bluff, he happened upon the stones Bryce had laid out, and had an idea so filled with possibility that his spirits soared. Executing it required patience until the right time, but with the plan came hope.

ᖇᖇ

Near the end of September, William traveled to Bozeman to represent Snake River at the inaugural meeting of the newly formed Dude Ranchers Association. The prospect of the trip was too draining for Cord.

On the first day of October, Cord awaited his son's return in a rocker on the Main's front porch. Out of sorts because his *Jackson's Hole Courier* had not come the day before, he sat and reflected on a newspaper story by Billy Owen a few weeks past. Some climbers had attempted the Grand by a route other than the one Billy had laid out when Laura and the kids went up. And almost died failing.

Cord had failed without leaving the trailhead. Looking back, should he have tried? Or had the same instinct that had kept him home from Bozeman been the right one? Hiding his increasing fatigue from Laura became more difficult with each passing month.

William's recent renewed mention of Texas was the worst of it. What did his son see in that faraway place of sweltering heat and rattlesnakes, when paradise lay at the foot of the Tetons?

Sadly, Cord knew what he sought there. Charlie had been right when he pointed out that, orphaned at six, Cord had never had to live in the shadow of a vital Franklin Sutton.

How had William and Bryce become so competitive? Had he and Laura encouraged it somehow? Having them race on Eli and Jacob should only have fostered a healthy desire to excel. And when William had been slow at reading, had he resented Bryce's facility with words?

Tears stood in Cord's eyes as he searched his heart.

How easy it had been that terrible day, to let William ridicule Bryce's desire to marry Francesca and live on the bluff, how simple to fall into the old knee-jerk reaction and brand Bryce too immature for love and commitment.

What chilled Cord was that this time they might have been wrong. If they hadn't all ganged up on Francesca and drilled her with how Bryce couldn't be trusted, would she have stood up for him ... with him?

Cord sighed. With Bryce God knew where, he must find a way to keep William in his life.

৩৽৵

William pulled his Model T up in front of the Main with Struthers Burt in the passenger seat. "There's Father." He honked the horn and waved.

"A shame he missed the meeting." Burt unlatched the car door.

William joined Father on the porch, hugging him more closely than he'd intended in front of Burt. Father settled back into a rocker and gestured at two more. "How was the meeting?"

Burt chuckled. "You wouldn't think, after all of us being in the business so many years, there'd be any question of what a dude ranch is."

"Indeed?"

"That's what we spent the most time on. Should we keep or drop the term 'dude'? After hours of wrangling, we decided to keep it. Then Dick Randall and the Eaton brothers proposed we define 'dude' as 'an outsider who pays for lodging, riding, hunting, or other services.' "

"They're outsiders, all right." William laughed. "Of course, we specified the term had no association with greenhorns or tenderfeet."

"Of course," Father said dryly, making it clear he'd seen his share of those as guests.

"We have to be polite; dudes are our bread and butter," Burt said. "The vote was unanimous that we adopt the definition and the name Dude Ranchers Association."

William jumped in, "But, it turns out we had three types of ranches represented at the meeting. Those who used to work stock and added dudes later—like Snake River—those like Bar BC—started for dudes—and the hot springs taking guests."

Burt brought out his cigarettes. "There was a lot of talk about needing to standardize practices."

"Don't see that," Father replied. "You show your folks a good time your way and I'll do it the way I see fit."

When Burt fumbled in his pocket, William stepped inside the Main for a box of their trademark matches and passed them over. Their neighbor went on, "Lately I've been hosting a lot of writers. And Katharine and I have been spending time on our private ranch so we can write."

"Times are changing. I don't know how long Laura and I will—"

"Father!" William interrupted. "You've got Charlie and me to keep things going even if you take it easy."

"A while back you were talking about Texas again."

Blood rushed to William's cheeks. He'd never expected Father to challenge him in front of Burt.

"Burt as good as helped raise you," Father pointed out. "He knows what's what."

Thankfully, Burt changed the subject. "When we put together the local chapter of the Dude Ranchers Association, they'll be openings for officers."

Father put out his hands. "I'm beyond all that." His sharp blue gaze fell on William. "How about it, son? You ready to help make sure someone like Dieter Gross doesn't run our local group?" He paused. "Or are you leaving?"

Father was right. Burt had been around since William was old enough to remember; he did know what was what.

Having decided his course on the bluff, William lifted his chin. "I've decided Bryce is the wanderer. I'll be happy to serve the Association."

At season's end, Francesca saw Rosa and Maria off to their winter work at the Excalibur in Salt Lake City. She wished Ned luck in his sophomore year at La Salle—Francesca didn't know it, but Ned had experienced a very successful summer, tutored by a waitress at the Bar BC—one Nellie from Nebraska.

This year, no one asked Francesca if she would go or stay.

Ironically, William solved the problem for her. He informed her that oil drilling, begun over in Driggs back in 1925, was continuing with some step-out wells to enlarge the field. A local driller had hired a rig out of Louisiana, with tool pusher B.J. Thibodeaux. The long and short of it was they needed a cook for the next few months, until the well either came in dry or winter weather shut down operations until spring.

Francesca would have agonized over the decision to leave Snake River, but William expedited her interview, applauded when she landed the job, and drove her over The Pass and up to Driggs in his Model T.

Apparently he couldn't wait to see the last of her. Laura, too, had encouraged her to "help out" and made no protest about losing her services. Francesca could only think William had decided to see Prudence Johnston or some other woman and wanted her gone.

Surprisingly, it stung. Not only stung, but when William dropped her at the drilling camp on the high plateau, with the wheat fields all golden stubble beneath October's brilliant blue sky, he smiled. Then leaped into his car, and, with a jaunty wave, deserted her.

Cast adrift, Francesca threw herself into work. The crew, comprised of strong young men, could not have been more different from the Wyoming cowboys. Their Texas drawls and Cajun patois set them apart, an itinerant band that followed the rig. Though they made her feel welcome, she didn't want to believe she had become a gypsy like them.

If she had only said no to this job, she'd be surrounded by her friends, the Suttons, Asa, Jim, Charlie, Ben and Anne, instead of listening to the crew carp about being away from home for Thanksgiving. But were the people at Snake Ranch her friends?

No word came for her from anyone at the ranch. Recalling her experience with the postcards at the Canyon Hotel, she took up pen and paper several times to write to ... Laura? William?

Each time she prayed her rosary, she gripped the blue beads and recalled William's shoulder warm against hers during the Christmas Eve service in the Chapel of the Transfiguration. Despite his mention of Texas, he was the one still at the ranch helping his folks.

Francesca's pain at Bryce's departure had metamorphosed to rage. How dare he toy with her? How typical that he'd shown her the same callous disregard he did his family.

Two days before Christmas, the well came up dry. Twenty minutes after word spread, B.J. Thibodeaux showed up at the kitchen hut; it was cozy and warm from both the coal-fired cookstove and the potbellied one on the hearth.

Thibodeaux twisted his winter hat in his hands. "Miss Francesca, I reckon we be movin' on." His black eyes turned bold. "You want to try a warmer climate, you come along with us to California."

Francesca's hand stilled in the dough she kneaded. "California," she repeated.

Thibodeaux nodded, his inky hair shifting above sharp black brows. "Will ... you be far from the wine country?"

"We be drilling in the inland valley, not far from Sacramento."

This move would take her where she had once wanted to go.

"So?" Thibodeaux asked respectfully. "What you say?"

Francesca closed her eyes to envision rounded hills covered with the contouring green of vines ... and saw the views from the bluff at Snake River Ranch—the Tetons, covered with snow, pearl white with deep bluish shadows.

"Thank you for the offer, Mr. Thibodeaux," she said, "but I believe I'll stick around here."

If she could.

When Francesca phoned Snake River, her palm was slick on the phone in the Rancher in Driggs. Wind whistled through the air gaps between the worn boards of the old bar; she must be crazy to want to winter over in the valley again.

The ranch phone rang for a long time. If William answered, would his voice reveal his feelings? Maybe Charlie would pick up and she could ask how the land lay.

"Snake River Ranch," said Laura.

"It's—"

"Francesca! Have they shut down drilling for the winter?"

"The well is dry. They have asked me to go to California."

A beat of silence. "Oh, dear, I know that's what you wanted."

And another. "I ... would like to come back to Snake River."

The seconds before Laura replied seemed an eternity, while Francesca waited.

Finally, unwilling to beg, she said, "I know you must have all the help you need there, so I'll just ...." She started to lower the earpiece.

Laura came back faintly over the line, "If you can get over The Pass, I'll have someone pick you up in Jackson Square."

Chapter Thirty-four
Christmas, 1926

On Christmas Eve morning, Francesca served the last breakfast of eggs, sausage and biscuits to the drilling crew. She gathered her belongings and Thibodeaux drove her down to Victor to take the mail sleigh over The Pass.

The last few days had delivered a bitter blast. Wearing the shearling hat William had bought her, her heavy coat, and the boots she'd climbed the Grand in—with extra wool socks—she hoped she was ready. Thankfully, clear weather blessed the day, the sun glittering on a fresh blanket of snow.

Everyone else must have reached their Christmas destinations; Francesca, the lone passenger, settled in beneath fur robes.

The ride began easily enough, the horses pulling smoothly up the long grade on the west side. When they reached the steep switchbacks near the top, the horses slowed.

By the time the tired animals achieved the divide, clouds had come up from the east side and ruined the excellent view of Jackson's Hole Francesca had been counting on. It began to snow, small stinging flakes that forced her to lift her muffler to cover everything but her eyes.

At Scott's Roadhouse on the crest, she and the driver alighted for a cup of hot tea and some warming time by the stove. Back outside, he went to a pile of snow-covered logs and attached one broadside with chains to drag behind the sleigh. "To slow us on the way down."

At the sight, Francesca's stomach fluttered. Too many stories of sleighs plunging off the road into deep drifts made her wary, especially with the swirling snow accumulating rapidly.

They started down very slowly, contouring the mountainside with a drop-off on the right and through a pair of sharp curves. Finally they reached the stretch of avalanche chute known as the Crater Lake run. Francesca imagined the Glory Bowl above, several thousand feet of steep, treeless slope carved by snow slides' repeated passage, and held her breath while the sleigh inched across the vulnerable zone. Back in 1913 and 1914, two mail carriers and a freighter had lost their lives in this very spot.

Suddenly, an unmistakable crack and boom .... A dull rumbling followed, and the driver whipped the horses and shouted for them to go faster.

Hampered by the log, they strained away.

In a minute they were past the chute's axis, but a cloud of snow mist enveloped them as the avalanche settled above the road.

They carried on; winter's early twilight and then darkness settled in. The snow squall let up, and when they rounded the final curve above Wilson, Francesca got a view of the valley floor. The cluster of town lights and scattered ones at ranches brought an ache to her throat.

Some of the lights came from ranchers placing lighted lanterns around the base of their hay piles to keep hungry elk away; if the animals just went to the refuge, they'd be welcomed and fed over the winter.

What kind of welcome would Francesca receive at Snake River?

What kind did she want?

After all the back and forth, was William to be her journey's end? No wild peaks and valleys, no passion that rose again and again in the night. Just warmth where she felt nothing but cold.

In Jackson Town, sleighs packed the square; the livery must be full.

"Christmas tree lighting tonight." The driver pulled up in front of the Crabtree Hotel's white clapboard length.

If no one from Snake River had made it in, Francesca might need their services.

The driver got her valise out; she looked around.

The sleigh had come in very late, if someone were here, they should come forward.

Just as the fact that the Crabtree and other Jackson hotels and rooming houses must be full hit her, she felt a tap on her shoulder.

She turned into a bear hug. William. She recognized him from the indefinable scent of his skin.

"I've been waiting hours," he declared, setting her back on her feet. "Now you're here, we'd better stay for the tree lighting. They have potluck and you must be starving."

He carried her valise and checked it, along with both their coats, then pointed out the groaning tables of food. Francesca had never thought she'd be happy to see beef and potatoes, but after the freezing temperatures on The

Pass, she loaded her plate with both. The heated Gymnasium, the chatter of everyone from little Benjy to his white-bearded great grandfather, the familiar valley faces ....

Folks talked about local fighter Mike Yokel's return from another tour in Australia. About the dwindling winter elk herd in the valley, down by half from 1925. And how Jackson Mayor Fred Lovejoy had suggested all the hoopla over extending Yellowstone or creating a new national park could be solved by making the Tetons a Wyoming state park. "Then we can keep it away from the bureaucrats."

"Is this an all-night event?" Francesca asked William.

He didn't look at her. "If we get weathered in, I've set you up with Anne and Ben in their suite at the Crabtree."

She was tired, but not too much to enjoy the pageantry. The American Legion, P.T.A., and churches had sponsored the big evergreen, and the program was all about children. The little people formed a nativity, piped carols in treble voices, and helped pass out sacks of candy, fruit, and nuts. Santa dandled Benjy and other youngsters on his knee to find out what they wanted delivered when he made tonight's rounds on his sleigh drawn by flying reindeer.

Jackson's former mayor, Grace Miller, joined Francesca and William in watching the children. "Snake River could use a few of those," she suggested.

It was as it had been last year, with everyone still waiting for what they believed was an inevitable announcement. Francesca's brief affair with Bryce had been hushed up by William to salve his pride, or dismissed as old news since Bryce had been gone again for months.

William draped his arm around Francesca's shoulder. "Some kids would liven the place up."

Had his sending her away been a tactic, the old playing-hard-to-get?

"How about it, you two?" Grace went on.

Francesca's cheeks warmed.

Grace turned to her. "What did you think of the—"

William cut her off. "We haven't been home yet."

Grace looked flustered. "Have you just come over The Pass from the drilling camp?"

"Yes, I ...."

Prudence Johnston materialized at William's elbow. Placing a possessive hand on his forearm, she said in her husky voice, "Have you been messing about in the kitchen again?" She looked coarser than the last time Francesca had seen her, wearing more makeup in an attempt to hide a bruise on her cheekbone. Below her knee-length hem, her chiffon hose had an ugly run. "I haven't seen you in too long," she told William in a suggestive tone.

Tiny Good's hand descended to grip her silk-clad shoulder, causing a clash of her beads. "C'mon, Pru," he growled.

Though the two of them left, Francesca felt as if the brightness had drained from the candles and Christmas lights. "I'm very tired," she told William.

At the Crabtree, the Raleighs welcomed her. Anne's bright eyes were clouded with sleep, a tousled toddler on her hip. Ben showed Francesca to a narrow bed in the room with J.C. and pointed out the sitting room sofa for William.

Exhausted as she was, Francesca couldn't sleep.

On Christmas morning, with the mercury plunging, William brought one of the Snake River sleighs to the front of the Crabtree. Francesca hugged Anne, kissed J.C., and greeted Romulus and Remus.

When William took the reins and settled beside her on the seat, she couldn't help but recall how his quick thinking had saved both their lives when the slide came down. He tucked the buffalo robe over both their legs. "Warm enough?"

They rode up the highway and across the winter bridge at Menor's Ferry. Snow began to fall. When they passed the turn to the Bar BC, Francesca inquired, "How are Burt and Katharine?"

"Gone east for the cold months."

As they drew closer to the ranch, she probed, "Your folks?"

"Father's hanging in; Mother's making sure he takes care of himself."

Once they reached Snake River, William guided Romulus and Remus toward the Main. At least Francesca thought so until he took the fork toward his parents' place. Maybe they were having a Christmas lunch in their home.

Before they had gone a hundred yards, William turned the team. there was no road here.

But there was, a new drive cut through the sage. "Where ...?"

William's laugh resounded. "You'll see."

The shape of a building materialized where none should be, a log house on the bluff by the lone cottonwood, where Francesca had prayed her rosary so many times.

Where Bryce had planned they would live.

Her heart started hammering. Bryce hadn't, he wasn't .... William wouldn't be taking her to him?

William helped her down from the sleigh. Brought out her bag.

She looked at the house. No one at the darkened doorway. Of course there wasn't. On the front porch sat a pair of rockers that someone ought to put away until warmer weather.

"This place is yours, Francesca," William said earnestly.

Bryce had laid out some rocks.

William had built her a house.

❧

William watched Fran as they walked through the house. Her eyes shone, her lips parted slightly.

Starting with the porch that wrapped all the way around, she exclaimed at each feature: the stained glass panel in the front door with a bunch of grapes in honor of her native Tuscany, the double fireplace serving the living and bedroom, the high windows at either end.

A new quilt in the wedding ring pattern covered the wide bed. Laura had made it while Fran was in Idaho.

In the kitchen, with the latest Glenwood cooking range in a creamy porcelain finish, Fran threw her arms around William's neck.

Though he wanted to drag her against him, he gave her a quick hard hug. "I thought you'd like the stove. It uses either wood or coal."

Fran's great almond eyes sought his. "It's all too much."

With an effort, he stuck to the strategy he'd determined. "It's all for you, with no strings attached. After the way my brother treated you, you deserve it."

❧

December 25, 1926

> It is difficult to believe 1927 is almost upon us.
>
> Last year brought joy and sorrow. Ascending the Grand at age fifty-two made me feel young again, but not having Cord with us provided a chilling preview of what I may have to face—life without my dearest love.
>
> Cord's role, and mine, in running the ranch continues to diminish, as Charlie and William take on more and more. Thank God Francesca has returned. We will see her in a little while at the Christmas dinner Jim and Asa are putting together.
>
> And William. While he was building Francesca's house, I have never seen him happier. He selected every log, directed the placement of every nail, and chose the furniture and lamps,

hoping they would be to her liking. I should like to have seen her face when he brought her in.

This past summer, when she fell for Bryce, I was of two minds. I hated to see William hurt, but my heart swelled with hope she might be the settling influence Bryce needed. How sharp my sorrow when he ran again.

After months of reflection, I must admit I can take no more of his senseless cuts. Though I will always love him, I shall harden my heart.

He may come back from time to time. He may write the occasional quick and breezy correspondence, telling me he has decided to go to sea and take up whaling. I will reply.

A blot of ink splotched the tail of Laura's "y." Of course she would answer, but never again would his leaving break her heart, or Cord's, if she could help it.

A new year is a time to look forward.

I pray Francesca sees the wisdom in choosing William. He may not have the flash, the gift of glib talk, but he has been Cord's and my rock, and he could be hers. Let them find happiness, let Cord hold a grandchild in his arms, so he might believe the cycle of our lives complete before ....

There are so many ifs. If William and Francesca do not make it this time, I believe he may leave for Texas, this time for good.

I must stop. I am writing myself into a depression with all these what ifs? Perhaps my dire mood stems from my freezing feet and ankles, though the fire burns in the grate. It is not as cold as in December of twenty-four (when it hit sixty below zero in Jackson), but in the past few days, the water pipes burst in the courthouse and my Christmas cactus froze inside the house. I have had enough of this winter, with months yet to go.

Charlie joined the family in the Main for Christmas dinner. The table was laid for seven: him and Harriet Lawrence, the Suttons and Francesca, and they expected Foster Case.

Jim and Asa served and then left to eat at their family tables. Bobby had gone to Idaho Falls two days earlier to visit his folks. Foster stopped by just in time to avoid holding up the blessing, and indicated he was seeing the cook at the Lazy D and would eat there.

As Foster left, the old fear roiled in the pit of Charlie's stomach, the feeling he got when his was the only black face in hostile territory. He tried to tamp it down; he was among friends, but he said, "I hope Foster doesn't say anything to Dieter Gross about Harriet being here."

"What if he does?" Laura said. "I mentioned to Foster earlier that I had invited Harriet since she was a woman alone. Why would he think she was with you?"

"People speculate," Charlie replied. "They see me on her street in Kelly, they wonder, even if I always wait until the coast is clear and go around the back."

Cord spoke to Harriet. "I still think you should move over here. We'll set you up in a private cabin, find some work for you during the season. That would make things less public and save Charlie a load of riding back and forth."

Harriet shook her head. "I'm proud of the house I bought in Kelly. I want to stay there."

Charlie groused, "We've plowed this ground, Cord. I read her the piece in the *Courier* the other day that warned how saturated the ground is after all the rain last fall. It's freezing up now, but Kelly's going to be in for it this spring. I've told her I don't want her in Kelly for snowmelt."

Harriet put her pale hand on Charlie's. "Everything will turn out all right."

Something in her inflection said she wasn't talking about moving to Snake River. Her plan was for them to move to Michigan, where they could marry legally.

Leaving Charlie with a tough decision.

Cord watched his foreman's consternation.

More and more lately, his life and Charlie's in the valley had become a house of cards. Pulling any of them might bring the whole thing down around their ears.

In 1920, Wyoming had passed a law against interracial marriage—it would have prevented Cord, as one quarter Nez Perce, from marrying Laura. Even now it questioned the legitimacy of their long union.

Michigan had approved interracial marriages in 1923. If Charlie heeded Harriet's obvious desire to go someplace where they might be accepted ….

The telephone on the stand in the far corner rang.

Cord shook off his mood and started to rise. Probably someone wanting to wish them a happy holiday.

"Keep your seat," William said.

He hurried over to the phone. "Snake River Ranch."

A beat. "Burt! Merry Christmas! How are things back east?"

Cord got up and went over.

When Burt spoke to Cord, his voice held a decidedly unhappy note.

"Everything all right? Katharine and the boys okay?"

"Sure, sure. I didn't mean to imply a problem with us. But," Burt hesitated, "there's some curious news from John D. Rockefeller."

"He's not dropping his interest in the valley?"

Another tug at one of the cards Cord had imagined.

"No, no."

Cord let out his breath.

"It seems Horace Albright has had a letter from John D., saying Horace must have misunderstood the area he intended to purchase. He wanted a much larger area included."

"How big?"

"I haven't seen the new request for ownership information, but I fear it may include some of the dude ranches we hope to see grandfathered in."

Chapter Thirty-five
May, 1927

For the third year in a row, it seemed spring would never come to Jackson's Hole. After the freezing dark days of December and a series of winter blizzards that caused every slide on The Pass to run, spring dripped with steady rain. By the first week of May, Jackson's Hole was usually relatively free of snow, but this year a thick covering lingered. The usual flowering of white phlox and elk sedge were delayed, along with the leafing out of aspen and cottonwood, while periods of warmth made mud season hell.

As the wet weather went on and snowmelt rushed to fill the streams and rivers, Slide Lake lapped at the top of its dam.

Everyone at Snake River Ranch became porcupines, impatient for warmth and sunshine. With only a month until dude season, Cord pitched in as he could, under Laura's watchful eyes. She bemoaned the lateness of getting the hothouse plants into the ground; it would delay the availability of fruits and vegetables throughout the season.

Francesca, though eager for warmer weather, found deep contentment in viewing the constant parade of change from her home on the bluff. She kept a vase filled with the offering of the day on her dining table before the big window looking up at the Tetons. In deepest winter, she cut bare branches, twisted them into abstract shapes, and threaded them with bright ribbons. As soon as new willow catkins appeared on bare branches, Francesca worked them into a new display. Soon she planned to revel in the explosion of wildflowers.

William, who visited at least once daily, pronounced her talent at floral arranging to be as advanced as her culinary skills.

He also continued to be her kitchen helpmate, but he had been as good as his word. The house was hers without strings.

Just as well. Though her anger at Bryce had worn itself out through sheer exhaustion, she had been sleepwalking since last August. The only thing she could have accepted from William was precisely what he offered—a warm and non-demanding friendship.

Though spring came late in Jackson's Hole, summer already gripped Morenci in a molten fist. The heat off the carryall's engine sent the temperature in the truck's cab soaring to at least a hundred forty degrees. Bryce's sweat evaporated in the desert air; he could not drink enough to keep up.

Most days, he didn't know why he bothered getting out of bed, but mine work formed a structure for his existence. By the time he had returned to Arizona, Charlene and his Model T were long gone. Instead of bunking in the company barracks with other workers, Bryce stayed in the local hotel, where he took meals and drank to occasional excess, making him likely to succumb to purchasing a whore and suffering the after-agony of self loathing.

Such scenarios hadn't affected him this way until Francesca.

With dude season in Wyoming looming, Bryce's recalcitrant curiosity reared its head. Had William won Francesca? Was Dad well? Did anyone give a rat's ass whether Bryce Aaron Sutton lived or died?

Expecting his mother to send letters to Morenci on the chance he'd come back, he'd alerted the postmaster, but there had been nothing.

Bryce pulled the carryall up and parked it outside the mine entrance. A sign on the wooden derrick over the shaft touted safety.

Safe as it might be, he hated riding down in the bucket, with the seeping rock walls rushing past and light from the surface receding, replaced by bare bulbs strung on wires. When he disembarked below, emerging into a long stone corridor smelling of rock flour, carbide, and the sharp residue of explosives, the walls closed in. His hard hat wouldn't be worth a damn in the event of a cave-in.

An injured man whose shift Bryce had been called to finish waited outside the elevator. Jaime Perez, whom Bryce knew by sight, cradled a hand wrapped in bloody gauze.

Mine manager Jake Gomez, known in company circles as a stern taskmaster and to labor as a nasty piece of work, stood beside Jaime, feet planted in a belligerent stance. "About time you got here."

Bryce touched the brim of his hard hat and kept his eyes down. The rock floor glistened; a line of bulbs led away into darkness. He would have liked to ask Jaime what had happened.

Jake led him over to a mule hitched to a small train of ore carts.

"Where's the iron horse?" The engine had to be absent because of poor air quality. Mules had gone out of general use at least twenty years earlier.

Jake scowled. "You've got Blossom. Head down to the face and bring back a load of ore." He stepped onto the bucket with Jaime, tapping his breast pocket where a cigarette box reposed. "Smoke break."

Bryce approached Blossom and reached for her bridle. The mule bared her yellow teeth and tried to take a bite out of him, revealing what he suspected had been Jaime's fate.

Being good with horseflesh, Bryce soon had Blossom pulling the empty carts down the rails, though she dragged her hooves and moved slower than he wished. The farther he got from the shaft, the more stifling the atmosphere became.

At the face, the miners had drilled a series of holes, loaded them with explosive, and prepared to set off a coordinated shot. Bryce kept Blossom and the carts well back, plugged his ears, covered his mouth and nose with his bandanna, and hunkered down.

Why wasn't he riding horseback beneath the cobalt bowl of the Jackson's Hole sky? Helping with spring calving, while cows hummed to their newborns, encouraging them to rise on wobbly legs. Walking the bluff above the Snake, while the sun made bright diamonds on the water.

With a muffled thump, the dynamite sectioned off a chunk of copper ore. A cloud of dust billowed.

It seemed to take a long time for the cacophony to still, for isolated rocks to fall and sandy particles to sift down, revealing a fresh face studded with reddish-gold chalcopyrite.

Still feeling as though he couldn't catch his breath, Bryce loaded the cart and urged a balky Blossom back to the lift.

Jake waited, pocket watch in hand. Grudgingly, he said, "You're faster than any of our other loaders. From now on, let's have you down here instead of driving a truck."

Bryce tried to sound pleasant. "I'm afraid being down here isn't for me."

Jake scowled. "Take it or leave it."

With the first perfect spring day—late as it was on Friday the thirteen of May—William's frustration over Fran came to a head. When he had built the house for her, he'd expected that, during the darkest chill of winter, she would turn to him.

He had waited like a cat at a mouse hole. No, like a baby bird needing sustenance. After twenty-six years of bumbling along, he needed Fran as he had never needed anyone.

Bryce had accused him of prejudice—of thinking Fran, with her foreign blood, wasn't good enough. Leave those sentiments to the Klan, thick-headed fools who couldn't see past a person's color or heritage to what lay beneath. To their ilk, he and Fran were the same, he with his Nez Perce blood and she with her "Eyetalian."

Take last month's cross burning in Kelly. In the darkest part of the night, in the middle of the street in front of Negro Moses Lander's machine shop. According to a livid Charlie, it had nigh frightened Harriet to death, what with her place right across.

The incident had sent shock waves through the valley, along with speculation.

When it happened, William had rushed to Francesca's side. Expecting to comfort her, he found her bearing the ugly news gamely, preferring to believe the perpetrators had come over The Pass to hit and run. She had assured him she wasn't worried about the Klan targeting her or the Mexican workers.

What was it going to take to make Francesca turn to him?

After nine months, she'd had every chance to stop thinking of Bryce. Surely now, with robins sitting on their eggs, baby moose appearing in the willow bottoms beside their mothers, and young badgers darting around their den entrances, the softer side of her would come through. She must want children, and William had come around to Mother's way of thinking. Father must hold a grandchild before it was too late.

His imagination went so far as to hope for a son and a daughter; they would get along with each other without the problems he and Bryce had.

William vowed that, when he took Fran to the Saturday night dance on the coming weekend, they'd make the announcement Grace Miller and the valley awaited.

Chapter Thirty-six
May 14, 1927

Cord invited Charlie down to the house for Saturday morning breakfast. Rather than risk Laura putting out cereal, he solicited Francesca for a nice coffee cake dropped off the evening before, and figured on frying eggs and sausage for Charlie and snagging a sample.

When Charlie showed up, Cord put a mug of strong black coffee in his hand and had him sit with him and Laura at the table. "Business first." He pushed some papers across.

Charlie groped in his breast pocket for his gold-rimmed reading spectacles.

"I probably should have done this last year on your twentieth anniversary, but ...." Cord sat back and swigged coffee. He'd snuck extra cream when Laura wasn't looking.

While Charlie read, Laura caught Cord's eye, cast a glance at the color of his beverage, and shook her head. He should have known better than to think he'd fool her.

"But," Charlie swallowed, "but ... this is fantastic."

Cord smiled. "One quarter working interest in Snake River, now, and to be included in my will in case of questions. The boys will divide the other three quarters of the ranch evenly, with the balance of my estate to Laura. Of course, she'll have the lifetime right to live here."

Charlie laid his hand on the papers and looked thoughtful. "Guess you must have figured I was studying on leaving."

"Laura and I thought you and Harriet might want to go someplace the law would permit you to marry."

Charlie nodded. "We've been putting it off because," he gestured at the window where the mountains raised their heads into a day threatening more rain, "I don't think I could bear leaving this place." He looked at the papers again, picked up the pen on the table and signed the agreement. Then offered his callused hand and shook Cord's. "Thanks, boss."

"You're going to have to learn to say 'partner.' "

A frown creased Charlie's broad forehead. "What do the boys think?"

Cord glanced at Laura. "As it happens, they don't know yet. Of course, Bryce—"

Laura broke in, "We thought it best to tell William after it was settled. But you know he loves you like an uncle."

Charlie's brows came together in a vee. "William loved his great uncle, but never forgot he was Nez Perce. He won't be happy at seeing a black man in his father's will."

Cord slapped the table. "Then he'll have to be unhappy."

When William returned from town on Saturday afternoon in his Model T, he ran into Charlie talking with Foster Case in front of the Main. With a wave, Charlie called, "Your father wants to see you."

William nodded his thanks and headed on to his bachelor house. He didn't have time to see Father, not when his shopping had already made him miss dinner. There'd be a potluck at the Gymnasium dance.

Whistling, William showered and put on his best suit. Combing his hair before the mirror after shaving, he caught his grinning reflection. Before he left his house, he slipped a small box into his coat pocket.

Francesca twirled in front of the full length mirror in her bedroom. Another little touch William had thought to put in for her. She had a feeling tonight was going to be another Cinderella occasion, only she didn't expect William to turn into a pumpkin the way Bryce had.

Adjusting a sage-colored wool dress and matching cloche hat made for her by Harriet Lawrence, she turned her head this way and that and wondered if she should bob her hair.

Probably not. The last time she'd mentioned it, William had run a finger down one of her long curls. "Don't you dare."

A rap at her door. His characteristic rhythm—three fast taps, a pause, and two more.

She went to the door, surprised to see his suit and silk tie. "Don't you look the dandy?" she said with a smile.

He handed over a bouquet of carnations he must have bought in town. Fresh flowers in the off season were dear, what with the freight over The Pass. Francesca took them and offered her cheek for him to kiss, his usual greeting.

His mouth lowered to hers.

In her surprise, she parted her lips. William probed with his tongue, warm and persuasive. He tightened his embrace so the flowers and her bent arms ended up crushed between them.

When they came up for air, he kept his face close to hers. "How long is this going to go on?"

Francesca smiled. "If it goes on too long, we'll miss the dance."

William slid his hands up her back to grip her shoulders. "Stop pretending you don't know I love you, Fran."

Her heart pounded like a drum and she lifted her chin. "I won't pretend."

"You once told me it was too late for me to tell you how I feel, but when I built you this place, I didn't mean it just for you, but for us, right up near the Main and the cookshack." Now that he had finally found words, they fairly poured from him. "You're everything good I've ever wanted and, after Pru, I don't deserve you, but I dare to hope."

William touched his lips to the side of her neck, first gently, then fervently. When Bryce had done that, she'd erupted in goosebumps from head to toe.

Tears gathered in her eyes. William's touch comforted; he'd never done anything to deserve her putting him through hell.

"I hoped," William said with a slight bitter note, "that maybe you could love me, too, at least a little."

A tear broke and rolled. Then another. William slipped his arms around her waist and pulled her against his powerful chest. "Don't cry, sweetheart."

She'd missed him terribly when she was working at the drilling camp, and she valued every hour they'd spent rocking on the porch. When she sat with him and his family at table, she felt she belonged.

William fumbled in his jacket pocket. "Look here." A jeweler's velvet box; he lifted the lid.

"Oh, my!" Never had she imagined a diamond like that might be hers. At least a carat, a single sparkling solitaire on a narrow band.

"It's set in platinum," he said with pride.

They were two people alone who might do better together. She should be the happiest woman in the world.

William drew out the ring. "Let's see if it fits."

Francesca permitted him to slip it onto her ring finger, left hand, where it fit as if custom made. She studied her hand, spreading her fingers. It was lovely.

William pulled her back into his arms and deepened the kiss. Her arms went around him, the ring box fell to the floor. His desire rose against her.

They would make love now. She would find out once and for all how it would be between them.

William urged her toward the bedroom and she went along.

With the utmost tenderness, he began to undress her. First her cloche; her hair tumbled over her shoulders. Next, the lace collar. He unzipped her dress. Unabashed worship in William's eyes darkened them to charcoal embers.

Her dress slid off her shoulders to pool on the shining hardwood floor. In the wall mirror, she caught their reflection. William, fully dressed, her in her camisole, chiffon nylons, and garter belt.

Their image blurred, replaced by one of her in another world, gasping and panting, tearing down Bryce's zipper.

No! She and William would be good together. She would be part of the Snake River family.

If only the telling made it so. In the mirror, she stood half naked with her hands at her sides; no fire sparked her eyes

Tempting as it might be to live a lie, she knew it wasn't about marrying the ranch or being part of the Sutton family. Not about having a home nobody could take from her. Not even security. It was about the breath and the blood and the passion she knew could exist between two people.

Because Bryce had gone, it would never be him.

The passive expression on her reflected face told her it would never be William, either.

She did love him. He was her friend, and hurting him would hurt her, too. But he could never fill her chest with the pressure and ache that the smallest thought of Bryce did.

William must have sensed her hesitation, for his hands stilled on her camisole straps. Looking down at her with his heart in his eyes, he asked, "Will you marry me, Fran?"

She shut her eyes. The ring felt hot on her finger, like a brand.

Bryce was gone, but what if he came back? Would she want to hide her hand, to slip out of bed in the middle of the night and go to him like a wanton, the way she had walked away from the campfire on the Grand?

Weighing her decision, she thought of spending the rest of her life with William. No leap of excitement seized her, no sense of longing, no feeling that if she could not be with him, she would die.

She'd chosen the man who made her feel that way before, and if she could not have it again, she would go it alone. If knowing Bryce had taught her anything, it was not to settle.

"No, William." She managed an agonized whisper. "I can't marry you."

୬୰ଏ

With the ring back in his pocket, William drove his Model T across the new steel truss that had recently replaced Menor's Ferry. He didn't know where he was going in the rainy spring twilight, only that he had to leave Snake River Ranch.

When he reached the turn for Jackson, he went north and crossed over to Mormon Row. Tonight, he'd take Pru to the dance.

Unless she had already gone with someone else.

Luck favored him. Or perhaps not, for she opened the door to his knock with a fresh bruise at the corner of her right eye and her eyes swollen from crying.

When she saw who it was, she tried to shut the door.

William put his foot into the space between the portal and jamb. "Pru! What the hell's happened?"

Her breath caught in a sob. "Tiny, he—"

"That sunnavabitch. I'll ...." What would he do, try to fight Tiny, who outweighed him by forty pounds?

Pru let him in. William glanced toward the kitchen and dining area in the rear of the house, "Where is everybody?"

"My folks went to town. I couldn't, not like this."

"What happened?"

Pru sniffled. "Tiny said he'd been to see Foster Case at your place and was in the neighborhood. Likes to make me feel small, as if he wouldn't come just for me. If we run into him, you have to promise not to make trouble."

"Why'd he hurt you?" William asked.

When she answered, he believed it was without guile. "Because he knows you're the only man I've ever loved."

Letting out his breath, he felt the weight of her truth.

"He ... made me do," she shuddered, "unspeakable things in bed, because he knew I wanted to show him off in town, so I could pretend I didn't love you ...."

William's ego began to recover. If Francesca didn't give a damn .... He'd always thought Pru cared and pretended he didn't know the full extent of it.

"I loved you, but you kept mooning over the exotic and oh-so-lovely Francesca," Pru finished.

William considered. "Not anymore."

Pru's wounded face brightened. "Oh, William, really?"

"Really," he said. "She's turned me down for the last time. Put some ice on your eye and get made up. I'm taking you out tonight, on my arm in front of God and everybody. If we run into Tiny, I'll—"

Pru put her palms on his chest. "You mustn't; he'd hurt you, too."

William extended his hands in a gesture of surrender. "If you don't want me to confront him about you ...."

She shook her head, setting her tangled blond bob swinging. "He said something about your family and Snake River. About your father cutting a nigger in on his business."

William's jaw dropped. "What did you say?"

"Said he'd stopped by Snake River earlier this afternoon and heard tell your nigger foreman got given a quarter of Snake River Ranch by Cord Sutton."

God, was that what Father had wanted to see him about? Recalling Charlie's relaxed smile and wave, he found his fists clenched. How dare Father let Charlie in on what rightfully should be William's? And even Bryce's?

Eyes wide, Pru went on, "I don't know what he meant, but he said there were some men in the valley who wouldn't sit by for it."

A chill walked down William's spine. Did Tiny mean the Klan?

After questioning Pru further and learning she knew nothing, he tried again to talk her into going out. In his arms, her head on his shoulder and her big breasts nudging his chest, he convinced her to gussy up and show Tiny and everybody else.

Except that ... alone with Pru in the house ... and with such pleasing propinquity, William found himself rising to the occasion.

By the time Pru had changed her clothes and fixed her makeup, he had emptied his three-condom tin.

It never occurred to him to give Pru the diamond ring.

Chapter Thirty-seven
May 15, 1927

Sunday afternoon, Francesca placed a last garment, the shawl from Rosa, into her valise and fastened it. Like closing the cover of a book, she was ending another phase of her life. Never again would she pretend she belonged at Snake River Ranch.

Ben Raleigh would be there in a few minutes to take her over to his and Anne's place. When they had spoken on the phone, Francesca had heard in Anne's voice that she thought all this amounted to a lover's spat.

Anne was bound to feel that way—as happy as she and Ben were, with J.C. and another baby on the way.

Picking up her bag, Francesca took a last look around the house William had built her. The brass-framed bed, stripped, quilts folded atop the mattress. There was the wedding-ring patterned one Laura had made, tangible symbol of a mother's hope.

Francesca blew out the bedside lamp against the dismal afternoon and went into the living room. Rain poured from a leaden sky, making rivulets down the window.

To leave seemed like defeat. The Tetons, though blurred by rain, appeared so rugged they defied taming.

But she had conquered the Grand, and summer thunderstorms, landslides, the flood at Circle X, blizzards, ice frozen in the water bucket in summer, tormenting winds.

Nothing she couldn't handle except the brothers Sutton.

The living room fireplace contained a pile of cold ashes. Setting her bag down, Francesca reached into her pocket and drew out her rosary. Though it was the Sabbath, she did not pray, merely clutched the blue beads in her hand.

When Ben knocked at the door, Francesca placed William's gift on the mantle and walked away.

The coward in Francesca had intended to phone Laura from Anne's, but when Ben reached the drive down to the Sutton's house, she said, "Turn here."

While Ben walked discreetly down to the stable to see Lucifer, Laura put on the tea kettle. "Anne called the Main and left a message you were leaving."

Francesca stood, uncertain what to do with her hands. "I should have told you first."

"You were afraid." Laura's direct gaze reminded Francesca of Bryce. "What's happened with you and William?"

"He asked me to marry him."

Laura's mouth twisted. "Forgive me if, as a mother, I'm not flattered by your reaction."

"I told him I couldn't—"

"Do you love him?"

"Of course, but—"

"You're in love with Bryce."

"Yes. I know it sounds daft, but I love them both."

"I'm sure you do." Laura gestured toward a chair.

Francesca obeyed. If only this woman could be her mother, without having to marry into it.

"I wish I could urge you to stay, and tell you that love could grow for you and William." The teakettle whistled. Laura set blue speckled mugs in front of them both. "What you have to listen to is what you said. You love William and you're in love with Bryce."

That evening over dinner, Anne started her campaign to keep Francesca in the valley. "Just because you want to get away from William ... for a while ... doesn't mean you should go off alone."

"If I want to break with him for good, I must," Francesca said.

But how could she leave the valley, when the goslings had begun to hatch, the male ruffled grouse to puff up his feathers and strut, and the time to search for morel mushrooms was coming back around? "Leaving is what I must do. Nothing has worked out here."

Anne speared a piece of pork chop. "You have friends here. Don't underestimate it."

Francesca tried the pork; her mouth was too dry to eat. "If I stayed, what would I do?"

"Help out at the school. Or deliver meals to the shut-ins. The church ladies try and keep up, but it's a burden."

Francesca shook her head.

All she wanted was to crawl into a hole and sleep for a thousand years. Having left the ranch, knowing Jim tended the fire in what she had come to view as her kitchen, brought back the heartbreak of learning the *castello's cucina* belonged to others.

Chapter Thirty-eight
May 17, 1927

With the heavy winter snow pack and wet spring, the Gros Ventre ran bank full through Kelly.

The roiling waters unsettled Ranger Duran so much that, though his wife expected him for dinner, he wouldn't be able to eat in peace without a check on Slide Lake's water level. As he drove up, he also surveyed the Forest Service telephone line; the wire had a nasty habit of going down when wet tree branches fell over it.

Premature twilight descended, and he switched on his headlights, reflecting the sheen of treacherous wet clay. When he reached a vantage point on the hill above the slide, gray light revealed the brimming lake, not only lapping at the top of the dam, but running over.

Duran stepped out of his car and peered through the murk, his guts hurting.

On their way back from doing some ranch shopping in Jackson, Charlie had Foster Case drop him at the Kelly Mercantile. "I'll find my own way back to Snake River."

"Staying overnight?" Foster suggested in a surprisingly ugly tone.

As time went on, more and more folks were on to Charlie and Harriet. Foster must now be one of them. He was leaving no doubt as to where he stood on it.

"Tell Cord I'll be in early tomorrow." Charlie jumped out and walked away, hunching his shoulders against the rain. As he crossed the wooden bridge over the Gros Ventre, the water level almost reached the bank.

Ten minutes later, he tapped on Harriet's door.

When he told her he wouldn't be leaving the valley, what would she say? Would she give him an ultimatum—move to Michigan where they could marry ... or else?

⊱⊰

On Tuesday evening, Francesca marveled at how full the Raleigh house seemed. With the addition of Benjy, whose folks were taking Larry to Idaho Falls for dental work, the noise level more than doubled.

Though Benjy had spindly arms and legs, he nonetheless had plenty of energy, getting J.C. toddling in circles until they both fell down on the rag rug. The boys' high-pitched giggles made Francesca smile ... and want to cry.

What kind of life should she make for herself and where?

Seeing Anne place a hand over her stomach in the universal gesture of pregnant women, Francesca was glad she had never lain with William. And sad that her union with Bryce, now nine months past, had not resulted in a child. No matter society's censure, she would have refused the remedies of the *stregas* and borne her baby.

An ache swelled her chest, one that never eased, not since Bryce had left her.

Ben rose and scooped up his nephew. "Time for bed, big guy." He smiled at Anne. "And for you, dear."

A knock on the front door; all eyes went to the hall. Ben set Benjy down and pointed him toward Anne with a gentle pat on his pajama-clad bottom.

The squeak of door hinges ... the amplified hiss of rain. "Ranger Duran!" Ben exclaimed. "What brings you out on a night like this?"

A murmur of voices and Ben came back wearing a somber expression.

"Did you invite him in?" Anne asked.

"I did, but he's making the rounds. Seems the good ranger thinks we may be in danger of a flood."

Anne frowned; her hand went to her stomach again.

Ben smiled. "I'm sure we don't need to worry. Our house is several feet above the river."

Anne collapsed in her chair, but didn't look content.

Without warning, an earth tremor sent shudders and creaks through the frame house.

Francesca jumped.

It seemed to go on for a long time, though it must have been only seconds.

Benjy planted his feet and started to whimper like a much younger child. Ben scooped J.C. up.

Though the seismic activity stopped, the joy had gone out of the evening.

Chapter Thirty-nine
May 18, 1927

Rain pounded the metal roof of the Raleigh house near the Gros Ventre. It poured from the sloped shakes covering the Episcopal Church in Kelly, puddled in the street, and kept the children at school inside.

Ranger Duran, wearing his sodden raincoat and Forest Service hat, drove through town. A few people seemed to have left, but most appeared to be taking a wait-and-see approach. Nobody wanted to look foolish by running for the hills—not after doing it for months after the earlier slide, knowing they could have been snug in their beds.

Perhaps this time they ought to take note, for one of the town bridges had washed away during the night. The greedy flood ate at the approaches.

At the other bridge, a group of men engaged in grim work. Though threatened by the rising river, they used pike poles to steer floating logs and tree trunks away from the wooden pilings.

Duran got out and joined them.

Francesca paced Anne's living room. Without her morning work of preparing breakfast for a group, she felt as if she would jump out of her skin.

Anne rose from her quilting frame and went to the window. "The river's come up some more."

As Francesca pulled back the curtain, the floorboards shifted under her feet. She clutched the lace and the rod pulled loose at the top. Glassware in the cabinet walked, making a tiny crystalline ringing. Anne's hand flew to her stomach.

When the latest tremor stilled, Francesca chose not to observe that it had been worse than the one last night. Nor did she mention her suspicion she'd awakened early due to another seismic disturbance.

"I hate to ask this," Anne began, "but would you mind going and getting Benjy out of school? He's my responsibility, and I'd hate for the waters to separate me from him."

Francesca didn't want to go out, but since Anne was both pregnant and needed to look after J.C., she donned her raincoat over her pink flowered dress. Out in the cart shed, she put the family's docile palomino, Sunny, into the traces.

Though she still lacked confidence when at the reins of a horse-drawn wagon, it was only a few miles to Kelly.

Duran looked up from his work, helping to shove a big log under the bridge, to swipe at the combination of sweat and rainwater dripping into his eyes. Then he blinked.

Too much debris poured down the river toward them.

Next to Duran, Jack Ellis swore an oath that would make Bobby Cowan blush.

"Maybe we ought to pry off the bridge boards," someone suggested, "before they get knocked off."

"Too late." Bobbing toward the bridge was a hayrack Duran recognized. Originally, it had graced a green slope overlooking the Gros Ventre. The last time he'd seen it, it had been floating in Slide Lake.

Duran shouted for help, and he and Jack Ellis took off for his Model T. If the hayrack had come over the dam ....

When they were about three and a half miles east of Kelly, Jack pointed out a wall of water tumbling down the canyon below the road. About six feet deep, it raced and tumbled; the dam must have collapsed.

Reaching the turnout where he'd stopped the night before, Duran had trouble believing his eyes. A veritable waterfall poured over the slide.

Heart racing, he reversed and put the gas to the auto, driving as fast as his Model T would take him on the dangerously slick road. He stopped at the first house on the way down and honked the horn furiously.

Leda Nygaard, mother of the young engineer, Sven, appeared from out back wearing denim trousers and a raincoat. "Mornin', Ranger. Couple of our calves are out of the pen—"

"Never mind them, the dam's breaking up!" Duran shouted. "Phone down to the Kelly Post Office. Warn the town and then call all the ranches along the way."

Leda blanched and ran for the house.

Driving toward town, every foot of elevation lost meant danger to Duran and Jack.

But their families were in Kelly.

The waterfall poured over, saturating what had been the dry downstream side of the thousand-foot-long earthen dam. On the south side, where the lake had already eaten a passage, a huge cut enlarged. Several more deepening channels speeded the process.

Like the fairy tale princess who felt the pea through twenty mattresses and twenty featherbeds, the mass sensed a void. No human eye watched, as, in dreadful slow motion, the south channel and the one down the dam's middle merged.

Water rushed in; the speed of events moved into overdrive. The flood gathered up part of the dam, with topsy-turvy trees and boulders. Constrained by the canyon, the released waters piled up until a monstrous serpent several hundred feet high weaved downstream on a quest for prey.

Duran rounded a curve and spied a group of cattle near the road, chest deep in a flooded field. They pressed against the barbed wire.

The ranger hit the brakes, sending the car into a long skid that ended at the edge of the water. With a surge washing down the canyon, the stock would drown.

Duran and Jack jumped out and went to the trunk for a tool kit. Using a pair of pliers, they improvised wire cutters and opened a hole in the fence.

The freed cattle pushed and shoved their way out and scrambled up onto a slope.

Only after they had taken the time for the rescue did it occur to Duran that the Forest Service phone line might not be working.

The Kneedy family, who ran the local gristmill on the Gros Ventre bank, had heard enough about the dangers of the dam. Nearly two years ago, Milt's wife, Anna, had elected to take her ten-year-old son Joe to sleep on higher ground every night. Milt slept at home in a decent bed and scoffed at their fears.

With today's rising water, Milt didn't mind moving some of his equipment away from the river, but there were limits. This phone warning from Leda Nygaard sounded like woman's hysteria.

෨෴

Francesca entered the Kelly school through a cloakroom smelling of wet clothing, mud, and manure on ranch children's rubber overshoes. She opened the classroom door.

The teacher looked at her. "May I help you?"

Around fifteen children turned their still winter-pale faces toward Francesca.

"I've come for Benjy," she said. "The river's still rising, and Anne wants him home."

Despite the teacher's obvious disapproval, she bundled the boy into the cloak room.

Bong.

Helping Benjy with his raincoat, Francesca lifted her head at the clang of the church bell. No glad melody or holiday tune this ....

Bong.

In Italy, the church bells had warned when bad news came from the battlefields.

Francesca shook off paralysis, zipped Benjy's raincoat over a blue and white striped shirt, and scooped up the boy's forty pounds. Cradling his head with the back of her hand, she rushed out into the gray morning.

A man dashed toward the school, slender and quick, drenched by the downpour. "Everybody out!" he shouted. "The dam's gone to hell!"

Francesca froze. "Bryce," she mouthed.

He slid to a stop in the mud before her.

For a moment, the craziness around them blurred. Beneath his saturated cowboy hat, droplets dotted his skin, his moustache dripped, and beads of water tipped his eyelashes.

"Francesca!"

Benjy's weight hurt her back as he squirmed.

Bryce took the little boy from her.

The teacher and the children came outside in a rush.

"The town's got to be evacuated!" Bryce shouted. "A call from Leda Nygaard .... Ranger Duran says the dam's falling apart."

Within seconds, the oldest children scattered in several directions. "Your coats," the teacher called.

A moment later, parents began showing up. "Go on," the teacher told Francesca. "In three minutes, I'll head up to the cemetery hill with any child left."

With a terse nod, Bryce looked at Francesca over Benjy's head. "I picked up Bayberry at the livery."

"I've got Anne's buggy and Sunny. Anne's keeping Benjy while his folks are in Idaho Falls."

Bryce tied Bayberry's reins to the rear of the buggy, while Francesca settled in with Benjy in her lap.

When Bryce climbed to the seat, Francesca asked tightly, "What are you doing here?"

"I'm back in the valley because last week I got a wake-up call, down in the Morenci mine. They wanted me underground and all I could think of was the sky over this valley...." He took his eyes off the horse and gave her an intense look, glancing at Benjy to remind her that the boy was listening. "Did Ben go over to Snake River this morning?"

"Yes."

"If you've got Anne's buggy, she's got no way out except on foot. If a big flood is coming, their house is too close to the river."

"Ben seemed to think it was okay last night."

"That was last night." Bryce turned the buggy toward the Raleigh place. "Now he's at Snake River and I'm here to look out for his family."

Francesca tried not to look toward the river.

Once Ranger Duran's wife and daughter were on the hillside, he kissed them and returned to his role of Paul Revere. Driving his Model T back across the bridge, he realized it was floating. Seconds after he made it over, the boards started popping off from the pressure of the water beneath.

Finding Kneedy still at the mill, Duran called, "You've got to get out. Flood's rushing down the canyon, worse than this."

Kneedy's jaw squared.

With nothing more he could do, Duran checked his watch. Almost eleven o'clock, over fifteen minutes since Jack had seen the wave of flood waters. God knew what might be coming on by now, so Duran got himself away from the river.

The serpent burst from the mouth of the Gros Ventre Canyon. With the blunt head of a poisonous viper, it slithered down the main channel, its belly scouring the riverbed to bare rock. On open ground, it flattened to one hundred feet high.

Directly in its sights lay Kelly.

Elderly sisters, May Lovejoy and Maud Smith received the telephoned warning at their home a few miles downstream from Kelly. May was all for leaving and harnessed their horse to the wagon. Maud went through the house, gathering things to take, bringing out load after load.

Mr. and Mrs. Frank Almy of Kelly got into their convertible and started driving away from the approaching danger, toward the Jackson road.

Along the Gros Ventre bank, Jack Moore rushed to warn Mike Meeks and Floyd True. With one horse among three men, Mike and Floyd mounted up together and Jack tied off to a rope on the horse's tail. They set out for the nearest hills.

Three miles downstream from Kelly, Max Edick and his hired hand Clint Stevens learned of the approaching flood. Because it didn't seem quite real to them, they took time to load up the pigs and chickens.

Bryce pulled the buggy up in front of the Raleigh house, leaped out and ran to pound on the door. With no answer, he twisted the knob and went room to room calling Anne and J.C.

Back in the buggy, he took up the reins. "She and the boy got out."

Which way now? Downstream followed the river across a sage flat. Bryce turned back toward the Gros Ventre Canyon, planning to take the turn onto Mormon Row that led north away from the river.

He wanted to ask Francesca why she had left Snake River. What had she planned on doing? Was William still on the ranch?

Though resolved to find out despite Benjy's chaperonage, he had no opportunity.

Francesca gasped, and he followed her stricken gaze. A wave of gargantuan proportion swept across the virtually flat valley floor toward Kelly.

Chapter Forty
May 18, 1927

The town of Kelly, with a population of nearly eighty, went down before the flood like bowling pins. The Mercantile, the post office, the Riverside Hotel, the blacksmith's shop, feed stable and livery, the garage ... all exploded into kindling, swept up in the maelstrom.

All were blessedly vacant.

No children remained at the school. The pastor had abandoned the sanctuary, and the livery people had herded the horses into the hills.

No one left in Kelly except Milt Kneedy, Anna, and her son Joe.

Did they see the approach of doom? If they huddled in their home, they must surely have heard the horrific din—annihilation accompanied by millions of gallons of water. If Milt stood outside in a last defiant gesture, he must have known he'd made his final mistake.

The wave swept over and crushed the sawmill, along with the Kneedy house.

May Lovejoy, beside her wagon, looked upstream. Sharp sounds of breaking and scraping assailed her ears, and she screamed, "Maud!"

Her sister dropped an armload of family quilts and ran for the laden wagon. With both women aboard, they started down the road. Thinking to outdistance the serpent, May drove and Maud seized the whip from its socket and flailed the horses.

Within seconds, they realized no team could outrun what pursued them. May turned at right angles to the flood, off road, bouncing and jouncing. A rancher on safe ground witnessed the mighty force seize and sweep them away.

Mr. and Mrs. Frank Almy lost their race as well. Sucked beneath the chaotic current, the elderly couple bumped into things unseen. She surfaced repeatedly, rolling along for a mile, fearing each submersion would be the last. Finally, she grabbed a rooted sagebrush. Separated from his wife, Frank swam for his life.

In the last moments before the serpent swallowed them, Jack Moore, Mike Meeks, and Floyd True abandoned their plan to escape on horseback and climbed a cottonwood. The horse washed away.

When the flood approached, Max Edick and his hired hand Clint Stevens gave up on the pigs and chickens and scrambled onto the chicken house roof. As the waters continued to rise, Clint panicked and leaped onto a passing hayrack. Max, left alone and shivering, waited to see how high the waters would rise.

The chicken house lifted from its foundation. It tossed and bobbed, corklike, while Max hung onto the rough shingles at the roof crest. Just as his numb hands threatened to open and send him tumbling, a ten-inch diameter spruce floated past. He leaped, grabbed some branches, and held on.

People came out all along the Mormon Row, watching from their homes and the Latter Day Saints' Church steps. The wall of water carried a sediment load that turned it black. Houses, barns, haystacks, livestock, and people all washed down the mile-wide channel.

❧

Francesca turned her eyes away from the flood that did not even resemble water; trees stuck out at crazy angles.

Bryce's white-knuckled hands held the reins, a muscle bunched at his jaw. "I may not get another chance to say this ...."

Her throat constricted at his admission of their probable fate.

"I was a pigheaded fool to leave you." He reached his hand and cradled the back of her head for the barest instant before going back to gripping the reins. "When I got in to Jackson, someone at Wort's Livery told me you'd left Snake River and gone to stay in Kelly."

Suddenly Benjy noticed what was sweeping toward them and emitted a shrill cry.

"Well said, little man," Bryce gritted.

Benjy continued to scream.

Francesca looked for the turn onto Mormon Row. And at their approaching destiny, ripping houses into bits, plowing them under, grinding, roaring, hissing, swishing. How much more hopeless this seemed than when the slide came after her and William. Eli and Jacob had nearly outrun it. Today there seemed to be no possibility of escape.

Dio, when it comes, let it be over quickly.

"Hang on." Bryce pulled on Sunny's reins for the turn onto Mormon Row. The horse, showing the whites of his eyes, refused to obey.

The buggy slewed toward the ditch.

❦

They were going to make it; they weren't.

Bryce should have done this differently; he should have done it the same. Benjy would grow up to be a strong man; Benjy would die today.

The hissing rush captured the buggy, slewed it sideways, borne up on the edge of the flood. Another hundred feet and they might have made it.

Bryce twisted in the seat and untied Bayberry. "Give me the boy," he shouted to Francesca.

With the child secured, Bryce slung an arm around Francesca's waist, and prayed for the spirit of Koyama to guide him.

"Do you swim?" Bryce asked.

"No!" Francesca cried.

Bryce passed Benjy back to her and pulled a knife from a belt pouch. "I'm going to cut Sunny loose. You and Benjy get on his back, and he'll swim you to safety."

"What about you?"

Bryce leaped over the dash onto Sunny's back. With swift motions, he slashed at the leather harness and turned. "Toss me Benjy. Then you jump."

Francesca started to stand, but the buggy rocked. Benjy's sobs were great gulps.

She tried again.

Benjy missed Bryce's arms and landed on Sunny's rump awash in the flood. Bryce reached back to grab him.

Too late. With a shrill scream, Benjy slid off.

Bryce leaped into the churning water after him, and found it foul, filthy, and freezing.

Before Bryce reached him, the child went under.

Keeping his eyes on where he submerged, Bryce put on a burst of effort and dove down. He felt around; no Benjy.

Chest burning, he surfaced. Circling, he looked hopefully for Benjy's dark head.

Though he'd only swum a few strokes, the distance between him and the buggy had widened to where he'd never be able to swim up current to it. Francesca still sat on the buggy seat, clutching the dash.

He cupped his hands to shout, "Get on the horse!"

She was looking around for him and Benjy and did not appear to hear.

Without warning, something hard and heavy struck Bryce in the back of the head.

๛

A great snag of tree bore down on the buggy, tipping Francesca into the flood.

Her long skirt and heavy raincoat threatened to drag her down, while she flailed, slapped, and gulped the taste of mud. She looked for the buggy.

Something long and supple, snakelike, touched her arm; she recoiled, though she knew the high country had no snakes. She tried not to inhale, but her rapid shallow breathing brought in water.

Something huge bumped her.

Her head went under again. She put out her hands and found a tangle of long hair, a wet flank.

Francesca got her head above the surface. Not Sunny, but Bayberry, her hands were in his mane.

Like a desperate child, like Benjy when he twined his arms and legs around her, she clambered blindly onto the mare's back. Eyes streaming, she dug her heels into Bayberry's sides.

A struggling pig appeared alongside, swimming for its life. A dead chicken floated by.

Bayberry kicked and struggled, and started to founder beneath Francesca's weight.

๛

Bryce, stunned by the blow to his skull, went under. Bright lights danced. What in hell had hit him?

He fought through the pain and swam up. Not ten feet away, a cottonwood reared and plunged in the current.

Bryce made it in four strokes, pulled himself up and hung, panting for breath.

Lifting his head, he saw a striped shirt floating, pale bare legs—Benjy facedown, caught in the tree limbs about twenty feet back.

Bryce dropped back into the water, fought his way over, and seized the branches holding Benjy. Head throbbing, he managed to get both of them up onto the trunk, where stout limbs forked.

Benjy's eyes were closed; his pallor was frightening.

Dammit, he'd only been under about two minutes. Bryce could hold his breath that long, and he knew Ben's brother, John, had taught Benjy and Larry to hold theirs if they fell in the river.

Bryce draped Benjy over a limb and pressed his back to expel water. A gush poured from the child's mouth, but he remained inert.

The flood claimed the valley.

It tore the Raleigh house from its place on the gravel bar and washed the base of Blacktail Butte. At the confluence with the Snake, it turned south and spread out, washing six feet deep through the town of Wilson.

At its broadest point, the swath of destruction spanned three miles.

When it reached Hoback Junction, twenty-seven miles from where the dam collapsed, water rushed upstream on the Hoback River for miles, flooding more ranches.

Nine hours after its birth, the serpent slithered into the uninhabited confines of Snake River Canyon south of Jackson, as if returning to its hole.

Chapter Forty-one
May 19, 1927

Three a.m.

When Ranger Duran warned of a wall of water bearing down on Kelly, many did not believe. Perhaps it is because the dam stood for almost two years and it is human nature to think disaster cannot happen.

This evening was a horror. Past dark, we searched for survivors amidst mud and rubble. Near midnight, William insisted Cord and I return home and rest.

Before we left what remains of Kelly (only three buildings left, including St. John's Episcopal, the vicarage, and the school), William promised to eat something and rest. I suspect he has kept searching for Francesca by lantern light.

On our way home, we stopped at the Bar BC. I don't think either Cord or I wanted to be alone yet, for we stayed late drinking coffee and talking with Struthers Burt.

I should sleep, but I keep listening for William's Model T. It is as though if I hope hard enough he may bring us Francesca, weary yet well.

❧

William slogged through mud-slick gravel by lantern light. By late afternoon, the Gros Ventre had retreated into its channel. Folks from Mormon Row had been first on the scene, followed by William, Ben, Asa,

Foster, Bobby, Jim, and his parents, who came across the Snake by the bridge at Moose, upstream from the confluence with the Gros Ventre.

Everyone at Snake River feared for Francesca, Benjy, and Charlie. Thankfully, Anne Raleigh had made it to Mormon Row on foot with J.C. before the worst of it; her affectionate reunion with Ben renewed William's determination to find Francesca.

Before dark, a searcher had located Mrs. Frank Almy and a fellow called Shorty, who'd been hauling wheat to Kelly when the flood tore him off his wagon seat. He and Mrs. Almy had managed to crawl out together onto firm ground. Her husband, Frank, had swum to dry land, as well.

Word had it someone had seen young Joe Kneedy atop a floating barn. No sign of his folks. No word on May Lovejoy or Maud Smith.

Mormon Row resident Allen Budge, who rode a good swimming horse, rescued Max Edick from the floating spruce before dark. No sign of the missing Clint Stevens.

After dark, many joined a refugee camp at Antelope Springs, a few miles north of Kelly's remains. They kept the campfires burning all night.

William couldn't believe he was still searching. Not with his fear of death, or to put it more precisely, of the dead.

He'd never told his father why he'd turned away from Bitter Waters. He'd meant to, just as he'd meant to do and say so many things.

One diamond bright winter day, nine-year-old William had been trying to get the Flexible Flyer to go down the bluff—the snow was too powdery for the runners to slide—when Father and Bryce had come down from the mountain.

William had abandoned the sled and run toward them. Father and Dan had asked him to go along cross country skiing, but Bryce was so much better and William didn't want to get shown up.

"Hey!" William yelled, "Where's Dan?"

Dan was William's favorite hand—the youngest and strongest on the place. Dan always made him feel safe, whether he was helping him learn to ride Jacob, or teaching him to shoot a pellet gun at rabbits.

William had never seen Father look the way he did when he gathered William against one long thigh and Bryce against the other. "I'm afraid Dan's dead."

Dead was something that happened to the rabbits when William's aim was particularly good. The light went out in their eyes and they lay still.

For months after Father's shocking announcement, he struggled to believe.

Dan couldn't be dead; he was just someplace else.

In the spring, William and Bryce came home from school to find a group of hands unloading a curious, wrapped bundle from a wagon.

"Stay back, boys!" Father shouted.

From listening to a murmured conversation, William surmised they had found Dan, up on the mountain where the avalanche had buried him.

Before the undertaker arrived, William decided he wanted to see if he was really dead like a rabbit. He asked Bryce if he wanted to come along, but Brother said he'd been on the mountain and believed Dan wasn't ever coming back.

After dark, William took a lantern and went to the ice house. He opened the door; shadows loomed on the sawdust-covered ice mounds.

Approaching the bundle, his heart in his throat, he set the lantern down and began parting the cloth.

What he saw did not look human. Like a picture Father had shown him of a shrunken head from some tribe, Dan had dried out and wrinkled. His eyes were open; whitened flesh stared.

William screamed.

In his precipitous rush to escape, his foot slipped on the straw and overturned the lantern.

He never told anyone he had set the fire.

William carried on through the dark ruins of Kelly, stumbling, righting himself and holding the lantern before him. In the wild, shadow-dancing darkness, every log sticking out of the sticky layer left by the flood looked like a human arm or leg.

Please, not Francesca.

How could he have been so stupid as to have gone to Pru? Francesca was his love, his life.

If God granted she be safe, he'd tell her he'd been a pigheaded fool. How thinking she might be dead had turned his world on its ear. She might have said she couldn't marry him, but she must stay at Snake River. Everyone there—Mother, Father, Charlie, Asa, Jim, Bobby, Ben and Anne—loved her.

Sooner or later she'd come to realize she belonged with him, too.

It was a wonder Francesca didn't succumb to hypothermia during the night. But at daylight, she awakened from a sleep so deep she had to fight her way up, as if out of dark waters. She lay where she had crawled out of the flood, too exhausted to move; cold had invaded her bones.

She looked for Bayberry, recalling the horse scrambling up the bank ahead of her. No sign of her.

During the flood, a fortunate eddy had brought the reins around to where Francesca could reach them. She had held on to them and Bayberry's mane, floating beside the horse. They must have been in the water a couple of hours, Francesca amazed at the dude horse's swimming power.

With a raging thirst and a muzzy head, she guessed the time at six a.m. A survey of landmarks told her the flood had receded, leaving her well above the river.

She'd fetched up on the south side of the Gros Ventre's confluence with the Snake, near the north end of West Gros Ventre Butte. At least eight miles down from where she and Bryce had been overtaken.

There must be searchers, but wouldn't most of them be up near Kelly?

Grimacing at the stiffness of every muscle and joint, she struggled to her feet. Her shoes had shrunk and hardened as the leather started to dry. Her pink-flowered housedress bore massive brown stains; long rips marked the skirt, leaves and twigs stuck out of her matted hair.

Daunted at the prospect of struggling back up the debris-covered plain to a dead town, she decided to hobble in her ill-fitting footwear toward the road to Jackson. Even that would be a couple of miles.

Bryce awakened, freezing, on a bed of gravel, exhausted from shivering in the night chill. The small, shaking form of Benjy curled against his chest; his arm covered the boy, who had miraculously revived.

The afternoon of the previous day, their tree had run aground near the west side of West Gros Ventre Butte. From the landmarks, he guessed they were about a mile short of reaching the Snake River Bridge on the road connecting Wilson with Jackson Town.

Before dark, Bryce ascertained that they had landed on an island, trapped by the still turbulent flood. Without any dry matches, he made a few futile attempts at playing frontiersman, but none of the river rocks would put off a spark and all the driftwood was so sodden he hadn't a hope of starting a fire.

Past midnight, the river's sounds indicated an ebbing.

Bryce woke Benjy, who began to cry, and held him until his tears slowed.

Then he circumnavigated the island again and surveyed the channels on either side. They'd need just the right place to cross, given that the Snake was already swollen with Yellowstone snowmelt and bolstered to even more deadly strength by the Gros Ventre.

It took a while to settle on a spot where they had to ford only about fifty feet. Rocks sticking out of the two to three foot deep braided channel provided stepping stones for all but about ten feet. The water there was deeper and plenty swift enough to sweep them away.

Famished and trembling with exhaustion, Bryce started ferrying stones to build a makeshift bridge.

In the morning, stupid with fatigue, William stopped by the modest frame LDS Church on Mormon Row for a hot meal prepared by the local women. Shoveling in fried eggs and sopping up the yolk with toast, William learned that with morning light the scoured scab lands had begun to give up the dead: Joe and Anna Kneedy, and Maud Smith.

Clint Stevens's body had wedged in a tree four miles from where he entered the water; William was glad he hadn't been there to see it. As the morning wore on, neighbors found the body of Mrs. May Lovejoy a half mile downriver from her house. A little later, Albert Nelson, plowing the drift piles with his son, Albert, Jr., spotted a hand sticking out of the sand. Thinking quickly, he sent young Albert on an "errand," so he wouldn't see the corpse of H.M. Kneedy uncovered.

By the time William dragged back to the church for lunch, folks from Jackson had begun to get through, fording the Gros Ventre at a makeshift low water crossing of rock; they brought an armload of newspapers.

William scanned the front page of the *Jackson's Hole Courier*:

Gros Ventre River Flood Takes Huge Toll in Life and Property

At Least Six Lives Lost; Many Homeless in Valley

Church and School Only Left Standing at Kelly

Wilson Inundated

Heavy Livestock Losses

Death and destruction came down the Gros Ventre River yesterday morning in a great wall of water that snuffed out at least six lives, wiped the town of Kelly off the map, ruined ranch after ranch and swept away several hundred head of livestock.

William read the names of the dead.

Snake River Ranch foreman Charlie Sanborn, who helped Mrs. Harriet Lawrence to high ground, returned to town to make sure everyone was safely out—this may have cost him his life.

God, no.

William put down a fork laden with roast beef and gravy. A hard ache in the back of his throat accompanied nausea.

Not Charlie.

When William had heard Father gifted Charlie with a portion of the ranch, he should have been glad for the man who loved him and Bryce like a second father. His first thought should have been a memory, of Charlie and Father laughing together, while each of them carried a small Sutton boy atop their shoulders. Of Charlie's marksmanship, making him the best shot at Snake River, a hair better than Father. Of Charlie's veterinary skills, whether turning a breech colt, pulling a recalcitrant calf, or placing his mouth to the nostrils of one of Sophie's pups to get it breathing.

Also missing is Snake River cook Francesca di Paoli and young Benjy Raleigh, whom she was last seen picking up from the Kelly school. A young man, whom the teacher could not identify, was with Miss di Paoli and is also missing. Word at Wort's Livery suggests he might be Bryce Sutton, who picked up a Snake River Ranch saddle horse there yesterday morning.

William stared at the page in disbelief. Then he was on his feet, adrenaline pumping. "I need to call my parents."

"Phones are out," Ben Raleigh's mother spoke from the food line. "Crews are working on it."

He fell back into his seat.

They wouldn't have the paper up at their place yet with the bridge out on the Jackson-Menor's Ferry Road. He'd have to hope Bryce turned up before Father or Mother knew the paper mentioned him.

Heart pounding, William kept reading.

This morning all available men are scouring the mud defiled flats, searching the heaped up driftwood, vast piles of uprooted and snapped off trees that the rushing waters moved as a sickle would mow the grass, searching with dread for what they might find, but searching.

William shoved the paper aside and went back to his own quest.

Chapter Forty-two
May 19, 1927

At two o'clock, Bryce spied men working on the washed out approaches to the Snake River Bridge. Carrying Benjy, he lacked the energy to shout to them.

Tiny Good, his blue work shirt sweat-stained, noticed him first and stabbed his shovel in the dirt. "Look what the cat drug in."

The rest of the men seemed eager to make up for Tiny's attitude. Someone pointed to a vehicle on the Jackson side of the bridge. "We'll get you into town quicker'n you can think about it."

"I've been thinking about it since yesterday morning." Bryce climbed into the passenger seat with Benjy clinging like a limpet.

Tiny strolled over for a parting shot. "Heard tell your nigger foreman's missing."

As the car started to move, Bryce's throat constricted. Charlie—constant presence at the ranch since he was a toddler—missing?

At two-thirty, William sighted a distorted human figure tangled in a heap of fallen trees.

Drawing closer, he made out that even beneath an earthen coating the man's skin bore a chocolate hue.

William began to run, stumbling through the mud-slicked rocks.

The body—it couldn't be alive and be twisted like that—moved.

"Charlie!"

A weak hand waved.

William screamed, "Over here! For God's sake, get a doctor!" He rushed to Charlie, whose left femur was clearly broken.

"Lost my watch," Charlie lamented, "and my lucky piece."

At two-forty-five, Francesca arrived at the Crabtree Hotel on Jackson Square, having caught a ride south with a searcher on his way home for a break.

Mrs. Rose Crabtree was another member of Jackson's early 1920's all-woman town council, having defeated her husband Henry in the election. As hostess, she greeted Francesca with a brimming glass of cold water.

"Is there news," Francesca choked, "Bryce Sutton?"

"They're still searching."

Francesca had a hot bath and put on a donated yellow flowered housedress and some low-heeled kid slippers. Next she ate every morsel of a roast beef dinner with mashed potatoes and gravy. Mrs. Crabtree barely suppressed the questions written all over her face.

How could Francesca encapsulate in a few sentences the terrible resignation she'd felt when the buggy rolled and tipped her into the freezing flood? Or how it had felt to see Benjy and Bryce swept away?

Hail Mary, full of Grace, the Lord is with thee. Holy Mary, mother of God, be with Bryce and Benjy ....

Charlie survived his rescue from the tangle of trees, blessedly passing out from pain while men strapped him to a board. A surgeon from St. John's Hospital in Jackson, who had made it up to the flood area, ordered Charlie carried into the schoolhouse.

Harriet Lawrence came as soon as she heard William had found Charlie. Her blue eyes huge in her pale face, she watched Foster, William, and Bobby lay her man out on a big sturdy table.

"You may not want to stay, ma'am," the silver-haired doctor told her, with a disapproving look over his gold-rimmed glasses.

Harriet's lips thinned. "I'm going to be with him from now on."

William caught the doc's negativity about a white woman making such a declaration. He also noted the same emotion written all over Foster's saturnine features. Time was when William would have felt the same way about a mixed race deal, but lately he'd found it harder to muster his old prejudices.

Especially when it came to family, as Charlie was.

The doctor began his examination. Charlie emerged from his stupor and started gritting his teeth against the probing. Panting with pain and drenched in sweat, he clutched Harriet's hand.

"I'll set this leg and send you home," the doctor said. "But I believe in being straight with a man, no matter what his color. The bone may heal with only a complaint upon a weather change, or you may never have full use of it again."

৩৵৬

Francesca lay on the hotel bed in mid-afternoon, unable to rest.

She needed to know about Bryce.

And she didn't. Better to linger in the no man's land of hope.

Pater noster ....

Per favore ....

Francesca shoved up from the bed. With Bryce and Benjy still missing, she had to do something. Even if she was in no condition to search the drifts and gravel bars, perhaps she could help put together meals for those who had lived in Kelly.

A newspaper on the table in the hotel room recounted those who had lost their houses.

> In as far as we have been able to ascertain the following are homeless, we doubt, however, if the list is complete:

> Ben Raleigh and family
> Mrs. Harriet Lawrence
> Wm. Woodward and family
> Mr. and Mrs. Harold Elkins
> David Abercrombie
> Elden White
> Fred Moyer and family
> Mrs. Ellen Hanshaw and family
> John Van Vleet and family
> Bert VanLeeuven and family
> Mrs. Walter Henrie
> Ray Shinkle and family
> Lawrence Clark
> Lawerence Carlson and family
> Mr. and Mrs. Frank Almy
> Ed Woodward and family

Chas. Rinehart
W. J. Kelly and family
Mr. and Mrs. Max Edick
Ranger Duran and wife
Albert Nelson and family
Mrs. R.H. Clark and family

All the above people reside at or near Kelly.

Mrs. C.P. Pederson and family
Jaimes Francis and family
F. J. Rowe and family
John VanWinkle and family
Mike Meeks
Harry Barber

All of whom reside along the lower reaches of the Gros
Ventre River north and northwest of Jackson.

Dave Cheney and family, Wilson

There will be a meeting of the Jackson Chapter of the
American Red Cross this Friday evening at the Rest House
at 8:30 p.m. All members and others interested are urged to
attend.

Francesca ran a borrowed brush through her hair, put her feet back into
the kid slippers, and opened the bedroom door. From the lobby, she heard
a commotion, voices raised. Someone laughing. "Praise be!" Mrs. Crabtree's
voice.

A low male reply.

Goose bumps broke out on Francesca's arms.

More unintelligible words in that compelling voice, grave-sounding,
ending with, "... any sign of her?"

Her hike through the countryside on aching feet forgotten, she ran down
the dusty carpet into the lobby. "Bryce!"

He turned, as grimed and filthy as she'd been an hour ago, and she threw
herself at his chest. "I thought you were dead!"

Before she could ask about Benjy, she saw a wide-eyed Mrs. Crabtree
holding a filthy child on her hip.

Bryce's arms came around Francesca, held her so hard against him she could feel his heart thundering. He kissed her; their teeth clicked together. She smelled the mud on him, tasted grit on his lips, and didn't care a whit that she'd just bathed.

"How did you manage to make it?" Bryce asked at her ear.

"Bayberry swam to me. I'd swear she knew what she was doing." She recalled the mare running off. "She got out of the river yesterday on the south side where it joins the Snake."

Bryce rubbed her back as if reassuring himself she was real. "Someone will find her. She knows to go to people."

Francesca wanted to kiss Bryce again, but she became aware of the audience they were drawing. She pulled away and brushed the sand off her borrowed dress.

"Three of 'em safe!" a man exclaimed.

"One left."

"Nope. Message came down from Kelly. Charlie Sanborn's found; got a broke leg."

Bryce released Francesca. "Thank God he's alive!"

The onlookers continued their jawing.

"Sure enough. Heard tell Harriet Lawrence lost her place ... reckon she might go to Snake River with him?"

Francesca waited to see if Bryce would quash the story, but he spoke into the rising murmur. "I hope she moves right over with Charlie."

Mrs. Crabtree tried to smooth things over. "How about a bath and something to eat for you and Bryce?" she asked Benjy.

"What's the word on Ben and Anne Raleigh?" Bryce wondered.

"The paper said they lost their house," Francesca replied.

"They're probably at John's place on Mormon Row. Nothing over there got it," a man offered.

And another, "More good news. Someone found your Bayberry and took him to Wort's Livery."

Bryce looked at Francesca. "Soon as we get cleaned up and fed, I want to take Benjy up to Ben and Anne."

Chapter Forty-three
May 19, 1927

Charlie lay in a wagon bed in the rain with Harriet at his side, Foster and Bobby on the seat, ready to drive to Snake River.

He steeled himself for the pain of taking the long way around up Antelope Flats road and around Blacktail Butte—too much debris on the southern route.

When they had brought him to the school, he hadn't seen the destruction, but as the wagon started to head north, he had a view out the back from where he lay.

"My Lord," he said. "Your place—"

"Is gone," Harriet replied softly. "My sewing machine, all the summer dresses I was working on for folks."

Despite his pain, Charlie's heart went out to her. "I know you set a store by your house. Maybe you can …."

Harriet looked bleakly out over the desolate landscape littered with mounds of river rock and ruined trees. Very little material from the buildings remained; it must all have been swept downstream.

"I won't try and rebuild." She tucked a damp blanket over Charlie and cradled his cheek with her hand. "Maybe I know a man who'll take me in?"

"God, yes, Harriet." Charlie's voice rose. "You know I've been angling for that all along."

As they passed the surviving Episcopal Church, a knot of men stood out front. One, who was all too familiar, put his fingers to his mouth and let out a sharp whistle.

Foster drew rein and Dieter Gross crunched over the gravel to peer into the wagon bed. A black hat covered his shaved head, the brim dripping rain.

Harriet gasped and drew her hand away from Charlie's cheek, too late.

Dieter's scornful eyes missed nothing. "You've gone too far, Sanborn, with your uppity ways. Getting Sutton to cut you in on the ranch and thinking you're entitled to a white woman." His malevolent gaze lashed Harriet. "Have you no shame?"

"None," she answered steadily. "It's you who ought to be ashamed."

Dieter looked back at Charlie, stuck on his back like a bug with his leg immobilized. "You take this woman to your house at Snake River and there'll be hell to pay."

Francesca, Bryce, and Benjy arrived at what was left of Kelly before sunset, having hitched a wagon ride as far as the rocky low water crossing of the Gros Ventre. On the north side of the river, one of the Mormon Row families offered to ferry Francesca and the boy up in an auto, while Bryce rode Bayberry.

A number of cars and some tethered buggies had parked in front of the LDS Church. Outside, six wooden coffins, in various stages of construction, sat on sawhorses. As she alighted from the car with Benjy, Francesca detected the scent of food and surmised the haves were serving the have-nots.

Seeing that Bryce was coming along slower on horseback, she took Benjy by the hand into the church.

And stopped.

"*Ave Maria*." On the altar, covered with dirty quilts, lay five adult-sized bodies and a smaller one that must be young Joe Kneedy. They evidently had yet to be washed and dressed.

The first few rows of pews held mourners. A woman with bowed head gave a muffled sob; a man pulled out a handkerchief and blew his nose. From the adjoining fellowship hall came hushed voices and the tink of cutlery.

Before Francesca could hand off Benjy or move to help the women with the food, William walked out of the fellowship hall. He didn't look at the bodies; Francesca recalled his aversion to death.

Prudence Johnston followed him, wearing a subdued dress, but as she moved to catch up with him, her crystal beads clashed.

"Francesca!" William gasped.

She'd thought word would precede them about her, Bryce, and Benjy being safe, but everyone turned and gaped.

"Our Lord be praised!" said the bishop of the local ward. "Call off the search."

As William started toward Francesca. Pru dug her fingernails into his forearm. "Don't you dare," she hissed.

She'd been dogging him ever since he came in for food, putting on "sympathy" for what people were beginning to believe was the certain loss of Francesca.

William threw Pru off and lifted Francesca off her feet, laughing. "You're here! I looked all night and day like a crazy man."

Freed by William grabbing Francesca, Benjy ran up the aisle toward the bodies.

The bishop snagged him. "There, young man. You must have had an adventure."

William realized how inappropriate his joy must look in this setting, and set Francesca down.

Over her shoulder, he saw Bryce coming up the aisle with a dangerous glint in his eyes.

ɕ∽ᶇ

Bryce glared at William and put a proprietary hand on Francesca's shoulder.

"Get away from her." A bit of spittle escaped Brother's mouth.

"William, you goddamned fool!" Prudence cried, to a collective gasp and dark look from the Bishop. She gave both William and Francesca stiff-armed shoves on her way to slam out through the vestibule—there she crashed into a weeping woman bearing a bucket of water to wash the dead and spilled the precious load.

Francesca trembled under Bryce's hand. God, what if she waffled again? What if William's entreaty made her turn back to him?

"Francesca's with me now." Bryce prayed she would not correct him.

William's expression darkened. He shoved Francesca out of the way and threw a punch that connected solidly in Bryce's midsection.

The breath driven out of his stiff, sore body, Bryce went down sprawling in the church aisle.

Francesca grabbed William's arm. "Stop it."

He shook her off. "Let go. This has been a long time coming."

Bryce scrambled up. "A damned long time. And Francesca's just the thing for getting it in the open." He glanced around at their audience and spread his hands open at his sides. "I don't want to fight you, Brother."

William's fist connected with Bryce's jawbone.

He reeled but stayed up. Fists raised, Bryce started to circle in the small space.

Francesca leaped between them.

The bishop grabbed Bryce's shoulder. "No fighting in a house of worship, not after what has happened to these poor people."

William and Bryce stared at each other, both breathing hard.

The first to look away, William gave Francesca a look of disgust. "He'll leave you again. You know he will."

Before Bryce could deny it, William followed Prudence's lead and slammed out of the church.

Chapter Forty-four
May 20, 1927

Bryce and Francesca arrived at Snake River Ranch at midnight. He was beyond exhausted, the knot on his head and the bruise on his cheek from William's punch throbbed.

Before he slept, he must see Mom and Dad.

Of course, William had probably stopped by and primed them to be negative. But if he hadn't, they might think he and Francesca were still missing, as the people in Kelly had.

The road in to the ranch seemed darker than he recalled, as Bayberry followed it at a slow and steady walk. Thankfully, it had stopped raining, the overcast breaking up to reveal a waning gibbous moon that lighted their way.

Bryce focused on the welcome feel of Francesca's arms around his waist as she rode behind him. He attributed her silence to the same deep fatigue that dragged at him.

The approach of hooves from the opposite direction—someone leaving the ranch—put him on alert. He wasn't ready to confront William again.

Horse and rider went by fast, reckless in disregard of the night.

"Who in hell was that?"

Francesca breathed at his ear. "I think it was Foster."

"Odd at this hour."

"He's been seeing a woman who works at the Lazy D," Francesca said.

On the lower river bench, Bryce stabled Bayberry with Lucifer, fed and watered her. Then he tapped lightly on his folks' door. "Hello?" he called.

A moment later, his mother flung the portal wide. "Bryce!" She threw her arms around him. "When Harriet came back with Charlie, they said you were still missing."

Dad came out of the bedroom with a lamp in hand. He set it on the dining table beside the newspaper. "Son!"

In his father's embrace, Bryce felt he'd been forgiven, but it wasn't enough. "Mom ... Dad ... I need to apologize for leaving you all."

Dad hugged him harder. "We owe you an apology as well. We should have believed in you."

৵৶

After being gone from Snake River only a few days, Francesca was overwhelmed by a sense of homecoming. In Laura's arms, then Cord's, she rejoiced in the family she had lost.

Laura made tea and they sat around the table. She touched the newspaper and looked at Bryce with moist eyes as if making sure he was real.

"William stop by this evening?" Bryce asked.

"No. We thought he was still searching." Cord glanced at Francesca.

She bit her lip, hoping neither of Bryce's parents would mention the house William had built her, or William's recent proposal.

"We saw him at the church in Kelly." Bryce touched his cheek. "When he saw us together, there were ... words."

"Oh, dear," said Laura.

The stillness in the room became palpable. Though they had forgiven Bryce for leaving in anger, his parents took this continued evidence of their sons' feud poorly.

"What happened?" Cord ground out.

"He slugged me," Bryce replied evenly.

Laura set her teacup down with a clink. "I'm sure that's what happened, but you have to understand how disappointed he is, after Francesca moved out of the house he built her on the bluff."

Bryce's lips set in a line. "How's that?"

Francesca met his eyes. "Last fall William built me a house. He stayed in his, of course."

"Of course," Bryce said dryly.

Laura looked troubled, and changed the subject. "Cord and I have been talking this evening. With Charlie laid up and just William here, we were going to have to cancel the dude season. Now you're here, we might be able to work it with the two of you, but there's less than two weeks, and if you boys can't ...."

Francesca sucked in her breath. How could Bryce and William possibly ... after ....?

To her surprise, Bryce lifted his chin, where a nasty bruise was beginning from William's blow. "We'll work together," he said grimly. "You can't cancel the season."

As soon as the door to his parents' place closed behind them, Francesca tried to put a hand on Bryce's arm, but he walked away stiffly. Moving quickly, he started for the road up onto the bluff.

Francesca followed. "Bryce—"

"You stop off at the fancy house Brother built you," he tossed over his shoulder. "I'll hit the bunkhouse."

"No!" she called. "Bryce, stop and listen to me!"

He dug his heels in and made it up the bluff without using the road. She scrambled up after him, the kid slippers Mrs. Crabtree had given her inadequate for the rough cobbled soil. Grabbing at sage to pull herself up, she made it to the top.

Bryce stood staring at her house, awash in silver moonlight. Deep shadows pooled beneath the porch. "I can't believe it," he declared. "William built the house I imagined." He shook his head. "That son of a bitch!"

"No," she said. "He's not."

Bryce rounded on her.

"He said it was mine without strings," she said. He'd also said he always intended to occupy it with her.

With a sinking sensation, she knew she owed Bryce the true state of her feelings for the brothers. "There's something I need to tell you." She swallowed. "I want you to know William will always be in my heart. I hate to see him hurt, when he's done nothing to deserve—"

"How about Pru?"

"Yes, he's been with her again this past week. I know that, but you need to understand why. Last Saturday, he finally asked me to marry him." Francesca stopped Bryce from pacing by putting her hands on his arms. "I told him 'no' because I knew that even though I love him like a brother or a friend, I would never be in love with him, desperately and completely, the way I am with you."

"Francesca! I—"

She put a finger to his lips. "From the first time I met an 'Idaho cowboy,' there was something between us. I didn't understand it, but it was always there, hiding in my heart when you went away the first time, and almost killing me last summer."

Bryce stopped pacing and dragged her into his arms. "God, I was so afraid I'd lost you in the flood," he murmured into her hair. "For all the times I wasn't there, I'm going to make it up to you."

Her knees turned to butter; the fiery sensations only Bryce could evoke poured through her.

Her pulse began a steady pounding. "Starting when?"

He took her hands as if making a vow. "Starting now." He looked at her place. "But not in that house."

"Where then?" Not the cookshack lean-to, and the cabin she had shared last summer with Rosa and Maria lacked appeal.

"How about a dude cabin?"

At two a.m. they walked into the heart of the ranch. Darkness reigned when they passed William's bachelor house.

It smelled musty inside the largest guest cabin. Bryce carried in kindling and a couple of logs while Francesca made up the double bed in the biggest bedroom.

Finally, there was nothing more to do.

With the fire shedding a glow, Bryce watched Francesca kick off her slippers and reach for the buttons on her dress. She held his gaze while she parted them, one by one, then slipped the yellow-flowered cotton off her shoulders and let it fall to pool on the boards.

Standing naked before him, she offered everything. He looked at her golden skin, burnished by firelight, her hair turned coppery. She was everything he had imagined on those restless lonely nights as a raw youth, discovering his appetites, through the years when he tried first one woman and then another, only to find something missing in each relationship. With this night, his years of wandering would end.

"I love you, Francesca," he said softly. "I want you to know I haven't been with anyone since you. I couldn't even imagine it."

Perhaps she had been with William; he didn't want to know. The odd thing was that if she had, if that's what it had taken for her to know whom she loved, then he was neither jealous nor curious.

He stripped off the white shirt, trying not to rush, unzipped the borrowed trousers. Never, not on the Timbered Island, not at the Canyon Hotel, had he felt such imperative desire.

When he seized her, his blood thundered, in his head, in his heart, in his sex. And he remembered. "I don't have anything ...." He should have picked up some condoms at the drug store in Jackson, but his mind had been on too many other things.

Francesca's eyes searched his. "Would it matter to you if—?"

"Matter?" What would a child of theirs look like? A lovely little girl with his eyes and her sleek hair? A boy with mischievous dark eyes?

He answered on instinct. "I think I'd be ecstatic!"

Chapter Forty-five
May 20, 1927

Snake River Ranch slumbered beneath a nearly full moon. Compared to the raw wound of the flood's path, its picturesque Old West ambiance lay untouched. In the bunkhouse, Asa, Jim, and Bobby slept soundly in separate rooms, worn out from their search for survivors.

Bryce and Francesca lay in a tangle, dreaming of the times they would have together.

Cord and Laura rested easier knowing Bryce and Francesca were safe, but they stayed awake a little longer, discussing Charlie's prognosis, and whether they would be ready to receive dudes in two weeks. Finally they slept.

Charlie breathed evenly to fool Harriet, but he'd palmed the doc's pills, hating the idea of being drugged.

In this darkest hour, he wished he'd not been so proud. His leg pounded in the soft flesh, and the bone screamed in agony where it had snapped in two. Despite the night chill, sweat popped out on his brow.

Lying with his leg propped in a cast, he considered waking Harriet, asking her to shake out some pills and bring him a glass of water. He could get used to having her help him.

Except a man wanted to be whole and help himself. And he would, if only his damned leg knitted up right.

Suddenly Charlie's ears pricked. He frowned and lifted his head.

If he could move, he'd investigate whatever did not belong outside his quiet home. A faint pounding as if someone hammered two boards together. He nudged Harriet.

The stars wheeled around the moon. The night smelled of sage and the pines on the Timbered Island, of earth and river ... and the stench of gasoline.

A match flared. And another.

Torches burst into bright life. An arm arced back.

And threw.

Asa woke to a crash of breaking glass.

He sat bolt upright, his heart racing. Moonlight revealed the dusty window in his bunkhouse room, intact.

Another crash, at the far end of the hall, where empty rooms awaited the summer outfit.

He jumped out of bed and opened the hall door to flickering orange light and the stench of fuel and smoke.

"Jim! Bobby! Fire!" he shouted.

Within seconds, the other men fell out, mouths gaping. "The hell …..?" Bobby cried.

Jim ran outside and the others followed.

"Would you look at that?" Asa yelled.

Five of the dude cabins were bright beacons of flame.

Bryce dreamed he and Francesca were on a bed before a lively fire. It crackled and popped, and shed a bright illumination visible even through his closed eyelids.

He opened them to hellish vermilion light.

And jackknifed out of bed. How could he have been so stupid as to let the fire get out of hand?

Standing, trembling, he looked at the fireplace wall and saw the flames weren't from the hearth, or the chimney.

"Bryce?" Francesca cried.

Through the open door between rooms, he saw the couch and curtains were ablaze, with fire licking up the front wall. It didn't make sense, unless ....

He stepped closer and smelled gasoline.

Good Lord, Brother had been livid but surely …. Recalling William's hesitation about saving him on the Grand, he felt a hollowness open in the center of his chest.

Francesca's fearful eyes met his.

"Let's get out of here." Bryce snatched up his boots and trousers and slid up the sash of the nearest window.

She rolled out of bed and grabbed her clothes. As she started to step into her dress, he put a bare leg over the sill. "Do it outside."

Francesca scrambled out after him into the night and struggled into her dress as she went.

Hopping on one foot, putting on his pants, Bryce heard her strangled gasp. "Look!"

She pointed at another blazing cabin.

A hard ache seized Bryce's throat. Someone was systematically destroying Snake River Ranch.

✢

Cord shocked into wakefulness with Laura shaking his shoulder.

"Dammit." He put a hand to his chest where his heart was suddenly racing. "Don't scare me like that."

She ignored his bark. "There's something wrong up on the bluff."

He heard it. Men shouting, horses' hooves drumming a stampede.

"I'm afraid there's a …."

Cord could see her strained face. With the curtains closed, there should have been darkness. Instead, a glow too warm for moonlight seeped in around the edges.

Sharing Laura's awful premonition, he threw back the covers and put his bare soles to cold boards.

Even as he rushed to the window, he wanted to retreat, to yank the bedcovers over his head and curl up in a dream. To go back to the night when he was six years old and deep in the untroubled slumber of the innocent, watched over by Sarah and Franklin.

Before the night of fire.

Cord drew back the curtain.

Up on the bluff, flames leaped for the sky. That was the Main; other torches marked the cookshack and the saddle shed.

"Dear God." Dancing light reflected in Laura's stricken eyes. She was up, pulling on her trousers.

He looked at the spectacle, unable to catch his breath.

From a hundred yards away, Francesca watched a flare arc through the darkness and land on William's front porch. A crash of glass and the front wall exploded into flames. Within seconds, they licked their way up onto the shake roof.

Then silhouettes against the flames, dark shapes of milling horses. The riders appeared strange, misshapen.

The moonlight caught two of them, in pale robes and peaked hoods with holes for the eyes.

Francesca started to run toward William's house.

Bryce caught her arm in a vice-like grip and jerked her to a stop. "Don't let the Klan see you!" he hissed. "We'll circle round the back."

Charlie poked Harriet for the second time.

She stirred and rubbed her eyes.

Through the thick drape, hung so Charlie could nap if he'd been up with a sick animal, came a faint flickering light.

Adrenaline shot through him. "There's something burning outside!" he said. "Go and see."

Grumbling, she pushed back the covers. "I don't see what—" She reached the window and pulled the drape open. "Oh, my God!"

Charlie struggled to lift himself on a pile of pillows. "What ....?"

She held back the heavy material to reveal a huge cross burning in his yard.

Bryce seized Francesca's hand. "We'll get William."

They took off, crouching low, taking a wide detour around to Brother's place.

When they passed the stables, Asa, Jim, and Bobby were getting the horses out. No fire there. "We managed to put out the one in the bunkhouse," Asa said.

"We're going to get William," Bryce told the hands. "Then we need to get into the gun room in the Main."

Bobby pulled a Colt .45 pistol from his waistband. "Here's one."

"Hold off until we're better armed," Bryce said. If Bobby showed their hand too soon, and they had only one weapon, they'd get themselves killed.

The five of them made a surreptitious approach to William's burning house.

When they got close without detection, Bryce started toward the window in the rear.

Jim clasped his arm. "I'll do it." No one could miss the flames leaping inside William's bedroom.

Bryce opened his mouth to argue, and Francesca's fingernails dug into his other bare forearm. "Let him."

Jim darted away in the darkness; his silhouette, head and shoulders, showed at the window.

"Say a prayer," Bryce whispered to Francesca. She clutched his hand so hard his fingertips went numb.

William had to have gotten out. He was somewhere in the darkness watching the horrors.

Jim's shadow returned, keeping low. He gasped for breath, unable to speak.

Bryce was holding his own breath.

"There's someone," Jim rasped, "in the bed. oh, God ...."

Francesca moaned.

The blazing pyre blurred before Bryce's eyes.

Brother.

In their last moments together, they had fought. Bryce had even had the gall to suspect him of trying to burn him and Francesca out. How in the name of God was he going to live with that?

Blind rage, as red and as hot as the flames, sent Bryce running in search of a weapon.

༶ঞ❀ঞ༶

Everything in Charlie screamed that he had to get up, but his broken leg rooted him to the mattress.

"Get down!" he warned Harriet, who knelt at the window. Light from the burning cross made a halo around her hair. "There's no telling what ...."

Any second, a torch would fly through the window. Blazing gasoline would spatter them both. To die by fire would be agony.

Or if the Klan targeted another window and set the place going, Harriet would have to try and drag him out.

What then? The anonymous cowards would be waiting outside with rifles, a noose ....

"Harriet," he said in a tortured voice. "Get out of the house, now. Try and find someplace to hide."

If they had the place ringed, it was already too late.

She turned, with the cross framed in the window behind her. "I'm not leaving you."

"You have to. You don't know how these things—"

"I won't leave you here helpless. If they set the house, you'll burn alive."

"It's worse than that. If they capture us, they'll probably lynch me. They may rape you and then kill you, too."

Her hand went to her throat. "Dear Lord."

"Go, Harriet. Now."

Her eyes blazed like the fire. "I said I'm not leaving you."

When Bryce, Francesca, and the hands reached the Main, the dining room and kitchen were fully involved. The gun room lay on the opposite side of the building.

Bryce, almost blind with rage, started for the front steps.

Asa threw his arms around him from behind.

Bryce tried to fight him off.

"Hold a minute," Asa gritted in his ear. "What's the plan?"

Bryce's head buzzed. William ....

Francesca circled around in front of him and forced him to look into her eyes, glittering in the reflected firelight. "Think!" she demanded.

Connecting with her tapped a valve that sent sanity coursing back into his veins. He had to settle down before he got them all killed.

When his breathing slowed, Asa released him.

"All right," he said. "Asa and Bobby, you take cover with Francesca. Jim comes with me."

Bryce started for the steps, turned back, and kissed Francesca; their lips clung. "We'll be in and out in no time."

He and Jim rushed onto the porch. On the boards lay a pack of Snake River's souvenir matches, Bryce saw them the instant before his boot crushed the box.

Inside, a wall of heat hit them; the fire was rolling up into the rafters. Curtains of purple, crimson, and vermilion wavered, formed and reformed, growing larger.

The gun room, which lay beyond the gathering area with the big fireplace, stayed locked, the spare key on top of the jamb.

With the heat at his back, Bryce reached the door, ran his hand along the top.

Nothing.

Heart thudding, he reached for the knob.

The door opened beneath his hand.

He looked at Jim in the dancing light, and saw he understood someone had beaten them to it. Bryce started to gesture him back, to begin his own retreat.

The door jerked open to reveal someone in the pale robe and hood of the Klan. They snapped a rifle up and trained it on Bryce's chest.

From the corner of his eye, Bryce saw an unarmed Jim melt away and head for the porch undetected.

Too late for Bryce. Who were these guys? All he saw beneath the hood were a pair of dark eyes reflecting hell back at him.

Eyes that looked familiar.

"Hold it there," said Foster Case from beneath his disguise, "I wouldn't want to have to kill you."

"You son of a bitch!" Bryce exclaimed. "I saw you ride away earlier."

"Met up with the boys at the Cottonwood Creek crossing," Foster said easily.

"I never would have thought you'd turn against us. Course I haven't been around much to know you," Bryce tried to keep a quaver out of his voice. He had to keep Foster talking. "If you're so inclined, I'm surprised you don't work at Lazy D with Dieter and his nest of bigots."

Foster laughed.

Behind him in the gun room, a window sash started to slide up. Praying it was someone from Snake River, Bryce yelled, "You've got a lot of nerve taking our money to work here and then burning the place down. With our own matches!"

One man, then another, came over the sill and pressed into the space beyond the gun cabinet. Despite himself, Bryce couldn't help flicking his eyes in their direction.

Foster whirled.

Flame belched from a barrel, the concussion cracked and sent a sharp pain to Bryce's eardrums, along with a high-pitched ringing.

A dark bloom spread on the Klan robe. Foster dropped the rifle from nerveless hands and crumpled to the gun room floor.

Bobby stepped into the clear, and plucked the hood off. "Shit!" Bryce read Bobby's lips.

Bobby and Foster had also worked together at Circle X, spent time jaw-jacking, bummed each other's tobacco, gone hunting in the fall ....

With a visible effort, Bobby shook off his shock and started helping Jim and Bryce pull rifles, pistols, and ammunition from the cabinets.

∾

Francesca heard the shot inside the Main and almost slumped to the ground. First William—she couldn't think about him yet—now Bryce?

Jim had come out and reported a Klansman was holding a gun on Bryce. Then he and Bobby had gone around the corner of the building with the pistol.

Running footsteps pounded across the wood floor inside the Main. Jim ran out, dumped an armload of ammunition boxes on the ground, and turned to go back inside.

"Wait," Francesca got out.

He didn't hear her.

Bobby ran out with two rifles in his hands and the Colt he'd had before stuffed in his belt.

A sudden huge crack came from the rafters. The flaming roof swayed, appeared to steady, then began to come down.

Two men emerged from the building at a run. "Go!" Bryce shouted. "Get back!"

Francesca and Asa ran with the others, while behind them, the crown jewel of the Snake River Ranch collapsed.

The men armed themselves and Bryce looked at Francesca. "Can you shoot?"

Recalling William's careful tutelage, she fiercely blinked back tears. "I can shoot."

Bryce handed her a Colt .45 and a box of ammunition. She'd never handled this particular pistol before, and the moon shadow hampered her, but she managed to figure out how to load it. Bryce nodded.

"Now, where are they?" he wondered.

The group looked around. Almost every building on the ranch was in flames, except storehouses, stables, and Charlie's place, set apart from the rest of the ranch against the upper bluff.

But as Francesca made out the dark shape, she noted a dancing light illuminating the sage. "Look." She pointed.

"Something's on fire behind Charlie's." Bryce exclaimed.

They moved across the flat until they had a view of a burning cross, not fifty feet from the house.

"Split up!" Bryce ordered. "Asa, you and Bobby and Jim go to Charlie. Francesca and I will check on Mom and Dad."

He led the way down the bluff to the lower bench. Clasping the loaded pistol, Francesca slip-slid in the soft riverine soil and turned her ankle on a cobble.

When they reached the bottom, all appeared dark and quiet around the Sutton house. Too dark and quiet.

Cord and Laura must have heard the commotion. So they were either hiding out, armed and ready, or ....

Beyond the house, from the river side, came a sudden repetitive sound, like hammering.

Bryce stopped, his hand lifted for silence.

Another clapping sound echoed off the bluff.

He put his mouth close to Francesca's ear. "Putting another cross together."

Klansmen on horseback surrounded Charlie's house.

They began to shout, "We can, we will, we must, fight back!" Along with insults aimed at a white woman who would sully herself with a black man. Any moment Charlie expected the conflagration to begin, or for the men to crash through the front door and drag him and Harriet out.

She huddled beside him, her face paler than he'd ever seen it. He should have stayed away from her, not let her risk herself.

His eyes fell on his holster and pistol, hung over the back of a straight chair against the wall. He'd never felt the need to sleep with a gun under his pillow; he'd felt safe at Snake River Ranch.

The shouting outside grew louder, as the circle tightened around the house.

"Harriet," Charlie whispered. "Get my pistol."

The terror in her eyes increased, but she brought it to him.

Something crashed through the window.

Charlie thought his heart would stop.

In the next instant, a thud. The men outside brayed like hyenas, while Harriet dodged the thrown rock.

Charlie looked at her. During the Civil War and the settling of the West, women had carried pistols, and not just to protect themselves. In the event of capture by an opposing army or Indians, they were prepared to kill themselves to prevent rape and torture.

If the men burst in and laid hands on Harriet, what would he do?

Outside, he heard the crack of rifle fire. Then more sharp reports and a man shouted, "Let's go!"

With a thunder of hooves, the terrorists rode into the night.

Francesca heard the shooting up on the bluff and the pounding of many hooves. Her heart thudded.

How many Klansman were in front of the Sutton house? Too many for her and Bryce to take?

Suddenly, from a thicket of fir about forty feet away came, "Pssst!"

Francesca froze.

"Son!"

Bryce was running toward the copse. Cord showed himself for a second in the moonlight and retreated. Francesca hastened to join them.

Laura was there, carrying a rifle, as was Cord.

"Where's William?" Cord hissed.

Francesca felt Bryce stiffen. She swallowed.

"Not with us," Bryce said shortly.

Cord gestured toward the house. "Bryce, the south side; I'll go north."

Laura stayed him. "That's not enough guns. I'm coming."

"And I," said Francesca.

Cord bent low and started creeping through the sage. Laura went with him. Bryce and Francesca brought up the rear.

Slowly, they angled up behind the house. There, they split up and started along the sides.

When they got to the corner, Bryce put a hand behind him and motioned for Francesca to wait while he investigated.

She crouched by the wall, while he disappeared around the corner into the shadows of the porch.

"Stand down!" Cord shouted from the other side of the house, "you murdering sons of bitches."

Francesca's chest clutched. Of course, a father would have understood Bryce's terse statement about William.

Cord's rifle cracked. Another report answered his. And another.

Francesca leaped up and moved to join the fight. She looked around the corner of the building and saw a Klansman taking aim at Bryce.

The training William had given her asserted itself—she raised the Colt, pulled back the hammer, and sighted on the center of the man's robed chest.

When she squeezed the trigger, the Colt kicked.

Before she could see if she'd scored a hit, someone seized her and knocked the Colt to the ground. A huge callused hand clapped over her mouth; she tried to bite, but it was cupped so it closed off not only her mouth but her nostrils.

More gunshots rang out.

The hand was suffocating her; the moonlight started to gray.

Without warning, a deafening report at point blank range. She must have been shot. She didn't feel any pain, but she'd heard stories of people in shock who didn't know they'd been hit.

Her captor's hands loosened, but he dragged her down with him as he crumpled to the earth.

Francesca struggled free, gasping for breath.

As things began to come back into focus, she saw a dark spreading stain on the Klansman's hood. She reached a shaking hand and revealed the staring sightless eyes of Tiny Good, shot through the head.

William faced her across the body, pistol in hand.

§◦❧

From behind Bryce, the concussion of another shot exploded. He turned to see what Francesca was shooting at, but she wasn't in sight.

"Francesca!" he called.

She didn't answer.

His heart in his throat, Bryce raced to the corner of the house and looked around.

William and Francesca stood over the body of Tiny Good.

She was staring at William as if he was a ghost. Brother looked green around the gills and the pistol in his hand shook.

"I killed him." William looked as if he couldn't believe it.

"You saved my life," Francesca said.

More shots from the south. A man shouted, "We're from the Bar BC. We've got you outmanned and outgunned."

From the porch, Cord shouted. "You heard them! Drop your weapons ... and your sheets."

Bryce turned back to the battlefield to find six Klansmen backing into a circle and raising their hands, while the men from the Bar BC approached.

From beneath their hoods emerged Dieter Gross and five of his hands.

§◦❧

William stepped onto the porch. Father saw him and his eyes widened. "William, thank God!"

Engulfed in a bear hug ... Mother's tearful voice from nearby. "Son, oh, son!"

She took her turn at pulling him into a hard grip, making him wonder aloud, "Why's everybody acting like they're surprised to see me?"

"You had us all petrified," Bryce replied, "We saw your house go up."

William registered that his house was gone, but he couldn't process it. Not with the magnitude of the night's destruction.

"I wasn't home," he said. "After we ...." Embarrassed at having thrown the first punch, he trailed off. "I stopped off at the Bar BC. I needed time to cool off before coming back to Snake River."

"I think we both did," Bryce said. "But if it isn't you lying dead in your bed, Brother, who is it?"

"In my bed?" William asked dully.

"Jim looked in your window and saw someone." Bryce's eyes were dark holes in the moonlight. "We thought it was you."

With a creeping coldness, William knew there was only one person who would have gone into his house, gotten beneath the covers and waited for him.

She'd been enraged, shoving her way out of the church.

Too late, he realized that what she had told him Saturday night before the dance had been the undiluted truth. All her posturing, all her drawing men in like a bright flower attracting bees had been to make one man jealous, to make him see through her bravado.

"Pru!" William gasped. He fell to his knees beside the wall and vomited.

Chapter Forty-six
May, 1927

The sun rose over the smoking ruins of Snake River Ranch, a lovely day soft with the promise of summer. The only buildings left were the bunkhouse, stables, hothouse, one dude cabin, Charlie's place, and Cord and Laura's house and barn.

The Bar BC hands had locked an unrepentant Dieter Gross and his accomplices in the barn to await the Sheriff's men. Cord said only one thing to Dieter, "I'll see you hang for murder."

For William was right about Prudence. He viewed and identified her by the melted glass lumps of her beads. Asa offered to ride and inform her family, but William insisted it was his responsibility.

With sweat popping out on his forehead, as thickly as it had when he entered the remains of his bedroom and saw the charred lump of flesh, he faced her parents. "I wasn't home. She came in ...."

Mrs. Johnston, her doughy fist pressed to her pursed mouth, fled the room.

Mr. Johnston looked down his narrow nose at William. "You treated our daughter like a whore. All she ever wanted was for you to love her."

William swallowed. "I know that ... now."

Mr. Johnston shut him out of the house.

William returned to Snake River to answer the Sheriff's questions about the killing of Tiny Good. Though no one accused him of being trigger happy, the little voice in his head wondered if there had been another way he could have dealt with Tiny.

Stupid with sleep deprivation, he holed up in the bunkhouse and pulled a blanket over his head.

What next? Father would probably want to rebuild, but William knew enough about the ranch finances to know it was a pipe dream.

Jackson's Hole prepared to bury their dead, the six victims of the flood, along with Prudence and Tiny. Foster's family had his body shipped over The Pass to Rexburg, Idaho, for burial in their family cemetery. It was just as well; few in the valley would have attended his service.

At many of the flooded ranches, cleanup began. Work started on a new bridge over the Gros Ventre to link Jackson and Moose.

In contrast, Snake River Ranch lay abandoned to the elements. When Jim, Asa, and Bobby, along with William and Bryce started in to work, Cord stopped them. "Leave all that for a bit," he suggested mildly.

In the early mornings, he and Laura walked amid the wreckage of their dreams. He sent Bryce to Jackson the day after the fire to telephone each of the dudes scheduled for the first two-week session. "We'll mail cancellations to the rest." Cord spoke matter-of-factly, as if each word did not drive a spike into his heart.

His house no longer felt like home. He and Laura had trouble sleeping, imagining each night sound to be another visit from the Klan. The group that had burned the cross at Charlie's house had ridden away without anyone discovering their identities.

He could only hope the fact that Dieter and his men were in jail awaiting trial acted as a deterrent to further violence.

William made his home in the bunkhouse, along with Jim, Asa, and Bobby. Charlie and Harriet stayed in his house, and Bryce and Francesca in the surviving dude cabin. She cooked in Laura's kitchen, where the Sutton family ate around their table, and delivered meals to Charlie and Harriet and to the hands.

On the day after the last funeral, Prudence's, Cord called a meeting of the family and remaining staff.

"I won't rebuild." Cord swept his sharp gaze around Charlie's front room.

Francesca, sitting on a straight-backed kitchen chair next to Laura, sucked in her breath. There it was. What she had feared since the fire.

"But you've got to," Bryce burst out from his place beside William against the wall.

Charlie, on the sofa with his foot propped up, glanced at Harriet, who sat at his side. Bobby, Asa, and Jim looked resigned.

Cord gave his youngest a weary smile. "We can't afford it, and I'm too old and tired to start over."

"I'm not," Bryce argued. "Tell them, William, we can put this place back together."

William opened his mouth and closed it.

"Tell them, Brother!" Bryce insisted. "We can do it together, you know we can." He looked at Charlie. "Your leg's going to heal. We can work this season and be ready for dudes this time next year."

Charlie looked at Harriet and spoke to the room at large. "I'm afraid that after what happened here I've promised my wife—we already think of ourselves that way—that we'll find a safer place to live."

Francesca's heart sank. It was all falling apart.

"How about it, William? We can hire help and ...."

William's silver eyes met Bryce's green ones. He shook his head. "I've been waiting to see what Father had to say, ready to respect his decision. Now he's made it, I've got to confess I'm relieved."

"Relieved!" Bryce exhaled an exasperated puff. "We're talking about the ranch here, our home."

Laura leaned forward. "We've been wondering about that. It was home, but it doesn't feel that way anymore. We've been ... violated."

William nodded. "I've been thinking about where I go from here." He looked at Francesca. "I need to get away." He turned to his father. "I've decided to make my life in Texas."

"Oh, dear," Laura murmured.

"I went to town yesterday and phoned Tom Lamar. I worked for him before outside San Antonio. His daughter, Anne, answered, and told me their foreman retired."

"No!" Bryce shouted. "It was just a fire and you're all acting as if it's the end of the world."

Cord rose and went to place a hand on Bryce's shoulder. "For me, it was more than the destruction of what I've worked for since 1898. It brought back another night of fire and violence."

∽✑

Six-year-old Cord heard the wolves outside his parents' cabin, a large pack calling each other home across the night. Wind whistled through the crack beneath the cabin door, and the draft ruffled his hair.

Rolling over in his flannel nightshirt, he removed a loose chink of mud from between the logs over his bed. Outside, a wash of moonlight turned sage to silver and the gray granite spires of the Tetons to pearl. The wolves howled again, closer.

Across the cabin, Cord's mother, Sarah, sat up in bed, one slender hand at her throat. Even in the dim light, her hair shone like a silken curtain. "Franklin!" she hissed at her husband. "Wake up."

Cord's father reached beside their bed for his Remington.

The front door of the cabin crashed back against the wall; a tall man stood silhouetted against the silver moonlight. He wore a breastplate of bones over a flannel shirt and trousers. Braids fell over his shoulders, and his hair was swept up in a startling dark wing from his broad forehead.

Two shorter men crowded into the doorway behind the first one.

"Stop!" Franklin shouted, pointing his rifle at the man in the lead.

Sarah gasped, "Bitter Waters!"

"We have been driven off our land," he said. "burned the white man's Bible and seek a new life." He spoke of war as if he were about to spit from the bad taste in his mouth.

"Then go to your new life," Sarah said, "and leave my family in peace."

"The army pursues and kills us at every turn. We need everyone in whose veins flows the blood of the People to stand with us. Leave this white man, bring your child, and come." He reached toward his trouser pocket, as if to pull out a pistol.

Cord's father raised his weapon and placed his cheek against the stock. He growled, "Get out," and reached to chamber a round.

"No!" Sarah leaped in front of her brother.

Cord would never forget the shock that transformed his father's face as the hammer fell and the Remington slam fired without a finger on the trigger. The explosion of sound filled the low log house.

Sarah clutched her side and brought her hand away, dark with blood. She muttered something in Nez Perce that Cord did not understand.

One of the two warriors with Bitter Waters reached to his belt. A blade flashed in the firelight. Arcing through the air, it struck flesh, a dull slicing thud.

"No!" Bitter Waters shouted.

Cord bit back his own cry as his father staggered, trying to grasp the wooden handle protruding from the center of his chest.

Sarah screamed. The sound seemed to bubble in her throat, a liquid agony.

His father went down.

Rushing to his mother, Cord tried to grasp her hands, but she fell silent and slumped across the body of her husband, mingling their blood where they lay. Cord gaped at the impossible sight, wondering if Jesus was holding it against him that his mother's people had burned God's Book.

Smoke assailed Cord's nostrils. Through a blur of tears, he saw one of the Nez Perce had stirred up the fire's embers and scattered them. The same man whose blade protruded from his father's chest. Flames climbed Sarah's lace curtains and licked at the bark on the log walls.

Bitter Waters snatched the painted elk hide from the foot of the bed and dragged Cord outside by the back of his nightshirt. Despite his struggles, Cord was wrapped in the blanket and taken up onto a big gray horse.

Fueled by the wind, fire turned the silver night blood red. The Nez Perce leaped astride their horses and barked as they had before, the sounds echoing over the terraced river bottom

Bitter Waters leaned over to speak to Cord. "Sarah was my sister. I grieve for her, even as you do, but you are strong. You are of the Nimiipuu, the People."

Cord looked at the full moon that seemed to fall endlessly through a bank of scudding clouds and listened to the unearthly howling that had wakened him only minutes and a lifetime before.

His home collapsed in a shower of sparks.

Cord cleared his throat to erase the thickness as he finished telling his story to his family. "Everything I knew was taken from me that night. I hated Bitter Waters, blamed him, ran from him and ended up in the white world."

Bryce's tearstained face lifted, anguish in his eyes. "What brought you back together with Uncle?"

Cord glanced at Laura. "During the summer of 1900, when I met your mother, Bitter Waters was in Yellowstone. He told campfire stories of the Nez Perce, until a bigoted Army Captain in charge of the Park sent him packing."

William spoke up. "You've been singled out by whites for being Nez Perce. That isn't fair."

"No, but that's the way it is. I tried for a while to hide my heritage, but it turned out badly. And taught me there was no use in deceit, that I should be proud of who I am."

William's gaze dropped, and Cord surmised he would be hiding his heritage down in Texas. Perhaps someday he would come to see another way.

Bryce rose and went to the window facing the Tetons. His hands fisted for a moment, then the view seemed to soothe him.

"It's the end, then," he said with resignation. "The end of an era. All of us need to figure out what comes next."

When Bryce left Charlie's place with Francesca, everything seemed at a distance, the way it had when Bitter Waters died. Only this time, he wasn't dealing with the loss of a man who had lived a long and good life, but the end of something he'd believed would always be here. No matter his wanderings, he had always known the ranch awaited him whenever he cared to come home.

He entwined Francesca's long fingers in his and walked her toward the bluff, steering clear of the pile of blackened rubble that had once been her house.

What was next? For him and for her?

He could think of only one thing that wasn't about loss and destruction and looking back.

"It's time," he told Francesca.

Her inquiring dark gaze upon him felt like balm on a wound.

"Time for us to get married," he said.

She blinked. "With everyone in mourning?"

Bryce's eyes moistened. He mourned for the chuck wagon dinners, for the towering timbers of the Main, for the delicious aromas in the cookshack, for Dad riding Lucifer during roundup, for the night he met Francesca and shared wine and *ribollita*, for Bitter Waters.

"Don't you see? That's why we have to do it now," he said. "For hope in the middle of sorrow. Charlie and William are going to start a new life. We will, too."

As they entered the Chapel of the Transfiguration, Francesca clutched Bryce's hand. This new life would bind them in the eyes of God and man.

Gone was the uncertainty of the past. She believed in Bryce, in his commitment and dedication. In his pocket were the shining gold wedding bands they had purchased in Jackson.

In a dream state, Francesca stood beside Bryce before the altar. At five in the afternoon, the picture window behind the dais showed off the peaks, framed by aspen with spring-green leaves fluttering in the sun.

Francesca's throat was almost too tight for her to speak, but when the time came, she recited her vows, clear and strong. Bryce's husky delivery brought tears to her eyes—his as well.

With the rings on their fingers—and the signatures of the minister and his wife to bear witness on the license—they were man and wife.

On the way back to the ranch, Francesca belatedly recalled she should be getting dinner ready in Laura's kitchen. "I completely forgot."

Bryce chuckled. "You had something more important to do."

They arrived at almost six and found Laura soaking a pot of beans. Cord sat at the table, reading the *Courier*.

"Sorry I kept Francesca from starting dinner," Bryce said breezily. "Or maybe I should call her Mrs. Sutton."

Laura Fielding Sutton, who never shrieked, let out a whoop. She rushed across the room and hugged Francesca, then Bryce. "Married!" she crowed.

Cord was on his feet. "Praise God."

Once the congratulations wound down, Francesca lifted the lid on the beans.

Cord laughed. "Bryce, why don't you run up to the hothouse and get us some salad vegetables and stop by the coop for a frying chicken?"

Francesca noticed the difference in her status before she served her first meal as a Sutton. Everyone insisted on pitching in. Laura put the salad together, bursting with her usual pride at whatever she grew; Cord and Bryce were less effective but also hovered.

William arrived promptly at seven.

Already leery of his reaction, Francesca watched him take in her ring and shift his eyes to Bryce's. He inclined his head in a barely perceptible nod, as if he'd been expecting it. "Looks like we're having a celebration," he said gamely.

After dinner, he announced he was leaving for Texas.

Chapter Forty-seven
Summer/Autumn 1927

Once William had gone, Jim Lovejoy went to work at Red Rock Ranch up the Gros Ventre. Asa Dean moved to his family place to take over the heavy lifting for his aging parents. Bobby left the valley to look for work, promising to keep in touch.

The flood cleanup along the Snake River proceeded apace. State and local authorities estimated the damage at half a million dollars. Some of the families who had lost their homes stated their intent not to rebuild. Ray and Anna Kent, who owned the Kelly Mercantile, decided to buy up land in the ruined town for subdividing when memories of the horror had faded.

In the East, John D. Rockefeller read about the flood and phoned Horace Albright in Yellowstone. "We aren't really interested in land along the Gros Ventre and the lower Snake," Rockefeller said, "but if the disaster has affected anyone's feelings about the valley, perhaps the time might be right to move."

Quietly, agents of Rockefeller visited Jackson's Hole. They hired local people, including wrestler Mike Yokel, to work for a land investment firm known as the Snake River Land Company.

July 15, 1927

Almost two months since the fire that ended life as Cord and I knew it. This time last year, we had a full complement of dudes and the outfit. From morning to night, the place sparkled with life.

This year, we live in a mausoleum.

Other ranchers were kind enough to buy Brutus, Romulus and Remus, and the rest of the cattle and dude horses. Bayberry, who distinguished herself by saving Francesca in the flood, earned a place of honor in our stable with Lucifer.

Bryce and Francesca stayed with us until a few weeks ago. They would have stayed longer, but since we have no prospect of work here, Cord sat Bryce down and told him we would be fine and there is nothing going on here for young people. "It's time you provided for your wife," Cord said.

When Charlie and Harriet left for Michigan last week, I felt total despair. I pretended to be glad for him and Harriet (he was walking pretty well) but their departure left Cord and me alone.

Cord is napping; he seems to do that more and more lately, perhaps because he doesn't want to face the decisions we need to make. If anyone had told me we would lose our pride and joy—our dude ranch—I wouldn't have believed them. Our insurance coverage wasn't much, because with the buildings so far apart, we never believed anything could happen to more than a few of them at a time.

At the sound of an auto coming down the bluff, Laura lifted her head. She put aside her pen and went to the door.

Young Mike Yokel, sturdy and fit, alighted from a new DeSoto sedan and came toward the porch with a smile. He wore a formal suit with a white shirt and matching spats over his shoes and carried a shiny leather portfolio. "Good afternoon, Mrs. Sutton."

"What brings you here?" Laura believed in getting to the point. Mike had never come here before, and she'd never seen him dressed to the nines, what with him being a freighter and a fighter.

"Cord around?"

"He's sleeping right now."

Mike's smile faded. "I can come back when it's more convenient."

Something in his manner made her say crisply, "Why don't you just tell me your business?"

"Of course." Mike reached a big hand into his portfolio and drew out a folded document.

Slowly, he opened it and held it at an angle where Laura could read.

Bill of Sale

The bold letters were in script. Close spaced typing covered several pages. Laura's chest clutched. The figure mentioned in boldface was more than generous.

"This would be an excellent time to sell, what with ... your trouble." Mike looked uncomfortable. Last week's hanging of Dieter Gross had raked up attention to their plight all over again.

"It's not a decision to be made lightly." Laura tried to keep her anxiety under wraps.

"Of course," said Mike for the second time. He held out the papers.

She took them and studied the bottom line. "Who or what is the Snake River Land Company?"

"It's my understanding we're backed by some eastern investors who see the potential in the valley."

Though she knew something had to happen to change her and Cord's situation, the mention of easterners put her back up. "You can tell them our ranch isn't for sale."

She stood outside until Mike drove up over the bluff and out of sight. Then she took the papers into the house and put them under the loose stone in the fireplace.

Over the next few months, the burden of her secret weighed heavily. Each time she looked at the fireplace, she imagined the papers would leap out and into Cord's hand.

Each day when she rose, she vowed that today would be the one when she told him. She needed to do it before Mike Yokel paid another visit and Cord ended up looking foolish and she dishonest.

Each night she lay down without having acted.

What was she afraid of? That Cord would want to sell, or that he would not? If only they could talk about it. But Cord seemed to have withdrawn into a place where she could not reach him. He continued to sleep long hours, ride to Moose for the weekly *Courier*, and make its study last several days. He responded readily to questions about what she might put together for meals, and turned to her in bed at night as always, but under his life-as-usual façade, she detected a desperation matching her own.

One afternoon, when they were sitting in rockers on the porch overlooking the Snake, a hand from the Bar BC brought a letter from William.

Cord drew out his pocket knife and slit the envelope. Laura expected he would read it to her as he usually did, but he handed it across.

September 5, 1927
Lost River Ranch, Texas

Dear Mother and Father,
I'm settled in now as ranch foreman for Mr. Lamar in a house big enough for a large family. Which brings me right to the point.
You are all alone there, with Bryce working in Idaho, and winter's coming on. I expect you'll be thinking of moving in to Jackson Town to the Crabtree like a number of folks do.

Cord cleared his throat and Laura stopped reading.
"I reckon we might want to consider it," he said, as if he'd been thinking of it all along. And not telling her.
Relieved at having the burden of silence lifted, she spoke rapidly, "That's right. Without electricity or a phone"—they hadn't rerouted the line from the Main to the house—"we'll be snowed in out here. No hands to ferry supplies, and I don't want you driving to town in the sleigh when it's ten below."
"No one to cook," Cord put in.
Laura smiled; it felt like the first time in months. "You've been a saint not to complain about my cooking." Not only had she never been good at recipes, but they both missed having their meals prepared after so many years of having a cook.
She turned back to William's letter.

I have a better idea. Why don't you sell the ranch and come south with me?

Laura lifted her head and found Cord looking thoughtful.

It gets hot here in summer, but the climate is wonderful. The ranch doesn't take guests, but there are many hands and their families. We have a building called the Chuckwagon, where everyone takes meals. The cook is fantastic, if a little opinionated. She's got a sign says, "You'll eat what I say when I say so." Of course, it's a joke; Mr. Lamar's daughter, Anne, plans the menu.

My house has a separate wing; you could move right in.
Say the word and I'll come up and drive you down.

Laura started to fold the letter, but Cord put out a hand. She passed it over and he put on his reading glasses.

He studied the words for so long she knew he wasn't reading, but thinking.

Finally, he sighed. "I've been sitting here amid the ruins feeling sorry for myself. Even when I figured we couldn't winter over out here alone, I didn't want to believe it."

"We can go to town."

"And live in a crowded hotel with folks walking across the creaking floor above? Babies wailing, people arguing or staying up later than we'd like? I need wide open spaces."

"Are you thinking we ought to go to Texas?"

"Have you got a better idea? We can't go on the way we have here."

"I know that, but do we have to rush—?"

"We're not rushing into anything. We've sat on our butts since May twentieth and that's plenty of time to see what's what."

"You've been thinking about leaving the ranch without telling me?"

Cord reached over and put his hand over hers. "Haven't you been thinking about things?"

"Of course, but I didn't want to—"

"Neither of us fancied facing it, but it's time we decided what we want."

Her gimlet eyes clashed with his. "You know what I want," she said.

Cord nodded. "The same thing I do. That Dieter Gross and his men had gone to hell before they attacked this ranch instead of after. You want to go out at dawn and see the sunrise reflecting on the Snake, to fly-fish in late summer below a ripple of rapids, to see the young bald eagles, and the osprey, the baby birds beating the wings so their parents will feed them. You want Humpty-Dumpty back together again, but we haven't the money or the will."

He sighed. "William's right about selling this place. It's not fair for Charlie to move and not get his share. And I'd like to give some of the proceeds to the boys, get them started on their new lives." He grimaced. "But who would buy it now with everything burned?"

Laura swallowed. "When you said you'd been thinking about things and not telling me ... I didn't tell you everything, either."

She went into the house and returned with the papers Mike Yokel had left.

Chapter Forty-eight
October 15, 1927

After midnight, Cord slipped out of bed, hoping he would not wake Laura. Who was he kidding? She always knew when he moved on the mattress, much less got out of bed.

She had clearly decided to let him say his goodbyes alone.

How he loved this woman who had given up her Chicago roots to follow him into what must have seemed to her a harsh and violent land. His father had been one of the first to winter over, but it had still been a rarity when he and Laura did it.

The ranch had seemed alive—a community of souls who came together and broke apart with each season. The hands: from career men like Charlie to college kids like Ned Hanson to the dudes who made it all worthwhile. Though a few bad apples came in the barrel, the mountains produced wide-eyed awe in almost every visitor. Children went from shying away from the horses to hand feeding them sugar lumps, from clinging to the saddle horn to developing the proper seat.

How could he leave this valley? In Texas, the Lost River would have horses and cattle, but no dudes or mountains with ever-changing light and shadows.

He reached into his pocket and, for the first time in his life, found that his obsidian talisman remained cold to the touch.

Tears blurred the silvery sage and turned a single moon to several. Even after nearly four months, the night wind delivered the stench of ashes.

Cord blinked things clear and walked up onto the bench. He moved among the ruins. Here was where that piebald pony had thrown a fellow from Gary, Indiana, hurting his pride more than his backside. There Struthers Burt had burst into impromptu song during a campfire evening. Over yonder, Cord had lifted tiny Bryce to Eli's saddle and let him view the world from horseback for the first time. William had watched from the fence rail with serious gray eyes and then demanded to show his little brother how it was done.

Cord kicked at a fallen timber, one of the great supports for the porch of the Main. In his mind's eye, it was no longer deep night, but bright midday, while a host of men with winches, pulleys and teams of oxen raised the first pillar of the building where he'd hosted dinners for almost twenty years. Where had the years gone?

Everywhere he looked, a thousand facets glinted back at him in the moonlight.

But even the moon's magic could not put his crown jewel together again.

In the morning, fog lay upon the meadow.

Laura waited at the big window in her and Cord's bedroom for dawn to touch the tip of the Grand. A draft circled her ankles like a beloved cat; mornings at the ranch had begun with its caress since 1900.

How could this one be the last?

Not wanting to wake Cord after his night wandering, she wrapped a shawl over her white cotton nightgown, slid her feet into fleece slippers and went into the living room. There she used less care about making noise, letting her leather soles shush across the boards. The day before she'd swept the floor, as if to leave a good impression on those who had taken title to this house along with the land and the ruins.

Laura bent to the woodstove and put a match to the edge of a page from the *Jackson's Hole Courier*. The little flame flared and licked its way up to set the dry kindling ablaze. In a few moments, the stove put off a comforting roar, a presage to warmth.

How many times had she and Cord discussed running electricity to the house and determined it best left for another year?

Now there were no years left.

Going to the silver box occupying a place of honor atop the mantle, she withdrew her leather-bound journal, placed it open on the table before the window and dipped her pen.

This book chronicled the past two years, starting just after the Gros Ventre slide. Around the time Francesca had come.

It is hard to believe that we are leaving today. The sun shines on the Tetons as though it were any other day, any of the thousands we have passed pleasantly at home over the last twenty-six years.

I sit facing what I have come to regard as my personal and private view of the Grand and wonder what we will do in far away Texas—a flat, baking land that Cord and I have never even visited.

Cord said his goodbyes last night. I woke in that darkest hour before dawn and found him gone from our bed. Through the window, I saw him in the autumn meadow before the house, his fine head of silver hair tilted back to look up at the mountains' shadow against the star-studded sky.

This morning our son is brusque and businesslike, but I saw his eyes darting this way and that, now to the corner of the hearth where Sophie had her puppies, then scanning the path to the barn. He could usually be found there, communing with the horses, when all his other haunts had been checked.

Everything has been loaded and there is no reason to linger. In just a moment, I will put this journal to rest where it belongs. I do not believe I could bear to read of our joys and sadness here, once we are in Texas. Instead, I will let time soften the edges of memory, in the same way it blurs the lines of our faces and fades the brightness of our hair.

And yet ... the mountains will not let me go, weaving their subtle spell of changing light and shadow. They invite me to stay, to watch the magic of clouds appearing from clear air and day fading to darkness.

William had been trying to put a good face on it, but now it came time to take his folks to Texas, he had a small boy's desire to sit down in the middle of the living room and refuse to let the people who'd bought the ranch—and the house—come in.

Mother stood before the fireplace with her silver journal box in her hand. A loose stone from the hearth lay on the floor next to a pile of dirt and a serving spoon.

She bent and placed the box in the hole and covered it with the stone, then scraped the dirt into the fireplace. When she rose with the spoon in hand, she looked surprised to see him.

Putting aside the implement, she dabbed at her eyes.

William almost went and took her in his arms, but if he did, she'd really cry. They looked at each other, all the childhood evenings between them—

sitting before the fire, playing checkers and cards, popping corn—in the days before they built the Main and took in dudes.

William might just cry, too.

Francesca sat beside Bryce in the Dodge truck Cord had given the two of them, along with the generous check from the ranch sale.

Behind the truck, they towed a double horse trailer to pick up Lucifer and Bayberry. And take them home. Not to the ranch in Driggs, but to their new home in the valley.

She still couldn't believe their good fortune. As soon as Bryce saw the amount on the check from Snake River Land Company, he had crowed, "Francesca, this is enough for us to buy a place in Jackson's Hole."

It hadn't taken any time. The flood had washed away one of the ranches along the south side of the Gros Ventre near Kelly, all except for the stables and two well-built cabins on the hillside well above the river. It was only about a quarter the size of the six-hundred forty acres of Snake River Ranch, but the price had been right and the owners eager to sell the site of their own disaster.

Bryce pulled up in front of Dad and Mom's and saw William carrying out suitcases.

"What in hell?" Bryce jerked the Dodge to a halt and jumped out. In dashing up the steps, he brushed past William, almost knocking a valise to the ground.

"You're going so soon?" he challenged Dad and Mom, who stood before the big window looking at the mountains. "I thought we were just coming to get the horses and have some dinner."

Mom looked around and he saw her tears. "William tells us he needs to get back to work in Texas."

Bryce heard William set the bags down on the porch. His boots marked his coming inside.

"Let William get back to work, then," Bryce said. "Don't go with him!"

"It's too late," William gritted. "It's all settled."

Francesca heard the ruckus from outside and came into the house, her heels tapping hard.

"Stop it!" she cried. "Your parents aren't pawns. They aren't one more thing for you two to fight over. Go to Texas .... Stay here ...." She mocked both Bryce and William.

Francesca turned to Cord and Laura. "Tell us why you decided to go to Texas."

They glanced at each other and Francesca saw the evidence of recent tears. "Because of being too far from town in winter and ...." Laura began.

"Because we couldn't feel at home on this place anymore," Cord said.

"That's why you sold," Francesca said. "But do you really want to leave the valley?"

Fresh tears welled in Laura's eyes. She looked through the big window at the mountains that would not let her go and through the open front door. The river's lively rush made music that had lulled her to sleep for so many years. She found her hand in Cord's again, the way it had been the day he signed the papers, clutching hard.

"We thought ...." she stammered. "William asked us and you and Bryce don't have a place, you live in the quarters on the ranch where he works."

"We do have a place," Bryce said. "We just bought west of Kelly, up Flat Creek Road on the east side of the Elk Refuge, an easy ride to town. With two cabins on the hill, you can have one—I'm going to start building a house right away. For us and the baby."

"Baby!" Laura burst out. The grandchild Cord—and Laura—needed to hold. How could she go to Texas and not see him or her born?

"She ...." Bryce glanced at Francesca. "At least Francesca tells me she's sure it's a she—Rachel—will be born in April and we'll need help." Bryce flashed his trademark grin, the one Laura always found irresistible. "I'm planning to put in some more cabins for guests."

Laura put her hand on Cord's arm. He looked down at her and their fate was sealed.

"This puts a different light on it," he said slowly. "We needed to sell Snake River Ranch, but leaving this valley has been weighing on me ever since we decided to try it."

Laura waited for the explosion, for William to accuse his brother of luring them to stay just to spite him.

William looked at Bryce. Odd, but his rage at Brother had drained away with his decision to make his way in Texas. The past months at Lost River had been everything he'd hoped. As foreman, he'd had the position where he could make a difference, and when he'd said goodbye to go on this trip, Anne Lamar had kissed his cheek. His cheek, but it was a start.

William belonged in Texas. And Bryce was right. Father and Mother belonged in this valley.

He could see in everyone's expression that they expected a protest.

"I think it's a good idea for you to stay," William said. He couldn't help feeling relief that Anne's family would now never have to know about his Nez Perce blood.

Father stepped up and embraced him. "It isn't that we don't love you, son."

"I know. But this is your home. This whole wide vista is your inheritance, as a child of one of the earliest settlers. It isn't a matter of which son you're choosing."

William went to Mother and hugged her. "I expect you to come down on the train during the winter sometime and warm up. See where I live." He forced a smile. "And don't forget, someday I'll have a child for you to dote over."

Dad looked at Bryce. "I've just got to ask. Are you truly ready to settle down this time?"

Bryce considered William's journey to Texas and realized he wasn't the least bit envious.

"I used to think moving around meant freedom," he replied, "but that kind of freedom has its price." He slipped his arm around his wife. "It took me years of wandering, and all of it brought me back to the place I began."

William scuffed his boot. "I guess I'll be taking off, then. Need to make some miles before sunset."

Bryce faced him. Offered his hand.

William drew him into a bear hug that included Francesca. Somehow, they were all crying and laughing.

"Take care, Brother." They spoke in unison and started to chuckle again.

Francesca followed everyone outside. William carried Cord and Laura's suitcases from the porch to the Dodge truck. Bryce stood beside the bed and took the bags from him, the torch passing from one man to the other.

William, the rock, had become the wanderer, and Bryce, Francesca's foundation. She recalled Charlie saying, "Folks don't know yet who's going to turn out how."

An awkward pause. Another round of hugs, with elbows getting in the way, of cheek kisses landing on someone's ear.

The cough of the Model T. Pale smoke of exhaust and the lone black car ascended the bluff for the last time.

Everyone left behind watched until the dust plume dissipated.

Francesca placed a hand over her stomach in the universal gesture of pregnant women.

As her future unfolded with Bryce, she would wake each morning and watch for the first rose finger of light to touch the tip of the Grand. Her little girl would push her way with chubby hands through the summer-fragrant sage on their Gros Ventre Ranch.

For she and Bryce had found, not the end, but the beginning of their journey.

Author's Note

As early as 1898, the Director of the United States Geologic Survey recommended the Tetons be designated a park, opening the way for a thirty-year battle. Finally, in July of 1927, President Calvin Coolidge signed Executive Order 4685, closing Jackson's Hole to future homesteading to aid the Rockefeller effort. John D. Rockefeller did secretly fund The Snake River Land Company and hire local wrestler, Mike Yokel. Many families who sold to Snake River were happy; others felt they had been cheated or hoodwinked when Rockefeller's purpose of creating Grand Teton National Park was later revealed. In this novel, I have taken the liberty of moving up the date of the first ranch purchase to the fall of 1927, rather than 1928.

In February, 1929, President Herbert Hoover signed the legislation creating Grand Teton National Park. Also in 1929, the Snake River Land Company purchased the Bar BC from Struthers Burt, giving him a lifetime lease.

This is a novel, and to separate fact from fiction I must reveal the following. The fictional Snake River Ranch bears no relation to the Snake River Ranch listed on the National Register of Historic Places. All members of the Sutton family, the Snake River Ranch and its outfit, and the valley Klansmen are fictional. No event such as the Snake River Ranch's night of fire took place.

The fictitious George Hall family has replaced Guil Huff, the man who really outran the slide, because I have attributed made-up opinions to the fictional wife, Vera. Ranger Dibble has become Ranger Duran for the same reason. However, I have used the written accounts prepared by both Mr. Huff and Ranger Dibble, and stored in the archives of the Jackson Hole Historical Society. Their eyewitness accounts describe their actions and observations during the real Gros Ventre slide and Kelly flood.

Secondary published accounts have differed as to details. I have tried to stay true to the primary references, except for inserting William and Francesca's adventures beneath the wagon and hers and Bryce's during the flood.

The real William Card ranch, submerged in Slide Lake above the Huffs the first night, has been replaced by the fictitious Circle X that survived longer. The flight through the night through a barbed wire fence actually belonged to the Ranger and his family. Foster Case, Lewis Pharr and Bobby Cowan have replaced real witnesses to the slide Farney Cole, Cole Peterson, and Boyd Charter. All of these characters' actions and traits are the product of the author's imagination. Wilhelm Bierer, who warned of the slide, existed, as did Struthers Burt. I have tried to capture Burt's spirit from reading his books and articles, especially *The Diary of a Dude Wrangler*. Those who died in the Kelly flood are also real, their stories based on historic accounts. To respect their memory, I have not attributed any characteristics to them that would necessitate fictionalizing. Grace Miller and Rose Crabtree were on Jackson's all-woman town council. For some characters, I have used common valley names, such as Raleigh and Lovejoy to promote authenticity—I intend no relationship to real persons.

About the Author

Trained at the Master's level in Geology, **Linda Jacobs** was one of Exxon Corporation's first women field geologists. After thirty years on the front line where new oil and gas fields are found, she turned her talents to writing novels.

Linda began writing stories as a child growing up in Greenville, South Carolina. In 1992 she returned to fiction after twenty years of technical writing and joined Rice University's novel writing program.

Jackson Hole Journey is part of The Yellowstone Series (*Summer of Fire, Rain of Fire, and Lake of Fire*). The Camel edition is the novel's first time in print, having been previously recorded by Books in Motion. The audio edition was a finalist in the 2011 Spur Awards from Western Writers of America in the Original Audio Book category.

Linda's personal love affair with Yellowstone began in 1973, when she attended Geology Field Camp near the park. She has visited the park in every season, for research and annual book signing tours. Linda also writes romance under the name Christine Carroll. *Children of Dynasty* and *The Senator's Daughter* are set in the San Francisco Bay area.

Married to fellow geologist Richard Jacobs, Linda divides her time between the West and the Shenandoah Valley of Virginia. They both enjoy adventure travel, having dived the Caribbean, taken three African safaris, and gone alpine hiking in New Zealand and the Spanish Pyrenees.

You can find Linda online at ReadLindaJacobs.com.

Linda Jacobs

Photograph by Nolan Conley